ARMY BRATS

By Michael G. Cerepanya

Published in the U.S.A. by
Michael G. Cerepanya
Hererford, AZ 85615
MichaelGCerepanya.com

Graphic Design and cover illustration by
Bazz Graphics
BazzGraphics.com

ISBN-13: 978-15347-7408-7
ISBN-10: 15347-7408-4
LCCN:

Dedication

*To my lovely wife, Cheryl
and my children, Elizabeth and Matt.*

.

Table of Contents

Acknowledgements

First of all I'd like to thank my wife, Cheryl, for being so supportive and patient for the four and a half years it has taken me to write *Army Brats.* I know she had to wonder if I would ever finish it.

I would also like to thank two fellow authors, Lucinda Sage-Midgorden and Maria Church. We all participated in a writers club that saw many other authors go in and out of it over the years, but the three of us stuck together until June of 2014, when circumstances made it impossible to continue to meet on a regular basis. The support and encouragement helped me to keep focused on my book. Also, Barry Midgorden, Lucinda's husband, for doing such a great job on the book cover and artwork as well as helping me with all the technical aspects of preparing the book for e-publishing.

To Cheryl's and my good friend, Maria Williams, for reading my book and giving me great feedback. Her suggestions on changing a word here and there or even eliminating words and sentences made a great difference in how well the book read.

Finally, I want to give a special thanks to Harvey Stanbrough, author, poet, publisher, teacher and just a great guy. The ten seminars I took of his over a year's time helped me go from a good storyteller into the writer I am today. I learned so much from him and enjoyed his classes immensely. Thank you, Harvey.

Credits

Edited by Emilie Vardaman, editsbyemilie@gmail.com.

Introduction

In the decade following World War II, the time of the Baby Boomers, life was much different than today for the children growing up. There was almost unlimited freedom for kids. They could go out and play without parental supervision. "Be home for lunch!" or "Be home by ten!" was often the only restrictions they had during the summer or weekends during the school year. It didn't matter if they lived in small towns in the Midwest, the cities of the east coast, or on military bases in the United States or Europe. They had plenty of friends to play with and the dangers of drugs or abduction wasn't even on their radar. The biggest fear of the day was whether or not the commies would release the A-Bomb on American cities. Rock and Roll was taking over the sound waves and baseball was the national pastime. It was a great time to be alive.

Europe was rebuilding after the war and the United States had a huge presence in Europe, especially in Germany. Growing up on military bases during the '50s and '60s left the door wide open for adventures and hijinks on a grand scale. *Army Brats* is a story of a young boy growing up as a military dependent during that time.

Chapter I

You're in the Army Now

As Lucas stared out the window of the car watching the rain lightly fall, it seemed like he was trapped in a whirlwind. Everything was spinning too fast. He was heading back home with his mother, two sisters and two brothers from the studio where they'd had their family passport picture taken in Connellsville, Pennsylvania. His mother didn't drive so Uncle Peter was doing the chauffeuring. Lucas' old man had already left for Germany. The rest of the family would be joining him in a few weeks.

It was September of 1958. The rain was coming down harder as they neared the Projects in Uniontown. Lucas' dad had just left after being home for two weeks. The last two weeks had been a blur. It hadn't really sunk in for Lucas that they would be leaving the only world he had known. Not that life in The Projects was that great, but anything else was filled with uncertainty and fear.

Now things got a little scarier. First there were all of those shots they had to get. Lucas was the oldest of the three boys. Ike was five and Joe was three. Their father, Sgt. Ivan Baryshivka, lived up to the nickname given to him by his fellow soldiers, Ivan the Terrible.

"Lucas," he ordered, "don't you dare cry when you get your shots. You're the oldest and I don't want your brothers to think it's okay to cry. You be tough!"

The old man hadn't been around much during Lucas' first eight years of life. He was in Korea for the first couple of years. Then he was in Ohio and a couple other places that never meant much to Lucas. He was just never around that often. He would come home on leave or on long weekends. It was never a good time for Lucas when his dad was home on leave. He would get lots of spankings every time his dad spent time there. He could never seem to do anything right in his dad's eyes. He got whopped for things he did when his dad was there and for the times he did things when his old man was gone.

"We're home!" Joe yelled, breaking up Lucas' thoughts for the moment.

Sensing the built-up tension brewing between Lucas' mother and his two older sisters, Karla (the oldest) and Susan, Uncle Peter dropped them off and left quickly. He didn't want to be around for that cat fight. Neither of the girls was happy about the move to Germany and somehow blamed their mother for having to go.

"You lived away from him for this long, I don't see what difference it makes if he's gone another couple of years," Karla shouted at her mother.

Maria replied, "It's been too long that we haven't lived as a family and the boys need to be around their father even if you think you don't."

"Then maybe just you and the boys should go. Karla could live with the Andersons and I could stay with the Tates," Susan said.

Maria glared at her. "Don't get fresh with me! We've been over this again and again. It is not open for debate. We are all going to Germany and we're going to be living with your father and that is that!" She turned to Lucas. "Lucas, take your brothers up to the bedroom and play until dinner is ready."

"Okay."

Lucas was actually relieved at the order. He often got saddled with taking care of his brothers but most of the time it was not too bad. They were both filled with a lot of energy and Lucas had fun wrestling around with them. Going up and horsing around with Ike and Joe would be a lot more fun than listening to his mother and sisters argue. It didn't make sense to him since the old man really didn't give anyone any options. They were all going to Germany in ten days and that's all there was to it.

Going to Germany would be a homecoming for Maria. She was a war bride, having met Ivan a year after the war had ended. This was the first time she had returned to Germany since she had left some ten years before. She had already had Karla, whose father had been killed in the war. Maria left behind a mother, brother and sister when she came to America. Her mother had passed away three years ago and although Maria kept in touch with her brother and sister, she had not seen them since leaving.

Karla was sixteen and starting her junior year in high school. She loved going to Uniontown High School and being involved with all of the high school activities. Lucas enjoyed when her friends came over. They always played their 45 rpm records. Lucas had eavesdropped enough to know all the gossip about Elvis, The Everly Brothers and just about all of the popular rock and roll stars of the day.

Susan was only eleven years old but acted as though she were sixteen. This caused a lot of friction between the two sisters. She was brash and opinionated and never hesitated telling her older sister and friends what she thought about just about everything. She also got away with more, and was allowed to do more, than the rest of the kids. Karla often got stuck babysitting her younger brothers and resented the fact that Susan never had to. Moving to Germany was one of the few times the two of them agreed on anything. Neither of them wanted to leave Uniontown and their friends.

A week later they loaded the last of the boxes into the moving van. Lucas looked at the last box as Uncle Peter closed the doors. *My toys are in that one.* Then Uncle Peter loaded the last of the suitcases into his car for the drive out to Peter and Aunt Sharon's house. The six Baryshivkas would be staying there for the next couple of nights before catching an early morning train to New York.

Lucas, Ike, and Joe had spent a lot of time at their cousins' house this past summer. Their cousin John was a few months younger than Lucas, and his brother Jeremy was only days younger than Joe. Rebecca was Susan's age. Their home was in the country and Lucas loved playing and hiking in the hills surrounding their property. A small creek ran through the area on the south side of the roadway. Uncle Peter and Aunt Sharon always had a couple acres of corn growing over there with tomatoes and green peppers, too. *I'm gonna miss John and Jeremy.*

"Let's go, Lucas!" he heard Uncle Peter yell cheerfully. "Your Aunt Sharon will have dinner ready when we get there. Better not be late."

Karla, Susan, and Joe were already waiting at the car. Ike was shoving Lucas toward the car. He was excited to get started on the big adventure. Lucas was more apprehensive. Mostly it was about living with his father.

No, this was not the life Lucas was looking forward to. He just wanted things to stay like they were.

"Life is always changing, Lucas." his mother would tell him. "Even when it seems like it remains the same. Someday you'll understand."

Maybe, but that someday ain't today.

It was crazy as the Baryshivka family boarded the USS Randall that September day. They were going to Germany on the same ship as Elvis Presley. Karla could hardly contain herself and Lucas could see her excitement. She had all of Elvis' records. We all heard them enough to know just about every song Elvis has done. Now they were going to spend ten days at sea with him. Karla was sure she would get to meet him at some point; after all, the ship is only so big.

The Baryshivkas managed to place their luggage into the cabins and went back out on deck as it neared the time for the USS Randall to depart. What they witnessed was total bedlam. The dock was covered with hundreds of screaming teenage girls pleading with Elvis not to go. The Military Police had their hands full trying to keep some of the more radical ones from jumping into the water.

"DON'T GO ELVIS"

"WE LOVE YOU!"

"DON'T MARRY SOME FRAÜLIEN!"

Lucas noticed they seemed to be shouting right at him. He looked over the railing from the deck he was on, hanging out over the rail from his waist up.

"Lucas!" shouted his mother in a panic, "get down from there before you fall!"

"I think Elvis is right below us, Mom."

With that, Karla, Susan and Ike all hung over to look as did everyone else around them that had heard Lucas. Maria caught Joe as he was trying to climb up to see, too. Next, she grabbed Ike and gave Lucas a look that didn't need any words to accompany it. He felt the daggers as he quickly moved back from the railing.

"Look, she knocked the MP's hat off!" Susan said as they all watched the hat fall the twenty-plus feet into the water, like a leaf falling from a tree.

The tide was out and much of the boat was below the level of the dock. The family was on the top level of the ship and almost even with the screaming fans across the way. It was the last image Lucas would remember from America for the next four years. He and Ike stayed on deck with Karla until they were well away from the dock. It was amazing how long they could hear the screaming fans. The sound echoed in his head as they left the railing.

Finally, they went below to their cabins. Ike and Joe were bouncing around on their bunk beds. Lucas stood for some time just looking out the porthole. What did life have in store for him once they crossed this vast ocean? His trance was broken by his mother's call.

"Boys, wash up and get ready for dinner."

She didn't have to say it twice. All three were famished from all of the day's activities. They quickly washed up and marched with their mother to the dining hall. Karla and Susan were already there.

"Luke, you sure are quiet," Karla stated.

"Just thinkin'."

Maria and the two girls started laughing.

"Lucas, when you start thinking," laughed Susan, "trouble always seems to follow. Remember how he kept thinkin' about how Grandma's automatic ice-maker in her new refrigerator worked. You thought you had to help it by filling it up with water."

"Yeah," piped in Karla "when the automatic fill kicked in, it flooded the whole kitchen. I thought Dad was gonna kill you!"

"It's a good thing Uncle Paul was home. He kept your dad from taking a strap to you," added their mother.

"Then remember last year when Luke locked us all out of the house after he got a spanking from Mom?" Karla asked. "When we kept trying to get you to open it, you said 'I'm thinkin' and then fell asleep on the floor."

"Yeah," added Ike, "Mom had to get Mr. Johnson to get the key to let us in. Boy was she mad."

Lucas smiled as he remembered. Whenever he was upset, he went into his cocoon and withdrew from the world. He would think about being a baseball player and playing for the Pittsburgh Pirates. He would go over and over in his mind the vision of Forbes Field where the Pirates played. His dad had taken him to a game at the beginning of that summer when he was home on leave. It was one of the few times he could really remember having fun with his father. That was a love they both had in common … baseball. He never saw his dad play, except for playing catch when he got Luke his first glove, but he knew how much the old man liked it. All of the Baryshivka brothers were baseball fans, especially fans of the Pirates. Ivan and his brothers followed every game they played.

"So what are you thinkin' about, Luke?" asked Ike.

"I was thinkin' of beatin' you up, Ike!" was his reply.

Ike just laughed and shook his fist at Lucas, who returned his laugh and shook his fist back.

With that, the subject was changed and the dinner conversation turned to the chances of his sisters seeing Elvis. The same conversation seemed to be going on around the other dinner tables, too. Luke was sure his sisters would manage to find a way to see Elvis again, especially Karla.

For the most part the boat trip was uneventful. However, there were a few days where the waves were high and a lot of people got seasick, Lucas being one of them. He never did very well on the carnival rides that had too much movement and the rocking motion in the high waves had the same effect. Fortunately, it only lasted two days, though it seemed like forever to Lucas.

There were a few exciting evenings, though. The first was when Karla finally got to meet Elvis. The ship had several "day rooms" or recreation rooms that had TVs and card tables as well as a piano in some of them.

On the night Karla met Elvis, she had gone with their mother to one of the recreation rooms when they heard that Elvis was going to a different one each night to meet people. Maria was not shy and when she and Karla found the one he was at, she had no problem asking him to pose for some pictures with Karla. Karla was in heaven. That was all she could talk about for the rest of the trip.

Several nights later, Maria woke the boys from their sleep.

"You want to meet Elvis?" she asked Lucas. "Get your brothers up!"

"We're in our pajamas, Ma," Lucas whined.

"That's okay; I promise you, Elvis won't care."

So there they were … Luke, Ike and Joe decked out in their pajamas, trudging up to the nearest rec room to meet Elvis. Mom might not think it was a big deal but Lucas hated the thought of meeting someone famous while he was in his PJs. *Maybe he won't be there.* They entered the room.

It was crowded, as crowded as Macy's the day after Thanksgiving. Elvis was playing the piano and smoking a big cigar. Lucas could see Karla with another teenage girl she had met. Lucas also took notice that Susan wasn't there. In fact he had not seen much of Susan the whole trip. She had met a girl her age and they seemed to spend all of their time together. Susan even ate with the girl's family on some nights. He didn't mind. Susan could be a pain in his butt. She thought because she was older she could tell him what to do and was always trying to do just that. Sometimes it was easier to just do what she asked or, he should say, demanded. Other times he would just ignore her. It really depended on his mood.

Lucas glanced sideways at his brothers. They seemed less impressed by this ordeal than he was. They both were having trouble keeping their eyes opened. Joe looked as if he were about to fall over when their mother picked him up and held him. *Okay, we've seen him, now let's go to bed.* Lucas was about to verbalize that thought when the music stopped and Elvis got up and started to head for the exit, which just happened to be right where Maria and the boys were standing.

"Boys, you're going to get to meet Elvis!" she blurted out.

Elvis walked right up to us and said, "Hello Mrs. Baryshivka! Did I pronounce it right?"

"Yes, perfectly," was her reply. "I want you to meet my boys. This is Lucas, Ike and this sleepy one is Joe."

"Nice meeting you boys," Elvis said as he shook Lucas' hand and proceeded to continue on his way.

"Nice meeting you too!" Lucas blurted out as Elvis walked away.

He might not have been that keen on meeting Elvis, but now that he had, Lucas was really excited about it. He was wide-awake as they walked back to the cabin.

"You'll remember that the rest of your life, Luke," his mother told him.

He instinctively knew she was right. There was something special about the guy. As he reflected back to the scene as they were leaving the dock in New York, Luke was now getting a little better appreciation of the excitement that Karla felt.

As excited as he now felt, he could feel his eyelids dropping like they do when he tries to stay up to midnight on New Years Eve. It did't take long for Luke to fall back to sleep. Two more days and we'll be in Germany. *Wonder what it's gonna be like there?*

Lucas was already awake when his mother came in to get the boys up. He was excited to be getting off of the ship. To him, it had been a long journey. He was ready to see something else besides the sea and the boat. At first, the ocean looked beautiful to him with its deep blue color stretched as far as his eyes could see. Most days the whitecaps kept it from looking flat. The ship was the typical grey of all the US Navy ships. It, too, became a little boring after the first few days. At the beginning of the trip he would watch the GIs on the deck below where most were quartered. One could overlook that deck without hanging on the rails from the upper deck where the dependents were. The upper deck didn't extend as far forward on the ship as the lower deck did. Now on the third day of the ten days it took to cross the ocean, it was like watching a movie he had already seen; he just wanted off the ship.

His mother had already laid out clothes for the boys and packed the suitcases except for the pajamas they had on. She rushed to help them dress and hurried them off to breakfast, the last meal they would be having on the USS Randall, so they could get back on deck. They were pulling into Bremerhaven, West Germany.

About that time, the ship blasted its horn. If there had been anyone on the ship still asleep, they were awake now! All three boys were beside themselves as the horn blast was followed by another … then another. People were dashing everywhere, everyone in a hurry. Susan was saying goodbye to her friend when Maria turned to her.

"Susan, you hold on to Ike. Karla, you have Joe. Lucas, you stay close to me. I don't want to lose anyone."

They went up on deck with their luggage and stood in an area close to where they had stood when they left New York. The entire Baryshivka family watched as the soldiers left the boat in single file. Elvis was with them, but none of the Baryshivkas could pick him out as he blended in with the rest of the GIs.

"There's Dad!" shouted Lucas as he pointed to an area just left of the gangplank.

They all began to wave and Luke could see his dad smiling and waving back. His dad looked the same as he had the last time Lucas had seen him only this time he was in his fatigues instead of his dress greens. He felt good about seeing his father. It was the first time he could remember feeling that way. Usually, when he heard his father was coming home, he was so filled with dread that he could never enjoy seeing him. This was different. There was some sense of security seeing his father waiting for them.

It seemed like it took forever before they could get off of the ship but finally it happened. Ivan seemed really happy to see everyone. *It must be make Dad feel good to finally be living with all of us.* In all of Lucas' eight years of life, that had not happened.

"Sprechen sie Deutsch?" Ivan said to everyone, as he kissed Maria. "You're in Germany, now." He patted the boys on the head and gave a brief hug to the girls.

Lucas could not imagine how his mother must feel being back for the first time since having left Germany, having the chance to see her brother and sister again after so many years. Both of her parents were dead. Luke could vaguely remember her crying a few years back when she got the word that her mother had died. He had cried too, even though he didn't know his grandmother. It hurt his mother and that was enough for him to feel pain, too.

For now, though, his thoughts were back in the moment. They were all climbing into a taxi and heading for the train station. One more ride after this one and he would be heading to his new home.

"Ouch!" yelled Lucas as Ike punched him in the arm.

"Whatcha gonna do about it?" was Ike's reply.

"You boys behave!" Ivan growled. "I don't wanna have to tell you twice."

"Oh, Ivan, give them a break," their mother said. "They've been good the whole trip. They're just excited now that we're here."

"Well, they are going to have to contain it for a while longer. We still have a couple hour train ride to go before we get to Zweibrüken. After we get home they can run around like crazy for all I care."

Lucas looked at Ike and smiled. *Oh, yeah, like Dad's gonna let us run wild!* He knew that there were limitations on how wild the old man would let them get. *Maybe it won't be so bad living with him.* Only time would tell.

Chapter II

Living in Germany

The train they boarded for the trip to Pirmasens was sparsely filled. There were several American families on board and the choices of traveling compartments were abundant. Ivan and Maria took one and kept Joe with them while Karla, Susan, Lucas and Ike were in the compartment across the aisle. It was a two-hour trip and after the excitement of leaving the ship had worn off, they were all ready to settle down for a while.

Lucas had dozed off and was awakened by the noise of a couple of children running down the hall of the car. Ike was asleep and Karla was reading. Susan had already slipped out and was wandering around the train. Lucas poked his head out of the compartment about the time the two kids came walking back down the aisle. They stopped when they got to Lucas.

"Hi, I'm Jimmy and this is my sister, Sally," the boy said as they stood in front of Lucas. Jimmy looked to be about Lucas' age and Sally, maybe a year younger.

"Hi! I'm Lucas."

"Where you from?" Sally asked. "We're from New Jersey."

"I'm from Pennsylvania," answered Lucas.

"We're exploring the train," Jimmy said. "Want to join us?"

Lucas wasn't too sure that his dad would let him and was a little timid about running around the train.

"Let me ask my dad," said Lucas. Then he popped his head into his parents' compartment. When he asked his dad, Ivan was half asleep.

"Don't get into any trouble … be back here in half an hour," he grumbled. "We're gonna be eatin' in an hour."

"Thanks Dad!"

With that, Lucas joined his newfound friends and went scampering down the aisle towards the back of the train. Two cars down they discovered one didn't have any passengers in the entire car. The three of them decided this was the place to hang out. Well, it was really Jimmy who decided. Lucas was just going along with the program.

They hung out and talked about their homes that they left behind them in the States. Jimmy then came up with the bright idea of opening all of the windows in the train car they were in. Unlike the train Lucas had taken from Pittsburgh to New York, in which you couldn't open the windows, these in the German train could be opened half way by pinching the latches at the top of the window and sliding the top half down.

The three kids had all of the windows down, which made it quite breezy, so they decided to close them again which was as much fun as opening them. They had closed fewer than half of them when the unexpected happened. The train went through a rather long tunnel. It all happened in seconds. By the time the train emerged from the other side, the entire car was full of smoke from the engine.

Coughing and blinking his eyes, which were as wide open as they could get, Lucas turned to look at Jimmy and Sally. Both looked back at him with panic in their eyes. Before Lucas could utter a word, Jimmy yelled at his sister.

"Let's get out of here!"

They both darted out the car towards the front of the train, leaving Lucas standing in the aisle, mouth wide open. He shot a glance back the other way and could see through the door window a conductor heading his way through the next car to the rear of the train. Even as the smoke was starting to clear, Lucas took off running in the opposite direction and as quickly as he could, got back into the compartment with his sisters and Ike.

Karla looked at him with a suspicious eye. He was gasping for breath and smelled like smoke.

"What did you do, Luke?" she asked.

"Nothing," was his response as he tried to squeeze up close to the panel next to the door so he wouldn't be seen by anyone walking by.

Outside they could hear some kind of commotion was going on. A conductor coming from the front of the train was passing their compartment, heading toward the back of the train. Susan, who had returned to the compartment and Karla were looking at Lucas very suspiciously as he quickly lifted a comic book in front of his face.

"I'm going to go see what's going on," Susan said, as she got up from her seat and went out. "I know you did something, Lucas."

Susan returned a few minutes later. She looked at Lucas as she told Karla, "I heard one conductor tell the other one that a couple of Army Brats opened all the windows in an empty car a couple of cars behind us and let in smoke from the engine when we went through the last tunnel. The second conductor said he saw a boy and girl fly past him into one of the forward cars. He was pretty sure it was them. They wouldn't happen to be your two new friends, Lucas ... are they?"

Lucas wanted to deny it but he had enough time to think about it and he knew he would get caught. If he lied about it, it would only be worse. He was terrified they would say something to their dad. The fear swelled up inside of him like an overinflated balloon about to burst.

"Yeah, it was us. We opened the windows, but we didn't mean for all of the smoke to get into the train. I never even thought about it. It was just fun to open the windows and have it real windy in there. There was nobody in the car so it didn't seem like it was gonna cause a problem," he said as he looked down.

"Are you going to tell Dad?" he asked.

"What do you think, Karla? Should we tell Dad?"

"I don't know. Do think you can behave the rest of the train ride, Luke?" was Karla's response as she grinned at Susan.

"I'll stay right here," blurted Lucas, "I won't leave the compartment. I promise! Please don't tell Dad!"

After a knowing look passed between the two sisters, Susan said, "Okay, Lucas, we won't tell Dad this time, but you owe us one."

Lucas could feel his whole body relax. *Wow!* He realized he had just escaped a possible spanking. *I better not do anything like that again.* Little did he know it was just the beginning of trouble that lay ahead of him.

The rest of the train ride was uneventful all the way to Pirmasens. From there, everyone loaded into a cab for the ride to Zweibrücken. It was pretty cramped with not much room to move. Adding to the discomfort was the fact that Ike and Joe had slept most of the train ride and were busting at the seams for some kind of activity. They kept fidgeting and making it harder for the rest of the clan to be comfortable. Joe was on Karla's lap and after the third time she told him to "hold still" the old man popped him on the back of the head.

"You don't want me to have to tell you to behave," Ivan said. The look in his eye said it all. That look was enough to make them act like angels the rest of the cab ride to their new home in Zweibrücken.

Sgt. Ivan Baryshivka was near the top of the waiting list for the next available opening for post housing for his family. He was stationed in Pirmasens and had signed up for the next available housing in either Pirmasens or the next two closest forts, the fort at Zweibrücken or at the hospital fort at Münchweiler. In the meantime they were renting a place in the town of Zweibrücken.

They arrived around 8:00 p.m. Their apartment was the third floor of a three-story house that was over 200 years old. As the boys went running through the house exploring, the landlady, Frieda, came up to check to see that everything was okay, following Ivan in as he and Karla brought up the last of their luggage. As Maria and Frieda engaged in conversation, Ivan grabbed Joe as he ran by.

"Hey, boys!" he yelled. "Settle down. There are people below us and some are already asleep."

The boys immediately stopped their running.

"Dad, why is the bathroom so big?" Luke asked, referring to the fact the bathroom was the size of a large bedroom with the actual facilities taking up just a small area of the room.

"They converted a bedroom into a bathroom for Americans. The rest of the house shares a bathroom. Frieda found out that Americans don't share bathrooms when she first tried renting the place. She converted a bedroom into one just for the apartment so she could rent to Americans," he replied.

"All the other families that live here share a bathroom?" Ike asked with an impish grin.

"Yep," answered his dad. "The owners have one in their apartment, the rest share one just off of the stairwell on the second floor."

"Boys, come with me," Maria instructed the three brothers as she led them to their bedroom.

Throughout the apartment were boxes of their household goods and clothes that Ivan had already brought over before the rest of the family arrived. This was not all of their belongings since this living situation was only temporary until housing became available on one of the forts. The unpacking would have to wait until the following day as the time was approaching 10:00 p.m.

"Okay, boys, here are your pajamas. Get ready for bed. Wash up and brush your teeth, then off to bed," she told them. "Lucas, you're in charge. Make sure your brothers brush their teeth."

"Will do, Mom," Lucas responded as his mother left the room.

"Lucas is in charge. Lucas is in charge," Ike kept mockingly saying to Joe after their mother left the room. That was until Lucas grabbed him in a headlock and gave him a knuckle rub, tackling him to floor. Joe couldn't resist piling on his brothers and joining in.

"We better get moving before Dad comes in," Lucas giggled as he pulled Joe off of Ike.

The boys quickly cleaned up and brushed their teeth, then went out into the living room to say goodnight, passing their sisters' room. Karla and Sue were busy unpacking and talking as they went by.

"Goodnight!" Lucas shouted to them as Ike and Joe did the same, mimicking Lucas.

"Goodnight, boys!" they both responded.

After telling their parents goodnight, the boys went back to their room. Their mother went with them to tuck them in on their first night in a foreign country. After the long and rather eventful day, all three drifted off to sleep very quickly. There would be new adventures in store for them tomorrow.

Lucas woke up to a lot of noise outside his window. As he got up to look outside his mother stepped into the boys' bedroom. Both of his brothers were still asleep but began to stir when Maria began talking to Luke.

"We're living right behind a German school," Maria told Lucas. "They must be on their recess break"

Joe was the next up, joining his mother and Lucas at the window. They were watching the German boys playing soccer.

The house their apartment was in was down a hill below the school. The schoolyard at the back of the building was on top of a large retaining wall made out of boulders, almost eye level with their apartment. The stone went the entire length of the house they were in, curving around the side of the road that went by the house. The road continued farther down to other neighborhoods. The wall turned uphill, tapering off until it met the road grade of the main street that passed in front of the school. The main street was made of brick instead of pavement, and as Lucas learned in his first week of school, was made by the Romans when their empire spread to northern Europe.

"Ike! Time to get up!" his mother shouted. "We have a busy day. Lucas, you and Ike get cleaned up and brush your teeth. Then get dressed. I put some clothes out for you both. Your father is taking you and Ike to school today to get registered."

The boys quickly got dressed and ready. It was not the excitement as much as the cold that got them moving. The bathroom was so big it didn't hold the heat very well. Lucas waited for Ike to finish, then they both headed for the kitchen.

As they stepped into the dining room, Ike grinned at Lucas and said, "Mush!"

That was what their father called oatmeal. It was Ivan's specialty. The boys only got it in the past when he was home on leave. It was a favorite breakfast for them and in Luke's mind, one of the few benefits of his dad's visits to Uniontown. Ivan was usually in a good mood when he fixed 'mush' for the boys. He knew they liked it a lot and it was always a pleasant time for all of them.

"You boys ready to eat?" Ivan asked.

"Yes, sir!" they answered in unison as they joined Joe who was already at the table.

That was how they had to address their dad, "yes, sir" or "no sir" when they answered him. Forgetting to add "sir" at the end resulted in a slap to the back of the head. It didn't take them very long to get into the habit of saying it correctly. That included three-year-old Joe. There were no exceptions to Ivan's rules.

The boys ate quickly, barely noticing their sisters talking with their father. The plan was for Ivan to take Susan, Luke and Ike to the American elementary school on the Fort at Zwiebrücken to register them. Then in the afternoon he would take Karla to the American high school in Kaiserslautern. Susan didn't look too happy because she would not be living anywhere near any new friends she would make.

Lucas and his brothers finished up with their breakfast. They could hear the kids in the schoolyard.

"Can we wait outside?" Luke asked his mother.

Ivan overheard his request and answered. "Yes, but stay by the car. We're leaving in about fifteen minutes."

"And don't get dirty!" added Maria. "Brush your teeth first!"

All three of the boys quickly brushed their teeth and bolted outside. As they looked around there were several of the students along the fence on top of the large rock retaining wall looking down at them, soon joined by other students. The entire fence was covered by children. Some of them waved at the boys. Luke returned the wave, which was followed with a lot of German chatter that Luke didn't understand, but he knew instinctively that they were talking about the three American boys. This lasted only a few minutes until a male teacher came over and began shouting at the students, dispersing the group. As he was about to walk away he shot a not-too-friendly look at the boys.

About that time, Ivan and Susan came out. Ivan caught the look by the German teacher. He turned to Lucas.

"You can expect a lot of looks like that from some of the older Germans. It hasn't been that long since the end of the war and a lot of Krauts still harbor resentment towards Americans. Hop in the car! We're going."

Maria and Karla had come down to see them off and Karla grabbed Joe by the hand as the car backed out of its parking space. Luke shot one last glance up at the schoolyard. *Wonder if any of the kids feel the same way as that teacher?* He wouldn't have to wait very long to find out.

The rest of the day was a blur. They drove to the school and walked into the office; Ivan filled out some paperwork and without saying a word to Lucas or Susan, left with Ike. Kindergarten was only half day and started in the morning. Class was almost over so Ike wouldn't be starting until tomorrow.

Susan and Lucas were given a piece of paper that had the

number of the bus they were to catch after school and another to give to the bus driver so he would know where to drop them off. Then a girl showed up and Susan followed her to her new classroom. It seemed like forever before the same girl returned and took Lucas to his. Except for introductions, there was really no conversation. Her name was Kathy. That was all Lucas would ever know about her. She knocked on the classroom door and entered, handing a slip of paper to the teacher, Mrs. Turner. Lucas had remembered reading her name on the bulletin board while he was waiting in the office. Her first name, he remembered, was Violet.

While Mrs. Turner read the note, Lucas stood in front of the class feeling a bit nervous as the kids in the class all began to whisper to one another as they glanced and stared at him. Finally, Mrs. Turner finished the paper and turned to Kathy and dismissed her.

"Thank you, Kathy, you can go now. Class, this is a new student that will begin with us today. His name is Lucas Baryshivka." Then, turning to Lucas, "Welcome to our class, Lucas! Did I pronounce your last name correctly?

"Yes, ma'am!"

The day continued with reading, arithmetic, and geography. After his extended summer vacation, he was trying to get into the swing of school again. He had missed the morning recess and was now getting his first break at lunchtime. He finally was getting to meet the kids in his class, but they came at him so fast, and with all of those new names to remember he couldn't recall any of them. He would have to pay attention to their names when Mrs. Turner called on them.

After lunch the afternoon went by quickly and Lucas was surprised when the bell rang, ending the school day. He walked out with several of his new classmates to the line of buses. He looked at his ticket.

"17" was looking back at him as he started to look at the numbers in the front window of the buses. As he neared the front of the next bus he heard, "Lucas!"

"This is our bus!" shouted Susan from the window of the bus he was approaching.

He quickly got in and started to sit next to Susan.

"Go find another seat!" she shot at him. "I don't want to be sitting next to my little brother."

Lucas moved a couple of seats farther back in the bus, taking a seat by the window. He sat in silence as the kids started piling in the bus. The last two people to load up were the driver, a G.I. named Scott, and the high school student monitor (each elementary school bus was assigned one), a pretty girl named Leslie. It was obvious to Lucas that Scott and Leslie liked each other.

"Okay, everyone settle down!" bellowed Leslie. "We're heading home!"

With that, Scott closed the door, and following the other buses out of the school parking lot, they were off.

Lucas sat back and observed the other students clowning around. Susan had already found a friend she was sitting next to. None of Lucas' classmates were on his bus. In fact, it seemed like he was the only third-grader that was on this route. That also meant there was no one his age in the German neighborhood where he lived. Finding friends his age wasn't going to be easy. It was a good thing he always had his brothers to play with.

After the first stop, the other kids on the bus began teasing Leslie and Scott. They began chanting.

"Scott and Leslie sitting in a tree. K...I...S...S...I...N...G! First comes love, then comes marriage, then comes little Scott in a baby carriage"

"Knock it off!" Leslie shouted, not very convincingly, as she looked lovingly at Scott. "Behave, you guys, or you'll walk home from here."

Before long, the bus came to a halt at their stop. Lucas, Susan, and two other older boys got off. One of the boys was in Susan's class and she stopped to talk to him as Lucas headed down the street to their new home. Some of the German students were yelling at him from the schoolyard above. He didn't understand them but the tone wasn't very friendly. He shot them a quick glance and then, head down, continued his walk home.

The rest of the school week was pretty much the same with the only excitement coming when Lucas called Mrs. Turner by her first name, Violet. She got pretty upset with him and sent him to the principal's office. Lucas didn't understand what the big deal was. He had only gone to Catholic school before now and all of the nuns were called by their first names. His last teacher was Sister Mary Ellen. After having the principal, Mr. Towsen, explain to him that was unacceptable, Lucas went back to class hoping this would not get back to his father. The rest of the school week was pretty uneventful.

That first Saturday, Ike and Joe went with their parents to the fort commissary to shop. Lucas stayed home to finish his homework. After finishing up he decided to take a little walk to explore the neighborhood.

"Can I go out for a walk?" Lucas asked Karla who was left in charge whenever both of Lucas' parents were gone.

"Okay, but don't go too far. I don't want to have to come looking for you," was Karla's reply.

Lucas took off up the street to the main road that ran in front of the school, which was in session. The Germans went to school half a day on Saturday. It was pretty neat to walk along the brick road. There were sections of it closer to the center of town that were paved over, but along this section it was still all brick.

After wandering around for about half an hour, Luke headed home. As he rounded the corner of the schoolyard heading down his street he came to an abrupt stop. Between Lucas and home were half a dozen German boys ranging in age from Lucas' age to a couple of years older. Lucas said "hello" and tried to maneuver around the boys. The biggest boy of the group blocked his path.

Lucas didn't understand much German yet, but he did know enough to know that this kid had just called him an American pig. The boy started to talk to Lucas in a menacing way.

"I don't speak German," Lucas said, as he again tried to get around the boy.

This time the boy, Karl, got in front of Lucas and gave him a shove in the chest. Lucas began to panic. His heart was pounding as his fear mounted. He again tried to get around Karl but now the other boys had closed ranks, limiting his movement. One boy bent over on all fours and knelt behind him. As he turned to glance at the boy, Karl shoved Lucas over the boy, sending him tumbling to the ground. Before he could get up, Karl was on top of him pinning his arms down with his knees.

Karl then began slapping Lucas in the face.

One of the other boys took off and ran back to the school. As Karl continued to slap Lucas, Lucas began to cry, much to the pleasure of Karl and the other boys. He struggled to get up but Karl was much stronger than Luke and began putting more pressure on his shoulders.

A few moments later, a man came around the corner, accompanied by the boy that had taken off earlier. He was a teacher at the school and quickly grabbed Karl by the ear, lifting him off of Lucas. Lucas didn't understand what was being said but he understood that Karl and his cohorts were now in trouble. The teacher lined them up against the wall and helped Lucas up. As he sent them marching back to the school he turned to Lucas and spoke in fluent English.

"I am sorry about what these boys have done. Many of them carry their parent's resentment from the war. They are not very fond of Americans. Nevertheless, you can be sure this will not happen again."

He then turned to the boy who brought him to the fracas and said in English, "Peter, will you please walk this boy home?"

"Ya, Herr Wagner!" was his response in a British accent. Then turning to Lucas, "My name is Peter, what's yours?"

"Lucas." He then looked at Peter and queried, "You're not German?"

"No, I am from England. My mother moved us here to work. She works for a British construction company. They are helping rebuild a lot of buildings that were destroyed by the bombing during the war."

They had reached the house and Lucas had managed to dry up the tears that had been running down his cheek. He felt relief but still had not been able to lose the feeling of fear. He turned to thank Peter for helping him.

"The chaps really aren't all that bad." Peter stated. "Karl is a big bully to all the boys. You were just a fresh target. They were pretty hard on me when I first started school. Since my German has gotten better, most of the boys and girls here hardly remember I am British.

"Well, ta-ta for now. If it's okay, I'll come by later today and show you around some?" Peter asked. "It will be fun to have someone I can speak English with."

"Okay," Lucas answered.

With that, Peter took off, heading farther down the street towards the bottom of the hill to an apartment complex. The first two apartment buildings were completed, the others were still under construction. Peter lived in first one with his mother and although Lucas couldn't play with Peter when he came by later that day, they did meet the following Saturday.

Lucas turned, let out a big sigh, and proceeded up the stairs to their apartment. When he entered the house, Karla took a look at his reddened face and scuffed up clothes and exclaimed, "What the hell happened to you?"

"Some German kids jumped me up the road," Lucas replied, trying to hold down the sob he felt was right there in his throat. It was easy to see he was on the verge of tears again.

"Where are they?" asked Karla. "I'll give them a smack upside the head for doing this to you."

"No, Karla, Their teacher took care of them."

"Well, you go get cleaned up and we'll tell Dad when he gets home."

"Do we have to tell Dad?" Lucas asked. He felt like he disappointed Ivan most of the time. He couldn't imagine how "the Mad Russian" would take it to hear some Germans just beat up his son.

"Yeah, Luke, we have to. He's going to see your face and know something happened."

About that time, Ike and Joe came into the living room and caught the end of Karla and Lucas' conversation.

"Luke got into a fight?" Ike asked excitedly.

"Did you beat 'em up?" piped in Joe as he bent his little body into a boxer's stance, trying to look as menacing as a three-year-old could.

"Guys, leave your brother alone. Lucas, go now and clean yourself up."

Karla was a good older sister to Lucas. She handled the responsibility of taking care of her younger siblings Susan not included, with few complaints and was very protective of the boys. It was a different story with her younger sister. Karla and Susan fought a lot. Susan thought she was a lot older than she was and liked to hang out with the older guys. This put sixteen-year-old Karla at odds with Susan quite often.

Then there was Joe. Friends of Karla would joke about Joe being her kid, which would just infuriate Karla. She was hoping once they moved to Germany, things would be different but so far it hadn't changed. She still had to watch over the three boys.

She really didn't mind watching over Lucas. He was pretty easy. He would play with his toys a lot and when she needed him to occupy Ike, Luke was more than willing to play with him. He played with Joe, too, much to Karla's delight. She could ask Lucas to keep his brothers busy while she was on the phone to her friends and as long as she didn't gab too long, things were fine. Sometimes, when she left them alone too long, the boys would begin to roughhouse, wrestling in their room. This usually led to some type of trouble. One of them would get hurt or they would just get too loud.

Lucas didn't get the total dynamics of the interaction between Karla and their mom, but he did pick up on the fact that Karla had to spend far more time watching them than her friends spent watching over their younger siblings. He felt sympathetic towards her without fully knowing why.

Lucas finished cleaning up and changing. His cheeks were still a bit red from being slapped by Karl but no longer looked like he had been in a fight. Although, from Luke's perspective, it wasn't really a fight. They beat him up and he did very little to fight back. He knew his dad was going to be mad at him. He used to listen to Ivan and his brothers, Uncle Paul and Uncle Dan, talk about the bar fights they would get into. They were a tough bunch of brothers that settled a lot of arguments with their fists. No ... Ivan was not going to be happy with Lucas.

Lucas' attention went to the front door as Ivan and Maria came in carrying groceries. Susan was with them and followed with more bags. "Come on, Luke!" she shouted, "Help us; there's more in the car."

With that Lucas sprang up and raced down the stairs with Ike on his heels. They both picked up a bag of groceries and rushed back upstairs as if it were a race, almost bowling over Susan as she was on her way down for another load.

"Watch it!" she barked as her two brothers flew by her. "And don't drop anything!"

Lucas and Ike both laughed as they continued upstairs. They just looked at each other when they set the bags down and headed down for more. They both had talked often about how Susan was always trying to boss them around. She was in charge if their parents and Karla were gone but that didn't happen too often. *Thank God!*

As Luke and Ike were climbing the stairs (a little more slowly this time) with the last two bags of groceries, they could hear Ivan shouting. As they got to the doorway, Lucas could see that Karla was telling their dad what had happened to Lucas.

"Lucas!" shouted Ivan. "Get your butt over here."

Lucas was feeling a whole different type of terror now as he moved quickly towards his father. When the old man called you, you learned that he expected you to come as fast as you could. If you took too long, you were rewarded with a slap up the backside of your head.

"You let some Kraut kids beat you up?" he asked as he glared at Lucas.

"There were four or five of them," Lucas replied meekly, again on the verge of tears.

"Don't you go cryin' now, boy, or I'll give you something to cry about."

"Yes, sir," Lucas responded, choking back his tears. His dad always would tell him that no matter what someone did to him, he better not cry. It was a sign of weakness. Lucas never figured out how not to cry when he was hurt but he had learned to control it somewhat around his dad. It would only make Ivan madder and he would smack Lucas and say, "Now you have something to cry about!"

Lucas told the story of how the boys blocked his way and tripped him, pinning him down. He also told him of the British boy, Peter, rescuing him. He could see Ivan was still mad but his body language indicated to Lucas that he had relaxed. Lucas was now out of danger of being hit by his father for failing to fight back.

The rest of the night, it was not brought up again. Ivan was unusually quiet through dinner. He and Maria talked softly.

Lucas could hear his mother say, "He never really had to

fight anyone in the projects. The Tanner boys would always look after him."

The Tanner boys were three brothers that were the sons of Maria's best friend back in Uniontown. The youngest was Susan's age. All three were well respected in the neighborhood by both children and adults. If they were protecting you, nobody messed with you.

Nothing more was said about the confrontation until the middle of the following week. Ivan came home with two sets of boxing gloves.

"Lucas," he roared, "no Kraut is going to kick your ass anymore. It's time you learned how to fight. Come over here and put these on."

Lucas was going through multiple feelings all at the same time. Part of it was terror as Ivan began putting the gloves on him and then putting them on himself. They didn't fit Ivan too well. Most of his palm stuck out of the gloves.

Lucas was also feeling excited. He knew Ivan used to box before he joined the Army. Luke had heard the stories at family gatherings about how his dad would earn extra money as a sparring partner in the Bowery in New York City. He knew Ivan was a decent boxer and now he was about to get lessons from him. This added a layer of anticipation to the fear and excitement he was feeling.

Ike and Joe were pretty excited, too.

"Can we box, too, Dad?" Ike asked.

"You'll get your chance," was Ivan's answer. "First I am going to work with Luke."

With that, Ivan looked at Lucas with an almost evil grin. Devilish would be a better description. He then got down on his knees to be closer to Lucas' height.

"I'm going to show you how to stand so your body is balanced." Ivan started, grabbing Lucas by the shoulders and positioning his body.

"Now, hold up you fists like this," he said, demonstrating the proper stance.

Then the lessons began with Ivan showing Lucas how to throw a jab first while keeping his feet in the proper position to best keep his balance and to throw the punch with the most power. After working with Lucas on the various types of punches he began working with him on blocking punches. That devilish look came over Ivan's face again as he popped Luke a couple of times in the face.

It wasn't as if Lucas didn't expect to get hit, but there was some snap to the punches his dad threw and he had to fight back that urge to run from the onslaught or just cover himself up. He knew neither were acceptable alternatives.

"Don't hurt him, Ivan!" Maria shouted as she sat down with Ike and Joe to watch the lesson. "Look, you've left a red spot on his forehead."

"I'm not hurting him, am I Luke?" was his response.

Lucas wanted to say *damn right you are,* but knew what his response needed to be or his dad would only be harder on him, so he glanced at his mom and said, "It doesn't hurt, Mom."

With that, Ivan grinned and popped Lucas again, only it wasn't quite as hard as the last two had been and this time Ivan showed him how to block the punch and to counter with one of his own.

"Smack him Luke!" shouted Joe as Susan and Karla joined the audience.

Ivan turned and looked at Joe, sitting on the end of the couch shaking his fist and as he was starting to say something, Lucas hit him in the mouth.

"Nice shot!" Ike screamed.

"Way to go Lucas!" Karla chimed in.

Lucas threw another glancing punch this time and Ivan countered with a punch that put Lucas on his ass. He quickly got up and to his surprise really didn't feel the punch even though he knew it must have been pretty hard. He could tell that Ivan was pleased at how quickly he got up and came back at him.

The lessons went on for another twenty minutes or so. Then as they took off the gloves, Joe and Ike were putting them on with Ivan tying the laces for them.

"Not too bad for the first day, Luke." his father said. "We'll work on it a little every night for awhile."

Lucas was hurting a little from Ivan's punches but he was feeling pretty good overall. Ivan never told him he did anything good, so to have him say "not too bad" was as high a compliment he could expect to receive from his dad. He felt even better when he heard Ivan tell his mom that Lucas did a lot better than he expected and that he picked up the technicalities of boxing pretty quickly. That feeling quickly turned to alarm when Ivan continued by saying Lucas wasn't mean enough but that he (Ivan) would fix that.

The lessons continued every evening for the first week. Both Ike and Joe joined in after the second day. They would box with their dad and Ivan would stop every time one of them did something wrong. Usually, he gave them a good pop with the gloves first then explained what they did wrong. They would end the session with each of them boxing each other for two rounds that lasted two minutes each. Surprisingly, Luke didn't mind being hit as much as he'd thought he would. When they had first started, he would cover up after getting hit and back away from the punches. By the end of the third week, he was counter punching and not backing up at all when he got hit, even when it was from his father.

A bigger problem for Lucas was boxing Joe. Joe was so little yet fearless. He would lower his head and come charging in, punches flying. Luke couldn't help himself from laughing so hard he couldn't really fight back. This reaction would make Ivan mad and he would put on the gloves and box Lucas.

"Boxing is no laughing matter, Luke!" Ivan shouted at him, following up with a couple of stiff jabs to Lucas' head.

Lucas would then have to get serious or he knew his dad would stick him pretty hard. Once, just after he finished suppressing his laughter he turned as his dad was pulling the gloves on with his teeth, as far as the gloves would go on his hand. As soon as Ivan looked up, Luke popped him in the nose. Ike, Joe, and his mom all gasped as Ivan looked at Luke with shock. Luke hit him again and then grinned at his father. That was a mistake. Ivan began jabbing Lucas with his left and following up with a couple of rights to the stomach, then finishing by hitting him with the palm of his hand, which was sticking out of the too-small gloves. The last punch put Lucas on his ass.

"Stop!" shouted Maria. "You'll hurt him!"

Ivan did stop but Lucas jumped up, and in a fit of anger, forgot about who he was boxing and came back after his dad punching as hard as he could. Ivan fended off the punches, and then began to laugh.

"Enough, Luke!" he hollered. "School is over for today."

Ivan looked at Lucas, standing in front of him, red faced from both the anger and the hits he had taken to the face. Lucas wasn't crying. He was mad and wanted to keep fighting.

"No, Luke," he said a little more softly, "we're done. That's the reaction I've been waiting for. When you're in a fight, you better be able to get angry, but now you have to learn to control it. Go get cleaned up and ready for dinner."

Ivan turned and grinned at Maria. She wasn't as pleased by the exhibit as Ivan was, but she slowly began to relax as she saw Lucas smiling as he and his brothers went to the bathroom. She could hear Ike and Joe's excitement with Lucas as they walked down the hall.

"You hit dad good, Luke!" Ike blurted out.

"Are you crazy?" Joe piped in as he hung on his older brother. It was like all three of them got the shot in on their dad. The two younger boys were, for the moment, in awe of their older brother.

The lessons continued throughout the winter, although with less frequency. Lucas didn't get a chance to get back at the German boys who had pounced on him but it didn't seem to matter. He had gained a self-confidence that he could handle them now if he had to.

He spent his Saturdays with Peter, exploring areas of the town that had been bombed during the war. The bombed-out buildings were being torn down to make way for new housing. It was fun as they played war and fought the imaginary German soldiers in the damaged buildings. Often, they had to hide from any adults they would see since they weren't supposed to be playing in such a dangerous area, but it just added to the fun of the war game. They seldom ran into a problem.

One Saturday morning, Lucas met Peter near the entrance to the school. Peter's teacher was sick and his class had that Saturday off. He didn't have to go the half-day of school he usually did.

"Look at my new slingshot!" Peter told Lucas, showing him it as they began walking down the hill.

"Fire it, you Bloody Limey!" Lucas joked.

"Okay, you damn Yank!" replied Peter as he placed a stone in the leather holder at the end of the thick elastic. He pulled it back and aimed at the wall and released it. Both the boys jumped as it hit the wall with a loud "whack." They looked at each other and Peter loaded it again. They began running down the hill with Peter firing the slingshot at the wall to his side. To their surprise, the rock caromed off the wall and went straight into Lucas' landlady's window, shattering the glass as the boys ran past. By the time they stopped, they were a hundred feet past the house.

"Oh crap!" Lucas blurted out. "We've gotta go back."

Peter didn't want to, but at Lucas' insistence, they turned and went back up to the front of the house to face the consequences. To their surprise when they got there, Lucas' landlady, Frieda ,was giving a teacher up in the schoolyard an earful. The fence was lined with students looking over at the shattered glass and a very unhappy Frieda.

Maria and Karla were both out front taking it all in. Apparently, Frieda thought the rock came from the schoolyard and one of the kids in the schoolyard had broken her window. The schoolmaster was trying to find out who did it and apologizing profusely to Frieda.

"What's up, Mom?" Lucas asked, as if he didn't know.

"One of the kids from the school threw or kicked a rock and broke that window," she said, pointing to the broken window as if Lucas couldn't see it without her pointing it out.

"Oh," he replied, looking at Peter who was now stuffing his slingshot in his pants behind his back and covering it with his coat.

"Well," Peter squeaked, "I'd better get home. Mum's waiting for me. See you later, Lucas."

Off went Peter, running down the street towards his house. Lucas was numb with fear and shock over the situation and said nothing. In fact, the two boys only mentioned it once on the following Saturday when they got together. They decided to never bring it up again for fear of the truth coming out. As it was, the school paid to have the window repaired and it seems that they were never able to catch the culprit. Obviously that was a great relief to Peter.

The next few months were pretty boring and routine. Lucas

would go to school, come home, do his homework, and on the nights that Ivan felt like it, he would get his boxing lessons in. On Saturday he and his brothers would clean their room, which would have to pass their father's inspection, and then they could play. Many of the Saturdays were spent with Peter in the old bombed-out building ruins. Often he would bring Ike and Joe with him.

They would play army in the ruins and only once did they run into a problem. Unbeknown to them, there were some German boys playing in the rubble too. As they were pretending to attack a German outpost, Ike yelled out,

"Kill the Krauts!"

Suddenly, three German youths stepped out from behind a wall. Lucas quickly yelled, "Shut up, Ike!"

Ike didn't need to have Lucas explain why. As the boys approached them, Peter walked over to intercept them. Lucas recognized one of the boys as being with the group that jumped him several months before. He spoke English fairly well and after he and Peter conversed for a few moments in German he turned to Lucas.

"So you want to kill Germans, do you?" he asked menacingly.

"We were only playing. Didn't mean anything by it," answered Lucas as his heart began to race. The German boy, Hans, was Karl's younger brother. He was a year older than Lucas and a good couple of inches taller.

"Maybe I make you cry and go running home to mama like last time?" Hans sneered.

As Hans neared Lucas, Lucas could feel his heart racing and his first impulse was to run. Then he remembered what his father had taught him during his boxing lessons, and as Hans was almost right in front of him, Lucas shifted his stance to be in a position to throw a punch. He was trying not to let his fear get the best of him.

Then everything happened so fast it seemed like a blur to Luke. Hans started to shove Lucas and before he even had another thought, Lucas hit Hans in the nose with a stiff left jab and followed it with a right to the stomach. Hans went down to the ground, doubled over. The rest of the boys all stood in shock as Hans looked up at Lucas, wide-eyed and bleeding from the nose. Lucas just stood there in the classic boxer pose.

"Hit him again, Luke!" Joe yelled as the two other German boys backed away.

"Nein, Nein!" shouted Hans from the ground. He had not attempted to get up yet. He was fighting back tears as he slowly got up holding his stomach. Peter said something to him in German and Lucas barely heard him say, "Ya, ya," to Peter as he joined his two friends and left.

Joe and Ike were all excited. "You kicked his butt!" Ike shouted, as Lucas stood frozen in the same position, feeling like it was all a dream. He fought back tears as he turned and looked at Peter who was standing there grinning.

"I don't think they'll be bothering you again, but you may have to watch out for Karl. I don't think he will really care. He is always slapping Hans around himself and ... I don't think he wants to face Herr Wagner again. Good bloody job, Lucas!"

At that, Lucas finally relaxed and said rather meekly, "Let's go home."

They all headed back, and although Lucas and Peter didn't say much, Joe and Ike kept talking about the fight all the way home, promising Lucas they wouldn't tell their dad. When they said goodbye to Peter, Lucas felt like his friend was looking at him differently - he was still grinning. Luke was trying to figure out what that feeling was he was getting from Peter that he couldn't identify. *Was it respect?* He couldn't quite pin it down. He was still trying to sort out his own thoughts. His body was jumping all over inside when they first left the ruins. *Why do I feel so good on one hand and fell like crying on the other?* He just couldn't make sense of it.

The next month leading into Christmas vacation was another boring time for Lucas - until his mother made the announcement that her German brother, Uncle Fredric and his wife, Aunt Helga, and their son Eckhart were coming to spend Christmas with them. Lucas was finally going to meet the Bachs, and his German cousin.

It was a wonderful meeting. Lucas could see how much his mother looked like Uncle Fredric. Aunt Helga was taller than

Luke had imagined and Eckhart was just like the picture Mom had of him. It was crazy as everyone was talking at once; half German, half English. Lucas couldn't help but laugh out loud as his mother continued to mix the two. She was trying to translate, even though all three Bachs spoke fairly good English. After awhile everyone was laughing as Maria began speaking English to Fredric, Helga, and Eckhart and German to Ivan and the kids. Lucas couldn't remember seeing his father grin so wide.

The Bach family spent two nights, leaving the day after Christmas. Eckhart's English was good enough for him to communicate quite well with Lucas. It was really a nice Christmas. Lucas was curious about Eckhart's life in Munich, bombarding him with questions as they sat in the bedroom talking. Eckhart talked about his love of skiing, Octoberfest, and hiking with his mother in the Alps.

After Christmas life went back to the same old humdrum for Lucas. He really didn't have any close friends at school and the weather had been so bad, he didn't get a lot of chances to play with Peter. He spent most of his time at home with Ike and Joe. When Ivan was home they had their nights of boxing. Ivan never said much to Lucas but Luke overheard him tell his mother one evening, "The boy's getting better. I bet he could kick that little Kraut's ass now."

Lucas had never told his dad about the fight at the ruins. Ike and Joe were true to their word to their big brother. They never said a word about it until months later when they moved out of Zweibrücken and then it came out by accident. Ivan overheard his two youngest sons talking about it one night and quizzed them on the specifics. He never said a word to Lucas about it.

Only once did anything exciting happen at school. It was late February and the ground had been covered by about ten inches of snow when the temperature warmed and a rainstorm came through. It melted all of the snow and everything was flooded, turning the ground into gooey red mud. The way the school grounds laid out, the buildings were spread out in two different areas. One area, where Luke's classroom was, was on top of the hill. The road was up there as well as the Administration Office.

The other cluster of buildings was down below on the terraced hillside. There was a basketball court on the side of the buildings facing the hill to the upper level. The area next to it was all dirt with a shortcut trail that went up to the top of the hill. The sidewalk that went from the lower buildings up took a much longer switchback route to the top. Many of the kids would take the shorter route.

On this day that dirt area was all mud by the late afternoon as classes were getting out. The first of the sixth-graders to come up began racing towards the trail going up the hill. They didn't get far. The first four went dashing in the muddy area and all got stuck. The leader was a big kid and he got the farthest, but when Lucas looked down to see who was doing all the screaming, the boy was up to his knees in mud and stuck solid. The second and third kids were also stuck but not as deeply. The fourth managed to stop just a few feet from the edge of the basketball court as he saw his companions get stuck in front of him.

There were several teachers there by the time Lucas got over to the edge of the hill along with most of the other kids from the upper buildings. Word had spread fast about the boys being stuck in the mud. One of the boys was crying loudly. He was afraid of missing the bus, but he needn't have worried. None of the buses were going to leave until the boys were out. About that time, everyone could hear the sirens as the fire trucks approached.

Lucas watched in fascination as several of the firemen got together on the basketball court. Within minutes they were all moving except one that stayed to talk to the boys. Moments later they were returning with ladders along with wood and canvas stretchers used to carry accident victims. They laid the ladders across the mud next to the first boy who was up to about mid-calf in the mud. The first fireman walked out to him on the wood stretcher and was able to pull him out of the mud. The ladder sunk a few inches while the fireman carried the boy to the other firemen on the court. As soon as they got off of the ladder another fireman took a second ladder and placed it past both of the remaining boys.

The first fireman turned from the boy he had just rescued and walked back out on the rescue plank. When he got to the second boy, he was in deeper than when Lucas first saw him. The big kid in front was in deeper too, with the mud now coming up to his crotch. Lucas could hear the fireman telling them to quit struggling. "It's only getting you in deeper." As the fireman, Danny, (Lucas heard his name being called by his fellow firemen) tried to lift the second boy onto the ladder the plank sank suddenly so the mud came to the top of the plank. The entire crowd of kids and teachers, and now some of the parents who were showing up as the word spread throughout the post, all let out a huge gasp, followed by an eerie silence. It was one of the strangest feelings Lucas had ever felt. He didn't have long to think about it, though, as Danny flattened his body out on the plank and continued to work on getting the boy's legs out of the mud. There was a big sucking sound as the second boy came out. As this was going on, a second fireman was on the first ladder lying down and reaching out to hold the boy's head and shoulders out of the mud, at least most of the way out. His back and the back of his head were covered with mud.

There was a second big sucking sound as the second fireman pulled the boy onto the ladder. Everyone cheered. Lucas looked around at the crowd. *This is really exciting.* Everything had been going fairly smoothly. That was about to change as Danny finally reached the last boy. By now, everyone knew his name was Paul. Several of the other firemen created another bridge on the other side of Paul. They ended up putting a harness under Paul's arms and several of them pulled ever so slowly as Danny from one side and another fireman on the other worked on getting his legs out. This took much longer than getting the previous boy out. Finally, after a good half hour (it was beginning to get dark), they got Paul out. His shoes and socks were gone! They were stuck in the mud and as far as Lucas could figure, they would be permanently.

All of a sudden, whistles began blowing as the teachers and bus drivers were now trying to get everyone on their buses and home. Lucas wondered if his parents would be worried about Susan and him. The buses were leaving forty-five minutes late. When Luke climbed on the bus, Susan was already there, impatient to get going. He had not seen her during the entire rescue operations. Lucas actually sat next to her on the bus, something that seldom happened.

"What a bunch of idiots," she said as she rolled her eyes at Lucas. "I have a ton of homework to do. I don't understand why they held all of the buses. They should've just let those little numbskulls' parents come get them for being so stupid in the first place."

Lucas just smiled. *I hope their dad isn't like mine. Boy, are they in for a beating.* He realized it could have just as easily been him in the mud. This made him smile even more. That would have really ticked his sister off.

It was the beginning of March when Ivan came home a little late one evening.

"Everyone come out here!" Ivan bellowed. "I only want to say this once!"

Lucas, Ike, and Joe moved quickly from their bedroom to the living room where they found their father grinning from ear to ear. Their mother was already sitting on the couch so the boys sat around her with Joe on her lap. Karla soon joined them, all staring at Ivan, trying to guess what this news was he was about to share with them.

"SUSAN! GET YOUR ASS OUT HERE!" yelled their father.

"I'm coming!" was the reply from the bedroom.

Finally, Susan joined them, sporting a sour face. She plopped down on the one remaining chair and folded her arms, looking quite bored.

"Starting tonight I want you to start packing up your stuff. We're moving," stated Ivan as a buzz erupted from the rest of the family.

"Did we get housing on the fort at Pirmasens?" Maria asked.

"No," replied Ivan, "but the next best thing. We got it on a hospital fort just five kilometers from Pirmasens, at a village called Münchweiler. We will be moving in next week. We need to have everything ready to go by Monday for the moving van to load up. Tomorrow will be your last day at your school. I have the paperwork you need to take in with you tomorrow. We'll have you at your new school by Tuesday of next week."

"Why can't we wait until the school year is over?" asked Susan.

"Because when the Army says 'move' you move," answered Ivan.

They had been on a waiting list to get military housing since before they came across the ocean. Lucas, Ike and Joe were excited. They would now be on an American fort where there were lots of kids their age and they spoke *English.* Only Susan seemed a little miffed by it all. For Karla it was no big deal. She was in high school and all three forts, Pirmasens, Zweibrücken, and Münchweiler, all sent their kids to the high school in Kaiserslautern so it wasn't going to affect her very much. For Susan, Lucas and Ike, who only went half a day to kindergarten, it meant moving schools. Since Lucas didn't really have any good friends at school, he was looking forward to the change.

"Jon Morton and his family are coming over Sunday night. They're gonna bring us some dinner since everything will be packed," Ivan informed the family. Sgt. Morton was Ivan's best friend. They had served in the war together and been stationed at the same post several times. Although Lucas had not met Sgt. Morton, he had heard enough about him and his family. He and his wife, Mary, had two girls Lucas and Ike's age. Ivan would talk about how smart the oldest girl, Tara, was. Now it looked like Luke was finally going to meet her. He was feeling a little funny about it. To be truthful, he was actually excited about it, but he wasn't going to let his brothers know.

It didn't take long for that to change. About ten minutes after the Morton's arrived. Lucas, Tara, Ike, Lilly and Joe went into the boys' room to hang out while their parents had a cocktail before dinner. Tara had this air about her that Lucas couldn't explain. Later, when he learned the word *arrogance,* he immediately thought of Tara.

"So you're from Pittsburgh?" Tara asked Luke.

"No, we're from Uniontown. It is south of Pittsburgh."

"How far south?"

"I'm not sure."

"What the population?"

As Lucas was pondering the question and trying to remember how many people were in Uniontown, Tara quipped, "That means how many people, oh slow one," which made the other three kids chuckle.

"I know what it means," Lucas shot back. He could feel he

was starting to get angry with this smartass girl. "And, I don't remember anyhow!"

"You're not very smart are you?" she snickered, again getting laughter out of the others.

"Smarter than your ugly face," was all Luke could think of, which was so stupid. Tara wasn't ugly, at least not on the outside, and everyone in the room knew it was a lame response.

Fortunately, before he could get into it any deeper, his mother called them all in to eat. "She got you good," Ike whispered to Lucas as they headed for the dining room. Luke just glared at him. He knew Ike was right. He just wasn't prepared for this girl.

They managed to get through the meal without too much more embarrassment for Lucas. Tara did shoot him a few jabs, very skillfully Lucas observed. It seemed like she knew how to take it to the brink of having an adult intervene, but always knew when to back off. Lucas didn't have a chance getting the best of her on any subject this night. He made a mental note to be better prepared the next time they met.

"See you around, Lucas!" Tara yelled from the doorway as they were leaving.

Not if I can help it. "See you," he responded.

After the Mortons were gone, Ivan kept going on about how smart Tara was. Susan looked at Lucas with a snide grin. She liked Tara. In a lot of ways they were alike. Lucas was glad they were different ages. He knew Susan wouldn't hang out with anyone that much younger. He could just imagine what it would be like if they both teamed up on him.

Fort Munchweiler
Hospital

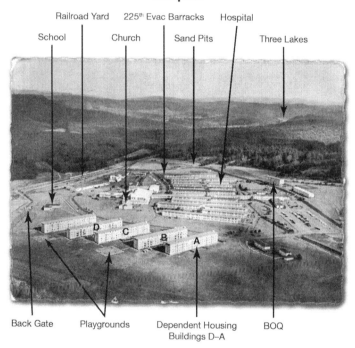

Railroad Yard   225th Evac Barracks   Hospital

School   Church   Sand Pits   Three Lakes

Back Gate   Playgrounds   Dependent Housing   BOQ
Buildings D–A

Chapter III

Moving to Münchweiler

The moving van showed up Monday morning and Ivan was there to direct them. It was a cool March day and about the time Ivan told the boys to get ready, it started to rain. It wasn't a very heavy rain but a light steady drizzle. As Lucas and his brothers climbed into the car for the drive, Ivan rolled down the window and yelled out the window, "Susan, come with us! Your mother and Karla can clean up here."

Lucas stared out the window looking at the beautiful scenery they were passing. He was barely aware of the conversation between Susan and their dad. The green forest and the lush hillsides rolled by. Most of the trees on the hillsides were pines, with other barren trees that had not yet leafed out dotting the edges of the meadows that ran along the roadside. Also, there were many reminders of the war that had taken place here not so long ago. As they drove through the countryside from Zweibrücken to Pirmasens, they passed many old farmhouses burnt down or destroyed from the ground fighting during World War II. Next to some of them would be a newly built house. Sometimes they would pass farm fields that were broken up by rows of concrete pillars that had been used as tank barriers during the war. These would stretch over large areas, often located in a field between two streams.

Lucas was just daydreaming about how it must have been during the war. He used to love going into the woods when they were at the projects or when he went to his cousins' in the country. The house in Zweibrüken hadn't given him access to the woods or a chance to get into the country. He was wondering if his new home would allow him to be in this beautiful country that was laid out before his eyes.

As they were driving through Pirmasens, Lucas could see a lot more evidence of the war here than he had seen going through the country. Some areas were like the ruins that he had played in while in Zweibrücken. There was scaffolding around a church steeple and more around a building that looked like it had a bank on the bottom floor. Most of what he saw looked like it was intact, but Lucas had no way of judging whether it was rebuilt or never damaged. He liked the look of the town. His mind just wandered as they drove through it until he jumped a foot off the seat as Ivan bellowed, "JUST FIVE KLICKS TO GO!" as they got to the end of the small city. Luke's heart was pounding as he looked at his grinning dad. They had all been traveling in utter silence, all with their own thoughts, when Ivan had roared.

"Scared shit outta you, didn't I boy?" laughed Ivan. "Look at his face," his father said to Lucas' siblings.

Lucas turned to look at his brothers and Susan. They were laughing hysterically. Lucas turned beet red and then burst out into laughter with them. His dad did scare the shit out of him … almost! He could tell by Joe's face that he wasn't the only one that their dad startled with his outburst.

The rest of the short trip was filled with chatter from them all asking questions of their dad and his responses, mostly about what they were passing. It was a history lesson of sorts, but as they all realized the more they were around their father, it was "History according to Ivan" that they were learning. A bit skewed at times and totally warped at others.

Finally, they pulled up to the gate of the fort at Münchweiler. It was a hospital fort close to Pirmasens. It had the first available housing within the parameters that were allowable under the Army distance rules for GIs to drive from their workstations to their homes.

The MP stopped the car for a moment before waving the Baryshivkas through. The rain had stopped but looked like it could begin again at any time. Ivan drove the car towards the dependent housing. They passed two houses, one a duplex.

"The Post Commander lives in the single house," Ivan told his kids. "The other house has the Chief Surgeon and the Commander of the 208th Signal Company."

Ivan continued as they passed the first of what were five apartment buildings. "This is where the officers' families live," he said as they continued past the cul-de-sac that had a second building facing it from the other side. After they went by the third building they turned down the cul-de-sac and drove to the end of it. As they drove along the length of the buildings, Lucas could see they each had three sets of balconies that went three stories high with windows at a fourth story, but no balcony. The moving van was sitting at the last stairwell of the fourth building.

Lucas got out of the car. *So this is going to be home.*

"We just started movin' stuff up, Sarge," the GI in charge of the movers said to Ivan. "Thought we could wait out the rain. So far, so good," he said with a grin.

"Come on, Luke!" shouted Joe as he grabbed Lucas' arm and started tugging him upstairs. "Let's look at our room."

With Ike following, they all ran up the stairs to the second story, dodging the movers that were coming back down for another load. They already knew which was their room. Ivan had laid out the plan for everyone as soon as he and their mother went to look at their new quarters. The three brothers dashed to the end of the hall and turned left into the end bedroom. The bunk bed was already set up. That was for Joe and Ike. Luke got the single since he was the oldest. His bed was leaning against the wall.

Luke went to the window and looked out. The moving van was below, stretched into the cul-de-sac. Painted in the cul-de-sac was a four squares game. It is a game where one big square was broken into four smaller ones, each about eight feet long on one side. A person is in each square with one person serving the ball, usually a basketball or soccer ball, into one of the other squares with the object being to get the people in the other squares to miss the ball. The receiving person tries to hit the ball into one of the other squares and this continues until the ball is missed and the serve is rotated. There are several variations to the game but two were the most popular with Lucas and his friends. One was to get points for each time a player missed your hit to them or the second, if you missed you were out. In the first scenario the boys usually played first to ten points. In the second there were often other players waiting until someone was eliminated, with the last one standing being the winner.

Luke looked beyond the cul-de-sac to a playground that was situated behind and in between the second and third apartment buildings. Later he discovered a second one between his building and the last one. The playground was like a huge sand box surrounded by a concrete curb with a swing set, monkey bars, and a sand box within the sand. The sand box had a concrete perimeter that was about eighteen inches high and wide enough to sit on. The sand in it was slightly finer than the sand in the rest of the playground. Luke was excited because he had never really had a playground so close to where he lived.

"Whatcha looking at, Luke?" Joe asked.

"Come see," was Luke's response. Both Joe and Ike joined Lucas at the window.

"Neato!" Joe yelled as he viewed the playground. "Let's go over there."

"We'll have to ask Dad," Lucas said as he turned from the window and headed back downstairs to where his father was directing the movers.

Lucas asked Ivan, who responded, "No, it's too wet and it looks like the rain is going to pick up again. I don't want you dragging wet sand into the house on our first day here. Besides, you're gonna have a lot of chances to play at the playground. We're gonna be here for awhile."

The boys were disappointed but they weren't down for long. They began exploring the basement instead. They followed two of the movers to a storage room that had their apartment number on it. The movers were placing some of the boxes in the storage locker. All along the basement facing the front side of the building were storage lockers. On the other side of the long hallway that extended the length of the building were two large laundry rooms filled with washing machines and folding tables. There were no dryers there; instead there was an area behind the building with clothes lines stretched across it. The area was surrounded by a tall wooden fence that, from the outside, made it look like an old army cavalry fort.

The brothers spent some time exploring the outside of the building, too, before it began to rain. The rain started lightly as they headed back to the moving van. Fortunately, the movers had just finished taking the last load up to the apartment and were picking up the moving pads and empty boxes, placing them back in the moving van as the rain picked up.

"Upstairs, guys!" Ivan yelled to his sons.

The boys dashed to the stairwell, pushing and shoving each

other as they went. This was the most fun and excitement they had had for some time. As they entered the apartment, Susan was sitting in a chair reading. Ivan entered shortly after them.

"I'm going back to pick up your mother and sister," Ivan stated. "Susan is in charge while I'm gone. I don't want to come back to any trouble, you hear?"

"YES SIR!" they shouted in unison. Joe broke out in a big grin and saluted his dad.

"Dammit, Joe, don't you be saluting me! I ain't no damn officer!"

With that, Ivan turned and left, and the boys started unpacking.

"Come on, Ike," Lucas said, "put your clothes away and then you can play."

"You're not my boss," Ike returned. "I don't have to if I don't wanna."

About that time, Susan came back to see what they were up to. "But I *am* the boss and I'm telling you put your clothes away or I'll tell Dad."

She was always threatening to tell on them. She used the fear the boys had of their father to control her brothers. This time it worked because Ike shot her a nasty look as he put down his toy soldiers and began putting his clothes away. Lucas helped Joey.

It was just about 4 o'clock when Lucas heard the school bus pull into the cul-de-sac. He jumped up from the floor and watched as the kids piled out of the bus in the rain and began dashing towards the apartments. Susan came in and stood next to Lucas at the window.

"The school here only goes through the third grade," she explained to Luke. "From fourth grade through eighth grade the kids get bussed to Pirmasens. The high school kids all get bussed to K-town." K-town was what most of the Americans called Kaiserslautern. "You'll only go here until this school year is over. After that you get bussed to Pirmasens."

As the bus rolled away, Susan exited the room. Within minutes, as Lucas was still staring out the window, his parents and Karla pulled up. By the time they ate dinner, helped with whatever assignment their parents gave them and hit their new beds, all three boys were exhausted.

"Tomorrow will be a busy day," their mother said as she came to tell them goodnight. "I'll be taking you to your new school in the morning, Luke. Ike's starts later in a different building, so we'll go there after you're in school." With that she turned out the light. Lucas tried to think about all that had happened that day but exhaustion took over and he was quickly asleep.

The elementary school, grades one through three, was a short walk from the last apartment building. The fort was a small one whose main function was the hospital. It was located about five kilometers east of Pirmasens. Upon entering the main gate of the fort, the road continued east past the gate. Less than a thousand feet into the fort was the bowling alley on the left with the baseball field behind the bowling alley. A road on the right went up a hill a short distance to the communications building and a picnic grounds east of the building. On the east side of the picnic grounds was the fence for the fort boundary and a row of trees with a soccer field on the other side of the fence and then more trees. Lucas learned that every Sunday the Germans would have soccer games at the field.

After passing the bowling alley, just a few hundred feet farther was the NCO Club on the same side of the street as the bowling alley. The road then came to a "Y" which was the beginning of the loop road that went around the entire fort. Going left at the split took you up a hill to the Dependents Quarters. This was also the highest area of the fort with the terrain falling off from the apartments towards the southeast. In between the third and fourth apartment buildings was a road to the right which went to a large cul-de-sac that brought you to the main hospital complex which included the troop's barracks, the hospital, the chapel, the mess hall, the PX, snack bar, movie theater and most of the entire fort operations. All of the buildings were interconnected by long corridors with the central one going from the main hospital entrance at the south end of the complex to the building at the north end that housed all of the utilities.

Continuing beyond this turnoff and the apartment buildings, the road started going downhill beneath the schoolhouse until it got to its northern-most point just past the school. There you could take a left turn to the rear gate of the fort but, it was always closed and the small guard shack was unmanned. Continuing on the loop road there were railroad yards and warehousing building on the left with the fire station to the right. The road continued for a short distance to the east before curving back around towards the main gate again, passing a materials pit, which was known to the kids on the fort as the sand pits. The road curved again just past the sand pits and continued towards the main gate passing the secondary entrance to the hospital on the right with the BOQ (Bachelors Officer Quarters) on the left. Just where the BOQ building ended was the main entrance to the hospital with a huge parking lot just beyond the entrance that went all the way back to the "Y".

Also a very important part of the fort, at least in the kids' eyes, was a large drainage ditch that started just behind a grassy field that was north of the parking lot. It collected all of the water runoff from most of the buildings, including the main corridor and the parking lot, taking it behind the NCO Club, bowling alley and ball field to a low lying area at the most western point of the fort. The drainage ditch was actually going against the slope of the terrain, getting deeper and deeper as it went west.

On the south side of the ditch near its western-most point was a large grassy hill coming down from the road and ball field elevation to the low lying area. This was the sledding hill when it snowed. It was a great one at that, being long and steep but not too long, so climbing back up it with a sled was not too difficult a chore. It was fairly flat with few bumps, so sledders could really pick up speed by the time they got to the bottom.

Farther to the west, on the right side of the ditch, was an area the kids nicknamed "Sewer Hill" because of the stinky smell that was emitted from large concrete boxes that were buried from ground level to about six feet deep. They never seemed to completely drain of rainwater, giving the standing water a very rank smell.

As Lucas would later discover, the loop road became a great route for the kids to have bike races. At this particular moment, as he walked the road with his mother to school, Luke hardly noticed. "Don't be nervous, honey. It will be fun," his mother assured him. He liked this much better than his father taking him to his first day in Zweibrücken. It was always good to be one-on-one with his mother. Lucas squeezed her hand *(she's the best)* as they strolled up to the front door. The bell had just rung and kids were racing into the school, many looking over at Lucas and his mother, some waving, others giving them a curious look.

Lucas and his mom did not spend much time in the Administration office. The clerk there, Miss Day, was expecting them. The school was too small to have a principal. It was part of the Pirmasens school system and the Pirmasens Principal oversaw the small school at Münchweiler, too.

Maria kissed her son goodbye and left. Lucas followed Miss Day to the third grade class. It was really awkward for Lucas as they entered the class. Everyone stopped what they were doing and there was complete silence as Miss Day introduced Lucas to his new class and teacher.

"Lucas, this is your teacher, Mrs. Shinn," as she turned to the class "and class, this is Lucas Baryshivka."

"Hello," Lucas said meekly and then almost fell back as the class in unison shouted, "HELLO LUCAS!"

Everybody laughed loudly at Lucas' reaction and then began talking amongst themselves. Mrs. Shinn began tapping her foot and said, "Class, let's all settle down now. You can all get acquainted with Lucas at recess. Lucas, take the third seat in the first row. It has been empty since Billy's father got transferred."

Lucas was happy to sit down and not be standing in front with everyone looking at him. That was really the first time that Luke actually looked at Mrs. Shinn and his mouth almost dropped open. She had a huge chin that was so disproportionate to the rest of her face it made her look both scary and funny at the same time. Lucas had to use all of his self-control not to stare at her chin. The boy across the aisle from Luke must have caught the look on his face as he smiled real big and nodded like he knew the shock Lucas had just gone through. Lucas put the thought out of his head and forced himself to concentrate on the math sheet in front of him.

At recess, a lot of Lucas' new classmates came up to him to introduce themselves, one of them being the boy across the aisle from Luke.

"Hi, Lucas! Yeah, that's her real chin!" he said smiling. "My

name is Jimmy Parker and this is Pat Simmons," he said as he
pointed to the boy next to him. The two were about the same
height and build, just a little shorter than Lucas. Pat had sandy
blond hair and Jimmy had black hair that looked like it wanted
to stick straight out of his head if it weren't slicked down by
some type of hair cream.

"We call her Mrs. *Chin*," Pat chimed in, grinning from ear to ear.

"But don't ever let her hear you call her that," Jimmy added, "or
you're dead meat."

Just then a boy shot in between Lucas and the two boys. "I'm
Ricky Mason. I live across the street from you in Building C. I
saw your moving van yesterday."

The other two boys just rolled their eyes and said, "See ya
later!" as they took off running across the schoolyard. Other kids
came up and introduced themselves but Ricky just sort of hung
on Luke.

"We can walk home together after school," Ricky said as Lucas
eyed the kids in the schoolyard. A couple of the girls from his
class were in a group looking at him and giggling. Lucas felt a
little embarrassed as he turned his attention back to Ricky. "Is
that okay with you?"

Lucas looked at Ricky and smiled. "Yeah, that's fine with me."

Ricky was a good inch shorter than Luke. He had black wavy
hair and an olive complexion. He had a bounce to his walk and
his blue eyes were wide with an excited look, which Luke first
thought was from meeting the new kid. As he soon learned, that
was the look Ricky always had.

Some of the other boys that had been tossing a football
around came over and introduced themselves. "Hi, I'm Bob
Ledahawski. This is Jason Sprint and Terry Smith."

Bob was a big kid, almost two inches taller that Lucas. He
wasn't fat but he was broad and barrel shaped. Standing next to
Lucas' lanky frame made him seem even bigger. Jason was short
and thin, looking slightly oriental. Lucas later found out his
mother was a war bride from Japan. Terry was the same height
as Ricky with thick red hair and plenty of freckles.

"I'm Lucas!" Luke blurted. He knew how silly that sounded as
soon as the words left his mouth. He realized they already knew
that. He had just been introduced to the whole class. He was

sure he was turning a little red-faced and it went a shade deeper when the group of girls went strolling past the boys laughing as they headed back to the classroom.

Bob let out a laugh as they headed back in. He turned to Luke and said, "I'm sure Jimmy and Pat told you to make sure you enunciate Mrs. Sssshinn and don't make it sound too much like Chin or you're in deep poop. We had a boy that was here last semester that accidentally pronounced it Chin and she grabbed him by the ear and marched him down to the office so fast he didn't even have time to figure out what he did wrong. Then she had his dad transferred right out of here."

"That's not true," Jason chimed in. "My dad said his dad already had his transfer orders before that happened."

"Believe what you like, twerps, but I ain't gonna take a chance. My dad would kill me if I got him transferred outta here."

The boys were the last to get back to class and Mrs. *CHIN* gave them a look that sent a chill up Luke's spine. *She looks like that creepy witch in the mirror from the Snow White movie.*

"Class, now we can begin," she said as the boys took their seats. She turned and looked directly at Bob. "Robert, don't be teaching the new student bad habits."

"No, ma'am," answered Bob. As soon as Mrs. Shinn turned to face the blackboard, Bob looked at Lucas and gave him a huge grin. Lucas looked back at him, *this could be scary fun.* He couldn't quite put his finger on why, but there was a sense of excitement that went through him as he thought about getting into trouble his first day in class. Unlike in Zweibrücken, here he already had some co-conspirators and friends. He continued smiling.

The day seemed to fly by. Lucas actually liked how Mrs. Shinn taught. Last week at Zweibrücken, Luke had just had some of the history she was going over, but she had a way of making it much more interesting. If her damn chin didn't keep becoming a distraction. She would turn just right and jut it out there so Luke would totally lose his train of thought. Finally, the bell rang and all of the class started to jump up and then, like they had choreographed it, they all sat back down (except for Lucas) and froze until Mrs. Shinn, breaking out with the only smile Lucas had seen on her all day, said, "Class … dismissed."

Ricky Mason was waiting for Lucas at the classroom door. As they walked out of the school, Bob, Jason, and Terry joined them. Just ahead of them were Jimmy Parker and Pat Simmons.

"So where you from?" Ricky asked. "What rank's your dad? Do you have brothers or sisters?" The questions just kept rolling out of Ricky. Lucas answered each question and the other boys just listened. When they got to Building D, Jason shot ahead to catch Jimmy and Pat while the rest of them turned down the sidewalk in front of the apartment.

"This is my stop," Bob said as they got to the first entrance into the apartments. "See you all tomorrow."

Terry got off at the next entrance and as they got close to Lucas's entrance Ricky shot across the street yelling, "Maybe you can come out later, Lucas? I live on the first floor, left side if you want to come over."

"I don't think my old man will let me on a school night," Lucas replied; besides, Lucas had a lot of homework to catch up on. Although he missed only a few days of school with the move, his new class, except for history, was a little ahead of where he was with his old class.

The next morning as Lucas got to the bottom of the stairwell, he found Ricky waiting for him. "Tomorrow is Friday; do you think you can play after school?" Ricky asked.

"I think so," replied Lucas.

"Great!" Ricky responded as they began their walk to school. They were joined by Bob and Jason. After they all said their hellos they mostly walked and listened to Ricky as he rambled on about a multiple array of subjects the rest of the way to school.

After school on Friday, Ricky wasn't taking any chances that Luke wouldn't ask to play. He showed up at the door about half an hour after they got home. "Lucas!" his mother yelled to the back room, "you have company."

Lucas came out of the bedroom with Ike and Joe following to see who was there. Lucas had told them about his new classmates and now they got to meet one.

"Hi, Ricky," Lucas said as he turned to his mother and introduced Ricky to her and his brothers. "Can I go out and play with Ricky for awhile, Mom?"

"Ok," she answered, "but be home by 5 o'clock."

"How will I know when that is, I don't have a watch?" This was another plug for Lucas who had been trying to get his parents to buy him a watch. He was hoping for one last Christmas but didn't get one. That didn't mean he was going to give up trying.

"Oh, that's easy!" Ricky piped in. "The flag goes down and the bugle plays at 5 o'clock. You can hear it anywhere on the fort. You know protocol, don't you? You have to stop and face the flag and put your hand over your heart. All of the soldiers have to stop and salute."

Well, Lucas didn't know. This was the first military installation he had actually lived on and he did remember it vaguely from the time the buses ran late when the boys got stuck in the mud in Zweibrücken. He had noticed that many of the people stopped to face where the flag was, but since a lot of the rescue people continued to work and he really couldn't see the flag, he didn't understand what was going on.

"Can I go with 'em? Ike asked.

"Me, too!" Joe shouted.

"Please, Mom, not this time?" Lucas pleaded. He had had to take his brothers with him on most occasions when he went out to play. It had begun to happen more and more as he played with Peter in Zweibrücken. He liked his brothers but wanted to play with his newfound friend for the first time without them.

"Maybe next time, boys," his mother told his brothers as Luke yelled out a "thanks" and bolted for the door, dragging Ricky with him.

Ricky was a little stunned by the speed at which Luke moved to get them away from the apartment.

"I don't mind if they come," Ricky said as they reached the bottom of the stairwell.

"I do," Luke shot back. "Don't worry; I am sure they'll come with us sometime soon. I always have to watch them. Consider yourself lucky today. I do!"

They went to the playground first. Ricky kept up a constant dialogue telling Lucas all about the fort and the kids in their class. On the swings were two girls. One of them was in Luke's class and he remembered her name was Bonnie Lee. Lucas thought she was the cutest girl in the class. The other, it turned out, was her younger sister who was Ike's age.

"Hi Bonnie! Hi Joan!" Ricky shouted at them as he and Lucas neared the swing. "You remember Lucas, the new boy in our class?"

"Of course I do … hello, Lucas," was Bonnie's soft-spoken reply. "This is my sister Joan."

"Hello," Lucas meekly replied. He was surprised at how that came out. It wasn't very confident, he knew, and he couldn't quite figure out why. He quickly realized he was staring at her and that he liked her. Not just the way he liked some of the other girls in his past classes. There was something different about the way he felt towards her. She was beautiful, with long blond hair that flowed just over her shoulders. Her blue eyes and high cheekbones were mesmerizing. He felt himself turning red and quickly ran over to the monkey bars and started swinging on them. He wasn't sure why but he was a little uncomfortable staying by the swings.

"See ya later!" Ricky yelled at Bonnie and Joan as he ran to catch up with Lucas. When he got to Lucas he asked, "Why did you run off so fast? I like talking to Bonnie. She sure is cute, isn't she?"

"I felt like it," was Luke's defensive answer. "Yeah … she is really cute."

"Hey … you like her, don't you?" Ricky asked.

"Naw!" was the only answer Lucas could muster up. Then the boys went on their way to see the neighborhood. Ricky was giving Lucas the rundown on the place with who lived where and what rank their fathers were. What Lucas did learn was that Ricky's dad was an officer and he shouldn't have been living in the building that he lived in. They were sort of in the same circumstance, both families were living "on the economy" which was military talk for living off the fort, while waiting for the first available quarters on post. Captain Mason didn't want to wait until quarters opened up in the Officers Building so he took the next available apartment, which is how he got to live in the building nearby. Lucas also found out that the other officers' kids didn't think too much of that, a reflection of how their fathers thought, and so Ricky didn't hang out much with them.

It seemed like they were barely getting started when "Retreat" began to ring out of all of the loudspeakers spread around the fort. Like Ricky had said, everyone stopped what they were doing and turned to where the flag post was. The soldiers saluted and everyone in civilian clothes put their hands over their hearts until the flag was down. Lucas covered his heart. *So this is what it is like to be in the Army.* As soon as the flag was down, Luke turned to Ricky and said, "See you tomorrow!" as he headed back home.

"Can you come out later?" Ricky shouted at him. "It is a Friday night. No school tomorrow!"

Lucas looked back and laughed as he saw Ricky standing there with this pleading look on his face. "Not tonight. I don't want to push my luck with my dad." And off he went.

The next morning at 8 o'clock Ricky was at the door. Ivan answered as the three brothers looked out of their doorway to see who was there. Lucas just smiled when he saw Ricky.

"Hello Sergeant Baryshivka, my name is Ricky Mason," he said politely. "I'm a classmate of Lucas' and I wondered if he could come out and play."

Lucas knew the answer before his father spoke the words. He and his brothers had just finished breakfast and were cleaning their room. They could never play on Saturday until the room was cleaned and passed Ivan's inspection.

"Maybe later," Ivan replied, giving Ricky a hard stare as he was trying to decide whether he liked him or not, "after the boy finishes cleaning his room and doing his chores."

"I could help," Ricky blurted.

"I don't think so," was Ivan's final word as he rather abruptly closed the door on Ricky Mason. Ivan decided then that he didn't really like the kid anyhow. Later when Ivan found out his dad was an officer he knew he didn't like him.

Luke, Ike and Joe ran to the window to watch Ricky walk dejectedly, home. Then Lucas turned to his brothers and said, "Let's hurry up and clean up the room."

After passing their father's inspection, including no dust on the window sill, Luke followed his father out to the kitchen where his mother was.

"Can I go out and play now, Dad?"

"Ask your mother."

"Mom?"

"Take your brothers with you," was Maria's answer.

"Do I have to?"

"You heard me, Lucas," she replied in a voice that Luke knew meant he wasn't going to win that argument.

"HURRY UP YOU GUYS!" Lucas shouted down the hall although he didn't have to. His brothers were listening in and they were off getting their jackets when their mother first told Lucas to take them. Now they were already running to the door with their jackets half on. "Hurry up slowpoke!" Joe yelled at his older brother as he passed him. Lucas laughed as he took off after his brother yelling "BYE!" to his parents as he closed the door behind him.

The three brothers had not gotten halfway across the street when Ricky came running out of the stairwell across the street. "Hi!" he shouted as ran up to them.

"Had to bring my brothers with me," Lucas explained. "This is Ike and this is Joe," he said as he yanked each by their jacket and pulled them in front of him.

"I don't mind," replied Ricky, "the more the merrier. Hi guys!"

With the introductions over, Ricky proceeded to give the newcomers a tour of the fort. First they checked out the two playgrounds. The one between the Baryshivkas' building and the last building was closest to them, but Bonnie Lee hung out at the one between Buildings B and C so that's where Lucas wanted to spend the most time. Ricky didn't let them stay long at either. After all, he had the whole fort to show them.

Next he took them down the street across from their cul-de-sac into the main hospital complex. The first building they came upon to the left was the chapel. "Each Sunday they have one Protestant Service and one Catholic Mass," Ricky informed them as they continued to the main entrance from the housing area, entering a breezeway with two sets of big double doors. They found themselves standing in an intersection of two major hallways with their typical military tile floors and white walls. To the right was a long uphill hallway that had a double door a hundred feet from where they stood.

"That goes to the hospital and all of the wards and rooms and training centers. Stuff like that," Ricky told them. "So are you Catholic or Protestant?"

"Huh," mumbled Luke as he was trying to take in all that his eyes were seeing. There were medical personnel and soldiers everywhere. It didn't seem overly crowded, but pretty busy. "Oh … we're Catholic."

"Me too," was Ricky's reply. "Neato!"

The hall to the left was perpendicular to the long hall to the hospital. Then, pointing, Ricky said, "If you go left it goes to the end there. Where it ends at this hall, you can see it goes right and comes out at the chapel. The library is at the end of that hallway, too, just before the double doors to the chapel. To the right is the fun stuff. Oh yeah, the huge room straight across there is the mess hall. They have big events there too." Ricky continued talking, like a babbling brook, as he pushed on with the tour taking them to the movie theater, continuing past it and reaching the end of the hall. Actually, it only ended in the direction it was going. Now it turned left and on the right was the snack bar, which was more like a small cafeteria. Across the hall on the left was the Post Exchange, better known to everyone as the PX.

"I'm getting hungry," Joe exclaimed.

"Me, too," chimed in Ike.

It was just about noon. "We better go home for lunch, Ricky," Luke stated.

"Okay," Ricky replied. "We can see the rest after lunch."

"Maybe, but we may have to practice boxing with our dad first. We usually do it in the morning but since we came out to play, he might make us do it this afternoon," Lucas said to Ricky as the boys headed out the double doors and onto the road back to their homes.

"Wow!" Ricky exclaimed. "You box?"

"Yep," injected Ike with a smile. "Dad makes us ever since some German kid kicked Luke's butt."

"I'm gonna kick your butt!" shouted Luke as he took off after his brother laughing and pretending to kick Ike's butt. Ike took off running with Joe, Luke and Ricky chasing after him. They ran all the way back home with Ricky lagging behind.

"We run a lot," Luke said to Ricky as they dropped him off at his house. Ricky was so winded it was the first time Lucas ever saw him at a loss for words. He just nodded and waved as the brothers took off.

After lunch Ivan was busy so he told his boys they would box after dinner. He also told them to be home by 5 o'clock. With that, the boys took off to meet with Ricky. They ran into him at the bottom of the stairwell.

"I thought I would check to see instead of waiting to hear from you," Ricky smiled. "And … I ran into Bob Ledahawski in the street. He's going to come with us."

"Neato!" Luke yelled as he raced past Ricky only to run smack into Bob's chest as he was about to come in. Bob was pretty big and it brought Lucas to a dead stop. Both of them broke out laughing as the five boys started across the playground. After introducing Bob to his brothers, he asked, "Where're we going?"

Ricky answered, "This is a shortcut to the ball field. We'll go to Sewer Hill first, then the bowling alley and all the way over to the main entrance to the hospital." Ricky had the afternoon planned. It was fun having Bob with them because he wasn't as intense as Ricky was and he liked Lucas' wise cracks as they continued the tour.

They were almost back to their homes when they heard the crackling of the loudspeakers as it hit 5 o'clock. Ricky and Bob turned to face the flag when Lucas yelled, "Oh crap, we gotta run." With that he shouted at his brothers, "Hurry up or we'll be late!"

Off the three brothers raced as the flag was going down. This was an event that would repeat itself many times over the years that the Baryshivkas lived in Münchweiler. It did lessen after Lucas got a watch for his tenth birthday but for now, his only way of telling it was time to be home was the sounds of 'Retreat' blaring over the loudspeakers and the flag being brought down for the night.

Over the next several weeks, Lucas got to be better friends with more of his classmates but Ricky pretty much dominated his time. One afternoon after school in early April, Lucas had no homework and asked his mother if he could go out to play with Ricky.

"Okay, but make sure you dress warm and wear your raincoat," was Maria's answer. It had been raining all day and it was pretty foggy out.

"I will!" Lucas shouted as he grabbed his raincoat and baseball cap and raced out the door before his mother thought to have him take his brothers. Not that she did every time he went out, but they had been with him a lot lately. It was nice not to have to take them for a change. In another rarity, Lucas was knocking on Ricky's door. Usually it was Ricky coming over to get Luke. Ricky's sister Kelly had answered the door. "RICKY!" she shouted to the back room, "It's your dorky friend." Then she turned back to Lucas, "Don't sit down, you're all wet."

Lucas had met Ricky's family a week after the tour. Kelly was a grade ahead of them, but acted like she was years older instead of just one year. Lucas didn't really care for her too much, but she was pretty harmless, so he just ignored her most of the time. Ricky's parents were very nice to him and didn't seem to have some of the snootiness towards him that some of the other officer parents did once they found out that his dad was only an NCO. Both Pat Simmons and Jimmy Parker's parents were that way. He could see how the boys got their "attitude" towards the other kids.

Ricky had been in his parents' bedroom asking them for permission to go out as Lucas stood by the door. "Let's go before you catch 'kooties' from Kelly," he quipped as he opened the door. Kelly just gave him a look as they left.

They cruised through the basement from Ricky's end of the building to the opposite end so they didn't get too wet. They played army for a while, pretending to fight the Germans as they went from building to building. As they were getting ready to leave Building B, Lucas looked down at the mat on the floor and saw a big rubber band. He could feel some bobby pins in his pocket, *Susan wore my raincoat,* and suddenly, he had an idea. Luke stooped down and picked up the rubber band. Ricky stopped.

"What's up?" he asked.

"I think I can knock out one of the street lights," Luke answered as they walked out into the mist.

"Really? How you gonna do that?" questioned Ricky.

"Just watch," Lucas said as they went to the street light that was at the intersection with their cul-de-sac. Lucas got directly underneath the light. All the streetlights were covered with a mesh to keep them from being busted out, which had been a problem in the past. Lucas had wondered if someone could still break the lights after Ricky had first explained the mesh covering to him. They were on due to the darkness of the day even though the sun had not yet set. It was about 4:30 p.m. and there wasn't much outdoor activity. There were some cars coming into the housing area as the soldiers were heading home but Luke hardly noticed. He was so fixed on what he was about to do that his focus was totally on the task. He pulled the rubber band back and let it go a couple of times before opening up a bobby pin and sliding it over. Ricky was watching with an uncharacteristic silence as Lucas pulled back the rubber band as far as it would stretch and aimed at the light above them. Without another thought he let it fly.

The bobby pin rocketed through the wire mesh, shattering the light with a loud 'WHACK'. As pieces of glass fell from above, the two boys looked at each other in utter shock and took off running to the first stairwell in Ricky's building. They didn't stop until they got to the other end of the building.

"Shit!" Ricky finally said. "We're gonna get in so much trouble." He was looking pretty scared. "I'm goin' home now. Do you think anyone saw us?"

Lucas' heart was beating so fast it took him awhile to answer. "I don't think so. I wasn't paying attention to see if anyone else was around. I really didn't think I would hit it on the first shot. I'm goin' home, too. We can't tell anyone about this, okay?"

"Okay," was Ricky's frightened response.

With that, Lucas looked both ways out the doors to the outside to see if anyone was coming after them. Seeing no one, he dashed across the street to his own apartment and went in. He took off his wet raincoat, hung it up and hurried to his room. Ike and Joe both looked at him as he looked out the window, nervously.

"What's the matter?" Joe asked.

"Nothing … don't worry about it," Luke responded.

Twenty minutes later Ivan got home. The boys stayed in their room reading comic books and Lucas started looking through some of his baseball cards when just after Ivan's arrival, the doorbell rang. Lucas looked out of the window and sitting there parked next to his father's car was a Military Police jeep. Lucas' heart sank. He could hear the men's voices at the front door. It didn't take him long to figure out he was busted.

"LUCAS!" Ivan shouted, "GET YOUR ASS OUT HERE ON THE DOUBLE!"

Lucas came out of the room with his brothers peeking out from behind the door. They knew by their dad's tone they didn't want to be out there with their older brother. They could see the two MPs standing in the doorway with Ivan glaring at Lucas as he walked towards him. Their mother was standing off in the dining room listening to the conversation. She had a very worried look as Lucas passed her and stood next to his dad. Before he could say a thing, Ivan backhanded him across the face, knocking him to the floor. Before Lucas could get back up on his feet, his dad booted him, sending him into the living room.

"Whoa, whoa … Sarge! Take it easy on the kid!" the older of the two MPs exclaimed.

"If I get a DR (Delinquent Report) because of this fuckin' kid, I'll beat the shit out of him," Ivan responded. "Don't you be fuckin' telling me how to handle my kid."

"Listen, Sarge, don't smack the kid around anymore and I promise I won't write it up," was the MP's response. "We'll just say he wasn't the one that broke the light and that we never caught the kid." You could see the shock on the MP's face as he stepped into the house and placed himself in between Ivan and his son.

Ivan hesitated as it looked like he was going to knock over the MP to get at Lucas again, but hesitated. "You won't write me up?" The Army in its infinite wisdom gave Delinquent Reports to the parent if their kids got into trouble.

"No, Sarge, got my word on it."

Ivan calmed down. "Get your ass in your room!" he shouted at Lucas. "There'll be no dinner for you tonight."

The words followed Lucas as he bolted for the bedroom crying as he ran past his brothers. They were both in total silence. It was broken a few moments later as Maria came in to comfort Lucas.

"I am so sorry, honey," she whispered trying to hold back her tears. "Your dad has such a temper." She then looked at the side of Luke's face, at the big red welt that covered his entire cheek. She then went out to the living room just as the MPs were leaving. Lucas could hear her yelling at Ivan, which didn't happen that often. He could hear her say that Lucas was only a boy and he couldn't be hitting him like he as a grown man. Ivan didn't say much, and then Luke could hear him walking down the hallway towards the boys' bedroom. Panic again hit him. *Am I gonna get another whopping?*

Ivan popped his head into the bedroom and looked at Joe and Ike. "You two wash up for dinner." Then turning to Lucas he said, "If I ever get a DR because of you I'll beat the living shit out of you, and your mother won't be able to protect you. Do you understand me, Luke?"

"Yes sir."

"Was that little Ricky shit with you?" his dad asked. Lucas started to shake his head 'no' when Ivan warned him, "Don't you go lying to me to protect that boy or I'll whop your ass again right now."

"He was with me, sir, but he didn't put the light out ... I did," Lucas confessed.

With that Ivan seemed to soften a bit and then left the room. Lucas was so relieved to be alone and out of harm's way, at least for the moment, he began to cry, hiding his face in the pillow so his father wouldn't hear him. He knew how much Ivan hated it when he cried. He was hungry but was glad he didn't have to go out and face the rest of his family. When his brothers finally came back in the room, Lucas was red-eyed, but had stopped crying. They just both looked at him and said nothing for several minutes. Finally, Joe blurted out, "Dad said he was proud of you for taking the blame and not giving up Ricky until he said he'd kill you."

"He didn't say he would kill him, Joey," Ike piped in. "He said he would beat you half to death." Then Ike broke out into a big grin and all three of them started laughing. They quickly stopped and looked at each other like they would all be killed for laughing about it.

The next day at school, Ricky came up to Lucas. He didn't walk to school with him as usual and seemed a little sheepish about approaching him now. It was obvious to everyone that

Lucas had a bruise that covered the entire left side of his face.

"I saw the MPs at your house. I guess someone saw us?" Ricky questioned.

"Don't worry, Ricky, I'm the only one they caught. They won't be coming to your home to tell your dad."

Ricky just stood there, staring at Lucas with some newfound admiration. He knew Luke got a beating for it, yet he didn't tell on him. Luke didn't really mention to him that he did tell his dad, but not the MPs. After Ivan's reaction, he never got the chance to say anything to the MPs. He wasn't sure if he would have turned Ricky in, but by the time the school day ended, he saw the respect he was getting from all of the other kids for not giving up Ricky. It made a deep impression on him. By the time they were walking home from school, all the boys were hanging out with Lucas as Ricky told the story of how Luke had put the light out. It was like he was some kind of hero to them. Lucas definitely liked the feelings he was getting from them. Besides, except for his face still being a little sore, he wasn't too bad off considering the beating he'd taken. *Survivable.* They all split up to go home.

The rest of the school year was fairly uneventful. Lucas flirted a lot with Bonnie Lee and expanded the people he hung out with, much to the dismay of Ricky. Luke spent most of his time with Ricky, but for Ricky it wasn't enough.

Lucas' mother became good friends with Bobby Ledahawski's mother Lena, so he started hanging out more with Bobby. He also hung out with Pat Simmons and Jimmy Parker after school on some days. He liked the diversity of his new friends. They were all so different, but he liked all of them. Lucas was Ricky's only true friend. That made it a burden at times for Luke. He wanted to hang out with some of the other kids but Ricky always looked so dejected that he hated to leave him, but he seldom could get Ricky to join him. He had figured that with Ricky's intensity, he had already burned through the other kids, at least the ones that liked Ricky. It was obvious that Pat and Jimmy didn't like Ricky, but Lucas thought they were kind of snobbish anyhow so he didn't think it was a big deal.

Overall, on the last day of classes before summer break, Lucas felt like the school year had been a successful one. He had managed to get good grades, transition from one school to another without any real anxiety, and meet new friends, with which he was able to form bonds like he had never had before in his young life. Now he was looking forward to his first summer in Germany.

Chapter IV

The First Summer

When school ended in June, Lucas felt he would have enough time to spend with anyone he wanted. He had his chores to do around the house and he did have to take his brothers with him a lot, but he still had a lot of "play time." This was going to be a good summer.

It was the middle of June, only a little more than a week into the summer vacation when Luke, Ricky, Ike and Joe were cruising the hospital halls. They were passing a waiting room where a young couple had just lit up cigarettes when their name was called. As they put their cigarettes out in the ashtray next to their seat, Ricky came to an abrupt stop. Lucas and his brothers went three steps farther before they, too, stopped. Lucas turned back in time to see Ricky grab the two cigarette butts and run towards them. He quickly passed the Baryshivka brothers as they turned and took off after him.

"What the hell are you doing?" Lucas said as he caught up to Ricky.

"Come on with me," he replied, grinning, "and you can see for yourself!"

"Where're we goin'?" Luke asked.

"Paint shack," Ricky bellowed as he led them all down the hallway and towards the mess hall. They all stopped to see if there was anyone around before they bolted across the mess hall to the exit doors on the other side. Lucas knew the post pretty well by now. They were taking the quickest way to the north side of the building.

They ran from the steps chasing Ricky as he continued to run all the way to the paint shack. When they got there, panting and gasping for air, the brothers looked at Ricky like he was some sort of nut.

"We need to catch our breath first," gasped Ricky.

Lucas looked around the shed. It was just that, a paint shed. Buckets of paint were stored there and the door was broken off the hinges so anyone could go inside. *I guess no one thought the door would need to be fixed. Who'd wanna steal paint anyhow.*

"Ricky, whatcha doin' with those cigs?" Lucas finally asked.

"We're going to smoke them," he exclaimed with wide eyes.

"What?" Ike blurted.

"Well, maybe not you two," Ricky said looking at Ike and Joe, "but Luke and I are."

"We are?" Luke asked incredulously.

"Yeah, unless you're chicken?" Ricky responded. "Your dad smokes and my dad smokes, don't you wanna see what it is they like so much about it?"

"But they're grown-ups," Joe chimed in.

"So what. That doesn't mean kids can't do it, too." With that, Ricky pulled out some matches and lit up the first cigarette. As he sucked it in he began coughing, and it appeared the smoke was coming out of his entire body. The boys were all laughing hysterically at him.

"Your turn, Chicken," Ricky said once he had recovered enough to speak. He handed the cigarette to Lucas who took it, wide eyed and heart pounding. He saw how big a draw Ricky had taken and took a much smaller one allowing him to suppress the slight urge to cough.

"That's how a man does it," Lucas said smugly as he handed the cigarette back to Ricky. After Ricky took his second draw, a much smaller one this time, he handed it back to Lucas, grinning as he did. They all laughed.

After Lucas took his second hit, he turned to his brothers and said, "You both have to take a drag off of this cig, too." Then, turning to Ricky, "That way I know they won't squeal on me to the old man. They can't say nothin' about me smokin' if they do, too."

They finished the first cigarette and lit up the second, passing it around from Ricky to Lucas to Ike and finally to three-year old Joe. After that afternoon, the paint shack was their secret smoking place. It never occurred to them that with the paint fumes in the shack they could easily blow up the shack, or at least catch it on fire. Fortunately for the boys, the shack was well ventilated. They didn't smoke that often over the next few weeks because they were usually too busy playing baseball or 4-square or just hanging at the playgrounds.

One day, all of that changed. It was a Saturday and Ivan had decided to take the boys and their mother to the Snack Bar for lunch. They had great hamburgers and potato salad there. It wasn't often Ivan took them out to eat so they were all eagerly looking forward to the treat.

The boys helped put two of the small tables together so they could all sit together as their parents went up to the counter and ordered their food. Ivan came back with a tray full of cokes and a coffee for himself. "Should be about ten minutes," he told the boys as they all sat down at the tables. The brothers sat quietly, listening to their father talk about his week at work.

"NUMBER TWENTY-THREE," came the shout across the snack bar about ten minutes later.

"That's us," Ivan said looking at the ticket in his hand. He had just lit a cigarette when he turned to Luke and Ike, "You two go get the food!"

The boys didn't wait for him to say it again as they bolted for the counter. Meanwhile, Ivan quickly put out his cigarette after just one puff. As soon as his hand was off the butt, Joe's was on it. He grabbed it and put it in his shirt pocket with Ivan and Maria staring at him, dumbfounded.

"Whatcha doin', Boy?" Ivan asked.

"Saving this one for Luke," Joe proudly replied, thinking how much his big brother would appreciate him getting such a big butt for him. It had hardly been touched. Joe adored his oldest brother and anything he could do to impress him, he tried.

"So where does Lucas go have his smoke?" Ivan said, pumping Joe for more information. Joe began to rattle off how they went to the paint shack with Ricky Mason and that all of them smoked, even Ike and he puffed.

"Oh my ... oh my," was all Maria could say as she looked towards the counter. Lucas and Ike were carrying the two trays very carefully, making sure they didn't spill anything. They approached the table grinning for having succeeded, but as Lucas sat the tray down he looked at his dad. Suddenly, everything changed. Ivan had an evil looking half grin. Lucas, terror written on his face and a tight feeling in the pit of his stomach, wasn't sure what was going on, but he knew that look on his father's face, and he knew he was caught at something. Ike knew it too. His eyes wide, he looked at his father, then at Lucas, then back again at his father as he instinctively backed away, out of his father's reach.

"Hey, Joey," Ivan said in a taunting voice. "Show Luke what you have for him."

"I got a big one, Luke," Joe said grinning from ear to ear. He was so proud of the size of the butt he'd nabbed for his big brother, still having no clue as to what it really meant. Luke's jaw dropped. Ivan's sinister grin got wider. Maria could only shake her head.

"What were you thinking, Lucas?" his mother finally asked. "In a paint shed? Do you know how dangerous that is? And letting your brothers smoke, too?"

"Sit down, boys," Ivan added, "and enjoy your lunch. I'm gonna pick up a cigar from the PX when we're done. Lucas, you're gonna get a special treat when we get home. You're gonna smoke that cigar, 'til it makes you sick."

Lucas sat down and continued to get lectured as he ate. He was upset but he was trying to figure out if he just had to smoke the cigar or was he getting a beating, too. It was sounding like the cigar was the only punishment. That seemed a whole lot better than he could have hoped for. His dad was in a good mood, but Lucas sensed this evil enjoyment his father was getting at the thought of Luke smoking the cigar. It didn't seem like it could be too much worse than the cigarettes were when he first tried them. He had to tell himself to remember to act like he hated it since it seemed like that was the result that his dad wanted.

They all walked back home, Joe seemed the most distraught. He now realized he had gotten Lucas in trouble and was trying to apologize all the way home.

"Its okay, Joey," Lucas said, trying to comfort his youngest brother. "It isn't your fault. We'd have got caught sometime. Someone was gonna see us in that shack sooner or later. Don't feel bad."

When they got home, the two younger brothers had to sit on the couch and watch their older brother smoke the cigar. Ivan unwrapped it, clipped the end and handed it to Lucas along with his lighter.

"Here you go, son. Light it up."

Lucas took the cigar and lighter and with everyone, including his sisters and mother watching, lit the cigar. He began coughing immediately but caught himself as he thought he was over doing it. He made faces like it tasted terrible and he puffed and puffed and coughed and hacked until he did almost feel like he could throw up. About half way through, Ivan took the cigar from Lucas' hand.

"Had enough?" he asked. Lucas just nodded yes. "I don't wanna catch you ever smoking again or you'll smoke a whole one of these the next time. That'll make you throw up. Now get your ass to your room. You're restricted to your room until dinner."

Lucas bolted for the bedroom, holding his stomach like he still felt like throwing up. He was soon joined by his brothers, both with concerned looks on their faces. As they looked at Lucas lying on his bed he looked back at them, winked and grinned. As they were about to open their mouths he quickly put his finger to his lips to quiet them.

"Our secret," he said smiling, and then looking sick again, then grinning again. His two brothers had to bury their faces in their pillows to suppress their laughter. So their big brother just pulled one over on their father. Ike looked at his older brother again. *Luke sure is brave or crazy. He's dead if Dad ever finds out.*

There was another "incident" that happened just after summer break began. There were not many colored kids in Lucas' class that past school year. The only Negro boy was Ronnie Clark. He didn't really hang with any one person too much but seemed to hang out with only one kid at a time. He was a very interesting boy who had spent most of his time in Puerto Rico where his dad was stationed. On a Saturday a few weeks after school ended, Lucas ran into Ronnie as he was heading to the PX.

"Hey Luke!" Ronnie yelled, flashing a big grin. "Are you doin' anything?"

"No," Luke answered, a little surprised that Ronnie was actually talking to him. Ronnie usually hung out with guys a year or two older than his classmates. He was good friends with Todd

Ledahawski and some of Todd's friends.

"I got some neato firecrackers, called Strikers. Want to blow some up?" he asked.

"Sure," Lucas answered. He was excited about it. Todd had fired off a few at the bus stop before school the week before. They had a top that was just like a match. You struck it on a matchbox and you had about six seconds to get rid of it before it blew up.

"Let's go by the guard shack," Ronnie told Lucas.

The two boys went past the school grounds and set off a few of the Strikers near the back gate by the guard shack. The boys soon got bored with just setting off firecrackers. Ronnie squeezed through the closed back gate.

"Come on, Luke," Ronnie shouted. "Have you seen the cemetery by the church in town?"

Lucas had not. He was a bit hesitant to go but finally, *what the heck, why not,* squeezed through the hole. He followed Ronnie to the cemetery on top of a hill overlooking the main street in the village of Münchweiler. They had a blast looking at the dates on some of the headstones. After half an hour they sat down on the rock wall that surrounded the cemetery. Below them was the main street that ran through the village. In the street was a horse drawn *honey wagon,* which was a wagon with a big tank of liquefied manure used in the nearby farm fields. Without warning, Ronnie stuck one of the firecrackers and tossed it to the street below.

BOOM!

Lucas jumped and so did the horse drawing the honey wagon, causing the wagon to tip over. Lucas stared in disbelief as the contents began spewing out of the tank.

"RUN," Ronnie shouted.

Lucas didn't need him to say it twice. Ronnie had already had a head start, but Lucas overtook him in seconds. As he took one last look at the carnage below he could see some of the Germans pointing at them as the dashed off. They didn't stop until they got to the back gate.

"We can't tell anyone about this," Ronnie said as he tried to catch his breath. Then he grinned as he looked at Lucas. "You run faster than any White kid I ever met."

Lucas just nodded. He had not yet caught his breath and when he did all he said was, "I'm going home." With that he took off for home thinking how lucky he was that they didn't get caught, or so he thought.

A couple of days later he found out that Ronnie had been caught. He was easy to identify since there weren't that many Colored kids on post and he had purchased the firecrackers in a shop in Münchweiler. Lucas kept waiting for the MPs to show up at his house, but they never did. Ronnie never gave him up and Lucas never got another chance to see him. Ronnie was grounded for a month (got quite the whopping from his dad, too) and the same day that they tossed the firecracker, Ronnie's father got his transfer orders. Within three weeks they were on their way to Fort Sill, Oklahoma. Lucas thanked his lucky stars that he did not suffer any consequences for the prank. Prank was too mild a word considering the smell stayed in the town for a good week.

Lucas tried out for the Little League baseball team the week after the firecracker incident. They had tryouts at the ball field and he was one of the youngest kids there if not the youngest. His friends all played ball but he didn't see them there. By the end of the day he found out why. He made the team but when he was filling out the paperwork the coaches told him he was too young. He was still only eight years old and the starting age was nine. It was all he could do to hold back the tears when he was told.

"You're a good ball player, Lucas," the coach said as he tried to comfort him. "There's always next year."

With that and a little harassment by Bobby Ledahawski's older brother Todd, Lucas headed home. Instead of going up by the road he decided to walk behind the buildings through the grass field. As he dropped down into the drainage ditch to cross it, he saw Pat Simmons and Jimmy Parker farther down the ditch. Tying his glove to his belt he decided to see what they were up to.

When he got close to them he could see they had their backs to him and they had a piece of wood or something in front of them.

"Hi guys," Lucas greeted them. "What are you doing?"

Both boys jumped into the air. "Christ, Lucas! You scared the shit out of us!" Pat exclaimed.

As Lucas came up beside them he could see they had a piece of wood with a couple of crickets held down on them with pins. He looked at Jimmy and Pat with a puzzled look. Before he could say another word Jimmy whispered, "We have a secret club called the Cricks. We sacrifice crickets as our club ritual."

"Seems kinda cruel," Lucas stated. "Who all is in your secret club?"

"It's just Pat and me and you, now, if you want to join."

"Do I have to sacrifice crickets to be in?" Luke asked.

"No, the club just has to do it once in a while. We kind of make up the rules as we go," Jimmy answered. "So, do you want to join us? You can't tell Ricky Mason or any of the other guys about it, though."

"Okay, I'll join."

"Good," Pat said. "Now you have to learn our secret passwords."

"Repeat after me," Jimmy said and began the secret code with Lucas repeating every line after Jimmy and Pat.

"Ricky ticky tombo … bosso rombo … holy itchatyro … holy itchatyro … by sen tow!"

With that Lucas sat down and watched them finish dissecting the cricket. *They better hope these little guys don't have a giant cricket brother that'll come and eat them for this,* and he began imagining a giant six-foot cricket bounding across the field at them. With a grin he jumped up and yelled "LOOK OUT, A GIANT CRICKET IS COMING!"

Both Pat and Jimmy jumped up and started to run. They looked back at Lucas, rolling on the ground, laughing his ass off and stopped dead in their tracks. Both started laughing with Jimmy falling to the ground pretending to be jumped on by a giant cricket. They got up and the three boys started for home. They asked Lucas how baseball had gone and he told them. "Too bad," was their response.

Reaching the first of the apartments where both Pat and Jimmy lived, they parted ways. "Don't forget to keep our club a secret," Pat shouted as they ran into their stairwell.

"I won't!" Lucas yelled back. After that day Lucas would meet with Pat and Jimmy every Monday of the summer vacation for their secret club meeting. Of course every one of the other kids knew there was a secret club, but Lucas would never give up any information. He wondered why since they really didn't do much of anything when they met. Pat and Jimmy were a bit boring to hang out with. Ricky, on the other hand, always came up with something interesting to do. Lucas had the same knack so between the two of them, they were always finding new things to explore and try.

Then in the end of June there was a change. Jimmy's dad got his transfer orders and his family was leaving in two weeks. Lucas should have been used to it already. If you're in the Army you go where and when the Army sends you. You got used to losing friends, but the flip side was you learned to make friends easily. Everyone was in the same boat so you made sure you helped the new kid feel at home right away. You knew you would be in the same situation somewhere down the line.

After Jimmy left, Pat was really down because Jimmy was his only real friend. Once when Pat was mad at Lucas, he told him it was Jimmy that wanted to invite Lucas to join the Cricks. Pat never wanted to let Lucas in.

A few days after Jimmy was gone, Lucas walked up to Pat on the swings in the playground. He was swinging next to Bonnie Lee so Lucas didn't hesitate to go over to them.

"Hi Bonnie. Hi Pat," Lucas chimed in his friendliest voice.

"Hi Lucas," they said in unison.

"Feel like having a club meeting?" Lucas asked Pat. He wasn't worried about saying anything about the club in front of Bonnie. Both Jimmy and Pat, like every other boy in their class went ga-ga over Bonnie. She knew all about the club, even before Lucas knew anything about it.

"It can't really be a club with just the two of us," Pat sighed.

"It was only you and Jimmy before you let me in," Lucas stated matter-of-factly.

"He's right," Bonnie piped in. "Besides, you should really do something to get out of this mood your in. You have been sulking around since Jimmy first got the news. Quit being such a baby."

Lucas' eyes almost popped out of his head. *Wow! Did she set him straight!* There was an awkward moment of silence before Pat finally said, as he was jumping off the swing, "Oh, what the hell. Let's go to my house."

The two boys said bye to Bonnie and took off for Pat's home. Lucas shot a glance back over his shoulder at Bonnie, smiling as their eyes met. *I really don't know her at all.* When Pat led them to his room, he brought out his Chemistry set and began working on a stink bomb he had concocted. Pat had been working for over a month on it and now he felt he finally had perfected it.

"Well, I'm ready to try it," he declared. "Where should we go?"

"Let's go to Sewer Hill!" Lucas blurted. "It stinks so bad there no one will notice. If it is really good, we'll go public," he chuckled.

On the way to Sewer Hill, Lucas asked Pat, "Why don't we ask Bob Ledahawski to join the Cricks? You like him okay, don't you?"

Pat stopped. He got a weird look across his face for a moment, and then he relaxed. "I guess I never even thought about it before. Okay, let's ask him, but it has to be a secret. He can't let anyone else know he's in."

"No problem," Luke said. "I'll have him come to our next meeting. When's that gonna be, Pat?"

"We'll make it tomorrow at one o'clock here at Sewer Hill!" Pat seemed genuinely excited. At least he wasn't moping around anymore.

After a successful test of the stink bomb, "Aaaaahhh ... that's horrible," Lucas shouted as they ran laughing and holding their noses, heading back to the apartments. Lucas immediately ran over to Bobby's house to invite him to join the club. The next day the three of them were at Sewer Hill.

Pat was already there when Lucas and Bob arrived. "Hi, Pat!" they both yelled as they approached.

"Quiet," Pat responded in what was a hushed tone, as he crouched down into the drainage ditch to get out of sight.

"Did anyone follow you?"

"No," Lucas responded, ducking down and walking like a duck, slid into the ditch next to Pat. Bob followed Luke's lead and did the same.

When they were all in the ditch together, Bob and Lucas could see the cricket on the board next to Pat. Lucas had warned Bob about the little sacrificial ritual with the crickets so he wasn't too shocked. Pat continued with his little sacrifice and went over the rules, not that there were many, except to keep everything they do secret. Then he said, "It's time for the secret password."

With that, Bob repeated after Lucas and Pat as they chanted,

"Ricky ticky tombo ... bosso rombo ... holy itchatyro ... holy itchatyro ... by sen tow!"

The "new" Cricks were formed.

That first summer in 1959 there were all kinds of discoveries for Lucas. Besides learning the layout of the Post, he began to understand what it was really like being in the Army. Nowhere did Luke notice the difference more than the Fourth of July. In Uniontown they had some great fireworks every Fourth, but the entire set-up of the event and participation by the public never came close to what he was now experiencing on this small Army Post.

Early on the morning of the Fourth of July, Ricky was at the door. Lucas was already up and eager to go out before his brothers were ready. As he was about to fly out the door with Ricky, he shouted back to his mother, "I'm goin' out, Mom!"

"Wait a minute, Lucas," she replied. "I want you to come back in an hour ... and pick up your brothers. There are a lot of activities today and I want them with you."

"Oh crap," Lucas muttered, and then to his mother he said, "Okay, Mom, I'll come back for them."

"Its okay," Ricky said to Luke, "your brothers are fun to have around."

"It's just more fun when they're not with us. After the cigarette deal with Joey, I'm always afraid they might let something slip at home. You know what my old man is like."

With that, they took off towards the ball fields. The different companies on the Post were setting up tents around the ball field. There were a couple of games that would be played today. The first was the Little League game, which Lucas wasn't planning to watch. He was still angry that he wasn't able to play. The other two games were softball games involving three of the companies that were stationed on Post and a team from Pirmasens. They had a regular fast pitch softball league that included teams from both Pirmasens and Zwiebrücken. The big game that everyone wanted to see was between the 225th Station Hospital Company and the 15th Evacuation Hospital Company. There were several players that had been in both companies at one time or another and the rivalry was great. They were also the two best teams in their league and tied for first place, so this was a big event for the Post.

There were also lots of contests for both kids and adults in between the games. Ricky and Lucas just wandered around and watched all of the activity … food venders, beer and soda stands. It was mass activity and the boys could feel the electricity in the air.

"I better head back and get Ike and Joe," Lucas stated.

"Let's hurry so we can get back here," Ricky replied.

They raced back to Lucas' home. His brothers were just finishing up their breakfast and were putting on their shoes as Lucas and Ricky were excitedly telling everyone about the activities. Luke's dad had to leave in the morning to help set up his company's tent at Pirmasens before taking off for the rest of the day.

"Mom," Lucas started, "we're gonna be there all day. They have free food and drinks so we can eat lunch and watch the games. Is that okay?"

"As long as you keep an eye on your brothers. I'll be coming down with Lena Ledahawski a little later today. And Lucas … be on your *best* behavior!

"I will, Mom," he blurted out, and with that the boys were out the door. Ike and Joe were having trouble keeping up with Luke and Ricky.

"Slow down," Ike whined. "Where's the fire."

"Quit your cryin' and hurry up," Lucas shouted at Ike.

The day turned out to be one they would all remember. Lucas and his brothers had never participated in something so grand. They began running into the other kids as every one of the boys and girls ended up there for the activities. They watched a little of the Little League game, which the Münchweiler team lost. Then they watched the first softball game between the Pirmasens team and the 208th Signal Support Company. On and off they would wander around to the different tents, checking them out or horsing around with their friends.

After the first softball game ended, there were a lot of contests for the kids. They had a contest where you had to eat three saltine crackers and whistle *Dixie.* Lucas wasn't sure why he entered that since he couldn't whistle anyhow, let alone after eating three of the crackers. There was another game with four-person teams that had to carry an egg in a spoon from first base to second base, pass it to a teammate who had to take it back to first base, pass it and do the whole thing a second time. Bobby Ledahawski and Jason Sprint joined Lucas and Ricky to form a team. They came in second and won some candy bars.

They also had a sack race which Ricky and Lucas finished dead last after falling and laughing so hard they could hardly get back up to finish. Then came the event that Lucas was looking forward to the most: the 50-yard dash. There were different age brackets that spanned two years. Lucas would run everywhere when he lived in Uniontown and usually could outrun all of his friends, but today there was a lot of competition. Luke was going to see how he compared to rest of the boys.

Just as he lined up he could hear his sister Susan yell, "Run like hell, Luke!" which made him blush a little. Not that cussing wasn't part of just about everyone's vocabulary, it was just he hadn't expected it from his sister.

"ON YOUR MARK! ... GET SET! ... GO!

Off they ran with the whole race taking less than ten seconds. Lucas bolted off of the line and in a few seconds couldn't see anyone in front of him or on either side. He easily crossed the finish line first. No one was close to him. He was rather taken aback by the large roar of the crowd and the applause he received.

"Wow, Luke!" Bobby exclaimed, "You're fast!"

He received a lot of other complements as well as first prize (a model plane). He headed back towards his mother, friends, and family. To his surprise his father was standing there, too. He was the only one not to say anything to Luke but he did give him a grin and a nod of his head. For Lucas, it was about the biggest compliment ever from his father. He was feeling pretty good.

After the race, they all hung around to watch the big game. Lucas could tell these guys were really good players. It was a close game with the 225th winning in the last inning as a soldier named Jim Cooke stole home. After the game Lucas and his brothers headed home. It was dinnertime, but they weren't really hungry since they'd eaten so much at the company tents.

"I think everyone is too full to eat a full meal," said their mother, "so I have some left-over potato salad and sandwiches for you. After you eat, I want you boys to rest in your room for awhile before we head out for the fireworks."

They all sat down and ate, with the boys still feeling full, taking only a few bites from their sandwiches. There was a lot more talking going on at the dinner table than was normal. Everyone had stories to tell of their day.

"Sgt. Kelly told me you had the fastest race time out of all the age groups, Lucas," Karla said. Sgt. Kelly was in charge of all of the activities and games. His daughter and Karla were close friends.

"Is that right?" Ivan asked.

"That's 'cause he has to beat the flag down the pole if he wants his dinner," Joe quipped.

Everyone broke out in laughter. It was common knowledge on the post that the Baryshivka boys would race home at 5 o'clock while everyone else was saluting the flag. By now Ivan's reputation had spread, and there wasn't a GI on post that was going to try to stop Lucas or his brothers and have them wait until the flag was down. The truth was it wasn't every night this would happen, but mostly on the weekends when Ivan was already home. During most weeknights Ivan didn't leave Pirmasens until 5 o'clock, so the boys usually would stop and pay their respects to the flag. However, it was always a gamble for them. Sometimes Ivan would come home early. The first time it happened, all three got sent to their room with no dinner. Karla and their mother snuck them some food later. Lucas had a feeling Ivan knew but wasn't going to say it was okay. They were only a few minutes late, but Ivan's rules were rules to be followed and he didn't allow much leeway with them.

The boys went to their room after dinner. Joe was playing with his toys; Ike was reading comic books and Lucas started reading a book he'd gotten from the library on the life of his hero, Mickey Mantle. At 7:30, Susan came in to let them know it was time to go. The entire family left together to walk to the hill behind the Post Commander's house. It overlooked the ball field and the area where the fireworks were set up. Maria had spread their blanket on the ground and Karla spread a second one so everyone could spread out on them. Right next to them were the Ledahawskis.

"Can we walk around and check things out?" Lucas asked his parents.

"I want you back here when the fireworks start," was Ivan's reply. "Ike, you and Joe stay here with me."

Lucas, Bobby, and Todd got up and wandered around through the crowd to find their friends. It was getting dark fast and it was hard to see but they got in some socializing before the first rocket was shot off. They had just made it back to their families when the first fireworks were lit. It turned out to be a spectacular display that lasted over half an hour. When it was over, they all headed home, the boys went straight to bed, exhausted.

"Pretty good day, eh Luke?" Ike said as he pulled his covers up over his shoulders.

"Yep, it was." Luke replied, it was a day that they would remember for a long time as they began drifting off. Joe was already fast asleep.

The following Sunday as Maria and the kids were walking to church, (without Ivan, as usual. He would always say his church was out in the wilderness). Ricky caught up with Lucas.

"I've been talkin' with Father Perkins and Robert, (the altar boy that would accompany Father Perkins from Pirmasens to serve Mass), about havin' altar boys from Münchweiler serve the Masses here. They're very interested. Do you want to be an altar boy?" Ricky asked.

Before Lucas could answer, his mother said, "I think that would be wonderful, Lucas."

"Well … maybe I should think about it," Lucas replied. After all, this was a new idea that he had never even contemplated before.

"What's to think about?" his mother asked.

"Yeah, Luke, what's to think about?" added Susan with a little smirk on her face. She knew that this wasn't the kind of thing that Lucas would be all gung-ho about, and she seemed to get some delight out of his uneasiness with the idea.

"I think you should be one," Maria stated. Lucas knew by her voice that he didn't really have a choice.

"We can talk to Father Perkins after Mass," Ricky shouted as he ran back to walk with his family.

Lucas didn't need to answer. He knew it was a done deal. It was like going to Catholic School in Uniontown. He knew his father wasn't for it since it cost money while Public School was free, but he'd lost that battle with Maria. Once she dug her heels in on something, it wasn't worth the fight to get her to change her mind.

After Mass, Ricky and Lucas went behind the altar to the room where Father Perkins and Robert were changing. It was the first time Lucas realized that Robert was a soldier, not that he was surprised, it was just new information. Robert was a Specialist 4th Class.

"I'm glad you two have decided to do this," Robert said. "It would really help me out with my other duties at the Pirmasens chapel if I didn't have to come here every Sunday."

"Robert," Father Perkins, who was also a soldier, said as he completed adjusting his Colonel's uniform, "let's set up training starting next Saturday. I think it will be a wonderful thing, and not just for your benefit. Having altar boys from the same post as the Mass takes place is very important in making the congregation feel like they are participating more. This is just wonderful!"

Lucas wasn't sure it was so "wonderful." On the other hand, he did like the idea of being up there right next to God. Although Luke wasn't crazy about going to church, he loved when they had a High Mass and there was more singing and the smell of incense; it made him feel very spiritual. He decided it would be okay to be an altar boy and after all, his friend Ricky was really keen on it.

Training started the next Saturday. Ricky and Lucas met Robert at the Chapel at 10 o'clock in the morning. First he gave them a tour of the back of the church starting with the vestment room. There was a cabinet that held the hosts, the altar wine, the chalices and several other items used during Mass.

"I'll bring down vestments for you both tomorrow when Father Perkins and I come for Mass. He wants you both to come a little early and sit on the stools that are against the wall on each side of the altar," Robert informed them.

"Wow!" Ricky exclaimed.

"We're going to start serving Mass tomorrow?" Lucas asked somewhat dumbfounded. He didn't think it would start so soon.

"No, no, no," Robert laughed. "You are just going to observe from there for a couple of weeks. We go through the training for the next three Saturdays and the Sunday following the last training day, one of you will serve Mass with me. The other will serve the following Sunday. We will do the same the two weeks after that. When we complete those, the two of you will be serving Mass together and I will no longer be needed here."

"Oh, yeah," he added, "you'll be collecting the money from the congregation starting tomorrow."

Lucas relaxed as they moved out to the altar. Collecting the money would be easy enough. He had seen Robert collect it and sometimes a GI from the congregation would help him. They would walk down each aisle with a basket at the end of a long pole, reaching down the pews for people to drop in money or envelopes.

Robert began the training. He showed the boys where they were positioned at each phase of the Mass, when to ring the bell and when to move "The Book" from the right side of the altar to the left side bringing it from the altar to the bottom center of the steps, genuflecting, then taking it back up to the altar and placing it on the left side. They went over how to help the priest serve Communion, holding the golden platter under the people's chin in case they dropped the host as the priest placed it in their mouths. After they had gone through everything several times, Lucas realized that it wasn't going to be too difficult.

The next day the two boys went to the church a half hour early, per Robert's instructions. When they got there Robert was ready for them.

"Here are the vestments you are going to be wearing," he stated. "They are the older type. We have the new ones on order, but don't expect to get them until the end of the year."

"What's the difference?" Ricky asked.

Robert went on to explain that the older vestments were made up of three parts: the cassock, which went up to about the middle of the boys' chests, was kept on by suspenders; the surplice that was a white shirt that was pulled over their heads and rested on their shoulders; and the collar, which draped around the neck and was fastened in back. The collar was about six inches wide and covered much of the surplice. The cassock and collar were red.

The newer vestments were much simpler. They consisted of a full body cassock that had buttons down the front with a surplice over the top. There was no collar. The full body robe was much like the one the priests wore, black with a high collar. The neck and collar of the robe were exposed by the wide opening of the surplice.

As the boys put on the vestments, Robert helped adjust them. Both Lucas and Ricky were on the small side compared to most of the altar boys. Father Perkins had mentioned he thought they were the two youngest that served with him. It became obvious to Lucas that the vestments were made for bigger boys. Using the suspenders to keep the robe off of the floor was quite a challenge. Lucas had a funny suspicion that the cassock did not typically go to the middle of the wearer's chest.

Lucas could hear the murmur created by the faithful coming into church. His heart was pounding so hard he could hardly hear Robert going over where they would sit and kneel at the benches against the walls along each side of the altar. He would give them a signal when it was time for them to pick up the donation baskets and take them down the aisles. Part of him wanted to run away and say forget it, but he knew he couldn't.

"Ready, boys?" Father Perkins said cheerily as he smiled at them. "Just relax. Everything will be just fine."

Lucas looked at the priest. *At least he didn't say "wonderful."* With that, the procession began with Ricky and Lucas, side by side, leading the way. Robert was a few steps behind them and Father Perkins a few steps behind him. The two boys walked to the foot of the center of the altar, genuflected and each went to his side of the altar to the appropriate benches. The whole time Ricky and Lucas could hear whispering coming from the congregation. This was new to them, too. Usually, it was only

Robert who served Mass with Father Perkins. Once in awhile there was a second altar boy who would accompany them from Pirmasens to Münchweiler to serve Mass with Robert, but this was a first, two boys from Münchweiler serving Mass.

Just as Father Perkins said, everything was just fine. Lucas was so focused on everything Robert did that he hardly noticed any of the congregation. It wasn't until they took out the baskets and went up and down the aisles collecting the donations that Lucas finally relaxed as he noticed many people smiling at him as he went through the pews. His mother was just beaming. Maria shot her son a little wave that made Lucas blush as he continued through the crowd.

When Mass was over, Father Perkins took the boys to the entrance of the church where he often went just after the service to talk with many of the congregation. Of course, Maria was there with Ike and Joey, Susan and Karla had already headed home, still beaming, so proud of her son, Lucas the Altar Boy. Lucas chuckled to himself. *I haven't even served Mass yet and Mom thinks it's the greatest.*

The next Sunday Ricky got his chance. Robert decided after their Saturday practice that the boys were ready and didn't need the extra week. Lucas told Ricky that Robert was motivated by the fact that once the two boys were both serving Mass, he wouldn't have to come to Münchweiler every Sunday. It didn't really matter to the boys. They both felt ready. Ricky's Mass went off without a hitch.

The following Sunday was Lucas' turn. Everything was going well until it was time to move The Book from one side of the altar to the other. Lucas had been having a little trouble with his cassock. It was old and the suspenders that held it up kept slipping so it would slide down to the floor. It had happened the Sunday before but Lucas only had to fix it once and it held the rest of the service. Today was different. He had already adjusted it a couple of times and he could feel it slipping again. As Lucas went to the center of the base of the altar, he genuflected and climbed the stairs going to the right side of the altar. He felt the cassock slip a little. As he came down the stairs, holding the gold stand The Book was on with both hands, he genuflected again at the bottom and started up the stairs. As he took his second step he stepped on the bottom of the cassock and began to fall over backwards. Lucas caught himself but watched in horror as he flipped The Book over his shoulder and onto the floor.

Robert was up in a flash and helped steady Lucas first. Then he picked up The Book and whispered to Luke, "Place the stand on the left side of the altar. I'll place The Book on it."

Lucas was in shock. He knew he was beet red. He couldn't believe it. *I DROPPED THE BOOK!* He could hear the murmur in the pews behind him. He thought his mother must be so embarrassed. As he placed the stand on the altar, Father Perkins was facing him, smiling.

"It is okay, Lucas," he said in a low voice. "It isn't the first time and I am sure it won't be the last time it's happened. Just focus on what you need to do the rest of the service, okay?"

Lucas muttered a low, hardly audible, "Yes, Father."

He went back to his position on the left side of the foot of the altar. The rest of the Mass was a blur. As Mass ended and he led Robert and Father Perkins to the Chamber Room he fought to hold back tears. Father Perkins gave him a hug and with Robert's help tried to make light of it.

"Make sure the eyes are dry now, Lucas," Father Perkins said in a jovial voice. "We don't want everyone in the front of the church to think anything out of the ordinary even happened."

Lucas knew that there was no possible way for that to be true when Ricky came bursting into the Chamber.

"YOU DROPPED THE BOOK!" he yelled.

"Hush, Ricky," Robert said in a very stern voice. "Little mishaps happen. We are not going to make a big deal out of it and I suggest you do the same."

Ricky stopped with his mouth wide opened, about to say something else, but there was something about the way Robert said it that froze Ricky mid-word. He had never heard Robert use that tone of voice before. Another word was not necessary as they all went out to the front of the Church.

Lucas put on his best smile as they greeted the people that had stayed to talk to Father Perkins. Maria gave her son a big hug and smile and whispered in his ear that she was proud of him for how he handled himself after the "incident." Lucas wasn't sure what she meant since he couldn't remember anything after dropping The Book until he was walking out in the procession.

By the time he left, he was feeling okay about everything. He could have put it behind him … that was until he got home. Susan had already told Ivan what had happened and Ivan was waiting for him with that mean, nasty grin he would get when he was about to tease him. Lucas had to put up with the teasing most of the rest of the day, but it didn't really bother him much. He had already put the incident behind him. He was curious why his brothers had not said anything about it to him so he asked them.

"Mom made us promise we wouldn't say anything about it while we were still in church," Ike said.

"Ike and I said 'we promise' but Susan said she wasn't going to promise anything," Joe added.

"Thanks, guys," Lucas told them. He also made a little mental note about his older sister. She couldn't wait to come home and tell their dad even though she knew he would give Luke a hard time. Oh well, he had put up with worse from his father. He could handle a little teasing.

As the summer of 1959 neared its end, Lucas had hung out less and less with Ricky. Ricky didn't seem to want to hang out with a lot of the other kids and he would try to dominate Lucas' time. Lucas talked to Ricky about it but Ricky wanted all of Lucas' attention and would leave pouting if they ran into some of the other guys and Luke wanted to do things with the boys. Besides, they all were a year away from playing Little League and the rest of the boys loved playing baseball almost as much as Lucas did. It seemed it was the same guys, Bobby Ledahawski, Jason Sprint, Benny Jefferson, Terry Smith and his older brother Robby Smith that all started playing ball together.

Terry had been in Luke's class in third grade. His brother Robby was a year older but had just flunked fourth grade. He had the same bright red hair Terry did. They had nine brothers and sisters. It was a huge family and they seemed to have more freedom to do what they wanted than the rest of the boys. Robby liked playing with Terry's classmates more than he did the boys his own age with the exception of Bobby's brother, Todd, who looked like a larger version of Bobby. They all spent time playing 500 in the large field just north of the cul-de-sac between Buildings C and D. 500 was a game in which everyone went out into the field, except one person, who would toss the ball into the air and hit it in their direction. If they were at the ball field they would all be in the outfield. Only one person could score points at a time, whoever caught the ball. If the ball was caught on the fly you got 100 points. If it was a one hopper … 75 points; two hopper … 50 points; and a grounder … 25 points. The first to 500 points gets to bat and the former batter takes a position in the field. There were no rules except for scoring. The boys were spread out but anyone could go after the ball whether or not it was going right at someone. Each player tried to catch it whether they were stealing it from someone else or not. If you made an error on the ball, you would have to deduct the same amount of points that corresponded to the type of catch had you caught it.

They also played a game with a tennis ball instead of a baseball, which the ball was bounced off of the wall of Building C. It was played with two players, one who threw the ball and the second who was the fielder. They played a six-inning game where the "batter" who threw the ball against the wall, tried to get base hits past the fielder. There was a line that marked a home run if you could get the ball to go over it as a fly. The end of the building was perfect for this game as the only windows on the end were small bathroom windows and they were off to one side. That left four stories of blank wall to toss the tennis ball off of.

Often other boys would play too, but the five of them were there consistently and soon started doing other things together. They would go watch softball games or the Little League games or go to the movies or snack bar together. Lucas still spent time with Ricky but it seemed like it was less and less.

"You just go hang out with your gang," Ricky would say, rather dejectedly.

"Come on with us, Ricky," Lucas would reply. Sometimes he would, but most of the time he would take off on his own.

Lucas felt bad that Ricky wouldn't join the "gang" as he called the group, but he had decided that he wasn't going to let Ricky's pouting keep him from enjoying his other friends.

It was the last week of August and the beginning of school

was just a couple of weeks away when Robby Smith came up to the rest of the boys playing 500.

"Hey, guys," he said excitedly, "I found out about a really cool place in the woods we should go."

"You know we can't go off post," Bobby stated.

"Yeah, that goes for all of us," Lucas added.

"Aw, you're all a bunch of babies," was Robby's comeback. "I found an old German bunker not far from here and it isn't blown up, except it looks like the door is blown off of it."

That got the attention of all of the boys. Robby went on to explain how far it was and how easy it would be to get there and back before their dads got off of work. Lucas didn't have his brothers with him. *It might be fun. But, shit, I'll get a beating if the old man finds out.* After weighing this in his mind and in the middle of the other boys justifying why they couldn't go, he blurted out, "I'll go."

Silence hit the group as they all looked at Luke, stunned. They knew how his dad was and they were in shock that he would agree to go.

"Really?" asked Robby.

"Yeah, really," said Lucas. "I'll go with you, but we need to make sure we're back here by 4 o'clock in case my dad gets home a little early. Terry, you have to come or give your brother your watch so we won't be late."

"Well you can count me out," said Benny Jefferson. Benny was a bit of a wimp and doing something his parents had forbidden him to do was out of the question for him.

"I'll go too," Jason said as he turned to look at Bobby with a little smile on his face. Jason was the smallest of all of the boys but had the heart and soul of a much bigger kid. The look he gave Bobby was one of 'if I can go you should be able to.'

With a droop of his shoulders, Bobby finally said rather meekly, "Me, too."

"I ain't givin' my watch to Robby," Terry said, "so I guess I'm goin' too."

So Benny took off to look for Ricky. They lived across the hall from each other, and before Luke's arrival Benny had spent more with Ricky than anyone else. The rest of the boys followed Robby as he headed towards the back gate.

The back gate was always closed. There was a guard shack there, but no one was ever manning it, and the boys could slip through the gate fairly easily. They followed Robby through the gate and onto a dirt road that went east of the post for a few hundred feet before turning south, following a power line for some distance. At what must have been about half a mile, a less used dirt road crossed their path.

"We take this road," Robby stated as the boys turned east again on the less traveled road. They walked for another twenty minutes or so when the road ended as the woods opened up to a meadow.

"Wow," said Lucas as he spotted the bunker across the meadow with its huge iron door hanging on one hinge. The bunker was not a troop bunker, but an old ammo bunker that was built into a small hill. The boys broke out into a run to get to it.

"Neato," Jason said as he looked around the inside of the one-room bunker.

"Not much left in here," Bobby noticed as he looked around. He was right, anything that could have been salvaged had been taken long before now.

"Rat-tat-tat-tat!" Lucas shouted as he picked up a branch and pointed it at his friends. "You Krauts are dead!"

"Oh yeah," Robby said as he returned Lucas' fire by picking up a pine cone and tossing it at him, "Take this grenade then!"

"BOOM!" Lucas shouted and flung himself up in the air as if he had been blown up by the grenade.

That was the start of half an hour of playing war at the bunker before they had to head back to the post. The group was pretty jazzed all the way back. It had been a new adventure for all of them and they had Robby to thank. Of course, they still had to make sure they didn't get caught going back on post. As it turned out, no one was around the back gate and the boys easily slipped back on.

Luke said his good-byes to his pals and headed home. He was home well before his dad got there. *Not a bad way to spend the last few days of summer vacation.* He decided he wouldn't tell his brothers about the bunker just yet. It was a secret for just the "gang" for now.

Chapter V

Fourth Grade

Summer was over and the Labor Day weekend ended the summer on a good note. Ivan had taken Maria and the boys on a drive to an old castle. Ivan had been in a good mood all day and they all had fun running through the castle with only an occasional yell from their dad to "slow down" so they wouldn't get hurt.

Now, Lucas woke up before his mom came into the room to wake him. It was always like that for him when he was starting a new school year or moving schools. This year he would be taking the bus to Pirmasens. For Lucas the bus ride was no big deal since he'd had to ride the bus when he was in Zwiebrüken, but he was excited about it anyway. He would be on the bus that carried the 4th, 5th, and 6th graders. There was a bus for the high school and another for the junior high school, all leaving at different times.

As Lucas was eating his breakfast, his mother was preparing his lunch in his new lunchbox. It was a Davy Crockett lunch box with a big picture of Davy on the front in his coonskin hat.

"What a dorky lunchbox you have, Luke," Susan said as she sat down next to him to eat her breakfast. Lucas just smiled. He knew she was just trying to get his goat and he wasn't going for it.

"Yes, it is, isn't it?" was his reply. Maria smiled as she observed the banter between the two. Lucas was her most easygoing child and she liked the fact that it was hard to get him upset. The bad consequence of that was that when he did get upset he was over the top and got a bit out of control. He could take his father's teasing better than the rest but it made Ivan tease him more, trying to get him angry. She had to admit that even though she didn't like fighting, boxing was a way that Ivan could get a certain amount enjoyment by getting Lucas mad, and the more they boxed the less he teased Luke.

"In fact, I think it is the most ridiculous lunch box I have ever seen," she taunted.

"Yep!" he said as he looked at her and let his cereal fall out of his mouth and back into his bowl.

"DISGUSTING!" Susan shouted. "Mom, your son is gross." With that she shot a big wide grin at Lucas and playfully bopped him on the head as she got up from the table and gathered her books.

"Gotta run, Mom," she said as she headed to the door to catch her bus. "Lucas, try to stay out of trouble the first day there. I won't be there to bail you out."

"Yeah, right," Lucas said as he waved goodbye to his sister. Although she was pretty protective of her younger brother when they were in Uniontown, he had not seen the same out of her since their arrival in Germany. In fact, she had ratted on him to their father several times and once, when some of her guy friends picked on Lucas at the ballpark, she didn't come to his rescue but instead joined in.

Lucas finished his breakfast and went to brush his teeth about the time his brothers were waking up. Karla had already left before Luke had his breakfast and now his mother was getting Ike ready for school. He was starting the first grade and she would be walking him to school that first day. Luke was picking up his new school supplies as he saw Susan's bus leaving the cul-de-sac. It was now safe for him to go out and wait for his bus. Some of the other kids were already gathering.

"Bye guys!" he shouted at his brothers as he ran to give his mother a hug and kiss goodbye.

"Enjoy your first day, Lucas," his mother whispered in his ear as she let him go.

"I will, Mom," he answered as he dashed for the door.

When Lucas got to the bus stop, he saw there were books lined up along the curb. Ricky, seeing the questioning look on Luke's face said, "That is how you save your place in line for boarding the bus. The 6th graders already are all in front of the line."

"Okay, I'll just put mine right here," he said as he placed his books behind the last ones in line. He didn't care about being first or last. He was just excited about going to school. He joined some of the other kids that were playing tag while they waited for their bus to arrive.

When the bus came, all of the kids ran to their books and got in line to board the bus. Several of the older boys that got there a little late cut in front of Lucas and the other 4th graders. "Hey! No cuts!" Lucas shouted at them.

"What are you gonna do about it, punk?" was the response from John Dolan as he stood next to Andy Kirkland, the other boy that cut in front of him. Lucas liked Andy okay but he wasn't very fond of John Dolan. John's older brother Jeff, was a good friend of his sister, Susan. Jeff and John were two of the older boys that liked to harass Lucas.

Lucas just glared at them as they entered the bus in front of him. John was right, there was nothing he could do about it, but it was another one of those incidents that Lucas would not forget. He would find a way to get them back. For now he was just going to let it slide and find a seat on the bus.

The five-kilometer ride to Pirmasens seemed to go quickly. Before they knew it they were unloading in front of the school. There were teachers and aides helping direct kids to their classes. The school building itself wasn't all that big, but attached to it were several Quonset huts that served as additional classrooms. Finding his classroom was pretty easy. The classes closest to the school office were the lower grades. As you continued down the hall away from the office the grades were progressively higher. Lucas found his room, one of three 4th grade classes. It was the last of the classes in the main building. As he was about to enter his class he heard a voice that made him cringe.

"Who let you in here, brainless?" came the smart aleck voice of Tara Morton. "I can't believe you passed 3rd grade."

"Hi Tara," Luke answered as he looked at the teacher's name next to the door of his room. "Are you in Mr. Knoll's class, too?"

"Thank God, no! I won't have to look at you every day, I'm in Miss Brady's class," she answered as she continued down the hall. That brought a smile to Lucas' face. He felt like saying "ditto" but decided to bite his tongue as he turned and entered Mr. Knoll's class.

A lot of his friends from Münchweiler were in the class. There were Bobby Ledahawski, Terry Smith, Jason Sprint, Benny Jefferson and Bonnie Lee. Lucas sat next to Bonnie. Ricky was in Tara's class. *Too bad for him.* Lucas turned his eyes on his new teacher. Lucas had never had a male teacher before. In

Uniontown he went to Catholic School taught by nuns, and since coming to Germany both of his teachers had been women. Lucas thought he would like having a male teacher.

Fourth grade was a good year for him. The year introduced him to African drums that Mr. Knoll had brought back with him from a safari to Africa. Mr. Knoll started the weekly "Tall Tale Award" which was a floating reward for the student that came up with the best "tall tale" story. Mr. Knoll told the class he was not promoting lying but rather he wanted the students to use their imagination. Lucas won the award more often than any of the other kids.

The rest of the year went smoothly for Lucas. He did get into a few confrontations at school. Some of the kids from Pirmasens resented the closeness of the "gang" from Münchweiler and Lucas nearly got into fights a couple of times, but both times there was a teacher nearby who saw the altercations and stopped them before they got too physical. The "gang" already had a reputation of being rough during their pick-up football games at recess or the lunch hour. It was supposed to be touch football, but the touching was getting a little close to tackling. Several of the teachers took notice.

There were also the days when it would snow. The end of the bus ride into Pirmasens was up a long steep hill. On a couple of occasions, after fresh snowfall, the hill became too icy for the buses to make it. The first time the bus tried it, but after sliding backwards downhill for about fifty feet or so, the bus driver turned around. On the other occasions, when the snowfall was heavier, the school called Mrs. Jefferson to let her know the buses were canceled. Lucas wasn't sure how she got to be the contact, but he guessed it was because she was closest to the bus stop. He really didn't care. All he knew was the Münchweiler kids had a few more snow days off than the kids living in Pirmasens.

It was now approaching Christmas vacation. Lucas' birthday had come shortly after school had started. He didn't expect a lot for his birthday but was surprised when he got a new baseball glove. He didn't get to use it much before the weather changed, besides all of the kids were into football during the winter. He spent the winter working his glove with saddle soap, softening it up for the next baseball season.

Christmas was even a bigger surprise for all three of the brothers. They got new bicycles! Lucas had never really ridden a bicycle before. He was the only one of his friends who didn't have one. His friends liked to tease him when they went off riding together. Even Ike was riding before Lucas. He would "borrow" a neighbor's small bike and ride it around the cul-de-sac. Much to Ike's dismay, Luke got to learn on Ike's smaller bike before getting on his, which was much bigger. Also, their bikes were German bikes and had shorter, straighter handlebars than the American bikes and they were a little different from the other bikes he had tried to ride. Fortunately, it didn't take very long or too many falls for Luke to get the hang of it. Much of the Christmas vacation was spent riding his new blue bike with his friends. Even though the weather wasn't the best, it had not snowed recently and the roads were clear to ride. The boys would bundle up and race around the loop road that circled the post. Lucas really enjoyed it, not just for the thrill of riding, but it was one of the few things Ricky would do with all of them.

"Let's race by starting at the same time, but going in different directions to see who gets back here first," Ricky suggested. Lucas smiled to himself. *Ricky really did come up with good ideas.*

"Neato," Bobby piped in. "I want to go first."

The boys ended up pairing off with Bobby and Ricky going first followed by Lucas and Robby Smith, then Jason and Benny and last was Terry and Todd Ledahawski. Todd wouldn't admit it but, like Robby, he liked to hang out with his younger brothers' friends more than kids his own age.

"You guys always come up with neat shit to do," he told Lucas once. "My friends are kind of boring."

It was true. They would still go to the bunker on the weekend and play army. Their newest game was to use pine cones as bullets, throwing them at each other. When one was hit he had to play dead until he counted to one hundred before joining back in.

This day, though, was all about riding. Bobby and Ricky sat on their bikes facing opposite directions. Ricky was facing west towards the main gate while Bobby was facing east towards the train tracks. Luke raised his hand, dropped it and shouted, "GO!" and off the two went. Soon they were both out of sight. The rest of the boys either rode around in a little circle or just joked around. Todd was putting Jason in a headlock and Terry and Benny were trying to pull him off. All in good fun, mind you. About five minutes later Robby yelled, "Here they come!"

It was real close, with Ricky appearing to be ahead, but he had a long uphill to finish. Bobby's approach was less steep even though he was a little farther away.

"GO … GO … GO … GO!" The boys yelled as the two riders approached. Lucas stood where they had started with his handkerchief held high in the air as the two flew by him almost at the same time.

"Wow, that was close," shouted Lucas, "but Ricky wins by a nose!"

"Really?" Bobby quizzed as he came back to the group, panting.

"Yeah," Todd piped in grabbing his brothers by the nose, "his nose is bigger than yours."

They all started laughing. Lucas was happy for Ricky. It was obvious he was tickled to have beaten Bobby. Bobby was bigger and stronger than Ricky, and Lucas for that matter, so he felt like he accomplished something by winning.

The boys continued their races. Lucas, novice that he was, still easily beat Robby. Jason beat Benny easily and Todd beat Terry. That set up the next round where the winners paired off. Ricky beat Lucas by just a slightly larger margin than he had beat Bobby. Todd out raced Jason, and in the final, beat Ricky by a couple of bike lengths.

They were all pooped by the time they called it a day and went home for dinner. This was a game that expanded to include a lot of the other kids and became a regular part of their weekends during the school year.

The beginning of 1960 was pretty routine for Lucas and the Baryshivka family except for a visit from Uncle Fredric, Aunt Helga and Cousin Eckhart in late March that changed their routine for a day. There was a late snow and although the buses were able to negotiate the hill in Pirmasens, the school was having problems with their heating systems in the main building as well as in a few Quonset huts. With all of the maintenance men running around trying to get it working, the Principal decided to shut the school down early for the day. While the children were having their lunch break, the buses started to assemble in the front. As lunch ended they were told, much to their delight, they would be starting their weekend early.

As Lucas sat in his cold classroom, bundled up in his coat and gloves, he thought about plans for the rest of the day. With the fresh snow, which could very well be the last of the season, he considered sledding for the rest of the day. Sometimes these late season snows began melting by the second day. Luke didn't want to miss the opportunity to sled one more time.

The bell rang and like cattle, the kids noisily began herding toward their buses or walking home. As the Münchweiler gang gathered on the bus, Lucas discovered he wasn't the only one to think about sled riding that afternoon.

"The sledding hill should be perfect today," said Bobby Ledahawski.

"I was thinking the same thing," Lucas replied. They all talked about grabbing their sleds and heading straight to the hill, which was just east of the ball fields on the south side of the channel that ran by Sewer Hill. As the bus pulled through the main gate at the Münchweiler post, Todd Ledahawski looked out of the window towards the top of the sled-riding hill.

"Hey," he shouted, "the Krauts are on our hill!"

Soon the whole busload of kids erupted in an uproar. Sure enough, the German kids had come through a hole in the fence not far from the hill and were sledding down the hill.

"We gotta run them out!" Todd declared. "Everybody, drop you school stuff off at home and meet me at the playground."

When the bus stopped at Luke's stop, he jumped off with Ricky, Bobby, Todd, Benny and the rest of the kids. He raced upstairs, quickly told his mom what happened at school and then raced back outside to the join the already gathered group of kids. Todd seemed to be the leader in the endeavor, and as they started heading towards the German kids he noticed with them was an older boy they all knew, Hans Mueller. His father was in charge of the German workers on the post. Hans was fourteen years old.

"Jason," Todd said as he watched Hans below, "go get Big Bert and tell him what's going on." The group started heading down towards the hill. Bert was the sixteen-year-old son of the post commander and he was big. He was the star football player for the US Army high school in Kaiserslautern. He had to be at least 6 4 , well built and big as a grizzly bear.

As the rest of the army brats neared the hill, the German kids picked up their sleds and began gathering around Hans. Lucas looked back towards the Commanders house and saw Bert running towards them as he was trying to put his jacket on. Jason was a step or two behind but keeping up pretty well.

"What? No school today, Todd?" Hans asked with a wry little grin on his face. Todd had met Hans before. Hans' father worked directly for Sgt. Ledahawski and he had met both Todd and Bobby before.

"Not today," Todd answered. "What the hell are you guys doing on our hill?"

"I'm so sorry," Hans replied sarcastically. "I didn't see anyone's name on this hill." His eyes then turned to Big Bert as he lumbered nearer the group. Hans was bigger than any of the other American kids there but he was a lot smaller than Bert. The rest of the kids there all turned and looked at Bert. He was an impressive site as he slowed to a walk a few feet from the group.

Looking right at Hans he said, "What're you Krauts doing on the post?"

Hans stepped forward to meet Bert a few feet in front of the rest of the German kids. Lucas was impressed with Hans. There was a good half a foot difference in height between the two, but there was no sign that Hans was the least bit scared. Lucas was scared just being in this potentially volatile situation.

"We, like all of you, decided to take advantage of this late snow and have a little fun before it melts. This is the best hill that is close for us," Hans responded. Luke was again impressed with how Hans carried himself and spoke such good English. He had an accent for sure, but his enunciation was better than a lot of American kids. "I see no harm in us sharing the hill," Hans continued.

"Well I do!" Bert shot back. "This fort is American soil and you aren't allowed on it."

"Oh, but I am," Hans replied. "I have an ID card that allows me to come on the post. I work sometimes for my dad at the mess hall when a worker calls in sick." With that, Hans reached deep into his pocket and pulled out his ID to show to Bert.

As Bert looked at it, Lucas could see him relax a bit. Luke also thought that Hans' calmness helped to ease the situation a little, too.

"Well I bet the rest of these guys (pointing to the other Germans) don't have passes." Bert said, but it was obvious to everyone that the intensity had gone out of him.

"Ya, this is true," Hans stated. "But what harm can be caused by a little sled riding? It seems like you have all come down here to chase us out or maybe fight us?"

"Yeah, maybe we have," Bert answered.

"Well, then, may I suggest we have one-on-one fights between us and if we win more, we stay and sled. If you Americans win, we leave," Hans said with a big grin.

"Okay," replied Bert. "That sounds fair."

Now it was Lucas whose heart began pounding. This isn't what was supposed to happen. Bert was supposed to show up, kick a little Kraut ass and it would all be over. Now it was looking like he was going to have to fight. No matter how many times he had fought, he never liked it and he always had a certain sense of fear that would come over him.

As Lucas was mulling this over in his mind, Hans and Bert stepped away from the others. After a little conference by themselves, they came back over to the two groups that were still facing off at each other.

"You guys are going to fight one-on-one with a German kid that's your age," Bert announced. "Hans and I are going to make sure each fight is a fair fight."

Hans was explaining that to the German kids. There was a mixed rush of emotion and fear on both sides. Then Hans and Bert began picking a boy from each side. Todd was the first and was paired against a German that was close to his size in height but a lot lighter. They began squaring off and then the German just jumped at Todd. They fought for a couple of minutes before Todd had the German youth pinned and unable to fight back anymore. Bert and Hans stepped in and declared Todd the winner.

This seemed to be how it went, with the bigger boys first. With the group that was there, Lucas was about the fourth biggest. The Americans were up two to one when it was Luke's turn.

"You will fight my brother, Fritz," Hans stated. "He is nine years old, too."

Lucas looked at Fritz in kind of a daze. *There is no way that kid is nine!* He was bigger than Lucas and he looked a lot stronger, although with all of their winter clothes on, it was hard to tell. Later, Lucas would find out he was actually 10 going on 11.

They squared off. Fritz lunged at Lucas, who instinctively sidestepped him and threw a jab to the side of his head. It staggered Fritz for a second as he regained his balance. For the next several seconds, Lucas held his own, boxing the German and avoiding his attempts to tackle Luke. He punched Fritz several times, but it didn't seem to have the effect on him Luke had hoped, and the bigger boy finally tackled Lucas. Once he did, the fight didn't last much longer. Fritz was decidedly stronger, and once he had Lucas pinned he began punching him when he was on the ground. Lucas tried to get free, but all he could manage were some not too powerful punches in Fritz's side. With all of the winter clothing they both had on, the body shots did not do much harm.

After a half a minute or so, Bert and Hans declared Fritz the winner and pulled him off of Luke. Lucas' face was red from both the punches and the cold. He felt he was about to cry, but held back his tears as he watched the rest of the boys fight. Fritz kept looking at him with an intimidating grin. By the time the last of the boys fought, they all realized it was getting late.

"Well, Hans, it looks pretty even," Bert said as he stood next to his new German friend. It was, in fact, the beginning of a good friendship between the two. No, this certainly didn't play out the way Lucas had thought it would. Bert and Hans decided that they could both share the hill for the rest of the day. If the snow was still there in the morning, the American kids would use the hill until noon and the German kids could use it in the afternoon. As it turned out the next day, they all shared the hill in the afternoon. Fritz even took a liking to Lucas and confessed to him his real age.

That afternoon, though, Lucas was still hurting, emotionally, not physically, as he headed home. As he got to the far end of playground, Luke could see his dad out on the balcony of their apartment. He could tell from his father's body language that he was pissed. *Had he been watching all of this from that distance? What was he doin' home on a Friday? He couldn't possibly have seen us from there?*

When he walked in the door his dad was there to greet him.

"So you let that damn Kraut kid kick your ass?"

Lucas's didn't answer and was quickly slapped upside the head by Ivan. "You answer me when I ask you a question, punk! Do you understand?"

"Yes, sir."

"Go get outta those clothes and get the gloves. I'm gonna teach you a lesson."

Luke went into the bedroom, still trying to figure out how his dad knew. He found out as he came back out to the living room with the boxing gloves. His dad told him that he left work early and was in the NCO Club when a GI came running in to tell them what was going on just down the way from them.

"How the fuck do you think I felt when I watched some Kraut kid kick my kid's butt in front of all of my buddies?" Ivan asked Luke.

"I don't know, sir," was Lucas' response. Now Lucas was scared. He realized that he had embarrassed his dad and he knew this boxing lesson was not going to be an easy one.

They put on the gloves and began boxing. This was unfolding like no other time Lucas could remember. His dad was really hitting him hard. He was trying to fight off the tears since he knew that only incited his father. Ivan would say, "So you think that German kid could hit hard? He can't hit you nearly as hard as I can." And he would smack Lucas with the palm of his hand, which was sticking out of the gloves that were too small for him.

Ivan continued to pound on Lucas for about ten minutes. Lucas kept hoping his mother would show up and stop it, but she didn't arrive with Susan and his brother until after they were done. By then, Lucas' face was puffy and his arms, chest and stomach were all sore. Ivan told Maria that Lucas got the bruises fighting the German kid, and Lucas was not about to call him on it.

The last thing Ivan told his son as he went to clean up for dinner was, "You remember the next time you get in a fight, boy. The kid you fight can't hit you nearly as hard as I can and every time you lose a fight, I'm gonna kick your ass just like today. Do you understand me, boy?"

"Yes, sir."

The rest of the school year was uneventful for Lucas. He liked Mr. Knoll's style of teaching, so he excelled in class. Luke was making the best grades he had ever had and was convinced it was due to having Mr. Knoll as a teacher, because he challenged all of the students and Luke took to challenges.

Getting good grades even helped shut up Tara Morton to a certain extent when the Mortons would come over for visits. They usually came over once a month. Way too often for Lucas, but his brothers got along with Lilly and on one visit Tara was even civil to Lucas. This was after Lucas and his friends had put on a play for all of the 3rd and 4th grade classes. Tara actually had given Lucas a very nice comment at the dinner table.

"You guys were really very funny. I enjoyed the play," Tara stated to a very stunned audience. It was quite obvious that Tara liked to pick on Luke. Maria would just smile and tell Lucas not to let it get to him. Ivan seemed to get some type of enjoyment out of it. Sgt. Morton just rolled his eyes when Tara would light into Lucas. Mrs. Morton seemed like it all passed her by.

"Must have been some damn play," Ivan roared. "I didn't think Tara would like anything you do, Luke."

"That's not true," Tara said with a pouty face. "I'm not that mean to Lucas."

Ivan and Jon Horton just laughed. Tara went on to tell everyone about the play as Lucas recalled how it all happened. Mr. Knoll had decided that all of the students would break up into groups of their own choosing and create a one-act play. Once people got together in the groups they wanted, Mr. Knoll would assign one of them to be the leader of the group.

"Okay, class!" Mr. Knoll shouted above the chattering from all of the students. "You have fifteen minutes to put your group together. I may assign some of you to one group or another to even things out if I don't think everyone is comfortable with the group they are in."

It was easy for Lucas. His pals Bobby, Jason, and Benny came over to Lucas' desk immediately.

"Okay, guys, I guess we have to come up with a story," said Bobby.

"Why am I not surprised to see you boys together?" stated Mr. Knoll, matter-of-factly. "Lucas, you are the group leader. I expect something good from you guys."

Mr. Knoll walked away smiling. It was no secret that he had a soft spot for the Münchweiler gang and not just the ones in his class. During the recesses and lunches Mr. Knoll would often hang around with the whole Münchweiler bunch, sometimes playing tag football with them. Sometimes he just told them stories of his adventures in Africa where he had spent two years. He would bring in his collection of African drums and all of his students would get their chance to play different ones during music class. He had great stories of near death and great adversity he had lived through. It was the adventure that surrounded Mr. Knoll that Lucas loved so much. He, in turn, loved the way the Münchweiler boys stuck together, looking out for one another. They reminded him of a tribe in Africa that he stayed with for six months.

He once told them at lunch time, "You boys have your own little disputes but when an outsider comes into play, you all stick together. You tougher guys protect the smaller and weaker guys. That is what being part of a tribe is all about. You are an extended family."

"Well," Lucas said looking at his friends, "what are we going to make a play about?"

It was Benny who came up with their theme. "How about we are soldiers in the war, fighting the Germans, only we make it funny?"

"How do we make the war funny?" asked Bobby.

"We can do it," added Jason. "Remember a couple of Saturdays ago when we were playing Army in the woods around the picnic grounds? It was all foggy and we were pretending to be a machine gun nest," he continued. "We were cracking each other up when we tried to scare each other after we started hearing those weird noises."

"Hey, I think that we can make that work into a play," Lucas finally chimed in. He had been listening … remembering and imagining as the others spoke. Now he had a vision of how they could do it. They all gathered around and began scripting the play, as did the other groups. This lasted another ten minutes before Mr. Knoll broke them up.

"You will need to work on your play after school. That's why I let you choose your groups. Look how you've split up. There are the girls from Münchweiler in one group, the boys from Münchweiler in another, and the Pirmasens groups have split up with kids from their housing neighborhoods. Normally, I would try to split you up so to mix the groups, but since much of this will have to be done on your own time, it will work better this way."

When school ended for the day, the boys all agreed to meet at Benny's to work on the play. As they left the bus Benny shouted, "I'll let my mom know you'll be over in about half an hour!"

Lucas ran up the stairwell and into their apartment to let his mother know what they were doing. After telling his mother about the assignment, he ate a quick snack, grabbed his toy machine gun and Army helmet and took off for Benny's apartment across the street. Bobby was coming down the sidewalk as Lucas was about to enter the stairwell to Benny's place. The two of them knocked on the door.

Mrs. Jefferson answered. "Hello, Lucas. Hello Bobby. Come on in. Benny told me about your project. Sounds like it'll be fun."

"Yes, ma'am!" they both answered.

"Can I get you boys anything to drink? I have Coke and grape Kool-Aid."

"I'll have a Coke," responded Bobby.

"Me, too," Lucas added.

The boys went to Benny's room as Mrs. Jefferson went to get their drinks. They began scripting their play much like their experience at the picnic grounds on that foggy day. Just as they got started, Jason entered the room with Mrs. Jefferson as she was bringing their bottles of Coke.

"Hi guys," Jason said as he began putting on his Army gear. "Starting without me?"

"Yeah, we knew you wouldn't contribute much," Lucas teased as he grinned at Jason. "Now that you've finally arrived, I guess we can finish."

He wasn't that far off. It didn't take the boys long to complete their one act play. They didn't write the script down except for a few notes that Jason took. The four boys went through the act several times to get it down to the eight to ten minutes the play was supposed to last. By the time they had to break up and go home for dinner, they were all confident they could pull it off. They would have another day to work on it if they needed to. It was Tuesday and they were to put on the play in front of their class on Thursday.

"Do you want to meet again tomorrow to go over it again?" Benny asked.

"I think we just need to get our props together," Lucas answered. There really wasn't much to gather. They all had their Army fatigues, helmets and their toy guns. They decided to use cardboard boxes for their machine gun nest. Mrs. Jefferson and Benny's sister Carol helped Benny paint them to look like stacked boulders. When the boys went over to pick them up on Thursday morning, they were truly impressed.

"Wow!" Jason exclaimed. "They look great. It looks like real rocks stacked up."

There were four boxes, one for each of the boys to carry. It was a little inconvenient on the bus ride, but they managed without any damage to their "scenery." Lucas brought his toy machine gun, a replica of a Vickers machine gun. The other three had toy rifles and Jason had a toy luger, too. Even though it was a German gun, they didn't think anyone would notice they had a weapon of the "enemy" as they put on their play.

The play went off with only a minor hitch. Lucas hit Benny on top of his helmet with the machine gun and the machine gun broke. Luke didn't panic but instead just acted like it was part of the act. He could stick the barrel of the gun back into the rest of it and it would stay if it didn't get banged against something. The class enjoyed the play and voted it as the best play of the class.

Mr. Knoll was beaming. He thanked all of the groups and told them all what a good job they did. The class might have liked Lucas's group's play best because it was so funny, but all of the plays were really good. Each group finished its play before lunch and after they returned from their lunch break, Mr. Knoll made an announcement.

"I have a surprise for everyone!" he exclaimed. "Tomorrow you will all be getting out a couple of hours early." Cheers erupted from the class. "We are having a teacher's conference in the afternoon so you will be getting onto your buses an hour after lunch. I have a second surprise for you. The Münchweiler boys will be putting their play on for all of the 3rd and 4th graders in the lunch room after lunch, before we end the school day."

Lucas' mouth dropped open. "What?" The other boys looked stunned, too.

"That's right," Mr. Knoll continued, "I spoke to the other teachers and have made the arrangements for it to happen. Don't look so scared, Bobby! You perform like you did today and it will be fine."

Well, that's how it came about that Tara got to see the play. It varied a little from the one the boys did for their class since they really didn't have a script, but it actually was a little better since they were prepared to incorporate the busted machine gun into the script this time around. No surprises except for Lucas seeing Tara give them a standing ovation.

Chapter VI

The Bowling Alley and Losing a Good Friend

There were a few more events before the end of the school year. A new boy named Lloyd Mize moved to Münchweiler. He was a tall, lanky kid with jet-black hair and a hawk-like nose. His mother, a real energetic person, was shocked to discover that there was not a Cub Scout or Boy Scout Troop on the post. She soon remedied that, and within a month there was an official Cub Scout Troop at Münchweiler. A year later, the whole Cub Scout Troop would become Münchweiler's first Boy Scout Troop. It became another chance for the "gang" to all get together one evening every week which led to many more opportunities to get in trouble.

The second thing that happened about a month before school ended was that Ricky Mason had spoken to the manager of the little four-lane bowling alley on the post and talked him into letting him work there on Saturdays.

"I asked for you, too, Luke. He said he thought bein' we're only nine years old we were too young, but he's gonna let us both try anyhow," exclaimed Ricky. He could hardly hold himself still. In fact, he couldn't at all. He was sort of hopping around Lucas as he spoke.

"You do want to do it don't you?" he asked Lucas. "You could make some money to buy sodas or ice cream at the Snack Bar or candy at the PX."

Lucas couldn't contain his laughter as he watched Ricky, "Alright, alright stop now!" he said. "I'll try it, Ricky."

"GREAT … NEATO … you won't be sorry, Lucas!" he responded.

"What will I have to do?" Luke asked.

"We will be setting pins," Ricky answered. "We have to be at the bowling alley by 9 o'clock Saturday morning. They'll show us what we have to do then."

"I hope I can get away that early. I have to pass inspection before I can go out," Lucas sighed.

"Tell your dad you have a job," Ricky chuckled. "I'll betcha he lets you go by nine."

Ricky was right about Ivan. When Lucas told him about the job he could tell he'd caught his father off guard. He started to respond three different times and stopped each time, trying to formulate what he wanted to say.

"Lucas, those bowling pins are big and dangerous," Maria interjected during the lull. "I don't think you should. You could get hurt."

"No, woman," (that's how Ivan often addressed Maria). "I think it would be good for Luke to have a job."

"But he seems too young," she replied.

"If he can't do it Sgt. Taylor won't hire him or keep him," Ivan answered. "Besides, it can't be for too long. I hear they're gettin' those automatic pin setting machines by the end of the year."

Lucas looked back at his mother. "Please, please, please Mom? I promise I won't get hurt."

Maria looked at Ivan and could tell that he was pretty set on Lucas doing this, so she knew it was useless to object. She finally agreed to let him work.

"Okay Lucas, you can take the job if they'll actually hire you," she said as if she really was hoping that Sgt. Taylor wouldn't.

"Boy, that doesn't mean you don't have to clean your room up. I expect to see your half clean before you go," Ivan stated.

"Yes sir," Lucas shouted, grinning and saluting his dad as he ran for the door. "I'm going to tell Ricky."

"Damn it, Luke!" his father shouted back, "don't salute me. I'm not a fucking officer."

But by the time those words were out of Ivan's mouth, Lucas was out the door and down the first flight of stairs. Ivan's angry look turned into a grin as he turned to Maria. "I think the little punk did that on purpose. He knows I hate it."

"I think he was just excited, Ivan," was her response. "I'm sure little Lucas would never do something on purpose to aggravate you." There wasn't much conviction in her voice. It did seem like Luke did those little things to piss his dad off just to see how far he could get before he got the slap across the back of the head.

Meanwhile, Lucas was across the street and ringing Ricky's doorbell. Ricky's sister Kelly answered. "What do you want Twerp?"

"Out of my way, Beanstalk!" Luke answered as he shoved by Kelly. Beanstalk was the nickname Luke had come up with when Kelly started calling him 'Twerp'. It didn't get to her that much at first. "Like I care what you call me?" But now she was a bit sensitive about it. Lucas started calling her that on the school bus and soon some of the other kids had picked it up. Now, anytime she heard it she wanted to punch the kid saying it and sometimes she did.

By the time Kelly turned around, Luke was already in Ricky's room. "Hey man, I can do it," he said to a startled Ricky who was lying on his bed reading a comic book.

"You scared the crap out of me!" Ricky shouted. Then he broke out into a big grin and the two of them began dancing around the room and acting goofy.

"You guys are a couple of fairies!" Kelly yelled at them as she passed Ricky's room on the way back to hers.

"I better get back home," Luke said as they settled down. "I can't wait until Saturday."

"Me either," Ricky said as Lucas was out the door and heading back home.

Saturday couldn't come quickly enough for the two boys. Lucas was up early. Only Ivan was up and had been for a little while. Lucas got up at five every morning. He could hear his mother in the bathroom. When he came out his dad looked surprised.

"You don't have to go to the bowling alley until nine, what are you doing up so early?" he asked.

"Too excited to sleep anymore, Dad. I even made my bed already," Lucas blurted.

Ivan looked at Luke and grinned. "Well, I was thinking of fixing some mush this morning, want some?"

Lucas loved oatmeal in the morning. There may have been a lot of things about his dad he didn't like, but his oatmeal wasn't one of them. "Yes, Sir. I'd love some."

Maria came out and joined them. Lucas actually got to engage in conversation with both his parents without any of his siblings around to interrupt or correct. Although, all said and done, he really didn't add that much to the conversation. But still, the half hour alone with his parents was a treasured moment.

About seven o'clock Susan drifted out, then Joey with Ike only moments behind him. Karla had been out to a movie the night before and stayed in bed until Lucas was leaving at 8:15. He tried to wait longer but couldn't anymore. When his dad said something to him about leaving so early he shouted back as he was going out the door, "I want to make sure Ricky is up and ready!" He heard all of his family laugh out loud and Susan say, "Ricky has probably been waiting an hour for you."

She wasn't far off with her assertion. When Lucas got halfway across the street, Ricky came bursting out of the stairwell doorway of his apartment.

"What took you so long?" he asked Luke. "I've been waiting in the stairwell since 8 o'clock."

Lucas grinned at Ricky and said, "Hey crazy man, we're not supposed to be there until nine and it'll take us all of five minutes to walk there."

"I know, I know, but my dad says you should always be early for an appointment."

"Ricky, your dad is a doctor! Of course he wants people to be early, but this would be early even for him. Let's take the long way, out by the town fence, sewer hill and the ball field. That may take us fifteen minutes."

"Okay. That'll help calm me down a little," Ricky stated.

The boys took the long way and got to the bowling alley at 8:30. The doors were open and Sgt. Taylor was inside sweeping the floor and arranging the rack of bowling shoes. The boys stood in the doorway a few minutes before he caught sight of them.

"Ricky! You're early!" he roared in one of the deepest voices Lucas had ever heard. It caused Luke to grin. "And you must be Luke, Ivan's boy. Served with your dad in the Pacific, son. Nobody I'd want to share a foxhole with more than your old man. Well, until Karl gets here you can help me clean up a little. Karl's the German pinsetter that's gonna teach you guys the job."

The boys wasted no time helping out. Lucas picked up the broom and finished sweeping for Sgt. Taylor and Ricky worked on the shoe rack while Sgt. Taylor started straightening out the bowling balls, talking to the boys the entire time. At 8:45 Karl arrived.

"Karl, these are the two new helpers I told you about, Ricky and Lucas," Sgt. Taylor told him as he walked in the door.

Karl turned to Lucas first and stuck out his hand, "I am Karl Bergman."

"Please to meet you, Karl," Lucas answered as he shook his hand.

Ricky came over and did the same. Then Karl said, "Give me a few minutes to get things set up and then I'll get started teaching you what you need to know."

"Take them with you now, Karl," Sgt. Taylor ordered. "I want them to see how you set things up, too."

With that, the three of them went to the back of the bowling alley behind the lanes. Otto, Sgt. Taylor's other German pinsetter left when he heard they were going to be getting automatic pin setting machines by the end of the year. He took a job on post in the mess hall when a position opened up. Sgt. Taylor was having trouble replacing him, which is why he was open to Ricky and Lucas working for him. He would rather have had older boys, but he thought he would give these two young guys a try. Besides, when Ricky mentioned Lucas as the second boy, Sgt. Taylor was more than happy to give Ivan's boy a chance. He and Ivan had a long history together dating back to his earliest days in the Army.

At the back of the four-lane alley there was a huge counter or catwalk that was about two feet wide and stood about three and a half feet tall. It had large rubber mats that looked like huge truck tire mud flaps behind each set of pins. Above the pins were racks that held the pins that were to be placed in the proper location on the alley. They had a large bar handle that came to about the boy's eyes when they stood behind it. The way it worked was when the bowler tossed his first ball, the pinsetter would have to jump into the pit behind the rack, pick up the ball and put it in the ball return. It would then go back to the top of the alley to the bowlers. Then the pinsetter had to pick up the loose pins and put them back in the rack above the alley. The pinsetter had to make sure he didn't place a pin in a location where there was still a pin left on the alley. Then he had to jump out of the pit until the bowler sent the second ball. After the second ball, the setter jumped in the pit, returned the ball, picked up the pins, placed them in the rack, and using the bar, placed both hands on the bar and pushed it down. This would lower the rack to the alley and release the pins in their designated spots. If the bowler left some pins remaining in place, the rack would simply slip over them. If the setter accidentally placed a pin in a rack above an existing pin it would shoot the pin up in the air and back towards the pinsetter.

"Always make sure the pins are on the spots on the alley," Karl told them. "If it is off a little, pull it out and put it in the rack or the rack will not come down. Sometimes it will cause all of the pins to fall out of the rack and you have to re-set the entire rack."

Karl went through his checklist explaining to the boys what he was doing. He was very nice to them and seemed to enjoy teaching them. He did a thorough examination of all of the pins. Any that had cracks in them or big chips out of them he tossed aside. He picked up a small grease gun and showed the boys the grease fittings on each side of the rack that needed greasing every day. "Don't put too much on them or it will get on everything. Just one squirt of the gun is enough," Karl told them.

Finally, Karl shouted out to Sgt. Taylor, "We are ready now, Sarge! Give us your best ball!"

"You got it," he responded, followed shortly by his first ball coming down the alley. Boy was it loud when it hit. Both the boys jumped and Karl broke into a deep belly laugh before jumping into the pit from the top of the catwalk. He moved quickly to place the ball in the return chute and scoop up the pins. Lucas noted that a couple of the pins were up the alley a little and Karl had to reach up the alley to pick them up without knocking down the remaining pins. He quickly jumped out of the pit. Seconds later the second ball came down, knocking down all the remaining pins but one.

"I am going to show you what happens when you put a pin in the rack where there is still a pin on the same spot," he told the boys. As he did, the pin in the rack came shooting out of the rack and almost hit Karl.

"These hurt very, very much if they hit you," Karl said in a heavy German accent. Then he turned to Ricky and said, "Now it is your turn."

After yelling to Sgt. Taylor that they were ready, Karl had Ricky stand on the catwalk. "You have to be quick so it is better to stay on top of the catwalk instead of waiting on the floor behind it. Besides, if you stand behind it you have to double the times you have to jump up to it and by the end of the day you will be dead tired."

Ricky did his turn without a hitch. Lucas then got on the catwalk and took his turn. His, too, went off without a hitch. Lucas was surprised at how hard it was to push the rack down. It took quite an effort. He had a feeling he would be pretty tired by the end of the day. They practiced a little while as Karl went out to the front to bowl a little. It was one of the side benefits of the job. Sgt. Taylor came back to watch the boys for a few minutes.

"We never did talk pay, Ricky, since we first talked about the job. I can pay you a quarter an hour and you get to split tips with Karl from the tip box." The tip box was a big box on the main counter that the bowlers placed tips for the pinsetters. "Today, Karl will get half the tips and you two will split the other half. You will each have an alley to watch and Karl will have two."

Neither of the boys was in any position to try to negotiate with Sgt. Taylor and to be honest, neither of them even thought about it. They were going to make some money and how much didn't matter too much when they had none.

At ten o'clock the doors opened and the Saturday league players started drifting in. From the back of the alley the buzz was exciting to Ricky and Lucas. Karl sat on the catwalk with his back against the wall at the end of it smiling at the boys. Karl was probably 18 or 19 years old. He had never worked with anyone as young as Ricky and Lucas. *This is going to be interesting.* He watched Lucas punch Ricky in the arm. He could tell they were all wound up in anticipation of their first day. He knew how tired they would be by the time three o'clock rolled around. That was how long they were scheduled to work. Another German boy would come in at 6:00 p.m. to help Karl finish the night.

The day flew by for the boys. They were very busy the entire time. They hardly had a moment to rest. Sgt. Taylor brought them back some cokes and there was a water fountain in the back, too. When he asked them if they brought a lunch, they both looked surprised. It had never even occurred to them to pack a lunch. The only time they did that was for school. At around one o'clock Sgt. Taylor ran next door to the NCO Club and got the boys a couple of burgers with fries. They took turns eating them with Karl helping to cover the lane of the one eating. When Ricky was eating, Lucas saw Karl jump in the far lane pit just as the ball came into Ricky's pit next to Lucas. He had just finished with his lane and seeing that Karl had just started in his pit, Luke jumped in and worked Ricky's. As he was climbing out, Karl gave him a big grin and a thumps up. That was about all the time they had before the next ball scattered pins.

When league play was over it eased up a little, but not much. By the time 3 o'clock rolled along, both boys were exhausted. It had been fun, too. They were able to joke with each other as they worked and they found out that if one of them had to go to the bathroom or get a drink, the other could cover their lane without having Karl help them. He had picked up on it, too, and pretty much left them alone to work their alleys. He seemed at ease with working two alleys. "A couple of nights I had to work alone. We had to close off one alley and I worked three of them. I was … what is the English word … exhausted … at the end of the night," he told them.

As the boys walked to the front, butts dragging, Karl walked out with them. He picked up the tip box and started counting out the money. Meanwhile, Sgt. Taylor came around from behind the counter with $1.50 in his each hand. As he handed it to the boys he turned to Karl.

"Well, Karl, what do you think? Think these two young men will work out?"

"Ya, ya I think they will do," he said as he winked at the boys. Then he handed each of them two dollars. "You both worked very hard and no complaints. Almost all of the new guys I break in complain at least a little bit. Here you go, you have earned this today. It was a busy day."

"Thank you, Karl!" they both said in unison. Little did Karl know that Lucas knew he better not complain. If that got back to his dad, he would be in deep shit.

"And thank you, too, Sgt. Taylor," Luke added. Ricky just nodded. Luke looked at him and broke into a big grin. He could tell Ricky was beat. When he wasn't talking all the time, you knew something was up.

"I'll see you both next Saturday, then?" Sgt. Taylor asked.

"You bet!" Lucas answered. Again, Ricky just nodded.

"It'll be a little easier next week. You'll only have to work until one o'clock. Karl's friend, Jacob, will be coming in at one on most Saturdays."

The boys waved and said their goodbyes. As they walked away, he reached his hand into his pocket and felt the money he had just earned. *Ricky and I are the richest kids on Post.* Lucas was happy about getting off early the next week. He liked working and making money, but this afternoon he was sacrificing playing baseball to work. It wasn't a trade-off he liked doing too much. He loved playing baseball.

On the way home, Ricky still was unusually quiet. Lucas was tired enough not to try to start up a conversation. "See you later, Ricky," he said as they got to their apartment complex.

"See you, Lucas."

When Lucas got home, his dad wanted to see his earnings. He acted quite impressed, which was something Luke didn't see often from Ivan.

"Whatcha gonna do with all that money, Boy?" Ivan asked.

"I don't know. I haven't really thought about it.

"You can buy us candy!" Joey shouted as he tackled Lucas and wrestled him to the floor.

"Ow, ow, ow!" Lucas squealed. "Don't grab my arms, they're sore!"

"Better leave your brother alone, Joey," His father ordered. "He worked hard today."

Lucas and Ricky continued to work at the bowling alley throughout the summer. (Bob Ledahawski joined them on the fourth weekend). That was after Ricky had gotten sick and couldn't make it on the third weekend. That day Karl helped Lucas with the second alley, handling his two alleys at the same time. After the first hour, Lucas pretty much handled the second alley himself with little help from Karl. He didn't mind working hard, and it kept him so busy he could hardly believe it when his workday was over. He made good money splitting the tips down the middle with Karl. He was able to buy his mother a birthday present from the PX with his own money. He felt pretty good about that.

There was only one time that Lucas got hurt, besides the occasional pinched finger. Karl wasn't working that day. It was

Bobby, Ricky and Lucas working. There were times when Karl didn't like it when all three would come in. He had no trouble working two lanes and he wasn't too keen on sharing his tips with a third person so Bobby didn't work as often. Usually it was just Luke or Ricky with Bobby filling in when one of them couldn't work or had to leave early for some reason. This particular Saturday Sgt. Taylor knew that Karl couldn't come in until 3 o'clock so he asked all three to come in.

"You boys figure out how you're gonna work it with the three of you and four alleys," he stated.

When they got to the back Lucas came up with a plan. "We'll all walk back and forth on the catwalk and whoever is closest to the pit that needs us will jump in and handle it while the others keep walking until one opens up in front of them."

It was a good plan and it made it more fun than usual. The boys would pass each other as they strolled back and forth and when a ball hit the pins in any lane, the closest boy would jump in and work it. A couple of times two of them would jump in at the same time but other than that, it worked pretty well. That was until late in the final games of league play.

There was one bowler that the boys always had to keep an eye on … Sgt. Miller. He tossed that bowling ball so hard that often pins would fly out of the pit and on more than one occasion hit the pinsetter. Neither Ricky nor Lucas had ever been hit but Karl had been and Bob got grazed the first time he worked the alleys. Karl ended up with a deep bruise on his bicep. In the back, the pinsetters would always let the others know if they saw it was Sgt. Miller up.

It was going into the final frame of league play when Lucas was just passing the third lane and had stepped even with lane two. Bob had just gotten off the catwalk to get a drink of coke and Ricky was just turning around at the end of lane one when Lucas heard the ball explode into the pins in what he thought was lane three, just behind him. He immediately turned around and jumped into the pit only to discover, to his surprise, that the pins were all in place. He landed and fell into a stoop so that he was peering out through the pins at the bowlers at the top of the alley. To his horror and everyone else's watching him as he peered through the pins, Sgt. Miller had just let go of his ball and it was flying down the alley towards Lucas. There was no thinking on Luke's part as he jumped up, spinning around as he did, towards the top of the counter. He heard screams from a few of the bowler's wives that were there at about the same time he heard the ball hit the pins. He was almost out of the pit when he felt the slam of a pin on his calf. Lucas didn't land on his feet on the counter the way he usually did but ended up tumbling over it to the floor beneath.

"SHIT!" Ricky yelled as he witnessed the whole incident in front of him. Bob dropped his coke, mouth agape, and just stared at Lucas.

Lucas immediately jumped up but fell again as he tried to put weight on his leg. Ricky was off of the catwalk and trying to help Lucas up as Sgt. Miller came flying through the curtains that served as the door to the back of the alleys. Sgt. Taylor was right behind him followed by most of the rest of the people in the bowling alley.

In the few seconds it took for all that to take place, Lucas had somehow registered everything that had just happened in his brain and realized how close he came to getting his head knocked off. As he started putting weight on his leg, still holding on to Ricky he managed to yell out to everyone, "I'm okay, I'm okay!" and then he started a hysterical laughter. He was close to crying but he knew he couldn't, so he laughed instead. Between the relief that had just come over him for surviving the close call and the pain in the back of his leg, it was the only thing he could do.

"Oh son, I am so sorry," Sgt. Miller said in a very concerned voice. "Are you sure you're okay? Let's have a look at your leg."

Lucas kept insisting he was okay and tried to get everyone to go back to finish their game but no one was leaving until they were sure he was okay. The good thing about being stationed at a hospital post was there was always some medical person close by. One of the bowlers was a medic and had run out and grabbed his emergency bag from his car as everyone else ran to the back.

"Move back Sarge," he said to Sgt. Miller as he moved next to Lucas, "and let me have a look at it."

After feeling to see if anything was broken and having Lucas go through a whole set of range of motion tests, he said to Lucas,

"You're gonna have one hell of a bruise but other than that I don't think there's anything serious. I'd put some ice on it and watch it close. If the swelling doesn't go down by the time you go to bed. Go to the Emergency Room at the hospital."

"It was my fault Sgt. Miller," Lucas said as the medic finished looking at his leg. "I jumped in the wrong pit."

"No shit, Sherlock!" roared Sgt. Taylor in that deep voice of his. Everyone burst out laughing. They were all relieved that he wasn't seriously hurt. "I'll call your dad and let him know to keep an eye on it."

Lucas almost panicked, "No, no, no … please don't tell my dad! He'll kill me for messing up."

"We don't have to tell him you messed up, Luke." Sgt. Taylor answered. "We'll just tell him you got hit by one of Hercules' balls," he said pointing to Sgt. Miller. "He knows Sgt. Miller's reputation. He won't have to know it was because you decided to play 'chicken' with him."

Everyone laughed again and they started to drift up to the front. Ricky and Bobby said they would handle the rest of the games. Lucas resisted their help but Sgt. Taylor interceded and there was no arguing with him.

"They're on the last frame and Karl will be here soon so you just sit on your ass, Luke, and let your buddies take care of the pits," Sgt. Taylor ordered.

It wasn't long before they were done. Luke had spent the time trying to walk out the stiffness that had developed in his calf. As the last of the bowlers were leaving, Sgt. Miller popped his head in the back to check on Lucas one last time before he left.

"I left my regular tip in the tip box for all of you but this is a tip just for you Baryshivka," he said as he stuffed a dollar in Lucas' pocket.

"Thank you," Lucas sheepishly replied.

After Sgt. Taylor left, Karl came in with a big grin on his face. "Ah so, you had a little excitement today I hear?"

Lucas didn't say anything but Ricky and Bob were happy to tell Karl all about it, embellishing the story as they told it. Then they said their goodbyes to Karl and went to get their pay.

"Wow!" Ricky exclaimed looking at Sgt. Taylor grinning from behind the tip box. "That's the most money I have ever seen in there!"

"Thank Lucas for that, boys," Sgt. Taylor said. "That's what you call sympathy money."

With that, he gave the boys their pay plus the tips, which he dumped in Lucas' baseball cap. When they got outside to split up the tips, Lucas pulled out the dollar Sgt. Taylor gave him and threw it in the kitty.

"That's your dollar, Luke," Bob said. Then laughing, "You earned it."

"It is all of ours equally, like we agreed when we started this job," Lucas replied. "Besides, it doesn't feel right that I get rewarded for doing something stupid."

"And, boy was that ever stupid!" Ricky shouted as he began to run home.

They all laughed and then Ricky stopped when he realized Lucas couldn't run with his injury. Ricky and Bob teased Luke all the way home. They challenged him to a race knowing that he was by far the fastest of the three and asked him if he wanted to play a little hopscotch before dinner. When Lucas did get home, Ivan was waiting for him with an ice pack. Lucas was taken aback by the show of sympathy from his father. It wasn't a side of Ivan he had seen before.

Lucas was playing baseball off the wall of Ricky's building with Mickey Mira, a new arrival that summer, when Ricky came running out of his stairwell. Mickey quickly assimilated into the group and was as passionate about baseball as Lucas was. He was a couple of inches shorter than Lucas with wide shoulders and a gold tooth that beamed as he broke out with a big smile. His sandy hair fell across his forehead and was a little longer than the rest of the boys'. They became instant good friends much to the consternation of Ricky Mason. Ricky was jealous of the relationship that Lucas and Mickey had developed even though Mickey went out of his way to be Ricky's friend, too.

Ricky saw Lucas and Mickey and bolted over to them. Lucas stopped throwing the tennis ball against the building. He could see Ricky had been crying. His eyes were red and puffy as he stood next to the light pole that was close to Lucas.

"What's wrong, Ricky?" asked Lucas, looking very concerned.

"My dad got his orders," Ricky sobbed. "We are leaving in two weeks."

"TWO WEEKS!" Lucas shouted. "Damn it, Ricky, you *can't go.*"

Ricky sat down on the curb. He couldn't keep back the tears. It made Lucas' eyes tear up, too. Lucas sat next to him and put his arm around his shoulder. Mickey walked over to them, but said nothing. He knew that Ricky and Lucas had been best friends and he also knew how hard it was when your best friend left. It was part of Army life. You had to get used to saying good-bye to friends every time your dad got transferred and it wasn't easy.

"Where're you goin'?" Lucas finally asked as he broke the silence that had enveloped them.

"My dad got transferred to Sam Houston Hospital in Texas," Ricky answered meekly. "I've never been to Texas."

"I'm sure it will be a neat place to be," Lucas said trying to comfort him.

"I don't want to leave here," Ricky replied. Then they sat in silence again. Lucas didn't feel like continuing the game and Mickey didn't press it. They all walked over to the playground and sat on the concrete wall that surrounded the large sand box. There were a lot of days they would come out with their toy soldiers and build forts in the sand box, choosing sides as they molded the sand into barriers. They would use a tennis ball as the ammo and take turns throwing it at the others soldiers until only one side had any left upright.

On this day, Lucas felt like throwing the ball at something to relieve his anger at Ricky leaving. He did realize that was what he was feeling after the initial shock wore off. He was angry with the Army for transferring Captain Mason. He was angry with Ricky for leaving. He was angry with God for letting it all happen like this. It just didn't seem fair.

The last two weeks the boys had together had their ups and downs. Ricky worked the bowling alley one more Saturday. He was there for another but was busy helping his family pack up for the movers. Mickey took his place for the rest of the summer and for the first few Saturdays in September before the bowling alley got the new automatic pinsetters. Lucas had mixed feelings when that happened. He liked having the money but he was tired of working every Saturday, especially when school was back in session. He would rather have the playtime.

The last day before Ricky and his family to leave arrived. It was sad to see him go but there was a nice send-off by all of the "gang" and a lot of other kids. It seemed like most of the time the kids that left just sort of slipped away. No fanfare, just gone one day. A lot of the kids from Todd's class were there too, which seemed odd to Lucas. Most of them thought Ricky was a twerp. Lucas smiled. *Well, Ricky certainly got noticed by a lot of people.* Then his thought was broken as he stood looking at Ricky a foot in front of him.

"Hey, man, I'm gonna miss you a lot," Lucas managed to say meekly.

"Me, too," Ricky sadly replied. "Thanks for being my friend, Lucas."

Lucas couldn't hold back his tears any longer. He gave Ricky a big hug and then spun away to hide his tears. Ricky stood there a moment, tears running down his cheeks. He had already said his good-byes to everyone else. He turned and got in the van taking them to Frankfurt. Lucas had managed to get control of his emotions for the moment. He turned and smiled real big and waved, locking eyes with Ricky one last time as the Mason family drove off.

"Bye my friend," he yelled. Then he turned and went home without talking to anyone. His friends watched him leave in silence. They all knew what he was going through. They had gone through it themselves at one time or another. After all, they were all Army Brats. It came with the territory.

Chapter VII

Off Post

When the Cub Scout Troop was formed in Münchweiler, Lucas wasn't sure he even wanted to join. Jason talked him into it. They met once a week for the first month, and then they met every two weeks. Tuesday evenings while school was still in session, Lucas missed a few meetings. He couldn't go until his homework was done and it seemed to be a good excuse for him when he didn't want to go to Scouts. The best thing about the Cub Scouts, as far as Lucas was concerned, was that next year it led to being in the Boy Scouts. He took to the Boy Scouts much more than to the Cub Scouts.

For Lucas it was a balancing act. He worked the bowling alleys on Saturday mornings until early afternoon. In the afternoons he had baseball practice and the team often had games on Saturday, too. The "gang" was constantly testing the boundaries of their freedom to roam about and play most of the day without supervision. He much preferred that than meeting with the Cub Scouts. To Lucas, it was plain boring. He'd rather play baseball from dawn to dusk if he could. Their team was pretty good with a lot of the younger guys like Lucas, Jason Sprint, and Bob Ledahawski being amongst the better players. Jason was the starting second baseman. Lucas was the starting shortstop and he was also the team's second starting pitcher. Their passion for baseball was contagious and all of the other boys in his group played. If they weren't playing with the Little League team they were playing pick-up games or 500 or baseball off the wall.

Also, over the course of summer vacation, two new boys besides Mickey moved onto the Post. The other two boys were Guy Henderson and Lester Horry. Guy was the son of an NCO as was Mickey. Lester's father was a Major and the new Chief Surgeon at the Münchweiler Hospital. He was also colored. Lester was a real nice kid and everyone hit it off with him right away. Guy was Lucas' height, but a little broader. He was also a little abrasive and combative as he tried to establish himself in the hierarchy of the group. The third day he was there, he and Lucas got into a fight while they were playing 500. It didn't last long. Lucas could tell Guy was strong, but hadn't fought very much. Luke soon had him pinned on the ground with his knees on Guy's shoulders so he couldn't move.

"You give up or do I have to hit you again?" Luke said to Guy as Guy tried to push him off to no avail.

"Okay, I give," Guy finally said as he relaxed and quit trying to resist. Lucas got up and let him get up. No one was hurt and they all went back to playing ball. It was the first of several times that they would get into it over the next couple of years.

During the second week of August, Todd had come up to the gang as they were hanging out in the playground, trying to decide what they were going to do for the day. Jason, Bob, Mickey, Guy, Benny and Lucas were trying to decide if they were going to play 500 or if they could get enough guys together to play a ball game.

"You guys want to see a really cool place Hans showed me yesterday?" Todd asked.

"What kinda cool place?" Guy asked.

"It's off post and it's a pretty long walk to get to it," Todd continued. "There is a small stream we follow to three different lakes. The first two are pretty small, but the last one is big and has a boathouse on it."

Now he got Lucas' attention. Todd usually never brought fun things to do to the group. He usually hung with them because most of his friends didn't do the fun adventures that Bobby and friends did. For him to suggest something interesting was highly unusual.

"Where is this place?" Lucas asked.

"We go out the back gate and follow the power line road for a little while. Then there is a path that follows the railroad tracks for bit. Then we leave it where it crosses the first small lake. The stream flows into the lake from above. It drops down the hillside in a bunch of small waterfalls that are really cool. Then we follow the stream as it goes into a meadow. When you get to the meadow there is a dirt road that follows the stream all the way to the biggest lake, but it's neater to follow the stream instead of the road."

Lucas was excited about it now. Listening to Todd's description had his juices flowing. "Let's go," he said.

"I can't go off post," Benny said in a flat voice. He looked a little dejected. None of the boys had permission to go off post but most of them did it anyway. Benny wasn't one of the more adventurous types and he sure wasn't one to challenge his parents.

"Won't we get in trouble for leaving the fort?" Mickey asked.

"Not if we don't get caught," was Todd's answer.

"We go a lot and haven't gotten caught, yet," Lucas added.

"I'll go!" Guy interjected. This was no surprise to Lucas. Guy was always trying to show he was as tough, or as brave, or as whatever the other guys were.

"How about you, Mickey?" Bobby asked.

"Yeah ... sure, I'm in," Mickey said not so enthusiastically.

"All right, let's go!" Todd shouted and off they went towards the back gate. Benny headed home after the others left for the Three Lakes, as they would forever be called by the boys. Lucas felt bad for Benny. He went out of his way a lot to include Benny in their adventures. The problem was Benny was "too good" of a kid. He did what his parents asked of him and he really never caused problems. Lucas always felt like he needed to include him and at times elected to do the "safer" thing and hang out with Benny instead of going off on an adventure with the group. Maybe it was the guilt Luke still felt from beating Benny up that one time. Maybe he just felt bad because Benny was missing out on so much fun by being "too good" to try anything that might not be okay with his parents.

On this day, it didn't matter. The discovery of Three Lakes was too good to pass up. It took the boys no time to reach the back gate and slip off the post. They followed Todd's lead as they walked along the rugged, two-track dirt road that followed the power lines and was bordered by pine trees that were only five or six feet back from the road. They were heading southeast of the fort. As they reached the end of a small green meadow on the right side of the road, they left the road and followed a narrow path that crossed the railroad tracks and wound up the hillside. The steep slope of the hill had only short, scrubby vegetation and many rocks and boulders sticking out of the side of slope.

As they climbed up the hill along the path, they could see the train tunnel below them. After traveling on the winding path up and down several hills, they could see the other end of the tunnel below them. At this point the path turned to the south for a little way before turning southeast again. They followed the path up and down several more hillsides before reaching a heavily wooded area. As they rounded the bend on their final drop down the hillside, they stopped in awe. Below them was the first of the lakes. It was really just a pond but it was beautiful. There was the waterfall coming into the lake from the left as they faced it. It was really a series of small waterfalls that dropped five or six feet at a time from the hillside above. The top of the hill where the falls originated was at least forty feet above the pond. Trees hung over it as it cascaded down the hillside, keeping most of it in the shade. Where rays of sunlight did make it through, they sparkled off the water in a dazzling burst of rainbows. The area was very lush around the lake. The boys stopped by a dam at the far end of it. The water dropped through a weir and continued as the stream flowed below.

"Hans said that the Germans spawn fish in this lake and release them into the stream. They eventually get to the last lake," Todd informed them.

"Wow, Todd!" Lucas exclaimed. "This place is so neat."

The boys hung out at the first lake for about half an hour before Todd said, "We better get moving if you want to see the other lakes."

Off they went, following the stream as it meandered back and forth flanked by the forested hillsides as the boys moved downstream and down the mountainside. They walked in the stream for much of the way. All the boys had their sneakers on and they were all soaked from the first lake so it didn't matter if they were in the stream or along it. It was only six or seven feet wide and narrower at times. The water was so clear they could see the fish in it. The boys would try to catch the fish with their hands from time to time as Todd kept after them to keep moving.

Before long they were at the second lake. Just before the lake, the hills rolled back on both sides, opening the area into the large green meadow. The surrounding area wasn't nearly as lush and neat looking as the small meadow at the first lake, but this second lake was about twice the size. They didn't spend much time at this lake as they walked around it and picked up the stream at the concrete dam on the southeast end of the lake. From there they continued to follow the stream through another, narrower, meadow. They could see a dirt road not far off the north and east side of the meadow. As they neared the third lake, they could see the end of the meadow was filled with reeds and cattails. The boathouse was visible now as the boys followed the path around the south side of the lake. There was a dirt road going the other way from the boathouse. As they got to the door, Todd tried to open it.

"It's locked!" he shouted back to the rest of the gang. "I want to see what's in there." He walked to the side of the door and tried to look into the window. He couldn't see much through the dirty window as he strained to see what appeared to be two boats inside.

"BOOOOO!" shouted Lucas as he shoved his face against the window from the inside. Todd let out a scream that startled the rest of the guys as they watched him jump back from the window. Lucas was howling with laughter from inside.

"YOU LITTLE FUCKING SHIT!" Todd yelled at Luke. "I'm gonna pound your ass!"

"How'd you get in there, Luke?" Jason asked.

"I just waded through the water to the front. It isn't very deep right there," Lucas answered, still chuckling. Then he began running as Todd came around and under the other side, chasing him. This continued for about five minutes or so before Todd finally gave up. He knew he couldn't catch Luke and by then he had gotten over the embarrassment of being scared. The boys hung out at the boathouse for half an hour before Bobby turned to the group.

"We shoulda brought some sandwiches. I'm hungry."

"Me, too," Todd added. "Let's head back. We can explore the rest of the lake some other time."

Luke wanted to stay but he was pretty hungry, too, and they had a hike to get back home. Following Todd's lead, they all started walking back to the post. This time they used the road for as long as they could before cutting over to the path just before the first lake.

They trudged up and down the hills finally reaching the train tunnel opening at the north end. Todd commented, "Hans says you can take a short cut by going through the train tunnel but he said you never know when the train comes through. I'd don't think we want to try that."

Of course, Lucas already had his mind churning. It was kind of like what happened with the streetlight. He knew he shouldn't even be thinking about it but something inside of him made him want to try. *Oh well, that's for another day. Right now I'm hungry.* Reaching the fort, they crawled back in through the back gate.

A week before school started Lucas had gone out to play with Mickey and Bob. They were playing 4-Square in the cul-de-sac and were soon joined by Robby and Terry Smith. Not long after that, the Clayton brothers, Earl and Dale, joined them too. Before long it seemed like all of the kids Lucas' age were at the end of the cul-de-sac. Jason Sprint, Pat Simmons, Lester Horry, Guy Henderson, and Benny Jefferson were all there.

They played 4-Square for about an hour when Lucas became bored by the game. There was too much standing around for the guys not playing at the time, Lucas thought. That really didn't bother him until he lost and had to sit out and wait his turn again.

"Let's play Army at the bunker!" Lucas shouted out at a break in the play.

"That sounds neato to me," Jason answered.

Soon all of the boys agreed to go, even Benny. That was a surprise to everyone since Benny never went off post.

"Really Benny?" Bobby questioned.

"Yeah, really," Benny responded. "I never do anything my parents forbid me from doin' and it's really boring sometimes. I don't wanna be the only one here while all of you go and have fun. My mom and sister are in K-town (Kaiserslautern) until late this afternoon. There won't be a better time for me to go off post."

Everyone cheered. Benny was well liked but was such a "goody two-shoes" that he missed out on a lot of fun that the rest of the boys had. Benny loved to play Army and when the group played by sewer hill or the picnic grounds or the sand pits he was always there. He would listen with envy when the rest of the gang would talk about their war games at the bunker. The lure of the bunker and throwing pine cones at each other was just too much for him to pass up.

"Let's get our guns and meet at the back gate in fifteen minutes," Lucas said with his most authoritative voice. They all took off for home to get their toy guns and rifles, yelling and cheering as they left.

Luke ran up to his room and grabbed his toy rifle and bolted back out.

"Where are you going, Lucas?" his mother asked as he started down the stairwell.

"Gonna play Army with the guys by the school," Lucas responded, stretching the truth. Well, in his mind it wasn't really a lie. After all, they were all meeting by the back gate, which was by the school.

"Okay, have fun; don't get hurt," Maria shouted to him out the door as Lucas was already at the bottom landing.

"I won't!" he shouted back as he exited the building. As he did, Benny was just crossing the street. The two of them walked to the back gate together.

"I hope nothin' happens while we're out there," Benny said as they walked. "I'll be in so much trouble if I get caught off the fort."

Lucas grinned at Benny and patted him on the back. "I won't let anything happen to you, Benny. I promise."

Ever since beating Benny up, Lucas had never gotten over feeling guilty about fighting with such a nice guy. He really did like Benny a lot and he even tried to teach Benny to box so the other kids didn't pick on him for seeming like such a wimp. Boxing just didn't fit Benny's personality and the lesson didn't last long before it ended with Lucas finally giving up and telling Benny, if someone picks on you, just tell 'em I'll beat them up." That actually worked pretty well. None of the kids at Münchweiler picked on Benny and in fact, also joined in on the "pick on Benny and you've picked a fight with me" bandwagon that Lucas had started. The Münchweiler crew already had a reputation at the school in Pirmasens as being quick to fight. Benny was probably the only one out of the old crew that had not gotten marched down to the Principal's office for fighting.

As the two got to the back gate, only Guy Henderson had beaten them there. Within a few minutes, all of the guys had showenup along with Todd Ledahawski, who had joined his brother. Once they were all there, Lucas again took the lead.

"Okay, guys, let's go!" he shouted and waved his arm like he was commanding a cavalry troop.

They all squeezed out of the back gate and proceeded along the dirt road that took them to the old bunker. Here they chose up sides and flipped a coin to see which team would defend the bunker and which would attack. Lucas was the leader of the attacking army and Todd was the leader of the defenders. Luke took his guys, which included Robby Smith, Jason Sprint, Lester Horry, Mickey Mira and Dale Clayton, through the woods to behind the hunter's tower that was at the far end of the meadow.

"You and Lester come in from the east side of the bunker," Lucas said to Jason. "Mickey, you and Dale come in from the other end and Robby and I will come in from the front. We are going to sneak as close as we can along the tree line before you attack, Jason. Give us time to get close. As soon as Jason and Lester attack, Mickey, you and Dale charge from the other end. Robby and I will delay attacking until we see where they're hiding. When you guys charge, they'll give up their location and we'll charge in from the front. Got It?"

All the boys answered at once, "Got it!"

They all began gathering their real ammo, the pine cones. It was a little awkward to carry their toy guns and try to carry a lot of pine cones too, but they managed by curling up the front of their shirts and carrying the pine cones there. It was harder for Robby Smith and Lucas to carry too many because they had to crawl a lot of the way so as not to be seen by the "enemy" at the bunker. On the other hand, they didn't need to carry as many since they were coming out of the wooded area that had plenty of pine cones all around.

Lucas and Robby got into position. They were well hidden at the closest point that the woods came to the bunker. Lucas could see Jason and Lester just about to charge from behind a small mound to Lucas' left. He couldn't see Mickey and Dale through the woods but assumed they were in place and ready to go. Lucas could feel the excitement of the pending charge when all of a sudden Todd shouted, "BOAR!" at the top of his lungs and began pointing in Lucas and Robby direction.

Neither of them moved at first. They both thought it was a trick to get them to reveal themselves. Then Luke noticed that all the other kids, including his team, were running out of their hiding spots and up to the top of the bunker or they began climbing trees. He turned his head in Robby's direction and there it was, a huge boar with large tusks lumbering down a barely discernible path, right towards them.

Lucas jumped up yelling, "BOAR, BOAR, BOAR!" as he started climbing up the nearest large tree that he could climb. Robby was staying hid, still thinking that they were trying to get him to give up his well-hidden position. That was until Lucas took off and started climbing the tree. Then he lifted his head and turned to look behind him. To his shock the boar was about ten feet from him. Robby shot out of his spot like a rocket ship and not only caught Luke going up the tree, but passed him on the other side of the tree, his eyes as wide as saucers.

When they both came to a stop, not a sound was coming from anyone. The boar sauntered into the meadow, coming to a stop a few times to root around the ground before coming to a stop in the middle. There he lifted his snout in the air and began sniffing. By this time, Lucas had calmed down somewhat even though his heart was still pounding a few beats above normal.

"Damn, Robby, you're white as a ghost," Lucas finally managed to say, much louder than he had intended. It got a snort and raised head from the boar below as it tried to "smell" where the sound came from.

"BEAT IT YOU FAT PIG!" Todd blasted like a loudspeaker.

The boar jumped and so did most of the guys. Then the boar started to move warily out of the meadow. Then the rest of the boys began to shout at the boar and it started to run away from the bunker and into the woods.

"YOU BETTER RUN YOUR FAT ASS OUT OF HERE!" Todd bellowed as he jumped down from his spot on top of the bunker. Then all of the boys started coming out of the safe places and into the middle of the meadow.

"Are you okay, Robby?" Lucas asked his friend.

Robby nodded his head then, broke into a grin. "Let's get out of this tree, Luke."

The two were the last to come down. When they got to the group, to everyone's surprise Benny stood in front of Robby and said, "Robby, I've never ever seen you run that fast. You better check your pants 'cause you were so scared you probably left a load."

The mouths dropped on half the kids there. That was so un-Benny-like that it floored everyone. Robby stood there, speechless, mouth agape, looking at Benny. Todd finally broke the moment by grabbing Benny by the head and giving him a nuggie and saying, "Nice one, Benny. Didn't know you had it in ya."

The boys started throwing pine cones at each other, not caring whose side they were on and then Lucas said, "Let's head back home. I'm getting hungry."

"Me, too," Bobby piped in.

"Robby, you go first and let us know if the boar is still there," Lucas joked. Robby flipped him the bird.

They all started walking back to the fort, pushing and punching each other as they went. When they got back to the gate, Lucas turned to Benny.

"So, Benny, how was the first time off fort?"

"Too much fun but a little *boar-ing* at the same time," he quipped.

They all got a hearty laugh out of that and then headed home to eat a late lunch. Benny was beaming all the way home. He now had a little better understanding of why Lucas would take the chances he took knowing how his dad would beat him if he got caught. Sometimes the fun and adventure was worth the risk. However, as much fun as it was, Benny had already decided he would never go off post again.

Chapter VIII

Back to School

A few weeks after the run-in with the wild boar, the boys were heading back to school. They received their class assignment once they got to school in Pirmasens. The first day was always hectic as the children looked at the list outside of each of the classrooms for the various grade levels. The year before, there were three 4th grade classes and three 5th grade classes. Lucas had checked on the three lists outside of the 5th grade. All of his friends except for Jason Sprint and Pat Simmons were listed for the first three classrooms. The three of them looked at each and Pat shrugged his shoulders as they got to the last room, or what they thought was the last one, without finding their name. Just then Tara Morton walked by.

"There is one more class but I am sure you dummies aren't in it," she said as she passed by them.

The three boys walked down to the next classroom. Most of the doors had the grade number on it next to the room number. This one did not have a grade number on it as the boys began to read the list. There were actually two lists, one that said "5th Graders" and another that said "6th Graders." They found their names on the "5th Graders" list.

"What the heck is going on?" Pat asked.

"I don't know," Lucas answered. "Whatever it is it can't be good if Tara is in our class."

"Oh, come on, Luke," Jason teased. "You know you like her."

Luke proceeded to slug Jason in the arm. "That's not *even* funny," he said.

The boys were still outside of the classroom when the bell rang. "Boys, are you going to join us or not?" was the question asked by a beautiful young woman that Lucas assumed was their new teacher. Her name was Miss Larkin. Lucas just stood there for a moment gawking at her. He found himself turn red when she smiled at him and with her outstretched hand indicated the way into the class.

"Come on in you Münchweiler punks!" was the roar from one of the 6th graders named "Big" John Paulson. Lucas had had a run-in with him the year before. He was picking on Benny during recess and Luke stopped him. They got into a fight that was quickly broken up by Mr. Knoll, and both of them ended up in the Principal's office. They had had words the rest of the school year but pretty much stayed out of each other's way. Big John didn't like the kids from Münchweiler and often tried to rally the Pirmasens kids to face off against them, but he really wasn't very well liked by anybody and the result was a lot of the kids from Pirmasens became friendlier with the Münchweiler kids. Lucas had a feeling that sometime during the school year he was going to have to fight Big John again.

The boys filed into the room and took seats close to each other. Lucas tried to avoid sitting next to Tara but Pat and Jason, with little smiles on their faces, grabbed the other two seats and left him no choice. Tara gave Lucas an evil little grin that gave him a chill.

"I think she likes you, Luke," Jason said as he backed out of arm's length from Lucas so he wouldn't hit him. Both Tara and Lucas shot him a look that made him shut up immediately. Jason decided he better not tease either of them about it anymore. He was more fearful of Tara's wrath then of Lucas punching him.

Lucas was befuddled. The start of this school year was not going the way he had anticipated. Most of his friends from Münchweiler were in other classes. Besides Pat and Jason, there were two girls from Münchweiler in the class, too. Katie Harley, who had been in Mr. Knoll's class with Lucas the year before, and Bonnie Lee. Although Lucas was happy that Bonnie was there, it did not offset the negative of having Tara in the class. Lucas still had a bit of a crush on Bonnie but she had made it obvious to him that the interest wasn't mutual, so they remained just good friends. In fact, since Ricky Mason left, Lucas had not seen much of Bonnie.

"Class, my name is Miss Larkin and I am your teacher this year," Miss Larkin began. "As you probably noticed there are two different grades in this class. It is an experimental class and you all are the guinea pigs. You all have been selected by your last year's teacher to be in this class. You were selected for a number of reasons. First, by your grades, and although you may not have had great grades in every subject, your 4th grade or 5th grade teacher felt that you could excel in a program like the one we are experimenting with. There were other factors in selecting you, such as leadership skills, an ability to think about things just a little differently, and mostly, a desire to learn. Now I am going to have you all move seats. The 6th graders on the left of this aisle," she said pointing to the aisle in the middle of the classroom, "and the 5th graders on the right side. Okay, class, let's all move now."

There was an instant charge of energy as all of the children got up and started moving. This benefited Lucas immensely. He was able to make sure his new desk wasn't next to Tara. He sat behind Bonnie and Jason took the desk next to him on one side and Pat sat behind him. His row was next to the 6th graders and Big John sat next to him. John gave him a huge grin as he sat and whispered, "Hey, Punk, we're neighbors."

Lucas thought this was going to be a long year. His fear that he and John were going to get into a lot of confrontations was manifesting itself again. As it turned out, the hostility Luke worried about from John never materialized. As they got to know each other, John turned out not to be as big of a jerk as Lucas thought him to be, and they became pretty good friends. They both were the kind of boys that no one would have thought would be in this type of class with the "brainy" kids. The other kids never really thought of them as "smart," but as Lucas found out with John, you can never judge a book by its cover. John was really a smart kid who tried hard not to let the other kids know. He liked the persona he had created for himself and much like Lucas, used his reputation to stay out of more fights than he got into.

Lucas loved having Miss Larkin as a teacher, and excelled. He also knew he had a crush on her that he was careful not to reveal. After a few weeks of school, it was obvious to most of the kids in the school that Miss Larkin and Mr. Knoll had a thing for each other. In a weird sort of way, that made Lucas happy. Mr. Knoll had been his favorite teacher until Miss Larkin. It only seemed fitting his two favorite teachers liked each other.

The mixed class wasn't as confusing as Lucas thought it would be on that first day. For the most part, the 5th graders worked on the 5th grade curriculum and it was the same for the 6th graders. The times they intermingled the classes were always fun projects and Lucas enjoyed that time most of all, even when Tara was in his group.

One of the activities was to split up into groups from both classes with an equal number of each grade in each group. They would pick a book out of several options Miss Larkin would give them and they would do a joint book report. The discussions about the book helped Luke look at the material he read a lot differently than he had in the past. What was the writer trying to say? What did a particular character symbolize in the book? What message could be hidden between the lines? These were all perspectives that Lucas had never had prior to this class. It made him want to read more than he ever had before.

The school year was passing quickly, and the only little black mark on Lucas during that first semester was when he volunteered to be on the School Patrol a few weeks into the year. Then, to everyone's surprise, he was elected Captain by the other patrol kids. It didn't last long. The second week into his new-found power Lucas began using his position to help his friends from Münchweiler. He also thought it was funny to make some of the other kids wait and not allow them to use the crosswalk until all of the Münchweiler kids had gone and even then, messed with some of the boys that he had played baseball against the summer before. It only took a few days for the complaints to mount before Lucas was relieved of his duties. He was hailed as a hero by the Münchweiler kids for his favoritism, but all of the good feelings he got from that were to dissipate the following day when Miss Larkin told him how disappointed she was with him. That night, Lucas went home feeling down. As he mulled over the entire situation that evening he realized what a mistake it was to misuse the power they entrusted to him. He vowed to himself he would be more responsible in the future.

Lucas didn't dwell on the School Patrol events very long. He had a new excitement that was dominating his thoughts. *His* Pittsburgh Pirates were in the World Series with the New York Yankees. Most of his friends were Yankee fans and Lucas' hero, Mickey Mantle was on the Yankees, but all of his young life Lucas was a die-hard Pirate and Pittsburgh Steelers fan. The

Yankees were always in the World Series. The Pirates had never been during Luke's short lifetime. It was more than fun for him. It was wonderful!

Another reason Lucas was so happy during the Series was that the Armed Forces Radio Network carried the games and Luke would listen to the ones he was able to, with his dad. He was in school during some of the games but Big John had a transistor radio with an earplug and would keep his classmates abreast of the score. Miss Larkin allowed him to do so, as long as it didn't become a big distraction. There were only a couple of games that started before school was out, because of the time difference, most were at night. Therefore, it didn't affect class much except for the day after a game as the excited baseball fans in class would spend the first fifteen minutes or so talking about the game the day before.

The Series was even at three games for each team. Game seven was on October 13th and Lucas couldn't wait. He and Ivan sat almost on top of the radio with Joey and Ike sitting on the floor. Both the younger boys got bored after about the third inning and went to their bedroom to play.

From Rocky Nelson's first inning home run, Lucas knew this evening would be like no other he had ever experienced before. Ivan jumped up and did a little "hillbilly dance" and just grinned at Lucas when an involuntary yell came out of him when the Pirates scored. The entire game was back and forth with Lucas or Ivan only leaving the radio to go to the bathroom. Maria would walk by and roll her eyes but inside she was so happy to see Ivan and Lucas together. Because Ivan was gone so much of Luke's earliest years, there was never a real bond between them. Not that Ivan had much of a bond with any of his children, but it always bothered Maria that the father/son relationship that she saw with many of the other families did not exist between the two of them.

The Pirates scored two more runs in the second inning, and Ivan and Lucas were feeling pretty good. Then Bill Skowron of the Yankees, led off the fifth inning with a home run.

"Bucs gotta score more runs." Ivan said to Lucas, using the short version of the Pirate's nickname, the Buccaneers. "You know those damn Yankees are gonna score more."

Ivan was right as the Yankees got four runs in the sixth inning capped off by Yogi Berra's two-run homer. Now the Yankees led the Pirates 5-4. It wasn't looking good for Pittsburgh when the Yankees scored two more in the top of the eighth inning and led 7-4. Ivan was pacing back and forth. Then the Pirates exploded for five runs in the bottom half of the inning to take a 9-7 lead. Ivan did his dance again. Lucas started trying to copy his dad's dance but decided against it. He had never had an experience like this with his dad before and he didn't want to do something that might upset him. If he looked all goofy doing the dance, Ivan might think he was making fun of his father.

In the top of the ninth, the Yankees scored two runs to tie the game at nine. Their last score was a bizarre play involving Lucas' hero, Mickey Mantle. Lucas had mixed emotions about the play. He loved the heads-up play Mickey made to get back to first base, avoiding a tag by Pittsburgh's first baseman, Rocky Nelson, and allowing Gil McDougald to score from third base.

"Damn it!" Ivan shouted. "What the hell was Nelson doing? He should have made the fucking tag!"

Pittsburgh got the final out in the top of the ninth. Ivan went to freshen his drink and ranted about the play that tied the score. Lucas didn't know how to react, so he just sat there and nodded his head in agreement with his dad. Then came the bottom of the ninth.

Bill Mazeroski was the first batter for the Pirates. The first pitch from Yankee pitcher, Ralph Terry, was a ball. Then the radio announcer, Chuck Thompson softly stated as the next pitch was about to be delivered.

"Well, a little while ago, when we mentioned that this one, in typical fashion, was going right down to the wire, little did we know ... Art Ditmar (this was a mistake by Thompson naming the pitcher that was warming up instead of Ralph Terry) throws ... here's a swing and a high fly ball going deep to left, this may do it. Back to the wall goes Berra, it is ... over the fence, HOME RUN, *THE PIRATES WIN!*"

That was the last of the announcer that Lucas heard as his dad leapt into the air and Luke joined him, jumping up and down around the room. Ivan grabbed Lucas and gave him a huge hug as he spun in a circle, yelling, "WE WON ... BUCS WON ...

WORLD CHAMPIONS!"

Now Lucas was really ecstatic. Not only had his beloved Pittsburgh Pirates won the World Series, but his dad had hugged him. He couldn't remember Ivan ever doing that since he was really little. He and Ivan continued to jump and celebrate as the rest of the family came to see what all the commotion was about. Ike and Joey rubbed the sleep from their eyes and soon were wide awake, too. It took half an hour before everyone settled down and went back to bed. Lucas lay in bed for a good hour before he drifted off to sleep.

The rest of 1960 was exiting with a vengeance. There were several back-to-back storms that were both snowy and cold, so Lucas and the gang spent more time inside. They did more things with the Boy Scout Troop that met once a week and they started to go to the gym. There they started boxing and lifting weights. They were just messing around at first but a GI, Sgt. Joe Brooks, was at the gym working on the body bag and speed bag and began working with them.

"I can see someone has taught you to box," he said to Lucas as he started pairing the boys off for a one minute round. "Well, let's see if we can perfect those skills."

That was the beginning of what turned out to be two years of a small, organized boxing group led by Sgt. Brooks. They trained and sparred a couple of times a week for the entire winter. In May, before the end of the school year, Sgt. Brooks set up a tournament with the help of some of the other soldiers. Lucas won his weight class, beating Lester Horry in the final but Sgt. Brooks wasn't very happy with him. Luke dominated the first round and most of the second, that is until Lester's nose started to bleed. Lucas couldn't bring himself to hit Lester anymore and when he did it was only body shots. Lester dominated the last round and Sgt. Brooks was furious with Luke for "quitting" and letting Lester win the final round. Lucas didn't care. He didn't get hurt and he felt good about not hitting Lester anymore. He didn't have that anger that his dad had taught him he needed in a fight. Lester gave him a big hug after Sgt. Brooks finished chewing his ass out. They sat together to watch the rest of the fights.

During the same time, Ivan was given a German Shepherd puppy. It was a female that they named Lucy. Lucas now had a new responsibility. Besides taking Lucy out to play it was his job to take her out at night before bed. Some of those nights it was very cold but Lucas loved Lucy and decided it was worth freezing now and then to have her. Lucy loved the kids, too. She couldn't stand it when they went out without her, especially Lucas. She loved it when he took her with him when they went sledding although a lot of the other kids didn't appreciate her presence. She would run after them as they slid down the hill, often knocking them off of their sled as she tried to catch them. Some of the older boys would get pissed and fire snowballs at her. Instead of bothering her, she tried to catch all of the snowballs they threw at her, only further annoying her detractors.

Just before Christmas, while the kids were on their holiday break from school, the family traveled to Munich and a small village on the Danube River called Vilshofen. It was where Lucas' mother grew up and where her German relatives were living. They met the rest of Maria's relatives and saw some of the most beautiful countryside in Germany. One of Maria's uncles lived along the Vils River just before it merged with the Danube. They could walk to the confluence from his house. It was like being in a magnificent painting. Lucas' senses could hardly grasp it all and it made Christmas vacation whiz by.

January and February seemed to last forever. Lucas and the rest of the boys didn't let the snow and cold weather keep them from playing outside, but it did limit the time they spent out. Unlike the summer, when on some days they would only stop at their home to eat lunch, the periods out in the weather were much shorter. As March rolled along they began to wander off post again. It was the second Saturday in March and the boys had been playing Army by sewer hill and the sled-riding hill. Most of the snow was gone except for patches in the shade and on the north slopes of some of the hills.

"Let's go exploring off post," Mickey said.

"That sounds good to me," Lucas answered.

"Me, too," Bob chimed in.

Lester Horry and Benny Jefferson decided not to go but the

Smith brothers, Terry and Robby, and Guy Henderson decided
to join them. They took off towards a hole in the fence that was
some 200 feet to the west of them by some trees. The boys slid
through the hole and followed the outside of the fence until it
met the corner by the road. Here they all put on their "war" face
and one by one, darted, unseen, across the road several hundred
feet from the main gate. Soon they were climbing the hill that
bordered the post along the southwest. As they traversed the
hillside, heading for the hill above the fort's picnic grounds, Guy
stopped and pointed.

"Look! There's a hole up there behind that boulder."

Lucas looked up, as did the other boys. He could see it, too.
It looked like some kind of cave. He began climbing up the hill
towards the opening. The others soon followed. When they
got to the cave they could tell it was well hidden from most
directions. If Guy hadn't looked up when he had they probably
would have gone right on past it.

"It looks like someone tried to cover up the entrance with
this big boulder. Bet it fell during the snowmelt," Lucas said
to the others, pointing to the boulder just below the opening.
It appeared that the weight of the boulder in the wet ground
caused a small landslide that exposed the entrance to the cave.
Lucas started digging out the entrance a little more by hand. The
opening was about two feet across and maybe eighteen inches
high. Robby and Bob joined him. It wasn't easy but the boys
eventually widened the opening to a size big enough for them
to crawl through. Bobby decided to poke his head in first. He
leaned into the cave, trying to see what was inside there. Just as
he was leaning and balancing himself so as not to fall into the
cave Robby touched him lightly on the back of the neck and
yelled, "BEAR!" at the top of his lungs.

"Aaaaah!" yelled Bob as he jumped back smacking his head on
the top of the cave opening much to the delight of the rest of the
gang. They all began laughing and literally, rolling on the ground.

"Good one, Robby," Mickey blurted out while laughing.

"YOU PUNK!" Bobby shouted as he began chasing Robby who
kept using the other boys as shields as he tried to avoid Bob's
grasp. Finally, Bob gave up chasing Robby and they both sat
down to catch their breaths. As they did, Lucas poked his head

into the cave. Then he threw a rock in it and listened as it hit the interior of the cave.

"Hey guys," he said, "this cave goes back a ways. We need to get some flash lights and our trenching tools and find out what's in here."

"What if it's a bunch of dead Germans?" Guy asked.

No one said anything for a few seconds. Up until then they were just excited to have discovered something new. What might be in the cave was not even in their thought process until Guy's question. They all turned and looked at Lucas. He was the leader of the Cricks now that Jimmy Parker was gone. Pat Simmons didn't want to be the leader even though he was a co-founder of the Cricks.

"I guess we'll decide what to do if and when we come across one. They would only be bones by now if we found anyone," Lucas said with as much firmness as his voice could muster. "For now, let's go back and get our gear."

The boys headed back to the fort. It was close to lunchtime so they all agreed to meet again at Sewer Hill at one o'clock. Luke raced home and got his flashlight and his entrenching tool. This was the small, folding shovel that soldiers carry on their belts or packs. It was a lucky thing for Lucas his father was in charge of *Property Disposal* in Pirmasens. He and his brothers got all the old Army gear they wanted. This gear was about to be thrown away or disposed of in some other fashion. The Baryshivka boys could also get gear for their friends since Ivan had no problem supplying their buddies. They all had helmet liners, pup tents, trenching tools, ammo belts, military flashlights and just about any other gear Lucas could think of asking for.

"What are you doing, Luke?" Joey asked as they were eating their peanut butter and jelly sandwiches. He had observed Lucas getting his gear ready before washing up for lunch.

"We're going to play Army at sewer hill," Lucas answered trying not to draw any attention to himself.

"I thought you did that this morning?" Joey continued.

Lucas was trying not to engage Joey but without much success. "We are picking up new sides and playing again," he answered. Then came the question he was hoping to avoid.

"Can I come and play with you guys?" Joey asked. Usually, Lucas and his friends didn't mind Joey or Ike or any of their friends playing Army with them. The more there were the more fun it usually was but he didn't want Joey or anyone else to know about the cave. Before he could answer he was saved by his mother.

"No, Joe, you are coming with me this afternoon," she said smiling at Lucas. "You'll have to wait for another time to play with your brother."

"Aw, Mom," Joey complained. "Can't I go with Luke now?"

"We are going to the PX in Pirmasens to get you new shoes when your dad gets back," she responded.

That effectively ended the conversation. Lucas finished up his sandwich and downed his glass of milk. He shot a quick, "Thanks, Mom!" as he ran to get his gear out of the bedroom. Joey was now five years old and he knew when there was something up with his brother. He watched inquisitively as Lucas put the flashlight into his coat pocket and carried his shovel out with him.

"Are you staying 'til dark?" he whispered to Lucas with a smile as Luke headed for the door. Lucas just shot him a look that said, "keep your mouth shut" to Joey and bolted out the door.

He met up with the other guys except for Terry Smith who had to help his mother with his younger siblings. There were eleven kids in the Smith Family and eleven-year old Robby was the oldest. There were two sets of twins and both Robby and Terry spent a lot of time babysitting their younger brothers and sisters. Robby had helped his mother with the little ones the last time so this time he got to go out since it was Terry's turn to help. Lucas felt bad for Terry. It made him feel better about the times he had to take Ike and Joey with him. There were a few times that Lucas thought he would help the Smith brothers out so they could get done quicker, but after the first and only time he did he could not make himself do it again. The Smith's whole house smelled like dirty diapers and it was hard for Lucas not to gag every time he walked into the house.

The boys retraced their steps up to the side of the road. They were about to sneak across when Guy, who was acting as the lookout, yelled, "Wait! Car coming!"

They all ducked down to hide from the passing vehicle. As it passed, Luke, who was at the head of the line to cross the road, peeked up to see the car. To his utter amazement it was his father's car and just as he looked at it his eyes met a wide-eyed Joey whose mouth dropped open as their eyes met. Lucas ducked back down as quickly as he could.

"Shit!" he exclaimed. "That was my old man! Joey saw me!"

"Do you think he would say anything?" Mickey asked.

"I don't think so," Lucas answered. He was pretty sure Joey wouldn't say anything. Joey knew they were not allowed off fort and Lucas drilled it into him the several times when Joey was with them off fort not to ever say anything to their parents.

"All clear!" Guy relayed to the rest of the boys.

Lucas jumped up and darted across the road, quickly followed by Mickey. They ducked down and waited as they heard another passing car. In a few moments they were all across and heading up the hillside. It took them a little while to find the cave again. It was well hidden, tucked away in a depression in the hillside with a big boulder the size of a car on one side and overhanging limbs from surrounding trees on the other and above it. Guy was very lucky to have seen it the first time. This time Lucas made some mental notes of landmarks he could use to help find it again.

"Here it is!" Robby yelled down to the others. He was about twenty feet higher up on the hillside than the rest and stumbled right into it.

"Let's start digging," Lucas said as he straightened out the spade portion of the shovel to line up with the handle and began tightening it. It didn't take very long for them to dig out the entrance so they could easily crawl in and out of it. Once it was big enough, Lucas took out his flashlight.

"Well, here goes nothin," he said as he ducked his head into the cave. As he got his whole body in, he shined the flashlight all around his immediate area. He could see the cave was tall enough for him to stand up, albeit bent over a little. That's exactly what he did. Then he shined the light down the cave. It wasn't a cave but a man-made tunnel. There were timbers along the sides holding up some cross-timbers in the ceiling of the tunnel. It was all dirt as far as he could see.

"Luke!" Bobby yelled. "What's in there?"

"Get your flashlights and come on in and see for yourself," Lucas replied.

The boys wasted no time in joining Lucas who had moved just far enough down the tunnel to let everyone in. They couldn't see how far back it went but about twenty-five feet into the tunnel it was partially blocked by dirt. Lucas slowly walked to that point. Lying on the dirt pile he shined his flashlight through the opening.

"It looks like it goes to the left another ten feet from here," Lucas relayed to the rest of the boys. "We need to move this dirt to go farther," Lucas said as he lifted himself from the dirt pile. "We'll need buckets to move the dirt out."

"I don't think we have enough time to go home and come back today," Robby stated. "We should plan on coming back tomorrow." Luke and the rest of the gang agreed. They crawled back out of the opening. They covered the opening with pine tree branches, and then they had to figure out how to mark it so they could find it again.

"We can stack rocks on the trail below it," Mickey suggested. "We know how to get back on that trail." So that was what they did. They also decided to stack some about twenty feet each side of the opening, which was about twenty feet up on the hillside above the trail. With the big boulder on the edge of the opening, they were sure they could find it again. Then they all continued on the trail in the original direction they were going when they had discovered the cave, playing Army as they went.

The hills surrounding the Münchweiler Hospital Post were beautiful. They were covered with a dense forest of mostly pine trees along the hillside and had several open areas that were a little too small to be called meadows. From those spots the views below looking across the post to the village to the north were spectacular. Along the dirt roads and meadows were a lot of trees that were still bare at this time of year. And, there were many patches of snow covering most of the north slopes completely. Lucas could never understand why more Americans didn't spend time out in this beautiful setting. Germans hikers would flood the trails and roads along the hillsides every Sunday. When the boys were out during that time they often were greeted with a, "Guten tag" as they passed the Germans on their Sunday trek.

The boys finally reached their destination, which was a hole near the southeast corner of the post by the sand pits. As they slid through the hole, Guy took off running toward the two old junk cars that were at the edge of the pit. He had never played at the pits before and had heard about the "Dick Tracy" cars. They were two cars built in the late '30s and looked like they were right out of some gangster movies.

"Wow!" Guy exclaimed. "These are so cool!" He then proceeded to jump behind the wheel of the first car. Lucas followed him and jumped up on the running board next to Guy and began pointing his finger at the other guys like he was shooting a gun. "Bam, bam, bam … gotcha ya dirty rats!" he shouted at them. They others followed their lead and got into the two cars pretending to have a gun battle as they zoomed through the streets of Chicago.

After half an hour of playing on the cars, Lucas turned to the other boys. "I'm hungry. I think I'm going to head home to get something to eat." It wasn't dinnertime yet but his mother would let him snack on something. The boys would often get wrapped up in their playing and miss lunch. It never seemed to bother them when they missed it. More often than not, Lucas would just eat a piece of fruit. If they were playing near the hospital they could go by some of the wards and the medics or nurses would allow them to grab a piece of fruit from a table they would have for the patients. There was always plenty of fresh fruit and juices. The boys were always careful not to pig out and take too much so the offer was always there for them.

On this day, Lucas knew his parents would not be back from Pirmasens yet so he could pretty much snack on what he wanted. The gang headed back by way of the road instead of cutting through the hospital complex. The road went past the train station and the fire station. They took a shortcut around the back of the power building and mess hall, across the field to the apartments. When Lucas got home, only Karla was there. He fixed himself a peanut butter and jelly sandwich.

"It's a little late to be eating lunch, isn't it?" Karla asked, as she got ready to go to work. She had been working at the Post Exchange since shortly after she'd graduated that past June.

"I'm starving and it isn't lunch. It is just a snack. I promise it won't spoil my appetite for later," Lucas answered.

Karla laughed, "What do you mean later? Dad and Mom were going to pick up some food from the NCO Club and bring it home with them when they get back from Pirmasens. They should be home in less than an hour." That was the first time Luke had looked at the time. It was already going on 5 o'clock. He gulped down his sandwich and a glass of milk, cleaned up his mess and smiled at Karla.

"All done! No evidence," he said as he cleaned up the last of the crumbs from the table. Lucas knew that Karla, unlike Susan, would never tell on him. He really liked it when Karla was left in charge. She was no pushover but she was easier to get along with and was pretty protective of all three of her brothers. Where Susan would have told his parents as soon as they got home, Karla would say nothing. Later, as the rest of his family returned, Karla was heading out the door. She said her goodbyes and whispered to Luke as she past, "Better eat all of your dinner, Little Luke." Then she was off with a smile and a wave. Luke winked at her as she left.

True to his word to Karla, Lucas had no trouble eating all of his dinner. His parents had picked up some hamburgers and french fries from the NCO Club. Lucas really liked the burgers from the Club. It was a treat. After helping to clean up when they were done eating, Lucas and his brothers went to their room to play.

Ike plopped down on his bed and began reading comic books. Joey sat next to Lucas on his bed and whispered, "Where did you go today when I saw you by the road?"

In a low voice, Luke answered, "We played Army in the woods and then went to the sand pits."

"You got to play in the old cars?" Joey asked, not so quietly.

"Yes."

"I want to go to the sand pits the next time you go," Joey pleaded.

"Okay, okay, but keep your voice down," Lucas said putting his finger in front of his lips. He knew he would probably have to take Joey with him the next day and he didn't want to take him to the cave. He would have to come up with a plan.

The following morning as Lucas was about to go out, his mother stopped him. "I want you to take your brothers with you," she said in a tone that Lucas knew was futile to argue against. He looked at Joey and Ike, both standing there in their winter clothing. Joey was eager to go. Ike seemed pretty indifferent about the whole situation but had nothing else planned so he thought he would tag along with his brothers.

"Okay, Mom, but just until lunch time?" he pleaded.

"Alright, just until lunch."

He turned to his brothers and waved his arm for them to follow him and out the door they went. When they got outside, they were met by Mickey and Jason. Mickey had told Jason all about the cave and he was excited to see it. As Jason was about to say something about the cave, Luke cut him off and rolled his eyes towards his brothers. Jason got the hint and said nothing.

"I've got my brothers until lunch time so I thought we could go to the sand pits and play this morning," Lucas said as Guy and Robby walked up to join them. They looked at Joey and Ike and got the picture. They knew that Lucas very seldom took his brothers off post since neither of them was allowed to go. Although Luke trusted that his brothers wouldn't say anything on purpose, he was afraid they would slip up like Joey did with the cigarette.

"Bobby can't join us anyhow. He and Todd have to go somewhere with their mother," Robby informed the group. Then they all headed toward the sand pits following the route they returned from the day before. As they passed the back of the mess hall and the power building, the boys saw three German workers come up the stairs from underneath the building. Curiosity got the best of them. Jason was the first to say what their expressions indicated they were all thinking.

"I wonder what's down there?" he questioned.

"Hold up a second," Lucas ordered. They all stopped. The three Germans went around the building to the door into the adjacent office. Then the boys zipped over to the stairs and were down them in the blink of an eye. When they got to the bottom they were amazed with what they saw. There was a hallway at the bottom. To the left was another set of stairs and a huge room filled with generators and all kinds of other machinery that none of the boys had a clue to what they were for.

To the right was a large tunnel filled with pipes and wiring that came out of the large generator room and hanging on the ceiling attached by metal bands, disappeared down the tunnel. "This is how they get heat to all of the buildings on post," Guy explained. "My dad told me about it when I asked him about the pipes that came into our building. He said all of the water lines, heater lines and electrical lines are under the buildings."

It seemed to make sense to all of them. Joey was the first to start walking down the tunnel a short ways. The others began to follow when Mickey said, "We better get out of here before those workers get back." About that time they heard voices and footsteps on the stairs.

"Quick, follow me." Lucas said in whisper. They ran down the tunnel for a few hundred feet when they came across the first cross tunnel. At the intersection of the tunnels, the boys ducked around the corner and peered back as the three German workers reached the bottom of the steps. One stayed near the entrance working on some control gauges as the other two descended to the next level in the generator room. It didn't look like they were going anywhere any time soon.

"Shit!" Lucas exclaimed. "We can't get out that way without being seen. It looks like this is the turn that would go to the Snack Bar and PX. I bet we can find our way around down here. We know the hospital well enough from above. I think we should explore more."

"Why not?" Robby answered. "Looks like we're going to be here for awhile."

With Lucas taking the lead, the boys began to explore the underground utility system. The tunnel remained fairly high ceilinged under the main corridors of the hospital. They spent the next two hours exploring the tunnels of the main hospital. There were many window openings along the way that were covered with mesh instead of glass. These were at just a few inches above ground level on the outside. It helped them keep their bearings as they moved throughout the network of tunnels.

As they returned to the main corridor Lucas decided to go left towards the library and church instead of right, back to the generator room. As they got fifty feet past the turn, the tunnel became smaller. It no longer had a concrete bottom but instead was all dirt. They could continue bent over for a few more hundred feet but they had to get on their hands and knees to crawl the rest of the way. They made the turn to the right that Lucas knew followed the hallway above to the Library. When they got to the end of that corridor, the tunnel took a left under the church. Just before reaching the church there was a mesh window that was opened.

"We can get out here," Lucas stated. "Let's look under the church to see where this ends, first." To their surprise, the tunnel didn't end there but became much smaller and continued past the church.

"I'll bet this goes to the apartment buildings," Jason said. The others all nodded in agreement. About that time, Joey began scratching himself.

"Something is biting me!" he said.

"Me, too!" Robby chimed in, as he pulled up his pant leg to see fleas covering his leg. "Let's get out of here."

That evening as they lied to the rest of the family about where they got the fleas, Ike and Joey looked at Lucas in anticipation. Lucas wasn't sure if they were anxious for the answer or they just wanted to see if their father got mad. To their surprise, Ivan's response was a favorable one.

"Well, I guess I could tell you boys not to go to the sand pits to play, but that means I'd probably have to beat you later 'cause I know you will. Those old car wrecks are pretty inviting." Ivan looked at the three of them trying to read their reaction. He grinned, as Joey's eyes got as wide as saucers. "I'll bring you a bottle of the DEET bug repellant when I come home Monday."

As they served Sunday Mass the next morning, Lucas told Bob Ledahawski about his dad getting them the bug repellant. After church Bob told Guy, who was the newest altar boy, as he came to the back of the church as the servers were changing. Guy took off to spread the word to the rest of the gang. The guys that weren't there heard about it and were hoping to be able to go under the hospital as soon as they could. "Guy, let 'em know we'll go back next weekend. I don't wanna get fleas again. I'm gonna wait 'til we get the bug stuff," Lucas said to him as he left the church.

Lucas wondered if any of the gang would decide to go without him and take their chances. Later that morning, they answered

Lucas' question. Todd had brought out his football and they spent the afternoon playing football between Building C and Building D. There was very little mention of the tunnels the rest of the day.

Over the next several weekends the boys had almost totally forgotten about the tunnel on the hillside. They spent their time outside playing 4-Square, hanging around the playground, and exploring more of the underground utility system to the post. They would also play at the sand pits for a short period each time they went under the buildings. Lucas figured that if they got fleas again he would be able to say they were at the sand pits again and he wouldn't be lying to his parents as long as they were at the pits for at least some of the time. As it turned out, the bug repellant Ivan gave them worked pretty well. It stunk, but after the initial shock of the smell, the boys got used to it and they only used it when they went underground.

By the middle of April, they had been under most of the buildings on the post. Their last great conquest was to follow the narrowest of the tunnels from the church to the housing area. Almost the entire way had to be done on hands and knees as they followed the pipes. It was also very hot as some of the pipes carried steam that was used for heating the buildings. It had been warm throughout the tunnel system but in most places there was more room and more ventilation so the heat wasn't as overwhelming as it was in this stretch. When they finally got to the basement of the middle building, Building C, they were exhausted and glad to be done with it. It would be some time before they decided to go back under the hospital.

Chapter IX

Spring Adventures

There were a couple of other notable things that happened during that spring. A family moved into the apartment on the first floor of Luke's building. Sgt. Bill Barton and his wife Rose moved in with their two kids, Joey and Sheila. Joey was the same age as Luke, and his sister was a year older and very cute. Joey was easily brought into the fold and soon was also a member of the Cricks. Both Joey and Sheila had different last names. This was their mother's third marriage. Sheila's last name was Wayne and Joey's was North. Lucas found this to be a bit unusual since he was brought up Catholic and in his short life, didn't know too many divorced people. He decided that it didn't seem to bother Joey or Sheila, so why should he care?

Todd Ledahawski and his best friend, Denny Mantra, whose father was the post Sgt. Major, the highest ranking Enlisted Man on the post, started hanging around Lucas' stairwell a lot more. They both took a liking to Sheila. Lucas also noticed that Randy Kirkland, who was a year older than Todd and Denny, also stuck around the area more. Randy lived above Lucas on the third floor of the building and hung out more with his sister Susan's group of friends.

A month before the Barton's moved in, a family moved in just below Lucas. It was an officer's family, Warrant Officer Jones. They had two sons, Steven who was Todd's age and Randy who was the same age as Lucas. Steven and Todd knew each other from school and some of the gang knew Randy but he had been in a different class than Lucas' and Luke didn't know him. They were only moving in for a few months until quarters in the officer's building or at Pirmasens became available. They had been living in the town of Pirmasens for several months, waiting for military housing, and took the apartment in the NCO's building due to problems the Jones' were having with their German landlord. Steven Jones was Todd and Andy's excuse for hanging out near their home, but all of the guys knew it was really because of Sheila.

The relationship between the Jones and the Baryshivkas family was not a very good one. Apparently, Mr. Jones was not accustomed to apartment living and having three rambunctious boys living above him. The first Friday they were there, the Baryshivka brothers were having their boxing lesson with Ivan. The noise upset Mr. Jones. He began banging on the ceiling with a broom and yelling from below, "Quit all that damn running around. It's like an earthquake down here."

When Ivan, who'd had a few drinks before he got home and was having another as he refereed the boys' boxing matches, realized what was going on, and began jumping up and down on the floor.

"Ivan, stop it!" Maria pleaded. "You're only going to make him madder."

"Screw that fucker!" Ivan shouted back at her. By this time the boys had quit boxing and were watching the scene unfold. "You think I'm gonna let that piss ant of an officer tell me or my boys how to act in our own home, you better think again." Ivan continued to jump.

"Boys, go clean up for dinner," Maria instructed them.

"I want you to all run down the hall to the bathroom," Ivan told them as Luke and Ike began taking off the boxing gloves. "You make as much damn noise as you can."

The boys enthusiastically followed their father's instructions. When they got back to the dining room things had calmed down. Ivan and Maria had been talking in the kitchen and the anger seemed to have left Ivan. As he walked out of the kitchen to join the boys, now at their places at the table, he grinned and winked at them.

"Well, that was an experience," Susan said in her usual sarcastic voice. "Seems like such a nice way to meet the neighbors."

"Watch your mouth, Sue," Ivan warned his daughter. She didn't press it and let the subject drop. That was the end of the incident for the evening, but it would be a reoccurring play that would be acted out again many times over the next three months while the Jones lived there.

After dinner Lucas asked his father if he could go out for a while. Ivan was pretty good about allowing Lucas some freedom from his brothers since his mother was always trying to have him take his brothers with him, so letting him go out on Friday nights was one of those times. His younger brothers were not old enough yet to go out after dark, at least according to his parents, and Luke was not about to help his brothers, especially Ike, argue their case.

It was unusually cold for a spring night, so Lucas put on his heavier coat and scrambled down the stairs where he ran into Denny Mantra leaving the Jones' apartment.

"Hey Luke, whatcha up to?" Denny asked.

"Nothing really, I was going over to Mickey's to see if he can come out," Lucas replied.

"Do you wanna hang out?" he asked. "Steve's dad was pretty pissed off this evening and Steve can't come out. I guess you guys and your dad got him in a foul mood. My other buddies are all busy," Denny said with a chuckle. Denny wasn't there when all of the stomping and yelling was going on, but Steve and Randy had filled him in. Denny usually hung out with Todd, but Luke knew Todd and Bobby were in Pirmasens with their parents.

"Okay," Lucas answered. "Let's go get Mickey." The two boys took off across the street and bounded up to the third floor of Building B where Mickey lived. It took Mickey about five seconds to grab his coat and scoot out the door.

"What's the plan?" Mickey asked. Lucas deferred to Denny since he really didn't have one. Denny just smiled at them and waved his arm in a forward motion.

"Follow me." Luke and Mickey quickly caught up to Denny who had taken off like a rocket and got twenty feet ahead of them before they took their first steps.

"So where we going, Denny?" Mickey asked. They were heading towards the main hospital complex. "Snack bar? Movies?"

By then they were just nearing the first building on their right. This was the barracks for the 208th Signal Support Company. "We're here," Denny said as he turned down the side of the building and ducked down by the corner. Lucas and Mickey followed his lead. They moved west along the building staying just below the windowsill level. Denny stopped below the fifth window they came to and reached up and grabbed a can of soda off of the sill.

"The GI's keep their drinks on the windowsills to keep cold," Denny told his companions. "We're going to help ourselves to some."

Lucas and Mickey looked at each other and raised their eyebrows. They knew Denny had a reputation for getting into trouble and having his father bail him out. Nevertheless, this little bit of thievery caught them off guard. The three of them continued sneaking along the building for a short distance when Denny stopped and used a downspout to pop the top off of the soda. After taking a drink he handed it to Mickey, who after taking his drink handed, it to Lucas. It didn't take long before the soda was gone. After a quick, "Wait here!" Denny scooted back to the windowsill that they took the soda from and put the empty bottle back.

"There aren't too many that I can see on the rest of the windows," Denny stated as he returned to the other two boys. "There usually are a lot more."

"Do you do this a lot?" Lucas asked Denny.

"Not too often. Todd and Randy and I have done it a couple of times."

"And you've never got caught?" Mickey queried. "I mean these guys had to be missing their sodas? I'd think they would keep a lookout for you guys."

"They think one of their buddies is stealing it from them," Denny answered.

"How do you know that?" Luke asked.

"My dad told me of a fight that happened one night after we grabbed a couple. One soldier blamed another for stealing it and they got into a fist fight," Denny explained. "They didn't have a clue it was a couple of Army brats."

The boys continued along the building. A few windows farther down the building there were several cans of beer on the sill. Denny reached up and grabbed a couple. This time he didn't say a word as he took off at a quick pace towards the far north end of the barracks. The 208th only occupied about half of the building so in the last part of the building the windows were dark. At the end there were several large bushes and small trees by the steps of the door into the barracks. The door was locked at this end of the building and there was no one around. This is where Denny stopped as the two younger boys caught up to him.

"You guys up for a beer?" Denny asked. Both of the boys looked at each other then back at Denny and shrugged their shoulders and nodded their heads yes. Neither had really drunk any beer before. The problem was it was a can and they didn't have an opener. Denny looked around as he asked his friends, "Do either of you have a knife?" He didn't really see them both shake their heads no, but continued to look for something to use.

"How about that nail sticking out of the fence?" Lucas asked as he pointed to a spot on the small white picket fence where one of the slats was missing. Denny turned to look at the nail.

"Well, I don't see anything else, so I guess we can give it a try," he said as he sat down one of the beers and walked over to the fence with the other. He aimed the top of the can at the nail, jabbed it into the nail and quickly pulled it away. Beer started spraying everywhere as Denny aimed the spouting liquid at his mouth and waved for the others to come over to him. After taking a big air-filled gulp, he handed it to Lucas. It was still shooting out pretty hard when Lucas grabbed it and aimed the beer at his mouth. It slowed to a gentle spew as he took a big gulp and passed it to Mickey. By the time Mickey got it, the can was half empty and no longer spraying everywhere. The boys polished off the can of beer and then went through the same ritual with the second can.

The three boys sat on the steps when they were done. They smashed and stuffed the cans into the stand up ashtray that was by the door of the unused section of the barracks. Denny looked at his two younger partners in crime and grinned. Then he asked his friends, "How do you feel?"

"I'm a little dizzy," Lucas replied.

"Me, too," added Mickey.

"Well, we better get out of here before any of the soldiers come out to see if their beers just fell. I don't want to be around when they start looking for them," Denny said.

The three boys got up and headed back to the housing area by way of the main road instead of the way they had come. They giggled a little as they went but there wasn't much conversation between them as each was caught up in his own thoughts. Lucas could smell the beer on himself. *How am I going to get by the old man.* He was feeling a little too giddy from the alcohol to worry too much about it.

"See you guys!" Denny said as they got to the first stairwell in Building B. "Don't get caught!" he shouted as he darted up the stairs. Mickey was next, and with a quick wave and "See you, Luke!" he, too scrambled up the stairs leading to his apartment.

Lucas paused at his front door. He was still feeling pretty dizzy from the beers. He opened the door and saw his parents sitting in the living room with the TV on although it didn't look like they were paying attention to it. Susan was working on some homework at the dining room table. Lucas headed straight for his bedroom.

"Hi!" he greeted his parent as he shot them a quick glance as he continued down the hall to his bedroom. His mother answered him with a wave. Fortunately for Lucas they were into a deep discussion about something and hardly paid any attention to Luke as he passed. He got to his bedroom where his two brothers had just gotten into their pajamas. He quickly got undressed and joined them.

"What did you do tonight, Luke?" Joey asked.

"Nothing much," he answered, "just hung out." Lucas went in the bathroom to brush his teeth. He noticed his eyes were pretty red. He began to feel fearful as he wondered how he would tell his parents "good night" without them noticing his eyes. His brothers didn't notice, maybe his parents wouldn't either.

Lucas went back into his bedroom and picked up a comic book as he plopped down on his bed. He had only read a few minutes when his mother came in to tell the brothers "good night."

"Lucas, quit rubbing your eyes," she said to Luke as she kissed him on the cheek. "You've made them all red." She kissed Ike and Joey and gave a final "Good night, boys!" as she exited the room and turned out the light. Lucas relaxed and let his spinning head take him right into a deep sleep.

The days were growing longer and warmer as May approached. The boys were playing 500 after school and on the weekends.

On the second weekend of May, the gang decided to play Army at the bunker as they had tired of playing ball. It was the usual group headed up by Bob and Todd Ledahawski and the Smith brothers Terry and Robby. Joining them were Lucas, Mickey Mira, Jason Sprint, Guy Henderson and the Clayton brothers, Dale and Earl. This was the first time Earl had joined them. Earl's best friend's dad had just transferred out and Earl had began hanging out with Todd and Robby more. He was their age but had been held back a year so was in the same grade as Lucas. Lucas got along with Earl, which was good since he had to beat up his brother Dale every time Dale would get into it with Ike. Earl always thought it was funny and, luckily for Lucas, didn't feel he had to fight Lucas every time Dale did.

It was just after 10 o'clock when the boys headed to the bunker. They did their usual game of picking up sides and attacking or defending the bunker depending on whose team they were on. Todd and Earl were the captains. The boys played for a couple of hours before deciding to head back home for lunch.

"Hey, what's this?" Earl said as he reached down to a spot where the ground had just been kicked up by the boys' playing. "It looks like a small bomb!" he shouted as the rest of the gang came running over to him.

"Be careful, Earl!" Lucas cautioned. "That looks like a mortar round." Lucas knew enough about weapons and ordinance since Ivan had given him a lesson on a lot the weaponry that the US Army used. He had several books on it at the Property Disposal Yard where Ivan worked. "If it's an old one from the war it could still go off."

"I don't think so," answered Earl as he began to uncover the remaining portion of the mortar that was still buried.

"I don't know if I would be pickin' … YIKES!" Todd exclaimed as Earl tossed the freshly uncovered shell right at him. Todd had no choice but to catch it as it came right at his chest. "Jesus, Earl! I oughta kick your fuckin' ass for that!"

"Oh, come on now, you aren't a chicken shit are you?" Earl teased Todd. "The thing has been out here for years. It's gotta be a dud."

"Whatta you gonna do with it?" Jason asked.

"I'm taking it home. Maybe I can sell it to a GI for a couple of bucks," answered Earl. "Those guys are suckers for any old war relics they can get their hands on."

"I don't know if that is such a good idea," Lucas added. "My dad told me how dangerous these can be." Earl ignored him as Todd tossed the shell back to him. They started walking back to the post, tossing the mortar back and forth as they went, mostly between Todd, Earl and Robby. Mickey, Jason, and Bobby decided to heed Lucas' words. They knew he was more up on this sort of thing than they were. Adding to their apprehension was the fact that Lucas wasn't afraid of being daring most of the time and he seemed to have a fear of this shell. If he wasn't going to toss it around, they weren't either. Dale joined them as they moved ahead of the older boys, putting some distance between the two groups. The older boys continued to toss the shell between them the entire trip back.

Once they got back on the post, they were hanging out behind the first set of apartments in Building D. The Claytons lived just above the Ledahawskis at the first stairwell to the building. The boys were right below the dining room windows of the apartments above. Lucas was about to head home when he heard this booming voice from the third story window.

"PUT THAT FUCKING BOMB DOWN, EARL, YOU MORON!" the shout came from Sgt. Clayton out the dining room window. "GENTLY … LAY IT IN THE GRASS! I'M COMING RIGHT DOWN!"

Earl had a horrified look on his face as he softly set the mortar in the grass below his feet. He was standing over it when his father reached him. With a quick smack on the back of Earl's head he yelled again, "GET BACK! ALL OF YOU!" He then looked up to see Sgt.Ledahawski looking out of the window. "HEY SKI!" he shouted to Sgt. Ledahawski as he opened the window. "CALL THE BOMB SQUAD!"

He then gently picked up the mortar and carried it across the street from the apartments into the field between the housing and the main hospital. By now word was spreading about the mortar, and a crowd of people were gathering near the road, a safe distance from the shell. Several of the NCOs from the buildings had come out and set up a perimeter to keep people back. Sgt. Clayton walked back to where Earl, Dale, Todd and Lucas were standing and again bopped Earl on the back of the head.

"What the hell were you thinking of, Earl?" he asked his son. "You're so damn lucky this thing didn't go off and kill all of you."

"Lucas told us to leave it alone," Dale piped in as Earl shot him a 'shut up' glance. "Well, he did Earl. He said it could go off at any time. I listened to him, Dad. I didn't toss it around like they did."

"Well, good for you Dale," his dad answered. "Glad to know I only have one moron son."

Sgt. Ledahawski came down to join the group. He said it would take the bomb squad a little over an hour to get there. By now the MPs had come and taken over the perimeter security around the mortar. They put up tape and stakes and made sure no one got close to the shell, not that anyone was trying to at that point.

Lucas decided to head home for lunch. He could see his dad coming down behind the building just as he went around the south end of the building. He thought about going back but decided to keep going home and walked down the sidewalk along the front of the building until he got home. He wasn't sure what he would say to his dad. Ivan was bound to find out that he had been off the fort when he asked where they found the mortar. He was able to give a huge sigh of relief when Ivan got home and it never came up. Luke found out later that Todd told him that he, Earl and Robby had found it knowing that Lucas and some of the others would get into trouble if their fathers found out they were there, too.

"I'm glad to hear you stayed away from the mortar, Luke," his father said. "That little punk, Dale said you told all of them it could go off at anytime. Sometimes you can drop one of those duds off on a concrete floor and it won't go off. Another time you can just touch it and it'll blow." Grinning at Lucas he said, "By the way, Luke, next time you have to beat up Dale, go a little easier on him."

Lucas nodded in agreement with his dad as he fought to suppress a smile. If his dad only knew of his arrangements with Dale when they fought, he wouldn't be too happy. Ike was always the one that started trouble with Dale and since Dale was older, Ivan would make Lucas fight him to protect his brother. Luke's heart was never in it since it wasn't usually Dales' fault, so after the first couple of times he fought Dale, they made a pact where they would fake a fight with Lucas ending up on top of Dale, appearing to be punching him until Dale would pretend to cry. They probably weren't the best actors, but from the distance Ivan watched from, it wasn't obvious. Luke had threatened Ike with a butt whipping if he told their dad. At least now he had his dad permission not to hurt Dale. Well … that was how Lucas was going to interpret it.

Lucas finished up with lunch. Taking his two brothers with him, he went back out to wait with most of the rest of the fort's personnel for the bomb squad to arrive. He went over to Earl, Todd and Robby who were joined by Andy Kirkland and Steven Jones. Soon the rest of the Cricks starting drifting over to the gathered group of boys. Earl was happy again as his father's anger had subsided. Lucas and the other boys thanked him for not ratting them out. "I know you guys would be just as tight lipped as me if it were reversed." was all Earl said.

It was close to two hours later before the bomb squad arrived. It was pretty anticlimactic at that point. Most of the boys were hoping the bomb squad would explode the mortar there, but instead they placed it in a big metal box, loaded in their vehicle and drove off. The excitement for the day was over.

★ ★ ★

It was the next weekend before anything exciting happened for the gang. Like the weekend before, the boys all started out playing 500. The older boys weren't around when Lucas decided that maybe it was time to visit the tunnel again. They had not been back since they first discovered it.

"Hey, guys," Lucas said as they gathered around the sand box in the playground. "Let's get our shovels and go back to the tunnel."

"Are you sure, Luke?" Jason asked. "I mean, I like a little excitement but after last week do you really think we should take a chance by going off post?"

"Sure, why not?" Lucas answered. "Nobody besides Todd and his pals knew we were with them last weekend. As far as anybody else goes, we never went off post." Lucas looked around to many heads nodding in agreement. Surrounding him were Jason, Guy, Bobby, Terry, Mickey, and even Lester Horry and Pat Simmons had joined them.

"Let's all get our trenching tools and meet at Sewer Hill in half an hour," Lucas stated. He looked at Benny and said, "Sorry Benny. You know you can always join us if you want to take the chance."

"No thanks, Luke! Thanks anyway, once off the fort is enough excitement for me. Besides, I think I have to go with my parents to K-Town this afternoon."

Half an hour later the gang began to assemble at Sewer Hill. Lucas had almost got stuck having to bring his brothers. As luck would have it, Ike wanted to play with Pat Simmons' brother, Kyle. Kyle was Ike's best friend. Joey decided he wanted to go with Ike so Maria made Ike take his younger brother with him instead.

"Okay, you all know the routine." Lucas told the group.

"I don't know it," Lester piped in. This was the first time he had gone with them off the fort in this direction. He had been off post before when they had gone to the bunker and to Three Lakes but he'd never had to cross the main road to the post.

"Well, just follow us Lester. You'll figure it out," Lucas replied as the boys headed towards the hole in the fence. As they did the last time they went to the tunnel, Guy acted as the lookout as they each took their turn to dart across the road. One by one they crossed until Guy finally joined them at the edge of the woods. They then proceeded up the faint trail that traversed the hill.

When they got to the area where Lucas thought the entrance should be, he stopped. The others stopped behind him.

"Are you lost Luke?" Guy asked.

"No, this is the right area. We need to look for the stacked rocks," he replied. The area looked different than it had on that winter day when they were there last. With the warm spring temperatures, the underbrush had grown up quite a bit and they were having trouble locating the tunnel.

"HERE IT IS!" Jason yelled down to the others from a spot that was just above them. "I found the rocks."

The rest of the boys scrambled up the hillside to join Jason.

Just like the first time they were there, it was easy to see once you were at the same elevation as the tunnel. The big boulder that was partially obscured stuck out like a sore thumb when you were level with it. Lucas pulled back the branches they had used to cover the opening.

"Let's get to work," he said as he took out his entrenching tool from its holster on his belt. He quickly straightened it out and tightened the knob that screwed the spade in place. Three of the other boys, Mickey, Bobby and Jason also had shovels and took out theirs, too. Lucas then instructed the others, "You guys will take the two buckets and hold the flashlights while we dig out the big dirt pile that's blocking the way."

Then the boys all entered the tunnel. It took them a few moments to adjust their eyes to the dimly lit shaft. Lucas and Bobby began filling the buckets while the other boys formed a bucket line. Jason went outside and spread the dirt around as Terry, at the entrance of the tunnel, was dumping it just outside of the entrance. Lucas told Jason, "We don't want anyone to see the dirt pile and find the tunnel. Spread the dirt around. Try to hide it as much as you can."

Although the dirt was powdery on top, the pile itself was pretty compact. It was taking Bobby and Lucas a lot longer than they had thought it would. After about fifteen minutes of digging they switched places with Guy and Lester. They worked for about five minutes, then switched with Jason and Terry. Five minutes became the rotation time. On Lucas and Bobby's third turn Luke's shovel struck something solid.

"Hey, I've hit something!" he exclaimed. Then he pointed said "Lester, hand me that big flashlight there."

Bobby grabbed the flashlight from Lester's hand and pointed it at the object that Lucas continued to dig around. Remembering the incident with the mortar shell, Lucas was being very careful. They could now all see it was metallic. Lucas started using his fingers as he got to what appeared to be a lip to the object.

"It's a helmet!" Lucas blurted. Then he started to use his shovel again. Getting the point of the shovel under the lip of the helmet, he gave a big pull up towards the ceiling. By now all of the boys had their heads around Lucas and Bobby when all of a sudden

POP! The helmet came flying out of the dirt pile accompanied with dirt flying everywhere.

"Shit!"

"Aaaagh!"

"Damn it, Luke!" Yelps and cusses came from the gang as they got showered by dirt. They began coughing and hacking for the next several seconds as the debris settled. As they looked around at each other they began to crack up laughing. They were all covered with this damp dark dirt to one degree or another. Then their attention turned to the helmet.

"Let's get out of here to get a better look," Jason suggested.

"Good idea," Lucas replied. They all filed out to the fresh air outside. Then he stated the obvious. "It's a German helmet."

"Wow!" Lester exclaimed.

"Whatcha expect, Luke, a Russian helmet? We're in GERMANY for God's sake," Terry sarcastically added. This got some chuckles out of the rest of the guys as Lucas turned red-faced but didn't respond. Then Guy broke the silence.

"What should we do with it?"

"I think we should take it to Coach Cooke or Coach Tyler," Jason said. "We can trust them to help us figure out what to do with it."

Lucas looked at Jason and smiled. He was thinking the exact same thing. He liked the way he and Jason came up with a lot of the same ideas. "Ok, then let's go by the way of the sand pits again. We can swing by their barracks."

The boys began their trek across the hillside towards the southeast corner of the post. It took them only a few minutes to be above the soccer field. They continued through the dense forest that blanketed the hillside, walking in silence, lost in their own thoughts. They often walked in silence for long periods when they would go to Three Lakes. At least it seemed like long periods to them. Lucas would, at times, concentrate on his breathing, as they would trek up and down the hillsides. This trance would be broken by someone uttering the first word or they would come up to a familiar point and be surprised at how quickly they got there. Those moments of silence were some of the things Luke like most about his hikes through the forest.

Through an opening in the trees the boys could see the

rooftop of the Bachelors Officer Quarters. Lucas knew the trail was going to take a sharp right just ahead of them. There it would go up hill for a few hundred feet before joining a small forest road that paralleled the fence line as it headed northeast where it would eventually intersect with the road they took to Three Lakes. It was along here that Lucas had to keep a sharp eye out for the small game trail that went back towards the post. If they missed it they would end up going all the way to the road to Three Lakes and have to double back.

"Here it is!" Lucas said as he spotted the trail. It seemed like a big deal to Lucas that he found the trail. To the rest of the gang it was as if it was no biggie. They were used to Lucas finding it and figured it must be pretty easy to find. They dropped down the hillside quickly and came to the fence just a little west of the hole. They scoped out the fort from the fence to make sure there was no one around to see them crawl through the hole. They didn't want anyone to find out about it. Unlike most of the other holes that were on the town side of the fort and were used frequently by the soldiers, as far as they could tell this hole was only used by the boys. If the wrong person found out about the hole, like Sgt. Major Mantra, they would close it and cut off a short cut the boys would use to head to the woods.

The gang passed through the opening with the utmost speed, headed west across the loop road that went around the fort and on across the huge field to the barracks on the other side. They now were eight young men side by side instead of single file as they had been through the woods. They had all taken turns carrying the German helmet but as they neared the barracks Guy handed it to Lucas. "You found it, you should take it in."

Lucas took the helmet and nodded. There was a group of GIs on the back steps of the barracks, four playing catch. Two of them were the boys' Little League coaches, Specialist 4th Class Jim Cooke and Corporal Gus Taylor, both with the 225th Evac. They stopped tossing the ball, and along with the other GIs, turned and looked at the approaching boys. It was quite the sight, the eight of them, side by side. It looked like a scene out of a Western movie where the posse was coming into town, or at least that was how Gus described it to the boys later.

"Well to what do we owe this great honor?" Jim shouted to

them as they crossed the helicopter pad and reached the wooden bridge that spanned the drainage ditch paralleling the barracks. The boys, without a word, paired off to cross the bridge. Lucas noticed that now everyone's attention was on the object in his hands. He felt a little surge of importance.

"We found this ..." Lucas started.

"I'll give you two bucks for that!" a GI named Connor shouted.

"I'll give you three!" yelled another.

"Four!" Connor responded.

"Five!" Cooke yelled, entering the bidding contest.

"Six bucks! I want that Nazi helmet!" Connor answered.

"Seven!"

"Eight!" Connor quickly countered.

No one bid higher.

"It's yours, Connor," Jim Cooke stated. "I was just trying to up the price for my team here. You boys did want to sell it didn't you?"

They all turned to Lucas, who with a combination of shrugs and nods appeared to say "yes, if you want to." Lucas looked at the prize in his hand. Part of him wanted to keep it but then he wasn't sure his old man would let him.

"SOLD!" he finally responded. "That's a buck each," he said as he handed the helmet to Connor.

"Here you go," he said as he fumbled through his wallet and handed Lucas a five and three one-dollar bills.

"Gotta be exact change," Lucas stated as he pulled back the helmet from Connor's grasp. "You need eight ones." Jim Cooke and Gus Tyler roared with laughter, joined by the other GIs.

"Come on, you can get change, can't you?" Connor pleaded. "I only have one other one in my wallet."

Lucas held his ground. "No, you need to get change if you want the helmet." The other boys were standing there in shock. What was he doing? Was he going to blow the whole deal? Lucas could tell how badly Connor wanted the helmet. He knew he would get the correct amount.

"I only have four ones. Does anyone have change for a five?" Connor asked as he spun around in a circle with the five-dollar bill in his hand.

"All I've got is four ones," Jim Cooke said holding up the four bills.

"Okay, I'll take those now and get the other dollar from you later," Connor stated.

"Not so fast," Jim replied. "I'll give you these four ones for your five and that's the deal. Take it or leave it."

"You asshole!" Connor shouted at Jim. "Damn you, give me the ones. Here's your damn five."

"See, everyone goes home happy," Jim said smiling broadly. The money and helmet quickly changed hands. Connor took off with his prize. The boys hung out for half an hour or so talking baseball with their coaches then headed home. They would take turns waving their one-dollar bills in front of each other. It was a good day.

It turned out to be a good night for the boys as they all decided to go to the movies with their earnings. *Sink the Bismarck* was playing at the Hospital Theater. They splurged on popcorn, candy, and Cokes. On their way home they sang the Johnny Horton title song for the movie. "We gotta sink the Bismarck to the bottom of the sea," they sang in unison, or at least, mostly in unison.

"We should go back to the cave tomorrow and see if we can find another helmet," Guy said as they finished the chorus.

"We can't do it on Sunday, Guy," Lucas answered. Then he said laughing, "The hills will be crawling with Germans."

"What?" asked a confused Guy.

"What Lucas means," interjected Jason "is that every Sunday after church the Germans go out into the forest and walk before they settle down to the soccer games."

"That's why all of those trails and roads are out there," Luke added. "If we're on the side of that hill they'd see us, for sure."

Guy had not been around long enough to go for a stroll off the post on a Sunday since the weather had turned nice but Lucas, Jason, and some of the other boys had. The German people loved to walk and hike on Sundays. One of the gang's trips to Three Lakes had been on Sunday and they remembered how many people they passed on their way back and how many times they said "Guten Tag" as their paths crossed. Lucas was right about the soccer games on Sunday, too. The soccer field was right across the fence from the post's picnic grounds. The boys had spent many days watching parts of soccer games while hanging out at the picnic grounds. No ... the return to the tunnel was going to have to wait at least until the next Saturday.

The week couldn't go fast enough. They would get a three-day weekend for Memorial Day with school out on Monday even though the holiday was on a Tuesday. The following week was the end of the school year.

Little League had already started practice. It had been light enough in the evenings for them to practice for about an hour after school. The Münchweiler team was going to be good this year. Lucas was the team's top pitcher and when he wasn't pitching he usually played shortstop. He also played right field sometimes, which was his mother's favorite position for him. "I love the way you snag those balls out of the air, Lucas," she would tell him. Last year he had taken away two home runs by reaching over the fence, which was about four feet high, to catch them.

Saturday finally rolled around. Little League practice started at 9 o'clock and lasted two hours. Lucas was really happy with the team's new name this year. They were the Pirates, his favorite team. "It's just the luck of the draw," Coach Cooke told them. "All of the uniforms are in different boxes and they just are handed out to the coaches without looking to see what the team names are. We just happened to get the Pirates."

The practice ended at 11:00 a.m. It was a long one but it was the first one they'd had on a Saturday, so the coaches wanted to get in as much practice as they could. The games started the first Saturday after school was out. The coaches handed out the uniforms at the end of practice. After the boys got their uniforms, Guy, Bobby, Jason, Mickey and Terry gathered around Lucas.

"Let's meet a Sewer Hill after lunch," Lucas told them. Then turning to Terry he asked, "Is Robby gonna be able to come?"

"He told me he was," answered Terry. "He had to baby sit until noon then he's free to go."

"Great! I talked to Lester during practice and he ain't gonna make it. His dad's taking him to the Ramstein Air Force Base today. Pat isn't coming either."

They continued to walk as they talked, dropping off guys as they passed their various apartment buildings. Lucas dashed up the stairs and into the apartment. "Hi, Mom!" he shouted as he headed for his bedroom to try on his new uniform.

"Wash up, Luke!" she said as he raced by. "I'm fixing grilled cheese sandwiches for you boys."

"Okay, Mom! I'm going to try on my uniform first."

"No, first you are going to wash up. Your sandwich will be ready in a few minutes." Joey and Ike were already at the dining room table as their mother was finishing up with the first sandwich. Lucas hurriedly washed up and put on his uniform before going out to the dining room to join his brothers.

"Wow! Neato uniform, Luke!" Joey exclaimed as Lucas sat down at the table beaming from ear to ear. "The Pirates? How'd you luck out?"

"It just worked out that way," Lucas answered as his mother brought him his grilled cheese sandwich. She was smiling as she sat the sandwich down.

"You must be pretty happy with that?" she asked, already knowing his answer.

"You bet I am! And look," he said turning around to show them all his number, "I got Roberto Clemente's number, 21! Where's Dad? I want to show him."

"You're dad had to go into work for a while today," Maria informed him. "He'll be home this afternoon sometime."

Lucas and his brothers finished up their lunch and went to their room. Lucas began to change out of his uniform. "What are you up to Luke?" Ike asked. He could tell by Luke's focus that he had something planned.

"Nothin' much," Luke answered trying to be as nonchalant as he could. "Just getting together with the guys this afternoon."

"You're goin' off post aren't you?" whispered Ike.

Lucas shot him a sharp glance and then said, "Never mind where we're going. You keep Joey busy so Mom doesn't make me take him. Can you do that?"

Ike hesitated, looking like he was in deep thought. *How can I get something out of this.* If Lucas wanted him to take Joe then he knew he was up to something secret. He decided he wouldn't try to leverage the situation then. With his father gone, Lucas might punch him if he pushed it too much. "Okay, but you owe me one."

"Thanks, Ike," Luke said as he finished tying his shoes. He then grabbed his entrenching tool and ammo belt and tucked it under his arm as he left the bedroom. As he passed the dining room he could see his mother in the kitchen. "Goin' out to play, Mom!"

"Okay, Lucas. Don't be late for dinner. Your dad will be home before five."

"Yes, ma'am," Luke was out the door and down the stairwell in a flash. As he headed through the playground on the way to Sewer Hill, he could see the Smith brothers in the field ahead of him about halfway between him and their rendezvous spot.

"Hey, Luke! Wait up!" he heard Bobby Ledahawski yell. Lucas stopped and turned, waiting for Bobby to catch up. In a few moments the boys were walking together towards Sewer Hill. Lucas looked back as they neared Robby and Terry. He could see Guy and Jason walking together a few hundred yards behind them. *Good. We're all here. No delay getting to the tunnel.*

"Hi guys."

"Hey, Luke, Bobby," Robby answered. Terry just waved. "What's Jason carrying?"

Lucas turned around again to look at Jason and Guy. He didn't notice the first time, but now he could see that Jason had more than his shovel in his hand. "Looks like a bucket."

Soon they were close enough to see that indeed it was a bucket. As they joined the group Jason lifted the bucket up. "Thought we could save time with this bigger bucket. My dad uses it when he goes fishing."

"Sounds good," Lucas said as he strapped on his ammo belt and entrenching tool. The rest of the boys put on their gear, too, and off they went to the hole in the fence. It took them a little while to get across the road because there had been a lot of traffic and they were being extra cautious. After all, before they were only going to a hole in the ground. Today they were going to try to make more money, and the tunnel was their bank.

Once the gang finally got across the road and into the woods, it didn't take them long to get to the tunnel. This time they didn't have to search for it. They went right to it.

"Let's set up the same way we did last time, okay?" Lucas directed the boys as he pulled out his flashlight. Lucas quickly got to what was the remaining portion of the dirt pile that blocked the way deeper into the tunnel. It only took a short while, just after Jason and Terry Smith took their turn at digging, that Jason hit something metal.

"GOT SOMETHING!" he yelled. The other boys quickly surrounded him as he slowly started to dig around the metal that was now exposed. "Yep, this is definitely another helmet!"

Jason dug gingerly around the helmet as the other boys watched. Jason eventually had enough of the helmet exposed to get the shovel under it and flip it up. As he banged the dirt out of the inside of the helmet he exclaimed, "Look! It has a bullet hole in it!" He handed it to Lucas.

"Hey! Get that flashlight out of my eyes!" Lucas shot at Terry as all the boys shined their flashlights on the helmet. Terry was still down on his knees by what was left of the dirt pile and was aiming his flashlight up at the helmet. It also was aimed right at Lucas' face. They all gawked at the helmet for several minutes, passing it around so all six of the boys could examine it closely. Finally, Lucas broke up the admiring of their newfound prize. "Well, let's see what else we can find!"

Robby was holding the helmet at the moment and sat it down just inside the entrance to the tunnel. He and Guy took up the task of digging out the rest of the dirt pile. The boys didn't find anything else of any value in the pile. By the time they had finished, they were all exhausted. They were so focused on finding another helmet or other artifact that they forgot the original reason they had started digging out the pile of dirt was to be able to go farther back into the tunnel. As all six sat down along the walls of the tunnels with their flashlights in hand, catching their breath, Lucas broke the silence.

"Hey, let's take a look a little deeper into the tunnel before we go. We could find something just lying on the ground," he said as he slowly got up and started moving down the tunnel. About every ten feet or so were shoring beams on the sides and top of the tunnel. It looked like there might have been wood planks placed across the top at some locations but most of the planks were either rotted out or hanging down and partially blocking the tunnel's walkway.

"To go much deeper we'll have to move these boards," Lucas told the others. "We'll have to be very careful so it doesn't collapse."

"I'm done digging or working any more today," Jason stated

matter of factly. As Lucas looked back at his companions he could see all were nodding in agreement. Lucas was ready to call it quits for the day, too.

"Ok," he said. "Let's go sell the helmet."

The Cricks filed out of the tunnel. Bobby picked up the helmet as they exited the tunnel. The dirt they took out of the tunnel wasn't as well disguised as the first time they'd been there when they blended the dirt into the surrounding landscape. They were all too exhausted to care. Lucas made a feeble attempt to kick down some of the dirt that looked like it was dumped there by a bucket. Guy and Bobby did the same as Jason and Robby placed the tree branches from the overhanging tree back across the tunnel entrance to try to hide it somewhat. It didn't cover it as well as it had before they'd started the day's work and many of the smaller branches had broken off as the boys moved the dirt from the tunnel.

They wasted no time and no chatter in hiking to the hole in the fence by the sand pits. This time as they crossed the field to the 225th's barracks there was no one playing ball outside. A couple of GIs that Lucas knew slightly were sitting on the steps in their white medical uniforms. It looked like they had just gotten off duty at the hospital.

"Howdy boys!" greeted one of them. "Cooke and Tyler aren't here."

"We're not here to see the coaches," Lucas replied. "Is Connor around?"

One of them stood up and tried to see what Bobby had behind his back. "Hey, do you guys have another helmet?" he asked. "I'll give you five bucks for it?"

"Connor gave us more last time," Luke answered. "We'll give him a chance to buy it first."

"Come on, kid, let me look at it?" the GI said, Lucas could see Connor walking towards the door behind the soldier he was talking to.

"What's going on, Luke?" Connor asked.

"We found another helmet," Lucas answered. "This one has a bullet hole in it."

"I'll give you ten bucks for it!" said the GI whose name, Jones, Lucas could read off of his name tag.

"Hey, screw you, Jonesy!" Connor shot at him as he reached for the helmet in Lucas' hand. "Looks like these kids brought it to me. I'll give you ten bucks for it, Luke."

Lucas pulled the helmet back away from Connor and looked back at the rest of the gang for some guidance. All he got were shrugs and "We're leaving it up to you, Luke," from Robby, to which the rest of the boys nodded their heads in agreement.

Before Luke could answer, Jones shouted, "I'll give you twelve bucks, kid."

"Luke, I'll give you fifteen dollars and I promise I will buy all of 'em that you boys find," Connor said, as he looked Lucas in the eye with a determination that had Lucas' attention. *He really wants this helmet.* "I mean it. We can predetermine how much I'll pay now and you don't have to try to *find* someone to buy them from you. It'll make it easy for both of us."

Luke took one last look towards Jones who was frantically trying to borrow some money from his buddy on the steps. "Well, I'm not sure about the future ones. We'll all have to talk it over and decide. I'll get back to you on that, but this one is yours for fifteen dollars."

"Great! That's a start. Let me go get your money," Connor said as he pivoted and raced back to his locker in the barracks. He soon returned with a five and a ten. "I don't have any change, Luke."

"That's not a problem," Lucas said as he took the money and handed the helmet to Connor, "we'll get change at the PX or Snack Bar."

"Thanks boys," Connor said as the gang followed Lucas while he waved the bills in his hand, grinning from ear to ear.

"Nice doing business with you!" Luke yelled as the six of them walked briskly towards the main hospital complex. Then, turning to his partners, he shouted, "Let's get some change so we can split this up."

After getting change from the Post Exchange, the boys headed home. They discussed how they were going to spend their two and a half dollars apiece as well as the business proposition from Connor. Most of the boys were good with Connor's offer, but Guy thought they might be able to get more if they let more soldiers know about it. He thought they would bid it higher if there were more. The problem Lucas and Jason had with that was they didn't want it to get all over the post or it might get back to their dads. If that happened, they would all be in trouble for being off post. By the time they reached the housing area they all were in agreement they would only deal with Connor.

The final week of school was excruciatingly slow for Lucas. He was sure the rest of the Cricks felt the same. Now in the last hour he was more irritated by Tara's constant know-it-all chatter all day than he had been for the entire year. It was like she could sense it and just sent more barbs at Lucas to get his goat.

Lucas felt his anger start to rise. Tara knew she wouldn't see Luke much now that school was out. More importantly, he wouldn't have to see her either except for the few times their families would get together. *She's gonna miss me! Shit, she just might like me.* That thought brought a smile to his face and his anger just melted away. He had been blocking out her words. Now he decided to listen but Tara was silent. The smile and look that Luke gave her totally disarmed her.

"You were saying?" Lucas asked in a very upbeat tone.

A puzzled look came over Tara's face as she watched Luke while formulating her reply. Luke just stood there smiling in the most serene way he could muster. Finally, Tara blurted, "Oh, screw you, Lucas Baryshivka!" as she pivoted and stormed off.

"Is everything okay, Lucas?" came a voice behind him. It was Miss Larkin.

"Oh, yeah," he chuckled, "everything is just dandy, Miss Larkin."

"Well that's good to hear. Tara seemed a little upset," Miss Larkin stated with a small grin. Everyone could get their fill of Tara from time to time, even Miss Larkin, although most of the time she heaped praise on Tara. Lucas had to admit it was probably well deserved *(she was pretty smart),* but he hated hearing it so much.

"She'll get over it, I'm sure," Lucas answered laughing loudly, no longer able to contain his joy in finally getting to Tara instead of it being other way around.

Then Miss Larkin changed the subject as she sat down on the edge of the desk and asked Lucas what his plans for the summer were. Did he like her class with both the 5th and 6th grades together? Would he be coming back for 6th grade to Pirmasens or was his dad rotating out? Lucas told her about playing ball being the biggest thing in his life throughout the summer. He shared with her that he and his buddies would be camping out both with the Boy Scouts and by themselves on the more remote areas of the Münchweiler Post. He also told her his dad was due to rotate out in August, but he had overheard him and his mom discussing extending for a year. Lucas was pretty sure they were but his parents hadn't made the announcement yet.

Then Lucas looked at her and began to turn as red as the ripe tomatoes in his Uncle's garden, as he told her how much he enjoyed her as a teacher. He'd had a small crush on Miss Larkin since the first day of class but would never admit it. He had a feeling that Miss Larkin knew.

"Well, Lucas, I certainly enjoyed you as a student," She said as she got up. "Mr. Knoll told me you had an active imagination and he was right."

Lucas had forgotten about Mr. Knoll and Miss Larkin's relationship until that moment. Even though it was never in the open, everyone including the other teachers talked about it. That thought brought Lucas back down to the reality that he was just a kid and she was an adult. He regained his composure and told her, "Thank you, Miss Larkin. I feel like I learned a lot in your class."

"Enjoy your summer vacation, Lucas," she said patting him on the back as she left. He knew he would as he watched her go. *This is going to be the best summer ever.*

Chapter X

Summer Returns

The first day of summer vacation was a Friday. The gang had all decided on the bus ride home that they would meet at the playground in the morning. Lucas ate breakfast and was out the door before his brothers were even out of bed. "Going out to play, Mom!" he shouted as he was leaving.

"Have fun, Luke!" she yelled back. "Don't get into any trouble!"

"I won't," he answered as he closed the door and shot down the stairs. He raced to the playground, excited for the day to start. He was the first one there. After standing by the sand box for a few moments, he decided to hop on the swing. As he pumped his arms and legs to get higher and higher, he didn't think about his friends or play or any of the other thoughts that always seemed to clutter it. Instead he felt the warmth of the sun as it came up on his left side. He could hear the tweeting of the birds as he gazed at the hillside through the buildings, then looking to the right, he could see the hillside where he would soon be climbing. *What a beautiful place this is. How terrible it must have been to have the war take place here.* His thoughts were shattered by a yell from the swing next to his.

"What the hell are you thinking about?" Robby Smith said looking warily at Luke. "I walked right up on you without you even seein' me."

"Just day dreaming," Luke replied. They both continued to swing without much conversation as Jason approached from their right and Bobby came around Bldg. C on the left. Lucas and Robby both jumped out of the swings at their highest points and briefly flew through the air before dropping to the sand playground below them.

"Oh crap!" Lucas said as the four of them sat on the low concrete wall that defined the sand box. "I forgot my shovel. If I go back my mom might make me take my brothers."

"We only need two shovels, Luke," Jason stated. "Bobby has his and I got mine. Only two of us have been able to dig at one time anyhow."

"Yeah, but that was on the pile. As we get deeper into the tunnel I thought we'd all be able to dig around to look for stuff," Luke countered.

"Well, I don't think you should go back home," Bobby added. "It would be a drag if you had to bring your brothers."

"You're right. If I had to take them, I wouldn't be able to go off post."

Just then Guy came trotting up from around Lucas' building. To the delight of the rest of the boys, he had a shovel in hand. A few minutes later, Mickey Mira and Terry Smith joined them and Mickey had another shovel. Terry had a second bucket. Now it was a no brainer, no need to go back home for his shovel.

"Okay, let's get going," Lucas said to the six other boys. With seven of them it was going to make splitting up the money a little more difficult if they found more helmets, but it would make the work go faster.

It didn't take the boys long to reach the tunnel. Getting across the road on a Friday was easier than on a Saturday when there seemed to me more traffic. They began setting up the bucket brigade as they worked deeper into the tunnel. They also had to re-prop up the inside shoring as they went. It was a dangerous situation and the boys were aware that the tunnel could cave in. They made sure they didn't go past a point where they thought the tunnel was safe enough. The truth of the mater was they were oblivious to the real chance and the consequences of a cave in. This troop tunnel was dug during the war and it had been over fifteen years since the end of World War II. There was nothing safe about it.

The gang kept working on it although they were moving less dirt out of the tunnel and doing more relocation of the dirt in the tunnel along the walls. It sped things up since they didn't have to carry the dirt so far. They had been working for about an hour when Jason went out to take a leak. He wasn't gone long when the boys heard him yell.

"We got company! Looks like Hans Mueller."

"Come on guys," Lucas said as he headed towards the entrance. "This could be trouble."

In the few moments it took Lucas and the other boys to exit the tunnel, Hans and three other German boys, including Hans' brother, Fritz were now at the tunnel. "What are you doing here?" Hans asked.

"I don't see where that is any of your business, Hans," Lucas answered as the other six Cricks stood behind Lucas with their arms crossed defiantly.

"These tunnels are dangerous. They could collapse on you and your friends, Lucas," Hans replied in more of a concerned tone rather than a confrontational one. Lucas had gotten to know Hans over the last few years. He really was a nice guy, and after they had established their boundaries for the sled-riding hill, there had not been another confrontation with the German kids. Lucas and Jason had sat with Hans and Fritz at one of the Sunday soccer matches to watch their father play. Their father was one of the soccer stars for the local club. Hans went on, "I had a friend that died in an old tunnel near Dahn when I was eight years old. I was about to follow him in when he bumped a shoring beam and the entrance caved in. By the time I got help to dig him out he had suffocated. You should not be playing in this tunnel."

"We're not just playing!" Guy blurted out.

"Shut up, Guy!" Robby shouted as Lucas turned to glare at him.

"What does this mean, you are not just playing?" Hans asked now sensing there was more to what was going on then he first thought.

"Hold on a second, Hans," Luke stated. "We need to talk amongst ourselves."

Lucas and the six other American boys stepped away from the four German boys to talk. They argued over whether or not they should let Hans, Fritz and the others in on what they were really doing. Guy and Robby were against it but the others agreed with Lucas who said, "If we don't they could collapse the entrance so we can't get back in. Besides, we have been on pretty good terms with the Germans and I don't want to start any problems with them. Hans could always say something to the Mess Sergeant where he works on post and we could all get in trouble."

They decided to vote on it and by a five to two vote decided to let Hans and his friends in on their secret. Lucas explained to Hans how they found and sold the first two helmets. Hans was intrigued by the whole situation. "They gave you double the amount for a bullet hole?" he asked. Then Hans pulled his brother and two friends aside for a private discussion before returning to face the Americans.

"I have proposal to make to you," Hans stated. "Let's work together on finding more helmets and we can all split the profits. It would just be the seven of you and the four of us. What do you say?"

Lucas stepped away from Hans and motioned to the other American boys to gather around him. They discussed it for a few moments then agreed to partner with Hans and his friends. They all shook hands, smiling as they did, to seal the deal. Then Hans said something to the two other German boys, Peter and Jakob. They took off towards the soccer field.

"Where are they going, Hans?" Bobby asked as they sped by him.

"They are going to get some wood to use for bracing," Hans answered. Then Hans followed Lucas and Jason into the tunnel to inspect it. He commented about the good job they had done in cleaning it up as they went deeper into the tunnel and he was impressed that they tried to shore up the walls and ceiling as they went. He had been in the tunnel before but had never gone past the huge dirt pile that the American boys had removed, so he was seeing parts of the tunnel he had never seen before.

The two German boys returned with six pieces of 2 x 4 boards, 6 feet long. Under Hans' instructions they began working in the tunnel alongside the Germans. Peter, Jakob, Robby and Guy went back to the soccer field and returned with some plywood and planks. They used them along with the boards to prop up the ceiling at a couple of locations. Then when Hans felt the tunnel was secure they began digging through the piles of dirt. They uncovered old food cans, some empty ammo clips and *two* more helmets. It was almost four hours later when the boys, totally exhausted, emerged from the tunnel.

"We can take the helmets to our buyer," Lucas said wearily. "Maybe we can sell some of this other stuff, too."

"You said the GIs paid twice as much for the helmet with the bullet hole, ya?" Hans asked. Lucas nodded yes. "Let me take the helmets. I have an old pistol that my father gave me. I can shoot a hole in the helmets."

Guy and Robby were not to keen on letting the helmets leave their sight, especially leaving them with Hans. Lucas on the other hand, completely trusted Hans at this point. Everything they had done throughout their day together was done in the spirit of a partnership and Luke saw no reason to not think it wouldn't continue. After a brief discussion it was decided they would let Hans take the helmets.

"Let's meet here again in a few days and we'll get the helmets from you," he said to Hans.

"I will need more time," Hans replied. "If I shoot a hole in the helmet it will look like it was newly done. I will have to wet it down and give it some time to rust."

Lucas was impressed. He hadn't thought of that, but it made perfect sense. Jason was the first to verbalize the thought. Even Guy and Robby, once they were resigned that Hans was going to take the helmets, agreed that this made sense. Not a one of them would have thought about it.

"Okay, Hans, when do you want to meet?" Lucas asked.

"You are out of school now so check with me when I am working at the mess hall next Thursday. We will see if they are ready. I think we should plan to meet here again next week to work on the tunnel some more. We will look at a couple of places I know of in the woods north of Münchweiler to see if we can find more helmets between now and then."

They had a plan. They all shook hands with a newly found trust and friendship developed over the day of working together. As the two groups split up they both started heading in the same direction for a short while. Then the American kids headed back to the Post the same way they had left it. They were filthy from the tunnel and dead tired by the time each got home. Their 'story' was the same. They had been playing at the sand pits again.

The partnership went well through the entire summer of 1961. True to his word, Hans brought the helmets to Lucas and the gang. It took a little longer for them to rust but the Germans had found two more at another site and by the time they brought the original two, all four had bullet holes that were rusted around the edge. They dealt only with Conner. Once, he did ask them how they found only helmets with bullet holes in them. Jason was the one to answer him.

"Guess only the dead ones left their helmets behind," he stated like it only made sense. Conner just nodded and never asked again. What did he care? Lucas had found out that he was sending them home to his brother who was selling them for ten times what he was paying the boys for them. That didn't matter to the Cricks or their German partners. They thought the money they got for them was plenty.

By the end of the summer, they had searched the entire tunnel, finding three more helmets, and the German boys had searched the areas they thought they would be able to find more. As the new school year was fast approaching, they had run out of places to look. They had found eleven helmets in all, and all with bullet holes, of course.

"Well Lucas," Hans said, placing his hand on Luke's shoulder during the last time the two groups met, "we have had a fine business together but it is time for it to end. It is not worth our time looking for them anymore. If we find more, I will find a way to get a message to you, but I think our days of searching for them are done."

Everyone was in agreement. Although they did not spend their entire summer vacation searching for old World War II German helmets, it had occupied a lot of their time.

When Lucas and his friends didn't spend time that summer on their business enterprise, playing baseball was their number one priority. Their Little League team was good. Joey North was a great catcher and hitter. Lucas pitched and played shortstop or right field when he didn't pitch. Jason played second base, Bobby Ledahawski played left field, Mickey Mara played center, Terry Smith played right field, and Don Davis played first base. They played two games a week and practiced twice a week in the late afternoon during the week. When they weren't playing a game or practicing they spent a lot of time playing 500 or bouncing the ball off of the side of Building C.

They also all participated in Boy Scouts. They met one evening each week in a wing of the main hospital that was used as a nursery and pre-school during the day. The Scout Master was Captain Harley. He was a dentist and his daughter, Katie, had been in Lucas' class the last two years. He had two more daughters and no sons. Lucas had overheard a couple of the GIs that helped out as Troop Leaders talk about how the women in Captain Harley's house drove him crazy, so his work with the Boy Scouts sort of made up for his lack of sons at home.

Lucas was bored with the Boy Scouts most of the time, but they did do a few things that were fun. They had a yearly campout, which took place at the picnic grounds during the second week of July. They all had pup tents and were in teams of two to a tent. Luke looked at the way all of the tents were lined up. *How neat is this!* He was teamed up with Mickey Mara in the last tent in a row of five. Their tent was at the lowest end of the sloping picnic grounds, which was near the northwest corner of the campground. Jason Sprint and Bob Ledahawski were in the tent next to theirs. There were trees along the entire east side of the grounds where it bordered the German soccer field. There were some shrubs between the row of tents that were set up along the west side of the grounds and the road to the communications building that ran parallel to the tents.

The day was spent on various games and contests using the different skills being taught by the Scouts such as knot tying and starting a fire without using matches. They had team contests ending the day's activities with the entire troop and Scout Masters participating in a large tug of war contest. That was followed by a cookout with hamburgers, beans, potato salad and watermelon. Then the Troop followed up the dinner with a huge bonfire where they toasted marshmallows and sang songs. As the evening wore on, the boys began to slip away from the fire and head to their tents. Lucas, Mickey, Jason and Bobby all left together.

Not long after they got into their tent, Luke and Mickey heard the sounds of a loud fart from their neighboring tent. Then they heard Jason yell, "Jesus, Bobby, that's the worst smelling fart ever!" followed by Bobby's laughter. Soon, Mickey and Lucas were unintentionally following Bobby's lead.

"I don't think those beans were too good of an idea," Lucas blurted out between farts. Soon Jason came flying into their tent.

"Man it stinks in there," he said pointing to his tent. Then after a slight hesitation, he looked at Mickey and Luke, both doing all they could not to burst out laughing as Jason took a sniff of the air in their tent, "Oh my god! It's as bad in here as it is in with Bobby."

The words were barely out of his mouth when Bob came diving into the middle of their crowded two man tent and ripped a big fart. "Aggghhh, let me out of here!" Jason shouted as he tried to crawl out of the tent. Lucas was holding his legs, forcing him to stay in the tent. The boys were laughing so loud that it began attracting some of the others in the area, including Gus Taylor who was a Scout Master as well as one of their baseball coaches. He flipped the tent flap open and stuck his head in.

"What the hell is going on ... oh, shit! Man does it stink in here!" he said in a rather stunned voice, much to the delight of the four Cricks howling in the tent. Jason managed to slip Luke's grasp and rolled out of the tent to stand next to Gus. By then the tent was surround by most of the remaining Boy Scouts and the Scout Masters. They were all suffering from the same effect the beans were having on Lucas and his pals. Even Captain Harley, who didn't normally laugh very much, was laughing uncontrollably.

"I guess we better take the beans off of the menu for next year," he said, his eyes filled with tears of laughter. At a later Boy Scout Troop meeting, Lucas heard the GIs saying they had never seen Captain Harley that loose before. They joked that he probably wasn't even allowed to fart at home.

Everyone eventually calmed down and the boys were instructed to turn in for the night. They had one more day of activities that would start early. As they all retired to their tents and crawled in their sleeping bags, Lucas and Mickey continued to talk quietly well into the night. After about an hour, Jason came in and joined them with Bobby right behind him.

"We can't sleep either, Luke," Bobby said. "We thought we would join you guys."

"Did you see anyone else out?" Lucas asked.

"I really didn't look," Bobby replied. "Hold on, let me take a look." He popped back out of the tent and after a few moments jumped back in. "It looked like someone near the top of the camp just finished a cigarette and I saw him go back in his tent."

"Good," Lucas said in a whisper. "Do you guys feel like having a little fun?"

"What do have in mind, Luke?" Jason asked.

Lucas shined his flashlight on all of their faces as his lips formed a mischievous grin. "Let's pull off a raid on the rest of the camp."

"What kind of raid?" Mickey asked, his interest aroused. Mickey had started to doze off but was now wide awake. Lucas always came up with good plans. He knew Luke had something fun in mind.

"We can sneak up to the top tents through the woods," Lucas said as he began sharing his plan with the other boys, "with Jason and Bobby going down our row and Mickey and I will go down the row behind us pulling out the stakes for the guide ropes holding up the tent poles. One will get the back and the other the front. We will use the flashlights to signal when to start. When I flash you guys twice real quick, you each start running down the row pulling up the stakes. Mickey and I will do the same. Got it?"

"Got it!" the three boys said in unison. Then they slipped out of the tent and, stooping over the whole way, made their way across the field to the woods on the east side of their campground. Once they got to the woods they were able to walk upright and quickly moved through the trees to the top of the campground. Lucas and Mickey stopped about twenty feet above the first tent in the closest row of tents as Bobby and Jason made their way to the same position above the second row of tents.

It was dark out with no moon, but the boys' eyes had adjusted to the starlight and they were able to see quite well. Lucas could see Mickey's eyes were open wide and excitement was written all over his face. Lucas could feel his mouth forming that impish grin as he aimed his flashlight at the other boys and flicked it on and off twice, quickly. There was no hesitation as the boys began running down the line of tents pulling up tent pegs and pushing the poles inward as they passed each tent. Behind them they could hear the surprised Scouts and Scout Masters yelling as they awoke to their tents collapsed on top of them. By the time the guys had reached the halfway point some of the kids from the first tents toppled were exiting. By the time they neared their own tents some of the boys in the tents they were now hitting were awake already from the cries and yells coming from the other campers.

At last they dashed into their tents, panting and gasping for breath. Then it dawned on Lucas to pull their tent pegs too so they wouldn't be suspected. Still unable to speak as he tried to catch his breath he pulled both the front and back pegs covering Mickey who was still inside. Bobby saw Lucas and quickly followed suit. Mickey's yell from in the tent helped Lucas' plan work even better. They could hear "What the hell?" and "What's going on?" from multiple voices as they stood next to their downed tents like everyone else. Flashlights were darting around everywhere. It took several minutes before everyone figured out what was going on. The GIs and Captain Harley went around calming everyone and then Gus' voice boomed out of the darkness.

"EVERYONE LISTEN UP! RESTAKE YOUR TENTS AND I WANT YOU ALL AT ATTENTION IN FRONT OF YOUR TENTS! DO I MAKE MYSELF CLEAR?"

There was a spattering of "yes, sir" but now the air was filled with laughter and accusations as to who was responsible. Most thought it was the Scout Masters pulling a fast one on them as they worked on fixing their tents. The quiet night was gone. To Lucas' and his comrades' delight, the whole camp was abuzz.

Lucas whispered to his companions, "Remember, we don't know nothin'." The other boys all nodded in the night with shit-eating grins on their faces. They were thankful that it was dark or there was no way they could have pulled this off and gotten away with it. As it was, their grins lit up the night.

By the time Gus, Captain Harley, and Connor, who also helped as a Scout Master, got to Luke's tent everyone was in a pretty jovial mood. Some of the boys had gone back into their tents but most were just lingering around trying to figure out who had committed this prank. As Gus shined his flashlight in each of their faces they covered their eyes from the brightness.

"Hey, you're blinding me!" Bobby shouted at them. The arm covering was more to not let the soldiers read their faces. The light really didn't bother them.

"So, are you delinquents responsible?" Gus asked. They all answered with the same set of denials they had heard from everyone else up and down the tent lines.

"Oh, no, not us," they said feinting innocence.

"Captain, if I were to put money on any of them, this is the bunch I would bet on," Gus said, shaking his head and suppressing a grin. "All right boys, you can all go back to bed now. Party's over!"

They went back into their respective tents. Lucas had to bury his face in his sleeping bag so he didn't burst out loud with laughter. Mickey kept shaking his head in disbelief that they actually pulled it off. A few moments later Bob and Jason dove into their tent to join them. It was a bit crowded but they didn't care as they bathed in the delight of their raid, whispering to each other for half an hour before Bobby and Jason started getting cold and left for their own tent. Within minutes after that, they all drifted off to sleep.

The next morning as the scouts were breaking down their camp, the midnight raid was the talk of the camp. There were kids accusing other Scouts of pulling it off but everyone denied it. At one point, Guy Henderson and Lloyd Mize came up to their good friends and Guy grabbed Lucas by the shoulder and swung him around.

"It was you guys, wasn't it Luke?"

Luke shot a look at Guy that said, *don't touch me like that again,* as Guy dropped his hand from Luke's shoulder, but he gathered himself and calmly said to Guy, "I guess you'll never know." It was another three weeks before the boys finally revealed it was they who had done it after all. Apparently, Gus was a betting man. The boys heard that he bet Connor five dollars that it was Lucas, Mickey, Jason, and Bobby that pulled the prank and Connor, unwisely, took the bet.

Lucas and the gang enjoyed the Boy Scouts' outdoor activities as well as their own outdoor activities, but nothing compared to playing ball. Little League was what they lived for. Lucas enjoyed the road trips to Pirmasens and Zwiebrüken. Ivan never went to the games, so Lucas and his mother would ride with the Ledahawski family. Sometimes Joey would go with them, but usually Joey and Ike only got to go to the home games. Sgt.

Ledahawski would drive, so he went to all of the away games. Lucas tried not to let it bother him that his father didn't go. Ivan would tease Lucas about being the water boy and why would he come to see Lucas sit on the bench. Lucas knew that his mother and others had told his father that Lucas was one of the star players of the team. He was their best pitcher. When he wasn't pitching he stayed on the field by playing shortstop or right field. Lucas loved to pitch because it put him in the action of the game with every pitch. He liked shortstop, too, because he got a lot of balls hit to him. Maria loved it best when her son was in the outfield. He was a much better outfielder than shortstop but there wasn't enough action for Lucas in the outfield and he thought it was boring. All of the times the gang had played 500 really had improved Luke's ability to catch fly balls. He had made several catches reaching over the fence to rob the opposing team of home runs. It seemed like all of the parents were much more impressed by this feat than Lucas was. To him it was just playing 500 by himself, and without battling the other guys for the ball, it didn't seem like such a big deal. However, he did love the attention that it got him when he came off of the field.

On this particular afternoon, the Münchweiler Pirates were playing a team from Pirmasens called the Yankees. Lucas was reliving the ninth game of the World Series in his mind on the drive to Pirmasens. He had told his mother that his dad should really come to this game. After all it was the *Pirates and Yankees!*

The Yankees were in first place in the League while the Pirates were tied for second when the day started. The team they were tied with had lost their game just before Lucas' game so they were now in second place with a chance to tie for first. The Yankees had beaten them earlier in the season. It was Luke's only loss pitching that year. Big John, *of all people,* had the winning hit off Luke in the top of the sixth to give the Yankees a 3-2 win. It was the fewest runs the Yankees had scored all season. That was of little consolation to Luke as Big John grinned at him from second base after his hit. Then to top it off, Lucas had had a chance to tie it with Jason on third with two outs in the bottom of the sixth. He hit the ball hard but right at the Yankees' shortstop, ending the six-inning game.

Today Coach Cooke was going to start Mickey Mira against the Yankees. The Yankees had a lot of left-handed hitters and Mickey was a left-handed pitcher. When Coach Cooke told Lucas at their last practice, Lucas was upset. "Coach, you know I can beat them this time," he said trying to change his coach's mind.

"Lucas," he said, "I am sure you can, but I'm going with the percentages. Besides, you threw a lot of pitches earlier this week against the Braves and I want a fresh arm out there." Lucas knew it was futile to argue with his coach so he dropped it. He felt like pouting but didn't want to seem like a baby to his friends, so instead he sat down with Mickey and started going over the Yankees batters with him and how he should pitch them. Coach Cooke looked at Coach Tyler and smiled.

As the teams went through their warm ups, Big John came strolling over to Lucas as he was running wind sprints along the right field line. "So Luke, afraid we'll kick your butt like last time? That why they put you in right field?" he said grinning from ear to ear.

"We'll see who has the last laugh!" Lucas shouted as he continued to warm up. Big John laughed and ran back to his teammates.

The game went back and forth for the first three innings. Joey North had hit a home run each of the first two times he came to bat. Both teams were hitting the ball pretty well but Coach Cooke stayed with Mickey. It was the bottom of the fifth. There were two outs and the bases were loaded with Big John coming to bat. Big John loved to be dramatic. He was a left-handed batter and considered himself the "Babe Ruth" of the league. As he strolled up to the batter's box, he did something right out of the history books. He pointed with his bat out to right field indicating he was going to hit it over the fence there, just like Babe Ruth had done. It didn't take long for the excitement to begin as Mickey sent a fastball right down the center of the plate. Big John connected. There was a loud "crack" as the baseball soared high and deep to right field. All of the Yankees fans were up on their feet. It looked like Big John was about to get a grand slam home run. However, he'd gotten under the ball a little too much and because Lucas was playing deep in right field when Big John came to the plate, he didn't have to go back too far before he was up against the fence. He could see the ball coming down. It seemed like it was up there forever. After the game, Lucas would comment that he didn't think he had ever seen a ball hit that high, and he got a lot of nods of agreement from many of the players and parents around him. The fence was a three-and-a-half-foot high chain-link fence, and Lucas was pressed against it as the ball came down. He reached back as far as he could stretch and gave a little lunge at the last second. Luke felt the ball slam into the webbing of his glove as he flipped forward again struggling to keep on his feet. As he steadied himself he looked at the ball in his glove. He had just taken a home run away from Big John. Lucas came sprinting into the dugout from the outfield waving the ball in the air as his teammates rushed him, slapping him on the back and cheering, as were the Pirates fans. Big John was still standing between first and second, stunned that the ball was caught. You could see the shock in the faces of their entire team. When that ball left the bat they thought the game was as good as over.

"Great catch, Luke!" Coach Cooke yelled as they all got into the dugout. "Guys, the game isn't over yet. It is still tied and we need to score."

Jason was first up and hit a little dribbler to the third baseman. Lucas knew they were still shook up when the Yankees third baseman fired the ball over the first baseman's head. Jason took second on the overthrow. Guy came up next. He bunted, moving Jason to third as he was thrown out at first. Lucas stepped to the plate as the Pirates fans cheered him loudly. Lucas stepped back and tipped his hat to the crowd the way he saw the Major Leaguers do. As he did he saw his father at the side and bottom of the bleachers. *Is that dad?* He didn't have time to think any more about it as he stepped up to the plate. Now he had a chance to be a hero at the plate as well as the field, but he never got the chance. Luke was walked on four pitches. It didn't matter as Joey North came to the plate. He had been the offensive star all game so it was only fitting that he hit the first pitch thrown to him into left field for a base hit, scoring Jason from third. The Pirates were ahead by a run! Bobby Ledahawski then came up and hit into a double play ending the top half of the sixth inning.

Just as the Pirates were about to take the field, Coach Cooke shouted, "Hold on guys, I'm making a pitching change. Luke you're coming in for the sixth. Mickey, you're in right field." He then took the lineup card to the umpire and the Yankees' coach. As Lucas walked up to the mound he was roundly cheered. "Strike 'em out, Luke!" Mrs. Ledahawski shouted as Lucas started his warm up pitches. His heart was racing as he stared in at the first batter. He shot a quick glance to the Yankees dugout and could see Big John standing at one corner. Lucas would not get a chance to face Big John since he had made the last out the inning before. Part of him wanted to, but there was a part of him that was happy he didn't have to. Big John was the most feared hitter in the league and had gotten two hits off of Lucas the first time the two teams had met.

Lucas stared in at the signal from Joey North. He threw a first pitch fastball. The Yankee's first batter swung at and popped it up to Jason at second base, one out. Lucas went to a full count on the second batter before getting him to ground out to Guy at third, two outs. The batter coming up was a kid from Lucas' 5th Grade class named Bobby Smith. He was a light-hitting second baseman but had gotten a hit off of Lucas during their last game, and it had tied the game. Lucas fired a fastball by him for strike one. Luke's second pitch was outside and in the dirt but Bobby went after it and missed it, strike two. The crowd was on its feet chanting "Pirates, Pirates, Pirates!" Lucas went into his windup. He knew he should be throwing a ball with two strikes and no balls but he wanted this to be his last pitch. He kicked his leg high into the air and fired a fastball as hard as he could. "THWACK. The ball slammed into Joey's catcher's mitt with Bobby just staring at it as it went by. "STRIKE THREE ... YOU'RE OUT!" the umpire roared as the game ended.

Lucas' teammates mobbed him and the Pirates parents and fans continued to cheer loudly as the boys lined up to shake the hands of the Yankees. Lucas looked for his mother in the crowd. *Is that dad walking away?* That was one of the problems when all of the soldiers were in uniform, it was hard to tell one from another at a distance. He did not dwell on it but for a moment; then he went back to enjoying their victory and shaking hands with the Yankees. As he came to Big John, John gave him a big grin and hug then said, "Great game, Luke!" Luke grinned back at him and answered, "Thanks, John."

The Yankees ended up in first place at the end of the season by winning all of their remaining games. The Pirates lost one and ended up in second place. Still, it was a good season for the team.

One of the other activities the boys enjoyed throughout the summer was camping out and not just the time they went with the Boy Scouts. On several occasions Lucas and his friends would camp out at different locations not far from the housing area. The first time, it was Lucas, Jason Sprint and Bob Ledahawski pitched their pup tent on the other side of the elementary school from the apartments. The campsite was located was kind of up on a hill with the post's loop road dropping below them. The tent was facing the road towards the main hospital complex. They had a good view of the railroad yard, too.

As the boys were finished setting up the tent, they were approached by a GI. He had a rifle draped over his shoulder and helmet on. Bob recognized him from the 225th's barracks. "It's Private Allen. Looks like he's on Guard Duty." Bob was right. Private Allen reached the tent and greeted them.

"Howdy, boys. Looks like you all are campin' out."

"Wow, how'd did you figure that one out?" Jason said sarcastically.

"Hey, ain't you Doc Sprint's kid? Don't be a wise ass," Private Allen answered, grinning so widely that his mouth looked like piano keys.

"So what's it to you?" Bobby tossed in keeping with the flavor of the conversation.

"I just thought I'd harass you guys until my shift is up at midnight," laughed Allen. "My route goes around the train depot and up to the back gate. Having you guys to pick on will make my night go a little faster."

"Maybe it's you that'll be harassed." quipped Jason.

"Yeah," Bobby joined in, "you don't know who you're messin' with." As the banter continued between the three of them as Lucas kept quiet, eating from a box of raisins, smiling as he was listening.

Private Allen then turned to Lucas and said, "What's the matter, cat got your tongue?"

"Better not mess with Lucas," Jason said to Allen. "He'll kick your ass!"

With that, all four of them burst out laughing, Lucas spraying raisins out of his mouth. Private Allen was a big kid from Wyoming. He stood 6□4□ and was well built. The thought of Lucas "kicking his ass" was so absurd that Lucas wondered how Jason had said it with such a straight face. When the laughter finally settled down, Private Allen turned back to Lucas and said, "Hey, aren't you Karla's little brother?" Lucas just nodded his head, still not saying a word. "Can you even speak?" Private Allen asked. Lucas answered with a loud fart that sent the other three to howling again. This time, Private Allen grabbed Lucas in a headlock as the other two boys jumped on Allen's back. After wrestling for a few minutes they all settled down sharing raisins and listening to Private Allen' stories about his ranch life in Wyoming. Soon they were calling him Chuck.

After awhile, Lucas looked at the darkening sky and asked Chuck, "Does anyone check on you to see if you're making your rounds?"

"Oh, shit!" Private Allen exclaimed. "I better get my ass movin'. I'll stop and see you guys a little later." He then took off at a near run towards the back gate. Once he was back behind the gatehouse he slowed down to his sentry gait and started heading towards the train depot. The boys settled in, talking about the usual things they talked about, like what they wanted to be when they grew up, girls, baseball and their friends, all the while continuing to snack on raisins and drink Kool-Aid from their canteens. The raisins were giving all the boys gas. Lucas was no longer the lone farter.

About two hours after leaving the three boys at their tent, Private Allen came back. It looked like he was trying to sneak up on them but Luke spotted him while taking a pee a few yards from the tent. "I see you, Chuck. You can stop trying to sneak up on us." Private Allen stood up straight and walked to them as Lucas was zipping his fly and heading back to the tent.

"Hi, guys," Chuck greeted them as he stooped in front of the tent opening. By this time, all three of the boys were farting up a storm. "Man, quit eating those damn raisins!" Chuck yelled as a wave of odor hit him in the face. He then grabbed the box from Luke's hand and tossed them as far as he could.

"Hey!" Bobby yelled. "What the hell are you doing? That's our food!"

"Cool your jets, Bob," Lucas laughed, "there were only a few left anyhow."

"Well I might have wanted them," Bobby whined.

"Here's a flashlight," Jason said. "Go find 'em if you want 'em that bad. I've had enough."

"I'm going to have to go again," Chuck told them.

"Aw, so soon?" Jason asked, again in his most sarcastic voice.

"My German girlfriend is gonna meet me at the back gate in about ten minutes then she and I are going to visit a special little spot behind the outer train."

"Sure you are," Lucas teased. "What're ya gonna do there? A little kiss, kiss?"

"Boys, it is going to be a little more than 'kiss, kiss' when we get there."

"Sure it is," Lucas continued to tease.

"Well, Lucas, believe what you want, I am going to get a little lovin' tonight. I want to leave you all with one last memento," Private Allen said and then he jumped head first into the tent, practically right on top of Bob, and ripped a long, drawn out fart that reeked worse than any the boys had cut. With shouts of "Oh, man!" and "Christ!" and "Damn it!" the boys baled out of the tent holding their noses and looking back at Chuck in both disbelief and admiration.

"Bye, guys!" Private Allen yelled as he picked up his rifle and took off towards the back gate. Lucas quickly opened the flap to the back of the tent to air it out. As they were getting ready to settle down again, Lucas could see a woman approaching the dimly lit back gate. Private Allen met her at the gate and quickly, the two of them walked to the train depot. Lucas reported his observation to the other two boys.

"Let's follow 'em and see if Chuck is really gonna get some sex from his girlfriend," Jason said.

"Okay!" both Lucas and Bob replied. They were looking for an adventure that evening anyhow. They had planned to sneak around the barracks and see what they could get into, but this plan was a better one.

As the boys slid out of the tent, they closed the flaps and headed towards the guard shack. Luke thought the best way not to be seen was to stay close to the fence and come up on the backside of the outermost train, using it to screen them from view. They did not converse as they slid stealthily along the fence, across the first two sets of train tracks, to the end of the last train car. They continued to move along the outside of the train. About midway down the train, Lucas put up his hand to stop his comrades.

"I think I hear them," he whispered. The three of them crouched in silence. They could hear both a woman's and man's voice. Then they heard nothing. Lucas motioned for Bobby and Jason to follow him as he crawled under the train and started moving towards the front. It was too dark to see very well in the little moonlight that was out that night. Lucas stopped again as he heard noise to their right. There was now a second train between them and the platform.

"Lucas," Jason whispered, "let's get under the other train to see if we can get a better look."

Lucas, straining to see, replied, "I don't know Jason. With all of the rocks here I don't see how we could do it without making a lot of noise."

"I don't think it would be any more than it is now," Bobby chimed in. "We've been crawling over rock and rail road ties. I've been in the back and it don't seem too loud to me, anyhow and they ain't heard us yet."

"Okay," Lucas finally conceded. "Jason, you go first. Roll out from under here. Keep low when you cross to the other train." Jason started to roll out from under the train when he suddenly stopped. Lucas didn't say anything but gave him a little nudge. Jason put his hand back to signal to stop.

"What is it, Jason?" Bobby finally asked. The suspense was killing him.

"What do you see?" Lucas asked, too. There was still no sound out of Jason as he stretched his neck to look. "Well?' Lucas said rather impatiently. Then he slugged Jason in the leg.

"OW!" Jason responded much more loudly then any of them

expected. "I SEE HIS WHITE ASS BOBBING UP AND DOWN!"

Then they heard a woman's voice saying in a heavy German accent, "Halt, halt I hear someone!" Then Bobby panicked and rolled out the other side of the train and began running, making all kinds of noise as he ran through the gravel along the tracks. Jason and Lucas took one quick look at Bobby and then back at the couple making love; then, they both bolted from the train, following Bobby back towards the back gate. Neither of them looked back until they passed Bobby. As Lucas passed Bob he looked back down the train to see if anyone was coming. To his relief, no one was, or at least it didn't appear that anyone was in the dim moonlight. The boys ran all the way back to the tent. When they got there, they got in their sleeping bags, breathing heavily from their run, and waited for what had to be the inevitable; Private Allen coming to get them for spying on him. But it never happened. As they lay there in their bags, Lucas lifted up on an elbow and said to Jason, "Why the hell did you yell?"

"I thought I was whispering!" Jason began to giggle.

"Whispering, hell!" Bobby piped in. "You scared the shit out of me!"

"Bobby and I didn't get to see anything, cause of your *whispering*," Luke chuckled.

"You didn't miss much, just Chuck's ass and his girl friend's knees," Jason said and then burst into hysterical laughter. The other two boys joined in, burying their heads in their sleeping bags to try to keep the noise down. They were still convinced Private Allen would be coming to get them, but they finally settled down. It was around 1:00 a.m. when Lucas could last remember looking at his watch. He could hear Bobby snoring and he relaxed. He remembered Private Allen saying his guard shift was until midnight. They never did see him again.

Chapter XI

Best Prank Ever

They camped out again several times over the next few weeks with different kids joining them at the different times. On a few occasions they had multiple tents. On this particular campout in early August, they had two tents. Lucas, Bobby and Jason were joined by Mickey and Guy. Guy and Bobby shared a tent with Lucas, Jason and Mickey in the other. It was a Friday night and a lot of the GIs were heading to town to the beer gardens as they did on a previous Friday night campout. Lucas had been woken up by drunk soldiers coming back to the post during the earlier campout and thought, there should be something he and his friends could do to have some fun with the men. He came up with a plan after playing Army at sewer hill the week before this campout. Lucas was on the side that was defending sewer hill. Todd was on his side and had come from his dishwashing job at the mess hall dragging along two cardboard boxes. At first they were going to try to use them as a defensive wall but there was a slight breeze and the boxes wouldn't stand up. Lucas had started digging a hole that he was going to hide in. As he lifted his entrenching tool into the air to slam into the ground, the wind blew the box in front of his swinging shovel, tearing a piece out of it. The piece landed across Luke's hole. He had an idea.

He tossed some dirt over the hole and discovered that it camouflaged it quite well. He and Todd began digging trenches around the base of sewer hill, putting cardboard over them, and covering them with dirt. When Andy Kirkland led the opposing "army" on an attack of Sewer Hill, the traps worked better than they had ever expected them to, sending Andy, Robby Smith, and Earl Clayton all sprawling across the ground.

When the five boys decided to camp out that Friday, Lucas came up with the idea to set similar traps for the GIs when they returned from town drunk. There were three main holes in the Post's fence along the town side of the fort, "We could split up and work on all three at the same time right after the sun sets." Lucas suggested.

All the boys were sold on the idea and began making plans to pick up the needed cardboard boxes that Thursday before the trash at the mess hall got picked up. They decided to store it for a day in Jason's family storage room in the basement of his apartment building. Each of the buildings had a storage space assigned for each apartment. Lucas' was full as was Bobby's and Mickey's, so Jason's was the logical choice. Guy didn't even know his family had a storage locker. Bobby and Jason picked up the cardboard and Lucas went home to get his penknife with Mickey joining him. They all met just outside of the basement entrance to Jason's building.

"How small should we cut these, Luke?" Guy asked.

"Let's just cut 'em along the corners of the boxes for now. We'll have to cut 'em to fit the holes later," Lucas replied. They quickly completed their task and placed the cut pieces in the storage room. Then they went to scout out their campsite.

On a few of their campouts, the boys had set up their tents north of the apartments, a few hundred feet from the fence. This day they decided to pitch the tents a little farther to the west towards Sewer Hill, just north of the Post Commander's house. It was about half way between two of the fence holes the GIs used to go to town. The first hole wasn't very far to the west of their tents. It lined up with a north/south road in town that dead-ended not far from the fence. The second was roughly lined up with Building A, the officers' apartments. The third hole was just a few hundred feet farther to the east of the one in line with Building C. Lucas told the rest of the guys he thought the tents would be just far enough away from the two holes not to be in the line the GIs would take from their barracks to the holes.

Once the tents were set up the five boys took turns running back to their homes to get their supplies and equipment. Besides their food, water and sleeping bags they also got their Army gear. They all had helmet liners, inside of the metal helmets that the GIs used for combat. Lucas helped get them through his dad. Again, having his dad in charge of the Property Disposal yard had lots of advantages. Ivan had supplied most of Lucas' friends with the items they were using.

Guy and Bobby went to help Jason with the cardboard. Todd Ledahawski came over to the tents following Bobby, Guy and

Jason as they lugged the pieces of cardboard to the tents.

"What the hell are you little punks up to?" he asked as he looked at the gear they had placed in the tents. "Are you setting traps?"

"We're not up to nothin'," Guy answered.

"Oh, bullshit," Todd shot back. "You're forgettin' I was in on the cardboard-over-the-holes traps at Sewer Hill. Looks like you're plannin' the same thing. Who are you gonna pull this on?"

Lucas took a deep sigh and told Todd of their plan. "Now you have to promise not to say anything to anyone, Todd," he pleaded.

Todd busted out laughing. "I wish I were hanging out with you guys tonight. It would be fun to see those drunken GIs comin' through there. You all better hope they don't catch you. They're going to be drunk and pissed. They'll forget 'bout worryin' who your fathers are, and probably kick your butts." Then he took off waving as he left. "Have fun!"

The boys continued preparing for their evening. The sun was starting to set. They weren't allowed to have a campfire unless they were in the designated spots at the picnic grounds, so the guys all had sandwiches and potato chips for their dinner with cookies for dessert. The two tents were about ten feet apart facing each other so when the tent flaps were pulled back they could all see each other. They were now sitting in a circle between the tents eating their dinner and talking baseball. The sun had set over the hills to the west. Darkness was starting to settle in.

"Everyone got their dark clothes?" Lucas asked, receiving a bunch of head nods and "yeah" responses. Most had old Army fatigue shirts from their fathers that fit them like coats. They were anxious to get started but it was still too early.

"When can we start digging, Luke?" Guy asked.

"We have to wait a couple of hours yet." Luke responded. "Most of the soldiers haven't even headed out yet."

"Luke's right," Mickey added. "I don't usually see them walking across the field until after 8 o'clock. I think we have to wait 'til around 9 before we start or we may have a couple of them surprise us."

The five boys settled down or at least four of them did. Guy was antsy and could hardly wait for another hour to pass. He paced around the campsite, shining his flashlight on his watch every couple of seconds. Lucas looked at his watch, which illuminated in the dark. He glanced at the fingernail of a moon setting in the west. "It's going to be a dark night," he said to no one in particular. Over the next hour their conversation rambled from baseball to the good looking girls in their school to who they thought they would get for a teacher the coming school year. Only twice during that time could they see a couple of groups of GIs heading towards the holes in the fence. A group of three went to the hole to their west and another couple of soldiers went through the hole on the other side.

"It doesn't seem like very many of them are going to town tonight" Mickey remarked.

"Don't worry," Bobby stated, "a lot of them go through the main gate if they have passes. But most of them take the short cut through the fence home. I heard my dad talking about it to my mom. He said the ones without a pass go out through the holes and come back the same way."

Finally, it was time. They decided to split up in two groups. Jason, Bobby and Guy would go to the biggest hole in the fence, the one to the west of them. Lucas and Mickey would get the center hole just to the east. Whoever got done first would head to the eastern-most hole to start and the other group would join in when they were done.

"Make sure the hole in the ground is as long as the hole in the fence," Lucas whispered as they were now in their stealth mode, "but don't make it too wide for the cardboard to bridge it. The dirt is going to make it sag some."

They were off. Jason, Bobby and Guy finished first and were coming up to Lucas and Mickey just as they were finishing placing the cardboard over the hole.

"Keep going," Lucas said in a low voice as they approached. "We'll catch up as soon as we cover the cardboard."

The three wasted no time continuing on to the third hole in the fence. They began their task immediately. By the time Lucas and Mickey joined them they were almost done with the hole. There were enough hands working on it so Lucas and Mickey just sat back and watched, keeping a keen eye on the other side of the fence in case a GI came wandering back a little earlier than expected. As the three boys finished digging, Lucas and Mickey slid the cardboard over the hole. Guy and Bobby began covering it as Jason smoothed over the dirt with his hand. "All done," he said as they all picked up their tools, and bending over at the waist, headed away from the hole and towards their tents. As they got a hundred feet or so away Jason stood up and the others followed his lead.

"Whew!" Guy exclaimed as he plopped in his tent. "Got through that part okay."

"What now?" Bobby asked, looking at Lucas.

"Let's put up our stuff except for one shovel," Lucas directed.

"What do we need the shovel for, Luke?" Mickey asked. "We already dug the holes."

"We'll need to fix the top of the holes after the first soldiers fall in," Lucas explained. "If they leave quickly enough we can cover the holes up again and catch the next ones."

Bobby began laughing. "Hell, I was happy just thinkin' of catching three GIs in our traps for the entire night. Luke wants to catch the whole damn Army!"

The other boys joined him in his laughter and Lucas, turning a bit red-faced, embarrassed a little for thinking about getting the most out of their little endeavor, just shrugged his shoulders. It had never even occurred to him that they would just plan to use the holes once. On the nights he was allowed to be out a little later, he had seen the GIs wander not far from the playground as they headed back to their barracks from the fence holes. They were usually in groups of two or three and often there were multiple groups that went by spaced out by anywhere from a few minutes to half an hour. When he first came up with the idea of digging the holes below the fence, he was always thinking they could re-cover the holes and catch several of the soldiers in the same holes.

After they stopped laughing the other boys again turned to Lucas for direction. After all, this was his plan and so far, they all loved it.

"I guess we can split up in the same groups we did to dig the holes," Lucas stated. "We have to remember not be too bunched together when we lay flat on the ground near the holes." Then turning to Jason, "You, Bobby and Guy should get close to the middle of the two first two holes. Mickey and I will get closer to the middle hole but far enough away that we aren't in the line they'll take back to the barracks. I think we can see the last hole from there because it will have the back gate light behind it instead of being in the total dark like the first two."

"Okay, Captain Luke!" Guy said as he saluted Lucas, grinning from ear to ear. "Deploy us to our posts!" The rest of the boys, including Luke, chuckled as they moved out.

As they reached a point midway between the first two holes and about fifty feet back from the fence, Luke stopped. "Right here," he said as he pointed to the ground. "Remember to stay about five feet apart and keep real flat so they don't see you when they come through."

"This looks a little too close, Luke," Bobby said in a low, concerned voice. "These guys are gonna wanna kick our asses after they fall into the hole. Don't you think they'll be looking right around here?"

Lucas was grinning as he answered. "I think they're gonna look close to the fence first, and then they're gonna look towards the lights from the hospital to see if they can see us. Go over by the fence Bobby and we'll lie down. See where your eyes go."

Bobby did just as Lucas said as the others all lay down. To his amazement, Lucas was right. You could only see close up, and then the lights towards the front of the hospital and the NCO Club back up the hill on the other side. The area that they were on sloped down towards the drainage way that ran a few hundred feet behind the NCO Club. Bobby couldn't see his fellow conspirators. He went back over to the rest of the guys.

"You're right, Luke," he said as he plopped down next to him. "It's still scary as hell. What if they have a flashlight?"

"If they come after us we just have to scatter and run," Lucas laughed. "They'll probably catch you, Bobby. You're the slowest of us all."

"Fuck you, Luke!" Bobby replied. He really didn't think it was very funny. Lucas was right. The rest of the guys could outrun him. Still, the excitement of the prank outweighed his fear of getting caught.

It was now a little after 9 o'clock. The boys were getting bored. Lucas figured they still had at least an hour at the earliest before anyone would be heading back to the barracks. They talked about all kinds of things in their low voices, catching themselves when they would get a little loud. Guy, as usual, was the most impatient.

"Maybe one of us should go on the other side of the fence and keep an eye out for them?" he suggested.

"I don't think so," Jason answered. "They might see you trying to get back to us."

"Jason's right," Luke chimed in. "It would be a pisser if after all of this waiting and preparing they spotted us."

"Even if they did," argued Guy, "they still wouldn't know about the holes."

"But they would be on alert that something was up," added Mickey, "and be looking for something."

Guy finally gave up on the idea. The conversation died down after awhile as they all were deep into their own thoughts. Lucas could hear Bobby snoring slightly. He smiled to himself as he fought off the urge to drift off to sleep as well. He could feel his head nodding as time drifted on, then suddenly he perked up. He could hear voices and laughter and quickly became alert. Lucas tapped Bobby next to him. The rest of the boys were alert, too.

"Shit!" exclaimed Guy in a low voice. "We didn't split up."

"Too late now. Doesn't matter anyhow, they are coming to this hole in front of us," Lucas stated. "Let's spread out a little." As he finished his sentence he began to crawl several yards to his right. Lucas would be the closest to where they should pass if they were heading from the hole straight to their barracks. Bobby, who was next to him, followed him, stopping a couple of yards short of Luke.

"58 bottles of beer on the wall ... 58 bottles of beer ... take one down, pass it around ... 57 bottles of beer on the wall." The boys could hear the two drunken GIs singing as they stumbled towards the hole in the fence. Lucas' heart was racing, his head pounding as they neared the fence.

"Hey Shithead! Here's the fence," one of the GIs shouted at the other. "And would you look at that ... we found the fuckin' hole right off."

"No shit you dumb fuck. The path goes right to it," said the second soldier as he slipped a little just before the fence. They both laughed hysterically. The boys couldn't see too much. The lights from the village were not very bright and trees between the fence and the village blocked out most of it. Still, they had been laying there long enough that their eyes had adjusted to the darkness as much as possible. They could make out the silhouettes of the two GIs as they reached the fence.

"After you, my dear," the first GI said jokingly to the second. Then the boys could see the silhouette of a man going through the hole. As he stepped through to the other side he quickly disappeared from their view with the sound of a thud instantly following. The next sounds were hard for the boys to decipher. It was mixed with curse words, accusations, moaning and laughter.

"You shit, Jackson!" the fallen GI could be heard saying. "You set me up!"

"No, honestly, Billy, I had nothin' to do with this. What the hell is goin' on anyhow? Someone had to dig this hole after we went into town."

"Had to be those fucking Army brats," Billy replied. "Who else would do something like this?"

"YOU LITTLE SHITS! WE'RE GONNA FIND YOU AND KICK YOUR SCRAWNY LITTLE ASSES!" Jackson yelled into the air.

Lucas' heart was racing. He knew his partners in crime were probably feeling the same. He was hoping they didn't panic and start to run. The two GIs were up and moving toward the barracks. Luke had a good look at the silhouettes as they moved between him and the lights from the cul-de-sac to the apartments. *Damn,* one of them looked pretty big. He remembered a guy named Jackson with the 15th Evac. *This must be him.*

"Let's stomp around here," the one called Billy said, "I bet they're somewhere close."

As all of the boys prepared to jump up and run they could see someone with a flashlight near the playground by the apartments shining it towards them. It was too dim to light anything up by the time the beam got out there, but it did dissuade the two GIs from looking for them. He could hear Jackson say to Billy that they needed to get out of there. Jackson thought it looked like Captain Harley, the dentist, walking his dog. The two soldiers almost stepped on Lucas as they headed toward the ball field instead of straight towards the barracks to steer clear of Captain Harley. In a few minutes they were gone.

Lucas stood up and said, "We have to fix the hole before anyone else comes." The rest of the brats all jumped up at once and headed to the hole. Guy got out his flashlight, and keeping it low to the ground, aimed it at the hole. He then lifted it to the faces of his comrades. They were all grinning from ear to ear. Mickey was almost it tears trying to hold back his laughter as they continued trying to be quiet. Finally, he couldn't contain himself as they straightened out the cardboard and dug out some of the dirt from the hole to begin setting up the trap again.

"Damn that was fun and scary!" he blurted through his laughter. The other boys all started laughing too, except for Luke who was focused on repairing their trap. He was grinning, but knew they had to hurry. The other soldiers would all start to drift back over the next hour or two.

"We need to split up more," Jason stated. "They could have stumbled into us if they didn't get scared away by Captain Harley and his dog."

"Your right," Lucas answered. "Let's go back to our plan. Mickey and I will move up to the next hole. If we hear 'em comin', we still have time to low crawl closer to the hole they're approaching. Same with you guys. If they're comin' towards our hole or the last one, stay low and get a little closer so you can see, or maybe I should say, hear 'em as they come through. The first one went off just like I hoped it would."

"No shit!" was Guy's reply. "I almost peed my pants when I thought they were going to stomp around on the ground looking for us. I thought Bobby would run."

"I thought you would run, you dork," Bobby shot back. "In fact, I think you shit your pants you were so scared."

"He always smells like that," laughed Jason. "We won't be able to tell when he does shit his pants."

"Fuck you guys!" Guy replied rather emphatically.

The bantering went back and forth until the trap was repaired. Then the boys split up per Luke's plan. They barely got into position when they heard sounds coming down the same path the two GIs followed. Lucas and Mickey stooped low and moved closer to the hole, crawling the last several yards. This time they were to the west of the hole with the other three boys in the same spot as before, east of the hole.

"Can you see Bobby and the guys?" Mickey asked Luke in a very low whisper.

"No," Lucas replied. "This is the perfect night. I just wish we could see our targets a little better. There they are … no more talkin', Mickey."

The lights from the housing area were behind and left of Mickey and Lucas. The boys had to be really still since the chances of being seen on that side of the fence hole were much greater than they were when they had been on the other side where the other three boys were. Lucas was worried that if the soldiers got low enough and looked back at the lights they might be able to see him and Mickey even though Lucas was convinced they would look like humps in the field. It was enough of a concern to him that his heart was pounding more now than the when the first two GIs came through.

The soldiers were arguing over whether or not one of them had a chance with some young lady they'd met at the bar when the other two dragged him out. They were pretty toasted and very loud. The first one stepped through the hole and went down with a hard sounding thump. Before he had a chance to react, the second stepped through the hole and immediately fell on top of the first GI. The first one let out a yell.

"CHRIST! What the hell is going on? Get the hell off of me!"

"My foot's stuck in the fence!" the second soldier shot back. "Let me lift up … there, now get out from under me."

The boys couldn't see what exactly was taking place in the darkness but listening to the soldiers gave them a pretty good visual as to what was happening. The third GI just stood at the hole in the fence. It took him awhile to assess what was happening to his two companions, and then he started to laugh. It was one of those deep down in the gut laughs that just increased as it continued, sounding like a roar that was really contagious. All of the boys were doing their best not to laugh out loud, too. That became even more difficult when the two soldiers on the ground began joining in on the laughter.

"Someone set a pit trap and caught a couple of drunk GIs!" exclaimed the standing soldier when he finally stopped laughing. The other two were now up on their knees. Lucas' heart was really pounding now. This was when they were most likely to be spotted since the men were so close to ground level. He could see them fairly well now, silhouetted against the lights of the village behind them. He felt a certain amount of relief when they got to their feet without looking back in his direction.

"Who in the hell do you think did this?" said the first GI to step through the fence.

"I saw there were some pup tents set up over there (pointing in the direction of the boys camping spot) when we came through here earlier. Bet it was some Army brats," said the GI that did not fall in the trap.

"Let's go get 'em." said the second GI.

"Are you crazy?" replied the soldier who was now going through the hole in the fence avoiding the hole in the ground. "What're you gonna do if we catch 'em? Their dads are probably fuckin' officers. No ... let's head back to the barracks. Chalk this one up as 'they got us' and forget about it."

"Easy for you to say, you didn't smash your face into the ground and have some asshole fall on top of ya." declared the first GI. Then after a slight pause, he cracked up with laughter with the other two joining in. They began brushing themselves off and walking towards the barracks with one final "FUCK YOU, YOU LITTLE PUNKS!" as they staggered away.

They were barely a hundred yards away when Guy jumped up. Not only did he jump up, he kept jumping up and down and saying, "That was great ... great ... great!!!!!"

"Go easy, Guy," Lucas could hear Jason say.

"Man, this is so much fun," Guy continued. "I gotta pee before I wet my pants."

"I bet Bobby did," Lucas jokingly said as he and Mickey got up from the ground and joined the others.

"Screw you, Luke," Bobby responded. "I was just about to shit my pants though." He let out a nervous laugh as Guy went over by the fence to take a leak.

"I think we all were," Mickey chimed in. "When they were kneelin' on the ground, all I could think about was what Luke had said about when they had the best chance of seeing us. I was getting ready to jump up and run."

"Let's fix the hole again," Jason reminded them.

The boys continued to chatter as they quickly got the cardboard reset and covered. It was a little harder to find the dirt to cover it this time. It looked like the soldiers kicked the dirt around more than the first two. The cardboard actually showed through in a couple of spots but Luke agreed with Jason that in the dark no one was going to notice. They finished up and went back to their positions. It was now close to 11 o'clock and once the adrenaline rush subsided the boys started getting sleepy. Lucas could feel himself drifting off. Then Mickey poked him in the sides and he immediately became alert.

"I think I hear somebody over near the middle hole," Mickey whispered. Just as he finished the statement Guy plopped down besides them.

"I think they're coming," he said to the two of them. "We're too far away over there to see anything, besides Jason and Bobby are asleep."

Just after the words came out of Guy's mouth the other two boys came crawling up to the group. "Let's crawl a little closer to the hole and spread out some." Luke instructed his companions. They all got up and, ducking down, moved another fifty feet or so closer to the middle hole. Now they could definitely hear the soldiers coming. There were two and they weren't as boisterous as the previous victims. Then shock overcame Luke as he recognized one of the voices.

"Oh shit," he blurted, "it's Coach Tyler!"

"Quiet!" whispered Jason rather emphatically. Then in a low tone, "Are you sure, Luke?"

"Listen," Luke said. These two GIs were not saying much, especially when compared to the other two groups that had gone through.

"Luke's right," Bobby piped in as he heard one of the men say "look for the hole over there." That's definitely Coach Tyler. Shit, what are we going to do?"

"Do? There is nothin' we can do now but wait and see what happens," was Lucas' response.

This added a whole new dimension to their adventure. It

had never occurred to them that they would be trapping their baseball coach. What if he got hurt? Would he find out who it was and kick them off the team? All kinds of thoughts raced through their minds. Even Guy was silent as he now peered nervously through the darkness to see if he could see their coach. There was not as much of the village lighting behind the GIs at the angle that they were watching from. Their eyes had adjusted well to the night and they could pick out two figures as they crossed the open area between the trees and the fence. Coach Tyler was a big, strong looking man and it was easy for them to pick him out of the two, even in the dark. There was not much conversation as they reached the fence. The smaller figure of the two went first and immediately fell to the ground as he stepped through the hole in the fence, into the hole on the ground.

"What the hell?" they heard him say as he partially caught himself with his right hand on the fence post and kind of rolled down to the ground slowly. This was a voice the boys also recognized.

"Are you okay, Connor?" Coach Tyler asked.

"Yeah, I'm okay." Then he did something the boys had never thought about as a possibility. He pulled out a small flashlight and shined it into the hole. Now the boys could see the two men in the glow of the light. "Who the hell dug this hole?"

The boys could see Coach Tyler turn in their direction. "There are only two kids who I know would come up with something like this," he said to Connor. "It had to be Luke or Jason!"

Lucas's eyes almost popped out of his head when he heard his coach. There was a small gasp from Jason. The other boys were trying to hold still but couldn't help but fidget with this new twist to their adventure.

"Give me that flashlight, Connor," Tyler commanded. Then he turned in the direction of the boys and began shining the light in a crisscross manner across the field.

"LUCAS! JASON! I KNOW YOU'RE OUT THERE!" he shouted. "COME ON BOYS, SHOW YOURSELVES!"

The light had passed over them without Coach Tyler seeing them. Lucas' first instinct was to keep hidden but then after hesitating for a brief moment, Lucas let out a big sigh and turned to his partners in crime.

"Let's go guys," he said to the others in a normal conversational tone. "I don't want the coach pissed off at us."

They all slowly got up and began walking towards the two men. Tyler saw them stand and covered them with the flashlight beam as they slowly walked forward. When they got to the men, their coach was grinning ear to ear. Lucas noticed that neither Coach Tyler nor Connor were drunk. They might have been drinking but they certainly were not drunk like the other GIs.

Connor was the first to speak. "What were you thinking? You could have broken my leg!"

"Easy, Connor," Coach Tyler interjected. "I am sure these guys were only having a little fun at the expense of a few of our comrades. I'll bet it never occurred to them that their prey would turn out to be their coach, right boys?"

The five boys all nodded in agreement and remained silent until Lucas finally spoke up rather humbly. "Sorry Coach. We weren't trying to hurt anyone. We do this to each other and our friends when we play army. I never thought that you might break a leg, Connor."

"Whose idea was this anyhow?" Connor asked.

"It was Luke's!" Guy blurted out to the shock of the other four boys. Lucas turned to glare at Guy. He was going to fess up to it, but he couldn't believe that Guy gave him up so quickly. He could see Bobby looking at Guy like he was going to kill him. He turned to face the two GIs.

"We were all in it together," Bobby stated as he stood up straight, ready to take his medicine. Jason and Mickey both chimed in, taking full responsibility for their part in the scheme. It didn't go unnoticed by the two men.

"Jesus, boys," Coach Tyler started, chuckling as he spoke, "it would've been damn funny if it wasn't that you could really have hurt someone. Is this the only hole or do you have more?"

"We have two more by that hole over there … and that one." Lucas said pointing in the direction of the two other holes.

"Where're your shovels?" Tyler asked.

"We have two over near the other hole," answered Lucas.

"Well, go get them. You need to fill these before someone does get hurt, okay?"

"Okay."

Guy left the group to get the shovels. He had not said a word after giving Luke up. He realized by Bobby's reaction he'd screwed up. There was nothing he could think of to make it right at the moment so he went after the shovels.

"You'll have to excuse me while I go take a piss," Connor said as he walked a few feet away and began relieving himself. "I'm lucky I didn't pee my pants."

Coach Tyler laughed and tried to lighten the boys' mood. He didn't want to take the fun out of their night so he began making light of the situation as he held the flashlight over the holes as the boys took turns filling them. They went from one hole to the next until all three were covered. By the time they were done all of the somberness they expressed earlier was gone. The five of them were back enjoying their night as the two soldiers accompanied them back to their tents. The two soldiers sat with them and listened as they told them of the earlier victims of their traps. Connor was telling them the names of the GIs they did trap as the boys described each episode. They all laughed together and as the two men got up to leave, the five boys were back in a good mood. They didn't say any more to Guy about giving up Lucas and he was able to join in the fun.

"It's after midnight. We got to head back to the barracks." Coach Tyler stated.

"I got one question," Bobby asked. "How did you know it was Luke or Jason?"

"Nothing personal, Bobby, but those two are the only two kids I could think of that would come up with a hair-brained idea like this. They have both shown a lot of imagination in how they approach baseball. It seems like any time there is a new idea for how we practice or how the *Coach* sets the lineup it comes from one of these two. I still think it was you guys that pulled the tent stakes at the Scout campout. Then there is the little Nazi helmet enterprise. As soon as I realized what we stumbled into my first thought was Luke, then Jason."

Then the two soldiers said goodnight and went on their way. The boys were exhausted by then. Without much conversation they all said goodnight to each other and climbed into their sleeping bags. They were still asleep the following morning when Robby and Terry Smith, joined by Todd, came to harass them at the tents. It didn't take the boys long to be fully awake as they told their story of the night before to the other boys.

"You should have gone back and dug the holes back out after Coach Tyler left," Todd told them.

"No way!" Bobby said to his brother emphatically. "I want to play ball, not sit on the bench. There was no way we were gonna disobey our coach." The other boys nodded in agreement.

"Besides," Lucas added, 'we were too damn tired to dig those holes out again.'

"I don't think anyone else came through anyhow," Guy said. "We had our fun watching those other guys go through."

The boys packed up their tents, sleeping bags and other gear. They shuttled their stuff home and ate breakfast. By the time they went out to play again, word of their adventure had spread and they were surrounded at the playground by most of the dependent kids, each of the pranksters giving their version of what happened.

Throughout the rest of the summer, Lucas and the Cricks were joined by different boys for more camp outs. They never set traps like they did that first time but they did manage to have other adventures. It was a very good summer for the boys.

Chapter XII

Altar Boys — No Road to Heaven

In late July Father Perkins named Lucas head Altar Boy for the Münchweiler Church. There were enough boys in Münchweiler to fill all of his Altar Boy needs and he no longer brought help from Pirmasens. There were the Ledahawski brothers, Mickey Mira, Guy Henderson, and Don Davis, who along with his sister, Sally, had moved to the fort during the summer. Don was in Todd's class and played on the Little League team for the last few games of the season. Sally was going to be a freshman in high school. Lucas was now in charge of setting the schedule of who would serve Mass each Sunday. It wasn't very difficult. He just rotated everyone so they could all serve with each of the other individuals. If anyone new came along he would just fit him into the rotation.

The boys that didn't serve on a particular Sunday would watch from the balcony at the rear of the church. It was blocked off to the remaining parishioners. The first time the boys were up there things went pretty smoothly. They followed the Mass as if they were in a pew below. Todd and Guy were serving Mass. The following Sunday wasn't quite as smooth. Lucas served with Mickey leaving Guy, Bobby, Todd and Don upstairs. Lucas could hear sounds from there and stole a quick glance as he was moving from one side of the altar to the other. Just as he peeked, Todd slugged his brother, Bobby in the arm. Todd was a bit on the loud side anyhow and when he laughed the sound carried. Lucas could hear that laughter from time to time. The previous week Lucas had started a program where they would all meet right after Mass and talk about any problems they saw during the Mass. The purpose was for the non-serving boys to point out things that would help those who served that Sunday. He didn't foresee that the servers would have to correct problems generating from the balcony.

They all gathered in the balcony after Father Perkins left for Pirmasens. Lucas stood in front of the others, facing them. He wasn't sure how to start it but finally decided the direct approach was the best.

"Todd, you have to cut that shit out," he stated.

A scowl quickly came across Todd's face as he responded. "You don't tell me what the fuck to do, Lucas. You're just a little punk."

"I'm the head Altar Boy and it's me that Father Perkins is going to come to if we have a problem," Lucas answered.

"Then don't make a problem, Luke, and no one will have to be talked to," Todd replied.

"You were the one causing a problem!" Lucas exclaimed. "You made enough noise for everyone in church to hear. I saw you punch Bobby."

"I'll punch my brother anytime I want to and it's none of your damn business," retorted Todd.

"It is when it happens in church as long as you're an Altar Boy and have the privilege to be in the balcony," Lucas pressed Todd. "You and Bobby want to sit next to your mom and sister and punch each other, fine, but not up in the balcony."

"Hey, wait a minute!" Bobby inserted. "I didn't punch anyone. It was my asshole brother that did all of the hitting."

"Sorry, Bobby," Lucas replied, "I was just tryin' to make a point." Then turning to Todd. "So are we clear?"

"Do you know what's clear?" Todd responded. "It's clear that I'm gonna have to kick your ass, you little punk."

"Maybe we'll all kick your ass, Todd!" Guy shouted.

"Yeah!" added Mickey as all but Don stood up and faced Todd. Don was fairly new and didn't want any part of this fracas.

After a short pause, Todd broke out into a grin and faced Lucas, "Hey, I was just kiddin' around, Luke. I promise I won't punch Bobby in church anymore. Besides, nobody else paid any attention to us."

"I saw Major Crabby turn and look up at us," Guy stated. Guy was very afraid of Major Crabtree. She had already gotten him in trouble with his parents by complaining to them once after a movie, telling them that Guy was 'unruly' and misbehaved at the movies.

"Well, try not to be so noisy up there, okay?" Lucas asked. "That goes for everyone."

With that, they all nodded in agreement and decide to go

home, change clothes and play some 500, however that was not the end of their problems in the balcony. Over the next month the boys were quieter but were not exactly well behaved. Lucas wasn't sure who fired the first rubber band into the congregation below. He had tried to be responsible and not participate but he couldn't help himself and soon, Lucas was also shooting rubber bands.

Then it happened. Todd and Don were serving Mass. Lucas, Mickey, Bobby and Guy all were in the balcony. Guy was aiming at his younger brother who was sitting with a group of his friends near the back of the church. Sitting in front of them was Major Crabtree. All four boys watch the flight of the rubber band as it left Guy's fingers, flying towards the pews below. Their lower jaws dropped in unison as the rubber band missed its mark and hit Major Crabtree in the back of the head. She whipped around at the young boys behind her, catching out of the corner of her eye, all four of the Altar Boys in the balcony darting back away from the edge and plopping down on the pews behind them. It took her no time at all to realize where the rubber band she was now holding in her hand had come from. Had the boys not moved simultaneously creating both a block of movement and a loud 'plop' as their butts hit the pew at the same time, Major Crabtree might not have noticed them and blamed Guy's brother and friends for the misdeed. Lucas' eyes were staring straight ahead at the altar. *Shit, we're in trouble now!* They behaved the rest of the Mass.

After Mass, Lucas saw Major Crabtree talking to Father Perkins. He gathered up his fellow Altar Boys and they all scooted out the back of the church, avoiding Major Crabby and Father Perkins. As they all walked away from the church they talked about what could happen. Would they be thrown out as Altar Boys? Would their fathers get DRs (Delinquent Reports) and beat the crap out of them? Would they get grounded for the rest of their lives?

It didn't take too long before the boys found out the results of the meeting Major Crabby had with Father Perkins. As he walked in the door that following Tuesday after school he heard his mother call out from the kitchen.

"Lucas!" she yelled as he headed for his bedroom. "Come in here!"

"Yes, Ma'am!" he answered as he turned and met her in the kitchen. "What's up, Mom?"

"What did you boys do in church last Sunday?" she asked. "I got a call from Father Perkins as did Lena Ledahawski, that we are to meet with him and Ellen Crabtree on Saturday after catechism classes."

Lucas felt a sick feeling in the pit of his stomach as soon as he heard Major Crabby's name. With a large sigh, Lucas told his mother what had happened. To his surprise she didn't seem too upset.

"You boys should be ashamed of yourselves for acting up in church," she said as she continued to work on preparing dinner for that night. "It's a good thing your father can't stand Ellen, and this doesn't sound serious enough to get him involved. Your father doesn't like any woman who out ranks him."

That evening at dinner Ivan told Maria that she could let him know if he needed to dole out any punishment after the meeting on Saturday. That was the only thing that was said on the subject the rest of the week, except for the quizzing he got from his brothers. Ivan seemed preoccupied and didn't want to get involved in anything that involved Major Ellen Crabtree if he could help it.

That Saturday, Bobby, Mickey, Guy, and Lucas walked out of the room in the building where they had their catechism classes, and made the short walk to the church, Todd and Don were already at the front of the church standing with their mothers and Lucas' mom. They all entered the church together. Mickey and Guy's mothers were already in the church sitting in the middle pew. Sitting in front of them was Major Crabtree, turned with her arm over the back of the pew, facing the group as they came in to join the others. Father Perkins was just coming up from the back of the church. He was smiling as he greeted everyone. Maria, Lena Ledahawski and Mrs. Davis joined the other mothers as all of the boys entered the pews across the aisle from their mothers. Father Perkins stood in the aisle in front of them.

Father Perkins cleared his throat, then started, "Well, I am sorry to have to have you all come in on this beautiful Saturday, but it appears we have had some shenanigans going on from our group of Altar Boys during the last couple of Masses. With that I am going to turn this over to Major Crabtree since she is the person bringing forward this complaint."

Major Crabtree stood up and began to glare at the boys as she went through her litany of offenses from the rubber bands shooting to just the general horsing around that the boys participated in during Mass. Lucas was amazed at the detail she went into for each one of them. *How could she have seen all of that?* The boys stirred uncomfortably. When she finished, Father Perkins turned to the mothers and asked, "Anything you want to add or any questions for Major Crabtree?"

They all shook their heads no as they looked around at each other. The mothers had already talked amongst themselves. It was hard to gauge what their position was. Lucas had overheard his mother and Lena talk about Crabby before. They knew she was kind of an extreme person and she wasn't very fond of kids but they both liked her. His mother had told him once when he was complaining about Crabby getting on them at the snack bar that he needed to be nicer to her. She had it tough in a man's world and she had to be as tough as she was just to get the respect she deserved as head nurse at the hospital. Lucas and his friends were not that sympathetic.

Luke was shaken from his thoughts by Father Perkins' question to him. He wasn't paying attention and it took him a second to react to his name.

"I'm sorry, Father, what was that again?"

"I said, Lucas, as Head Altar Boy, what do you suggest to resolve this problem and see to it that it doesn't come up again?" he repeated.

Lucas was not prepared to have any input into this meeting. They were all there to hear what their punishment would be. He and his buddies did talk about it during the week and had thought about what they guessed would happen. After a few moments of silence he finally managed to speak.

"I think we need to close off the balcony again and we can celebrate Mass with the rest of the congregation when we are not serving. All of us will promise to behave from now on."

"Excellent," Father Perkins stated. "Well, I guess this meeting is over." Then, looking at the Altar Boys, "I expect you all will behave without incident going forward."

All of the boys were nodding in agreement with their heads bobbing up and down and mumbling, "oh, yes Father" and "sure" and "of course" coming from all of them. Father Perkins clapped his hands and said, "Meeting adjourned!"

"WAIT! WAIT A MINUTE!" Major Crabtree shouted as she stood up. "Is that it? These little brats get away with only a 'don't do it again" and they are off Scot free?"

Now Father Perkins turned and gently put his hand on Major Crabtree's shoulder. "Ellen, what more do you want from these young lads? They admitted their guilt and have promised us they would not do it again. Their crime was not so severe to warrant any other action as far as I am concerned. Their mothers are here to see to it that they behave themselves in church in the future. I think this is how Jesus would have handled it."

Lucas looked at Crabby and try as he might, could not contain the smile that was spreading across his face. She was red in the face and the most animated Lucas had ever seen her. You could almost see the steam coming out of her ears. He glanced at the other boys, noticing they were looking down at the ground, trying not to look too happy over how things were turning out. Todd and Bobby knew they still had to deal with their mother, knowing that there would be some punishment that would be doled out by her for the embarrassment of being called to a meeting by the parish priest for their misbehaving. They knew they could deal with that. Before the meeting they were worried that they were going to be kicked out of the Altar Boys. That would have really meant a much worse punishment that would have included a whipping by their dad. They could tell by their mother's expression that this was going to be minor, probably a grounding for a week, maybe two. Lucas wasn't worried about any punishment. His mother would make him sit by her during church if he wasn't serving Mass. He could tell she was irritated by Major Crabtree's reaction to Father Perkins' decision. He could see that look on her face whenever she got into that "mama bear" protective mode regarding her kids. She didn't like Ellen calling her son a "brat".

"Well, Ellen," she said as she turned to Major Crabtree, "I believe Father Perkins gave his decision and I'm okay with it. I say we close the book on this chapter." Then turning to Lucas, "Let's go home, Luke."

Lucas was more than happy to obey his mother. He hopped up from the pew and saying good-by to Father Perkins and the rest of the group, followed his mother out of the church. They didn't say much on the walk home. Once they got home Maria sat Lucas down at the dining room table.

"Lucas, I am disappointed that you boys horsed around in church. It is God's House and you should show more respect. I want you to promise me we won't be going through this again."

"Oh, yes ma'am, I promise," Lucas answered.

"I wish Ellen had come to me first instead of going to Father Perkins over such a trivial thing. In fact, if she had gone about it differently you might have been given a bigger punishment from me. I just didn't like the way she handled it."

Susan had been in the kitchen making some lunch and had overheard her mother. "I think you should ground Luke for at least a week!"

Lucas shot a glare at his sister. "Why don't you eat crap you fart-face!"

"LUCAS!" his mother shouted. "You will be grounded for a month if I ever hear you talk to your sister like that again."

Behind their mother's back, Susan stuck her tongue out at Lucas and gave him her smug grin. Lucas knew better than to respond. For now, he was just happy that his mother wasn't too upset about the incident. He would let his sister get in her little digs and keep his mouth shut.

For the next few weeks the boys behaved in church. When Todd and Bobby were not serving Mass, they had to sit with their family. Lucas was fortunate. His mother gave him no such restriction nor did Mickey's mother. The two of them sat in the back of the church instead of up in the balcony. To say they behaved might have been stretching the truth a little because at every opportunity the boys would make faces at Major Crabtree behind her back. She suspected something, as she kept shooting glances at them during Mass.

"We have to find some way to get even with her," Mickey said to Lucas as they were leaving church. Bobby had just caught up with them.

"Let's get together this afternoon and come up with a plan," Bobby suggested. The three boys agreed to meet if they could, at around 3 o'clock. Sundays were hard for Lucas to plan things. He never knew if his father would decide to take the family on a Sunday drive or if he wanted Luke to go with him to watch the Germans play soccer. That Sunday his dad decided to take them all to the snack bar for a late lunch. Lucas joined his parents, brothers and Susan for burgers and fries. As the Baryshivka family started walking up the road from the main building complex they ran into Mickey, Bobby, and Jason walking down the road towards the Hospital complex.

"Dad, can I go play with the guys?" Lucas asked his father.

"Sure," he answered as he continued the story he was telling Maria. "Be home by five o'clock."

"Stay out of trouble, Lucas!" Susan shouted as Luke took off with his friends. He just gave her a sly grin and said nothing. Susan watched the four boys take off. *They're always up to something.*

"I left my jacket in church," Bobby said as the boys neared the building. He had served Mass that morning and wore a light jacket to church. It had warmed up enough after service that he forgot all about his jacket until that moment. They all turned and followed Bobby through the church to the back where they kept their vestments. Jason had never been in the back part of the church so Lucas gave him the tour. They met up with Bobby in the "Catholic" side.

"Hey!" Lucas exclaimed as he looked at the cabinet where wine and hosts were kept. "Father Perkins forgot to close the cabinet. You're supposed to check on that before you leave, Bobby."

"I thought Guy was taking care of it today," Bobby answered.

"No big deal," Lucas said as he started to close the cabinet.

"What's in there?" Jason asked.

"The altar wine and the wafers that we get for communion," answered Lucas as he opened the cabinet for Jason to see.

"So that is God in those things?" he asked incredulously.

"Well, not now," Lucas replied.

"The priest has to bless them first," Bobby added.

"What's the difference between the big ones," Jason said as he pointed to the container of the large wafers the Priest used during mass and then pointed at the smaller ones used in communion, "and those small ones? Do they taste different?"

"I don't know if they taste any different but the big ones are the ones the priests use during the mass and the small ones are the ones we get when we receive Holy Communion," Lucas answered. He now wondered if there was a difference. "Maybe we should taste them to see if they are different?"

"No way!" Mickey blurted out. "We'll surely go straight to hell if we do!" Bobby and Lucas broke into laughter.

"They haven't been blessed yet, Mickey. It wouldn't be a sin until they were," Lucas stated matter-of-factly, although he really didn't know. He just decided that was the way it was.

"I think I would wanna know if the one the priest gets is different than the one that you guys get is all I'm saying," Jason said egging Lucas and Bobby on to try one. By this time it didn't take much encouragement to get Lucas to eat one. He took one of the large wafers out of the package, broke a piece off and looking at Mickey's horrified expression, ate it. Everyone waited in silence.

"Taste the same as the ones we get," Lucas finally said as he finished swallowing. "I need something to drink to chase this down."

There was a small sink with water there but no one could find any glasses except for the chalices the priests used for the Eucharist. "Don't even think about it!" Mickey said to Lucas as he saw Luke's eyes focus on the Chalice in the cabinet. "I'll find you a glass."

But by this time the wafer was stuck to the top of Lucas' mouth and he needed something quickly to wash it down. Without hesitating he grabbed the bottle of altar wine that was opened, pulled out the cork and took a swig, much to the horror of Mickey and Bobby. "Ahhhh, that hit the spot."

"WHAT ARE YOU DOIN'?" Mickey shouted at him.

"He's going straight to hell, that's what he is doing," Bobby chimed in.

Meanwhile, Jason, the non-Catholic of the group, was thoroughly enjoying the drama he was witnessing. He never really understood the "eating God" part of the sacrament of Holy Communion and could not quite understand why Mickey and Bobby seemed so upset.

"It's okay, Mickey," Lucas said trying to calm Mickey down. "They don't become the body and blood of Jesus until Father Perkins blesses them during Mass and changes it to Jesus' body and blood. Father Perkins told me that himself." Then turning to Bobby and Jason and offering them the bottle of wine he said, "Want to try some?"

Jason took the bottle from Luke's hand and took a swig and passed it to Bobby. Bobby held the bottle in his hand for several moments before finally taking a drink as Lucas started to reach for the bottle. He then passed it back to Lucas who took another drink before passing it to Jason again. This time Jason handed the bottle to Mickey.

"That's okay, Mickey, you don't have to drink any. I know how much this bothers you," Lucas said as he reached for the bottle. Much to his surprise, Mickey pulled back the bottle, put it to his lips and took a big swallow, nearly choking as the alcohol rolled down his throat. The other boys just laughed and Jason patted him on the back. Then Mickey did the unexpected and grabbed one of the large wafers and ate it. He then took out two more and handed them to Bobby and Jason.

"Guess we can all go to hell together," he said as he chased the wafer with another swallow of wine. The boys laughed and passed the bottle around a few more times. Then Lucas looked at the bottle, which was near empty now.

"Oh shit!" he exclaimed. "We drank most of the bottle."

The boys were all feeling the effect of the wine. Lucas looked in the cabinet and saw there were only two more bottles left. He knew if they finished the bottle and got rid of the evidence Father Perkins would know one was missing. After a brief discussion they decided to put the bottle back with what was left, hoping that Father Perkins would not know how much was in it, only that there were three bottles, an open one and two unopened ones. Then Lucas closed up the cabinets and the three boys, all feeling light headed, left the church. They were all in such a good mood that they decided retribution to Crabby probably wasn't a good idea.

"Let's just put our hands in a prayer position and look serene every time we see her," Lucas said, trying to look serene. "That'll just drive her crazy."

Bobby and Mickey, in their buzzed state, agreed.

That next Sunday church went smoothly. Lucas and Mickey served Mass. Neither of them saw Father Perkins preparing the wine for the service and nothing was said. After Father Perkins headed back to Pirmasens, Lucas and Mickey went back in the church and to the cabinet that kept the sacraments. It was locked. They looked at each other and they instantly knew Father Perkins knew the wine was missing. They thought for sure they were going to get in trouble as they shared their discovery with Bobby. All three boys were looking fairly glum when Todd came up to them.

"What are you punks looking so down for?" he asked. Lucas decided to tell Todd what had happened.

"And you Jackasses didn't ask me to join you?" he laughed. "I should turn you three idiots in."

"You don't have to," Bobby said. "We're sure Father Perkins knows we did it."

Todd looked at the three younger boys, shook his head and smiling said, "I should let you sweat it out a little more but I'm such a nice guy I can't. I overheard Father Perkins telling Mom that he had to lock the cabinet up because he thought a GI had gotten into the wine. He never even suspected you turds." Then he spun around and left the three boys as Guy came over to the group.

"What's going on?" Guy asked.

"Nothing! Nothing at all!" a relieved and smiling Lucas said as the boys headed back towards the apartments. "Let's go play some 500."

Chapter XIII

Sixth Grade — Another School Year Begins

When school started that fall Lucas found out he had Miss Larkin again as his teacher. The school did not renew the one-year experimental program of combining 5th and 6th graders in the same class so Miss Larkin was teaching 6th grade this year. Much to Lucas' delight, most of his friends from Münchweiler were in the class. Bobby, Mickey, Jason, Lester Horry, Joey North, Terry Smith and Lloyd Mize were all in the class. Benny Franklin was in a different class and Pat Simmons had moved back to the States in August.

There was one person that was in class that Lucas would have preferred were in another class; Tara Morton. When Ivan had extended his tour in Germany, Sgt. Morton did, too. He and Ivan were good friends, having served together much of their Army careers. Lucas didn't understand all of the details of how his father got assigned to different locations and he really didn't care. All he cared about at this time was he was happy living where he was and enjoyed the companionship of his buddies. He could put up with Tara during school if he had to.

It didn't take long for Tara to dig into Luke, but, Miss Larkin put a stop to it right away. "We are going to learn to respect one another this year," she started. "I will not tolerate name calling, bullying, or teasing. Well, at least not malicious teasing. I want you all to enjoy this class and hope you come out of it with both knowledge and be a little more prepared to join a civil society."

It was obvious to all that Miss Larkin was pleased to have Lucas in her class again. Sara Carson, who had been in Miss Larkin's class with Luke last year, was in his class again. Lucas liked Sara. She was nice, smart, and had a good sense of humor once she opened up. During the first six weeks, Miss Larkin used Sara and Lucas to help her with her new class. Much of the early lessons were things Sara and Lucas already had been taught in the combined 5th and 6th grades class. When the class would break up into study groups there were usually three groups with

Miss Larkin leading one and Sara and Lucas each leading one, much to the dismay of Tara Morton. Lucas really didn't want to be a "student teacher" but it didn't take long for him to see the wisdom of this assignment. Much of that first six weeks was boring to Lucas and to Sara since it was all material they already knew, so it would have been hard for him to stay engaged in the class if he wasn't helping teach it. The two of them spent some of their recess time staying in class with Miss Larkin helping to set up their teaching lessons. Lucas found himself liking Miss Larkin more and more. He knew even before his buddies began to tease him about it, that he still had a crush on his teacher. Luke was also smart enough to know that nothing would come of it. He had to laugh at himself when he imagined Miss Larkin paying any kind of romantic attention to an eleven-year old boy. Besides, she was still dating Mr. Knoll and he did have to admit they made a good couple. Sometimes, though, his mind would imagine him growing up and being with Miss Larkin.

This didn't last too long. Near the end of the first grading period a new family, the Durbins, moved into Münchweiler. They had four kids, two in the 6th grade, Molly and Henry. Henry was older but had been held back a grade. Molly ended up in Miss Larkin's class. She had dark red hair that didn't quite make it to her shoulders. She was a few inches shorter than Lucas with deep dimples and an infectious smile. Lucas started developing a fondness for Molly and Molly for him. He had never had a girl pursue him before and he liked the thought of it as much as he liked Molly. It wasn't exactly a burning hot relationship. They liked to hang around together, and the rest of the Cricks liked her, too. Molly and Henry hung out with the boys and had become good friends with Todd Ledahawski. Lucas and Molly would ride the bus together, go to the movies, and spend time at the snack bar, but when it came to being with his buddies, Luke put the romance on the back burner. Molly didn't seem to mind too much. It was one of the things Luke liked about her. Often, she acted more like one of the guys and didn't mind the time Lucas spent with his friends. She would just spend time with her girl friends.

One Saturday afternoon, the whole gang was hanging out next to the playground between Buildings D and E tossing around a football. Earlier in the morning they had played "Kill the man with the ball" which was a simple game. The game was started with the football being tossed in the air and everyone trying to catch it. If you were the lucky or unlucky one, depending on your perspective, who caught the ball you had to avoid being tackled by everyone else. Once you were tackled, the other players would form a circle around the player who was just tackled and he would toss the ball in the air for the next person to catch. It was usually a game the boys played while waiting for enough boys to show up to put together a pick-up football game. That usually required a number of the older boys to show up to have enough players to have two teams with at least six members on a team.

On this particular day they did not get enough guys to show up to have a game and after exhausting themselves playing "Kill the man with the ball" they had gone home to eat, agreeing to try again after lunch. Lucas was the first to get back outside and he had Ike and Joey with him. Lucas figured if none of the older boys showed up, some of the younger ones could play and they could still get a game together. Both of his brothers liked playing football, and they were better than some of the older boys. Lucas thought that was because the three of them were always wrestling or boxing each other. They got used to being hit or strong armed and did not shy away from the physical play of football. Luke liked the way that Ike could weasel his way into the backfield during pass plays and tackle or force a quick throw from the opposing quarterback. Joey was a fearless tackler, and playing with older boys didn't seem to bother him in the least. He was faster than most of the older boys, too. Lucas would brag about his youngest brother, telling people that next to himself, Joey was the fastest kid on Post.

Soon, Mickey and Jason showed up followed by Molly and Henry. Bobby and Todd were heading their way as Molly came up to Lucas and kissed him on the cheek.

Luke's two brothers broke out in a little jingle, "Molly and Luke sitting in a tree. K...I...S...S...I...N...G! First comes love, then comes marriage, then comes Little Luke in a baby carriage!"

Lucas punched Ike in the arm as Joey quickly got out of harm's way, laughing as he put ground between him and his older brother. Henry repeated the jingle and was quickly slapped in the back of the head by his sister. "Watch yourself, big brother. I don't want to have to hurt you."

They all broke out in laughter as Bobby and Todd joined the group. Todd looked around and then looked back by the buildings before saying, "It doesn't look like we're going to get enough guys to play. I just saw Joey North and TJ heading towards the hospital and I know his older brother, RT, is hurt and can't play. I checked on Andy Kirkland and his mom said he was bowling with Denny Mantra and Jeff and John Dolan."

"I don't feel like playing "Kill the man with the ball," Lucas said as he tossed the football to Joey.

"How about a little Stretch or Chicken?" Todd asked as he pulled his penknife from his pocket and unfolded it.

These were two games played with a knife and all of the boys had one. It was part of what Lucas liked calling "standard issue," a phrase which he picked up from his dad. "Stretch" was a game where two players faced each other and stood about six feet apart with their feet together. One would start by tossing and sticking the knife in the ground near, but to either side of the person he was facing. If the knife stuck in the ground that person would have to move his foot to that spot. Then it was his turn to throw the knife. It would go back and forth eventually leading to the opponents using their hands to stretch to the knife. The game ends when one of the players can no longer stretch enough to reach the knife.

"Chicken" was a little more dangerous. In this game the two opponents would again face off at about six feet apart with their legs spread to a little more than shoulder width. The knife would be tossed in between the legs of the opponent and if it stuck in the ground the person on the receiving end of the toss would have to move their feet to the spot where the knife stuck. As the feet got closer and the area to stick the knife got smaller, the first one to move his feet as the knife was tossed would lose.

"I'll play," Jason said.

"Okay," Todd answered, "you and me first, Jason."

"I got winners!" Henry shouted.

"I'm next!" Luke yelled as the rest of the boys called out for their positions to play. "Ike, you and Joey can't play. Mom would kill me if you got stuck."

"Aw, Luke," Ike whined, "that ain't fair."

"That's just the way it is," Luke stated. There was no more argument from his two younger siblings.

They started out playing stretch, going through everyone with Henry ending up the final winner. Henry then decided to change the game. "Let's play chicken now."

"I'm out," Jason declared.

"Me, too," Mickey added.

"I'll take you on, Henry," Todd said as he stood up from the spot in the grass where he was sitting and moved to stand in front of Henry.

"I'll go next, again," Lucas added. He was still bothered by the fact he got eliminated in his only game of stretch.

"Lucas, don't play this game," Molly pleaded as she tugged on Lucas' arm. "Henry never loses and I don't trust him."

"He has to get by me, first," Todd declared. "And that ain't gonna happen."

Henry just grinned at Todd as he took the knife by the blade and tossed it between Todd's feet. It landed just about in the middle. Todd moved his left foot to the spot where the knife was stuck in the ground, picking up the knife as he did and placing the blade in his hand. He threw it between Henry's feet landing it just inches from his right foot. Henry didn't budge. He then moved his right foot to the knife, picked it up and looked at Todd.

"That was pretty damn close to my foot, big guy." As he placed the blade between his thumb and fingers he said, "Now I'll show you how close I can come to your foot."

He flipped the knife between Todd's feet landing a few inches from his left foot. Todd flinched a little but did not move his feet. Then it was his turn again and he placed the knife just in the middle, between Henry's feet. As the distance between their feet narrowed, each of the boys grinned at each other. This time as the knife left Henry's hand, Todd moved his foot.

"Hey, you asshole!" he shouted at Henry, "You would have stuck me if I hadn't of moved."

"Aw, you're just a sore loser," he replied. "Come on, Luke, your turn."

"Lucas, don't play this game," Molly pleaded.

"Go ahead, Luke!" Ike shouted. "Show 'em you're not afraid."

"Yeah!" Joey chimed in as his oldest brother got up and moved into position in front of Henry.

"You're the champ, Henry," Lucas said. "You go first."

Henry quickly stuck the knife halfway between Lucas' feet. Luke followed with a similar placement between Henry's feet. They were on the fourth round with very little space left between either of their feet. Everybody stood up and circled the two contestants.

"I'll bet you a dime Luke moves this time," Bobby said to Mickey as Henry prepared to toss the knife.

"You're on," Mickey replied.

The words were barely out of Mickey's mouth when Henry cocked his wrist to throw the knife. Lucas did not take his eyes off Henry's face as he watched him make his toss. He was still looking at Henry as he felt this sharp pain in between his second and third toes. He was still looking at Henry when Henry's mouth dropped open, then, looking up at Luke's eyes, he turned and ran. Lucas looked down as he heard the cries from his friends and brothers. There it was, the knife sticking into his tennis shoes. He could feel the blood running between his toes and he still did not move. Finally, Molly came leaping over Joey who had bent down to look at the knife in his brother's foot, and grabbed the knife, pulling it out of the shoe and Luke's foot.

"Oh, Lucas!" she cried out, "Does it hurt?"

"No, not really ... well ... maybe a little bit," he answered as he finally moved his foot. Then he sat down in the grass as Molly helped him get his shoe off. The others gathered around to look at the wound as Molly then yanked his bloody sock off. Once Lucas raised his foot the bleeding almost stopped. As Molly dabbed away the blood with Luke's sock they could all see the small cut in between his toes where the knife had been. Another inch towards Henry and it would have missed him altogether. It didn't take long after Molly held the pressure on the cut for it to stop bleeding altogether.

"You going to the hospital, Luke?" Ike asked.

"No, I don't think so," Lucas replied. "It really doesn't hurt that much. It stings more than anything. I'll put some iodine on it and a Band-aid. It should be fine." Then turning to Molly, "I'm gonna kick your brother's ass."

Molly broke out into laughter. More as a relief than anything as she realized Lucas was okay. "I'll help you!"

That December during the Christmas vacation, a huge snowstorm hit the area. The kids loved it. That morning there wasn't a grade school or high school kid who wasn't sledding or watching the kids sled down by Sewer Hill. The German kids came too. Lucas got to try out his new ski glasses he had gotten from his German cousin Eckhart as an early Christmas present when he, along with Uncle Fredric and Aunt Helga, came for a visit a week earlier. There was almost eighteen inches of new snow on the ground and it was blinding. For those that had a good sled run and made it all the way to the drainage ditch, they found themselves digging their sleds and themselves out over two and a half feet of snow. Lucas had to laugh to himself as he watched some of the younger kids just trying to make their way through the deep snow.

By noon, most of the kids were heading home for lunch or just leaving due to exhaustion. Lucas could not remember when he'd had so much fun in the snow. Besides the sledding, there were multiple snowball fights. While sledding down the hill, Lucas got into one after he was hit on the side of the head by Hans. The strike caused him to flip over and the sled rode him down the rest of the way. The snowball fight ended with Hans and Lucas rolling in the snow, pushing clumps of snow in each other's faces.

When Lucas got home he had to change clothes because he was completely soaked. Ike and Joey had been with him and had to change, too. All three of the boys quickly got into dry clothes and sat down to a hot bowl of chili their mother had made. They ate quickly, and began to get their boots back on.

"Whoa, boys!" Maria said as she entered their bedroom. "You all have had enough for one day. I don't want you getting sick."

"But Mom," Lucas objected, with a whine in his voice, "we may never have another great snow like this. All of my friends are going to be back out there."

"Well ... okay, Lucas," she said, giving in to him. "But Ike and

Joey should stay in."

Both of the younger brothers began complaining and pleading their case when Lucas stepped in, "I will watch them so they don't get too cold or wet, Mom. You should let them go back out, too."

Maria was taken aback by Lucas' statement. Usually, he was trying to get out of taking his younger brothers. "Are you sure, Luke?"

"Yes, ma'am. I'll keep a close eye on Joey and if he is getting too cold or wet, we'll all come in."

"Okay, you better, Luke."

"I will," Lucas answered as his two younger brothers cheered and both hugged him around the waist saying "Thank you, thank you!" several times over. Then all three finished lacing up their boots, put on their heavy sweaters, which were still a little damp, and their coats. After hugging and kissing their mother and thanking her for letting them go, the two younger boys followed their older brother out of the house.

"That was really cool of you, Luke," Ike said to his big brother.

Lucas smiled at him and said, "Hey, this is the coolest snow day of our lives. I wouldn't want you two to miss out on enjoying it … even if you are a pain in the ass, Ike."

It was around 1:30 p.m. when the boys got back to the sled hill. Most of the kids were back out but the ranks had diminished some. A lot of the other mothers felt the way Maria had only they hadn't given in to their children. This time the boys were only there for a couple of hours. The clouds had left and with the clear sky, the temperature started to drop quickly as the afternoon wore on. Lucas could have stuck it out longer but Joey was beginning to look a little blue, and between sled rides, Lucas could see him shivering. Keeping his word to his mother, he gathered up his brothers and their sleds and, over their weak objections, headed home.

As they were leaving, Bobby and Mickey came up to Luke. "Hey, Luke. Can you come to the Teen Club tonight?" Bobby asked. The Teen Club was a bit of a misnomer since they let in anyone eleven years old and older. There were not enough teens to justify operating the club if Special Services didn't allow the age limit to be lower than a typical Teen Club would normally be. It did bug some of the true teenagers, Susan being one of them, but there wasn't much they could do about it. Lucas' age group had the largest numbers and a lot of the older teens didn't attend much anyhow, so without them, the club would have been closed.

"I'm not sure if my mom will let me," Lucas answered. " I had to beg her to let us come back out."

"I know what you mean," Bobby said. "I don't think my mom would have let me and Todd come back out if my dad wasn't home. If he hadn't told her she should let us come back out, I don't think she would've."

"I didn't have any trouble with my mom when I asked," Mickey added.

"That's cause she doesn't love you," Lucas said jokingly as he and his brothers waved and headed home.

Surprisingly, to Lucas, his mother said he could go to the Teen Club after dinner. She had him run some of his wet clothes down to the dryer in the laundry room, but he had to wait until Mrs. Barton, Joey North's mom, was done using the two dryers. Use of the dryers was always a problem in the winter. There were a lot of clotheslines behind the building and plenty of washing machines, but there were only two dryers and they were always in demand. Mrs. Barton was kind enough to let Lucas dry his clothes in one of the dryers before she put her last load in it. She said she could wait until the other dryer was finished and put the clothes there. Lucas put the load in and went back home, returning 45 minutes later to get them. When he got to the laundry Mrs. Barton was gone and his clothes were folded and stacked on the counter. He made a mental note to remember to thank her when he saw her again.

Dinner was fun that night as his brothers told their father all about their day. Lucas didn't say much, letting the two of them do most of the talking. Once in awhile, Ivan would ask Luke a question, but for the most part he just listened to his two youngest sons rattle away. Lucas was happy his dad was in a good mood. He knew the whole time he was preparing to head out for the night, that Ivan could veto his mother's approval of him going out.

After dinner, Lucas helped clear the table, then went and got bundled up. His glove inserts were still a bit damp but he figured they would be getting wet again when he began throwing snow balls and that, he knew, was a given.

"Home by ten!" Ivan shouted at him as he headed out the door.

"Yes, sir!" he answered as he closed the door and flew down the stairwell. He went to the Ledahawski's to see if Bobby had left yet. He hadn't. He and Todd were just getting their coats on when Lucas arrived.

"You guy's ready?" he asked.

"You bet." Todd answered. "Bye, Mom. We'll be home by ten o'clock."

As the three of them exited the apartment building Mickey was just crossing the street to see if they were ready. The four boys then headed towards the main hospital complex where the Teen Club was located.

As they walked down the street nearing the first barracks they noticed a couple dozen GIs in the area between it and the next wing of the hospital. In fact, there were a lot of the older kids there, too. Andy Kirkland was there as well as Susan's friends, Jeff and John Dolan. Lucas didn't care much for either of those two. Robby Smith, Earl Clayton and Don Davis greeted the three boys as they got closer. They were all Todd's age.

"We're getting ready for a giant snowball fight," Earl Clayton told them as they reached the older boys.

The soldiers of the 208th Signal Company were constructing a huge snow wall between their barracks and the building to the east. There was a large open area between the buildings. As Don Davis explained, it all started by a few of the GIs from the 208th rolling up huge snowballs to build a giant snowman. Somehow that had changed during the building of the snowman and a large wall began to take shape. A few of the soldiers from the 15th Evac had come by and started throwing snowballs. One of the soldiers came up with the idea of a snowball fight between the companies with the wall being the defense that would be manned by the 208th. As the wall began to grow so did the participants as more and more of the soldiers from the other barracks began to show up along with the teenagers and younger kids heading to the Teen Club. Now as the wall was getting to be around six feet high, people were beginning to make their arsenal of snowballs. Two Sergeants took charge, began setting up the rules, and splitting the kids into two different groups. Lucas, Todd and Mickey were assigned to the defense of the wall.

As some of the other kids got wind of what was going on, more and more of Luke's friends were joining the imminent battle. Guy joined the defense, as did Henry Durbin, Lester Horray and Lloyd Mize. As the boys exchange "hellos" excitedly, the Sergeant from the 208th got out in front of the wall and hollered at the top of his lungs, "THE BATTLE OF MÜNCHWEILER ARMY HOSPITAL WILL BEGIN IN TEN MINUTES! PREPARE FOR ATTACK!"

Just as he completed the last word, several of the GI's from the 225th and 15th pelted him with snowballs. He quickly headed for the shelter of the wall, cursing the attackers as he ran. The battle didn't wait ten minutes since no one let up after the initial tosses. The younger boys were mostly relegated to making snowballs for the GIs but they took it upon themselves to throw some, too. The battle lasted over half an hour as the attackers charged and retreated trying to take the "wall" while the 208th fought them back.

"This is a blast, Luke!" Mickey said as they both released snowballs at their enemy.

"It sure ..." but before Lucas could finish his sentence a snowball caught him on the side of his head, knocking him down in front of Mickey. "IS!" he finished as he jumped up laughing and wiping the snow off of his cheek.

The snowball fight finally ended as the attackers breached the wall and the snowball fight transformed into wrestling matches and small skirmishes that covered a lot of the open field towards the housing area. There was no "official" ending of the battle. It just petered out as the tired, wet, and cold participants began to drink beer, talk and leave, most laughing as they went. The boys went to the Teen Club for a short while to warm up and drink some hot chocolate, the whole time telling their tales of the battle.

"I'm wet and cold," Lucas said to the others as he put his coat back on. "I need to go home and change to something dry. See you guys tomorrow!"

"I'll go with you," Mickey said as he followed Lucas out. Todd and Bobby caught up with them shortly after they began their trek up the snowy street towards the housing area. Lucas was happy to get home and get out of his wet clothes. His mother suggested he take a warm bath, which he did. He went to bed early that night after telling Ike and Joey all about the snowball fight. It didn't take him long to fall asleep. It had been a fun day and night that he would remember for a long time.

Chapter XIV

1962 — A New Year of Adventures

The end of 1961 was pretty uneventful after the big snowball fight. Lucas was having a good year in school and the Cricks played on and off (mostly off) the post through the Christmas vacation. They explored the entire fort, underground, through the heating tunnels. By this time they had learned where the cats were that carried the fleas and managed to stay away from them. The hikes they took to Three Lakes were fun in the snow, with the creek almost iced over, only flowing down the middle of the creek. The lakes were frozen over but not thick enough to walk on.

The kids also got to go to the skating rink at Ramstein Air Base through the Teen Club. Lucas had never skated before and was reluctant to get out on the ice after falling on his first two attempts to get into the rink. The rink was huge, built in an airplane hanger with a high, arched ceiling. There were windows near the top at each end of the building and florescent lights hanging from the ceiling. He was about to give up when his sister Susan and Andy Kirkland dragged him out and pulled him around for a few laps. After putting up a little resistance, Lucas gave in, and by the time the day had ended he had learned how to skate and had one of the most fun times with his sister that he could remember.

Through the whole winter the Boy Scouts met once a week on Tuesday evenings. Captain Harley had coaxed Private Albert Tate into helping him as one of the volunteer Scout Masters. Albert was nineteen years old and an avid hiker. He had crossed paths with the boys several times on hikes they did to Three Lakes. He would always stop and talk to them and tell them about the history of the area. Captain Harley wanted to get the Troop into more activities than their annual campout and the few Scout Round-Ups they went to in Kaiserslautern and Ramstein. Private Tate insisted all of the boys just called him Al. He made plans with Captain Harley and Specialists Cooke and

Tyler, their baseball coaches, to hike to a castle near the village of Merzalben. In spite of the war, it was mostly intact, but it was abandoned and did not get many visitors. They had planned the hike for the last Saturday of January.

The weather forecast for the day of their hike was for clear skies and cold temperatures. It had been snowing on and off all winter. They had just had a warm spell that melted much of the snow on the ground … it was mostly patchy with some large drifts along the north-facing hillsides. They all met at the back gate. Lucas and some of the other boys exchanged glances and smiles as they waited for Coach Tyler to come with a key to the lock that was on the gate. Lucas thought it best not to show Captain Harley how to get through the gate without the key.

"It's damn cold," Bobby yelled as he jumped up and down to get warm.

"Watch your language, Bobby," Captain Harley shot back at Bobby. "Scouts don't cuss."

"Which ones don't?" Guy wisecracked, as Lucas just turned away, shaking his head and stomping his feet in an attempt to keep warm. Albert looked at Guy, shook his head and smiled, saying nothing as he snapped an icicle off of the roof overhang on the guard shack. He knew the boys often went off Post through the back gate. As cold as it was, they all wanted to get moving. Albert could only guess how much self-control it must be taking for the boys not to show Captain Harley how they get through the gate so they could get this show on the road.

"It's about time," Guy said as he spotted Tyler and Cooke approaching. The rest of the Troop all turned to look in the direction Guy was facing. They began cheering as the two GIs reached them.

"What? Are you babies cold?" Tyler teased them as he unlocked the gate. The boys began pouring through the open gate.

"Hold on Troop!" Captain Harley yelled, trying to get control of the situation. "We need to do this as an orderly group not as a mob. Private Tate will be in the lead. Then the rest of you need to hike two abreast as long as we are on the dirt roads. Once we get to the path, it is single file. Specialist Cooke, you take up the rear and make sure we don't lose anyone."

"Yes sir," Cooke responded. With that said the boys quickly paired off.

"Can I hike with Al?" Lucas asked.

"Sure you can," Private Tate answered before Captain Harley could respond. "I'd love to have you hike with me." Al knew from his previous encounters with the boys in the woods that Lucas was usually the leader of their hikes unless one of the older boys like Andy Kirkland was with them. They talked as they hiked down the road at a pretty good pace. Lucas knew Al was holding back more for Captain Foley than for the Scouts. He called it his "leisurely" pace. Lucas had to chuckle to himself. He wasn't sure he wanted to see Al's fast pace if this was his leisurely pace. It was easy enough for all of the boys to keep up. Benny Jefferson and Lloyd Mize were the two slowest and the pace had to be set based on their ability to keep up. For Benny, this would be his only hike with them. His father had orders for the States and he would be leaving in a couple of weeks.

When the Troop reached the trail they needed to take off of the road, they stopped for a break. "How's everyone doing?" Jim Cooke asked. Most gave a thumbs up or nod or just yes. Cooke turned to Benny who was sitting behind him on a boulder. "How about you, Benny? You doin' okay?"

"Yeah, Coach, I'm good," he answered. Benny was pretty red in the face, which prompted the extra inquiry from Jim Cooke, but Lucas could tell he was feeling okay. Luke was used to Benny's red face. He had a light complexion and when he was in the cold he got pretty red, but it was no reflection on his stamina.

They didn't linger long. It had warmed up some, but it was a biting cold as the Scouts gathered their packs and began following Private Tate down the trail. Lucas had dropped back to the middle of the group to be with Mickey and Jason. The three of them, along with Bobby and Guy, had spent a lot of time hiking in the hills that surrounded the post and village of Münchweiler. They knew the area fairly well but this was an area that was new to them. There wasn't much conversation, but as they passed certain rock formations or remnants of bombed out structures from the War one of the boys would state, "we have to come back here" as they made mental notes of where they were and noted some type of markings that would allow them to find these "neat places to explore" that would not be as easy to locate during the warmer months when the vegetation was thicker. Many of the structures appeared to be old farmhouses or out buildings. They had vegetation growing in and over them that, at this time of the year, were leafless. It would certainly look different when the plants leafed out.

The castle was about four miles from the post. It took them an hour and a half to get there with a couple of rests on the way. The trail met an old road going up to the castle. As they got to the road the boys could see parts of the castle sticking up through the trees. The last few hundred yards was a very steep uphill climb.

"There it is," Al Tate said, stopping and pointing, more for Captain Harley than for anyone else. The boys cheered. Lucas took off at a run up the hill. The rest of the Troop charged after him. They were all yelling as they ran. Captain Harley started to stop them with a "wait ... wait" when Gus Tyler put his hand on his shoulder and said, "Captain, I think you better just let them go. I don't think they'll hear you anyhow."

Captain Harley turned to Gus and said, "Yeah, I guess you're right. There's no stopping them now. Let's gather them all in the main courtyard after they've burned off a little of their energy."

"Yes, sir," Gus Tyler answered. He then turned to his good friend, Jim Cooke. "Let's gather up the Troop before they get too scattered." They both went out to round up the boys who were already exploring the castle. It took a good fifteen minutes for them all to finally reach the courtyard in the center of the castle. The castle was a fairly small one, at least by the standards that Lucas had seen in the various castles he had been able to visit since living in Germany. Most of the ones he had seen were renovated and were set up as tourist attractions. This one was unoccupied and it was obvious there had been no repairs or upgrades done to it. It was interesting to see one that hadn't been restored not badly damaged. There was some evidence of bullet holes in a few of the exterior walls, but nothing to indicate anything more than small arms had been used around it. The moat was heavily overgrown with vegetation but easily distinguishable as the castle moat. Most of the castle was covered with moss and vines. It also had a lot of areas that had large icicles hanging from it where rainwater or melted snow had run off the turrets that made up the corners of the castle's wall. The stone that made up the walls seemed to have multiple colors in it as the sun danced off it where it poked out through the moss and vines.

"Gentlemen, may I have your attention?" Captain Harley bellowed. He cleared his throat as the buzzing of the boys' chatter quieted. "We are going to spend an hour here. Have fun exploring the castle and the surrounding grounds but do not go too far away from the castle. The rule is you have to always be able to see it if you explore the surrounding woods. Also, lets all plan to eat lunch together in forty-five minutes from now. I will let you know what time to gather back here by blowing my whistle like this ..." Captain Harley blew on the whistle three times emitting a sharp, shrill sound so loud that all the boys and the GIs instinctively covered their ears with many of them letting out moans as they did. "Any questions?" He asked as he finished. When he was met with silence, he declared, "Okay, Scouts, go and have some fun!"

The statement was greeted by cheers and an immediate disbandment of the boys as they began to scatter throughout the castle. Lucas, surprisingly, did not race off with the others. He saw Private Tate sitting off to the side on a rock slab. Tate had just finished packing a pipe and was now lighting it up. Lucas broke out in a grin as he approached him. He had seen several pipe smokers in his short life, but never one as young as Al.

"I didn't know you smoked, Al," Luke said as he sat on the slab with Private Tate.

"I don't smoke cigarettes but I have always liked the smell of a pipe," Al replied. "Why aren't you out exploring with the other Scouts, Luke?"

"I have time. I thought I'd see what you were up to," Lucas answered.

Al laughed, "I'm just kicking back enjoying my pipe and this beautiful spot. Reminds me a little of home, except the castle of course."

"Where's home?" Lucas asked.

"Colorado, in a little place not far from Telluride called Ouray. The mountains there are a lot higher and steeper, but the vegetation is similar and breathing this fresh air comin' up from the valley below … well it just allows me to close my eyes and think that I am home."

"Are you homesick?"

"Man, you sure have a lot of questions." He paused for a moment, "No, not really. I wanted to see other places in the world and here I am. This is a beautiful place and I've been able to visit Munich and Paris since I've been stationed here. I think about home sometimes but I'm not really 'homesick.'"

"What did you do back home, Al?"

"Wow, you just keep 'em coming, don't you?" Al said, shaking his head. "I used to ski a lot in the winter and hike and climb a lot in the summer, mostly with my two older brothers and my dad. We'd hunt a lot, too. My two brothers were always real protective of me. We had an older brother, Jonathan, who was killed in the Korean War. Really affected my dad a lot. He didn't want to lose any more of his sons. He didn't want me to join, but my mom was the one who convinced him I had to live my own life and follow my own path. I know she grieved over Jonathan, but seemed to put his death behind her easier than Pop."

"What about you, Luke? Are you homesick?"

Lucas thought for a moment and then slowly said, "No, Al. This is my home. I may have lived in Pennsylvania for more years, but I've lived here for most of what I can remember best, so that makes this my home. Does that make sense?"

"Yeah, Luke, it does. It's hard to remember a lot of when you were really young and those earliest years fade more the older you get, and heck, I'm not that much older than you."

Lucas started laughing, "Bullshit!" He started shaking his head as he got up to go find his friends. "You're almost twice *my* age and could never keep up with me … OLD MAN," he said, punching Al's arm as he ran off.

Most of the boys were exploring in groups. Lucas saw Guy and Jason up on the wall above the courtyard next to the largest of the four towers at the corners of the castle. Luke bounded up the stone steps that curved up to the tower and seeing his two friends with their heads in the window of it, snuck up behind them and, grabbing them by their belts, yelled "BOO!" and pretended to push them through the window, which was about three feet tall and eighteen inches wide.

"DAMN IT, LUKE!" Guy yelled. "You scared the shit outta me!"

Jason just gasped and shot Lucas that look like 'I'm gonna get you for this' as he pulled back from the windows.

"Careful, Guy, Scouts don't cuss, besides, you're always shitin' your pants. So, what are you sissies looking at?" Lucas inquired as he moved to the window to look for himself. He could hear voices of the boys below in the bottom of the tower.

"Mickey, Benny, Lloyd, and Robby are down there in the dungeon," Jason answered.

After carefully checking the location of Guy and Jason, Lucas peeked down into the dungeon. It took a few seconds for his eyes to adjust to the darkness. He was able to hear them before he could clearly see them. They were talking about what it must have been like to be jailed in the dungeon as Lucas backed away from the window. Turning to his two friends he said, "Too bad we don't have any water balloons."

Both Jason and Guy's eyes lit up. "Oh, man, really!" Jason blurted.

"Hey, we can use those." Guy said as he pointed to some four to six inch icicles hanging off the bottom of the rock ledges that ran across the bottom of the north windows.

Without really putting much thought into it, the three boys began breaking off the icicles and dropping them through the window at the boys below. Amid the yells and hollering below, the three could see the icicles shattering around the Scouts in the dungeon as they scurried to get out of the one opening they had used to get in, emerging in the courtyard below.

Lucas, Guy and Jason backed away from the window to look at the fleeing group just as Gus Tyler came leaping up the stairs shouting at the three.

"What the hell are you doing? You want to get someone KILLED?" he screamed as the three boys shrunk away from the intensity of Gus' anger, mouths agape, unable to answer him. "Is everyone okay down there?" he yelled to the group below.

They all nodded yes or answered yes as Gus regained his composure. The three boys had never seen their coach so angry. He took a couple of deep breaths then turned to the three of them and in a calm voice said, "Hey, I'm sorry I yelled at you guys, but do you realize you could have seriously hurt one of your friends? Those icicles from this height could have gone right into one of their skulls."

It was obvious to Gus by the expressions on the boys' faces it was not a thought that had crossed their minds. After giving them a short lecture regarding thinking about the consequences of their actions before they act, he gave them all a pat on the head and had them join the others in the courtyard for lunch. The whole incident could have put a damper on the rest of the day, but being the resilient kids they were, they soon put it behind them. After all, Lucas thought, no one got hurt. He did think about it enough to realize that Gus was right and he would have felt terrible if he had hurt one of his friends.

After the boys ate their lunch, Captain Harley told them all they had an additional hour before they would be heading back to the fort. The boys were all happy they got to spend the extra hour there. This time the Troop did not split up into small groups but decided to play "Army" and split into two groups, one defending the castle and the second attacking it. They had a blast, using pine cones as bullets, although they were harder to find then they were around the bunker since the pine trees were a little farther back from the castle. They battled for the next hour and were pretty beat by the time they started their four-mile journey back, this time at an even slower pace than their trek up. Benny managed to keep up, but just barely. Lucas walked Benny to his stairwell at the end of the trip before crossing the street to his own home. As he left Benny he patted him on the shoulder, smiled at him and said, "Good job Benny. You did really good on this hike."

Benny smiled back and nodded. He was too tired to say anything. Lucas was totally exhausted himself. He cleaned up and got ready for dinner when he got home, but he didn't have much to say to his brothers who were bombarding him with questions about the hike. He helped clear the table then went into his room where he only got about halfway through his new Superman comic book before falling fast asleep.

It was the first Saturday of March 1962. Lucas had just finished eating lunch and was reading *The Mickey Mantle Story* on his bed when Ike came in the room. Lucas looked up at him and thought he was looking a bit sad.

"What's up, Ike?" Luke asked.

"Nothin'," Ike answered with his head hanging down as he plopped on his bed.

"Come on, Ike, you can tell me what's buggin' you."

After a big sigh, Ike finally told Lucas why he was so down. "Billy Washington's dad is getting sent to somewhere call Vet Num and he has to move back to Georgia."

"You mean Viet Nam," Lucas corrected him. "I heard dad and mom talking about it the other day. Some kind of war going on and we have to bail out the French again, dad said. He said that the Army was sending over advisors to show 'em how to win the war."

"I don't care what it is," Ike responded. "I don't see why Billy and his family can't stay here until Sgt. Washington gets back. Billy says his dad has to go for a year."

Lucas let out a soft chuckle, remembering overhearing conversation between Ivan and Sgt. Morton talking about the Army way of doing things. "The Army doesn't work that way, Ike. If dad went, we would have to go back to Pennsylvania and be near Uncle Peter and Aunt Sharon."

"How do you know?" Ike asked.

"When I heard mom and dad talking about Viet Nam, I heard dad say if he were called to go, that's what would happen," Lucas answered his younger brother.

"Do you think Dad will have to go?"

"I don't think so," Luke responded. "I heard mom say he was getting too old to be going off to another war. That made dad kind of mad and he said he just might volunteer but it was such a piss ant war that he wouldn't waste his time," Lucas smiled. "I wouldn't mind if he did go away for a year."

"What?" Ike asked, not believing what his older brother had just said.

"Just kidding, Ike!" Lucas said as he closed his book and hopped up off of the bed. *Sort of! It would be nice not to have the old man around to whop me for a whole year.* "You better go play with Billy while you can."

Lucas then smacked his younger brother on the head as he left their bedroom and took off to play.

★ ★ ★

The last weekend in March was an unusually warm one. Saturday morning after cleaning their room Ike asked Lucas, "Do you want to go out and play catch, Luke?"

Luke thought about it for a moment before answering. He had plans to meet with the guys after lunch to hang out. "Okay, Ike. Let's play."

Joey, who was playing with his toy soldiers on the floor, jumped up and yelled, "ME TOO!" and grabbed his glove.

"Wait, Joey," Lucas commanded. "Pick up your toys first."

Joey didn't hesitate. He scrambled to gather his toy soldiers and place them in the shoebox he kept them in. Lucas and Ike waited. They both wanted to make sure their younger brother didn't get them in trouble with their father. They had already passed Ivan's Saturday morning inspection. The boys had worked on their room the night before so they had very little to clean up after breakfast. Ivan was a bit surprised when Joey had come out to tell him the room was clean and ready for his inspection. They passed with flying colors.

Lucas and Ike picked up their gloves and a baseball and headed towards the door. Their parents were sitting at the dining room table having coffee. Ivan nodded as Lucas told his parents they were going to play catch out in the back of the building. They scrambled down the stairwell, through the basement, and out the back door. Joey and Ike stood on one side and Lucas stood about thirty feet away facing them. They began tossing the ball back and forth. Within a few minutes, Susan showed up with Jeff and John Dolan as well as one of their friends from Pirmasens, Terry. He had come to Münchweiler to hang out with the Dolan brothers.

"Why don't you little punks scram and go play somewhere else," Jeff Dolan said.

"Why don't you scram," Ike shot back.

"Yeah!" Joey added in support of his brother.

Susan looked at Lucas and said, "Luke why don't you, Ike and Joey go play ball somewhere else."

"Why should we?" Lucas replied. "We were here first."

"Because we have some other friends that are going to meet us here in half an hour or so. If we leave they won't know where we went. So be a good little brother and leave."

Lucas thought about it, but there was something he just couldn't stand about the Dolan brothers. They were giving him a smug look that made him not want to cooperate even though his sister was asking him fairly nicely. At least for her it was. He looked at all of them and shook his head no and tossed the baseball to Ike.

"Guess we will just share the space," Luke finally said.

"The hell you will," Susan said. "Now beat it before the guys here pick you up and drag your butt outta here."

Ike and Joey shot a nervous glance at their older brother. They knew Luke well enough to read his body language and it was saying loud and clear "I'm staying." Luke peeked at them out of the corner of his eye as he continued to toss the ball.

"LUKE! I'm not kidding!" Susan shouted.

Without thinking, Luke flipped her the bird. Both Ike and Joey's mouths dropped open. They were used to seeing the Cricks give each other the finger but they had never seen Lucas flip off anyone else, let alone their older sister. It was a reaction that Lucas didn't think about. Like Pandora's Box, now it was out and he couldn't take it back. He could feel his heart start to race. This was new territory for him. He had let his distain towards the Dolan brothers cloud his judgment.

"Oh you little shit!" Susan shot back. "Wait until I tell Dad! You are in *so* much trouble."

Lucas knew she was right and the smart thing to do was to apologize and leave. Then maybe she wouldn't tell their father, although he knew she would have it over him forever. Then he looked at the grins on the faces of the three boys with her and he, again, couldn't help himself. "Screw you!" he responded.

"Come on, Luke!" Susan shouted almost shaking. "You and I are going up to Dad right now."

"Go yourself!" Luke shouted back. "I ain't goin' nowhere."

"That's what you think!" she said. Turning to John Dolan, "Can you guys drag my punk ass brother up to our apartment?"

"With pleasure," John answered. "Come on guys. Let's grab him."

They thought Lucas would try to run and started to surround him but instead he held his ground, dropping his baseball glove and clenched his fists. "I told you, I'm not goin' anywhere."

No sooner had the words gotten out of his mouth, Jeff jumped at him. To his surprise, Lucas swung at him and caught him flush on the jaw, sending him sprawling backwards. Then Terry and John were on top of him. Lucas kept swinging and kicking as Jeff got back on his feet. He grabbed Luke's feet and wrapped both of his arms around them so Luke couldn't kick anymore. Terry and John now each had an arm and shoulder, halting Lucas' ability to swing at anyone.

Turning to her two youngest brothers, Susan told them, "Go home, now!"

Without hesitating, Joey grabbed Lucas' baseball glove and the ball and took off through the basement, to the stairwell and up to their apartment on the second floor. Ike hesitated for a moment, but seeing no way to help his older brother, took off after Joey.

"Bring his ass upstairs," Susan ordered the three boys. Lucas had relaxed once he realized he couldn't get out of their grasp. The three boys picked him up and headed into the building with Susan leading the way. As they reached the bottom of the stairwell going into the basement and started up the first flight of stairs, Lucas could feel Jeff loosen his grip on Luke's legs. Lucas quickly began kicking again catching Jeff just under the chin. With the other two boys squeezing his arms it didn't take long for Jeff to regain control of Luke's legs. They repeated this dance on the landing between the first and second floors with Susan shouting at Lucas to stop fighting as they finally neared the second floor.

They were about three steps from the floor when the apartment door swung open. There in the middle of the doorway was Ivan. The boys stopped in their tracks as Ivan glared at them. Susan started to say something when, without moving the gaze he had on the three boys, stopped Susan in mid-sentence.

"Shut up, Susan!" Then told the boys in a very icy tone, "Put my son down."

Jeff was the first to let go of Luke's legs and as they dropped, Lucas gave him a swift kick in the thigh. Terry and John both let go of him as Lucas gained his footing on the step. Lucas just stood there as they released him. No one wanted to move as Ivan loomed over them.

Turning to Susan, Ivan asked, "What the hell is going on?"

"Lucas flipped me the bird!" she answered.

"What?"

"The bird, dad, you know … he gave me the finger!"

Now, turning his attention back to the three boys standing on the stairs, "If I ever catch any of you little assholes laying a hand on my son again, I'll beat the living shit out of you. Then I'll find out who your fuckin' dads are and I'll beat the shit out of them, too. You got me?"

Jeff, John and Terry turned white. Susan turned red. The three boys began nodding their heads up and down and repeating, "yes, sir … yes sir" over and over again as Ivan looked at Lucas. Luke couldn't really identify the look. It didn't really make him afraid. He already figured he would get a beating for this, but even resigned to that fact, Lucas was surprised Ivan didn't give him that look that just about scared the piss out of him.

"Luke, go to your room and take your brothers with you," Ivan instructed him.

"Yes, sir," Lucas answered. As he started walking by his father, he glanced back at the three boys and glared. *I'm gonna find a way to get you guys!* As he entered the apartment, he saw his two brothers standing at the edge of the dining room, listening to the whole incident unfold. He didn't have to say anything as they turned and headed into the bedroom in front of him.

As they entered the room, Ike turned to Lucas and said, "Sorry, Luke. We shoulda jumped on those punks when they grabbed you."

"Yeah," Joey chimed in.

"No, that's okay, guys. They were too big for you two. You would have only gotten hurt and then I'd have been in more trouble than I already am."

"Dad's really going to take the belt to you, isn't he?" Joey asked his voice shaking.

"Yeah, I expect he will," Lucas answered. The fear he didn't have before was beginning to swell up in him like a big balloon as the reality of what was about to happen started to sink in. He could already feel the belt stinging his butt.

"Do you think, he'll beat us, too?" Joey asked, knowing how many times they all got the belt when one of the three brothers would mess up.

"No, no, Joey, don't worry," Lucas said trying to calm his youngest brother. "This is something, like the cigar, where I'm the only one that'll get it."

All of a sudden, Ike popped into the conversation. He had been peeking out of the door and listening to what was going on with their dad and Susan. "Wow, Dad really yelled at those guys and he is yellin' at Susan now. I think he is on his way back here."

The two younger boys both jumped onto their bunk beds. The door swung open. Ivan stood there looking at Lucas who stood up to face his father. He didn't look mad at all. In fact, he had a nasty looking smile on his face. It was quiet for about half a minute. Lucas' heart was pounding, waiting for his father's wrath.

"Boy, next time put that bird in a cage!" Ivan finally blurted out so suddenly all three of the brothers jumped. Ivan laughed.

"Huh?" was all Lucas could muster.

"I said put the bird in a cage." Then Ivan raised his middle finger of his right hand and took his left hand, curled in a claw like position, and cupped it over the middle finger of his other hand. "See, Luke? Put a cage over it."

Then Ivan spun around, laughing, turned down the hall and closed the boys' bedroom door as he left. The three brothers were all left with their jaws dropped to the floor like a drawbridge to a castle, and their eyes as big as saucers. It took a few moments before it sunk It. Then Joey was the first to break the trance. He cupped his left hand over the right hand of his middle finger and began jumping up and down in front of Lucas singing, "Put it in a cage, put it in a cage, be a good boy and put it in a cage."

Lucas and Ike began cracking up. Lucas didn't want their dad coming back in so he pulled his pillow over his mouth to muffle his laughter, much of which was a release of tension for what his body had just been through. Ike started to mimic Joey and the two of the danced around Lucas mouthing the words so as not to be heard. Lucas had tears as he begged his brother to stop, which they finally did a few minutes later when their mother yelled down the hall that it was time for dinner and to wash up.

When the boys arrived at the dinner table, Karla and Ivan where sitting down and their mother came walking out of the kitchen with a bowl of mashed potatoes in her hands. Susan was not there. Both Maria and Karla were looking at Lucas as the boys sat down. They had this strange look on their faces. It was like they were trying to look at him with a disapproving look but were also trying not to grin.

"Where's Susan?" Joey blurted out, sporting a big grin as he did. He wanted to see her face. She had to know his big brother didn't get punished.

"She's having dinner at a friend's house," Maria replied, which the boys took as "she stormed out," since that was how they described her behavior the last time she got into a argument with her mother and stomped out of the apartment.

Dinner went on as usual. Ivan talked about the upcoming maneuvers he dreaded participating in. Karla talked about her job at the PX and Maria talked about all of them visiting her sister during the Easter vacation. As dinner ended, Karla and her mother cleared the table. The boys asked to be excused, which was mandatory before they leave the dinner table, and started to get up, expecting the almost automatic response from their father. Instead they were stopped in their tracks.

"Hold on boys!" Ivan commanded. "On second thought, Joey, you and Ike can go. Luke, you stay awhile. I got something I wanna say to you."

The two younger boys hesitated a moment, then catching a look from their father, darted for their room. Lucas' body stiffened. *Oh-oh, now it's coming.* After not getting punished for "flipping the bird" he figured he would at least get a lecture from Ivan. Ivan waited until the boys' door shut then turned to face Lucas.

"You popped that goofy lookin' kid pretty good, didn't you?" he started. As Luke nodded affirmatively, Ivan continued. "Yeah, I think he's going to have a pretty good bruise on his cheek. If you had hit him in the eye, it would be quite the shiner by now. Those boys are a couple of years older than you, aren't they?"

"Yes, sir," Lucas answered.

Then Ivan bent over and in a low voice said to Lucas, "You

know, in the Army when you have a guy that screws things up
for the rest of the company, you pull a blanket party on them. Do
you know what that is, Luke?"

"No, sir."

"Well, you wait until you get the guy coming out of someplace
alone, then you and your buddies toss a blanket over him and
beat the crap out of him. He can't identify anyone with the
blanket covering him so no one gets singled out. Are you getting
my drift here, son?"

The light was going on for Lucas now. His dad was telling
him how to get even. He began to slowly nod his head as a slight
smile began to form on his face. Then a new thought hit him,
and looking straight in his dad's eyes said, "Well, if you just have
a bunch of guys and you don't care if the person knows who you
are, do you still need a blanket?"

Ivan burst out laughing! "No Luke, you can just beat the crap
out of him straight up if you like. Make sure you go after one
at a time, though." After a short pause, he said, "Go join your
brothers, Luke."

The next day, Sunday, Lucas got with his fellow Cricks and
told them what had happened. All of them were shocked
that Ivan didn't beat the crap out of Luke. They started firing
questions at him.

"You mean he didn't even bop you on the back of your head?"
Bobby asked, as Lucas shook his head no.

"I would have thought your old man would've broken your
fuckin' finger!" Jason laughed. "Then stuffed it back down your
throat."

They all laughed hysterically with Guy and Mickey adding a
few barbs to the conversation when finally, Robby Smith popped
the question, "So what are you gonna do to get back at those
assholes?"

Everyone stopped laughing and looked at Lucas, waiting for
him to answer. He told them what is dad had told him about a
blanket party, but the entire group felt just the way Lucas did
when his dad told him. They wanted to just thump them openly.
The Dolan brothers were older but there were only two of them
and Lucas was pretty sure he could take the younger one, John,
by himself. They didn't have many friends so the boys weren't

too worried about them getting their buddies to get back after the Cricks. It was Mickey that came up with a suggestion.

"John has been working at the Teen Club, cleaning it up every Saturday morning. He gets done around ten. We could wait for him then."

Lucas thought about it for a second then began to smile. "I think that's a great idea, Mickey. I've seen him come out of there, and he always cuts close to the last barracks and then cuts across the field instead of going up the road. We could wait for him there."

"We have a plan!" Guy shouted. "Now let's play 500!"

With that, the boys all went home to get their baseball gear. Although it was March, it was the warmest Saturday that year, and all of the boys were dying to play ball. Once they got playing, getting back at the Dolans was no longer on their minds. They did begin to think about it as the school week neared its end. When any of them crossed paths with John Dolan, they would look at him, grin and nod their heads, which led to him ask, "What the hell you punks looking at? I'll knock that shit eating grin off your faces," to which they would just continue to grin and nod at him as they went on their way.

Saturday finally came. The boys had agreed to meet at the playground at 9:30 that morning, but Lucas was late. Ivan was tougher than usual with his inspection of the boys' room and made his sons redo their beds and clear the stuff out from under the bed. Joey always thought he could hide his toys there and not get caught, but it never worked. When the boys finally passed inspection, Lucas sprinted out of the house before his mother could tell him to take his brothers. When Luke got to the playground, he was the last one there. Also, to his surprise there were additional volunteers. Besides Bobby, Jason, Mickey, and Guy, Joey North, Robby Smith, T.J. Carson and Don Davis were there, too. T.J. and Don were in the 7th grade with John Dolan. They found out about the plan from Bobby's brother Todd. T.J. had heard about the Dolan's dragging Lucas up to his dad from one of his sisters, Mary Sue.

"I can't stand that punk, John," T.J. stated. "Thought we could help you out, Luke, just in case any of his friends try to jump in." Then T. J. started laughing along with Robby, Don, and Joey.

"Why is that so funny?" Guy asked.

"Because John Dolan doesn't have any friends!" Don Davis shouted out. "We all would like to kick his ass."

Lucas nodded and thanked them for joining in. Then he laid out the plan. It would work even better than he had thought now that there were more of them. Robby, Bobby, Joey and T.J. would wait near the Teen Club for John to come out. They would tell him they were going to kick his butt and force him to run in the direction of the gap between the last two barracks, where the huge snowball fight had taken place. Don, Mickey and Guy come out from the back of the end barracks to force him to turn. When he turned into the gap, Lucas and Jason would be waiting for him. They all left the playground and hurried to their positions, barely getting in place just before ten o'clock. T.J. and his group were still walking towards the Teen Club when John came out.

As John exited the building he looked warily at the four boys approaching him. He cautiously greeted them, "Hey guys. What's up?"

It was T.J. that spoke for the group. "We're gonna make you pay for what you and your brother did to Lucas last weekend."

John's eyes got wide as saucers, then he did just what they were hoping for, he took off running towards the housing area along the edge of the barracks. Joey and Robby stayed in the street and ran parallel to John, making sure he did not run back out that way while T.J. and Bobby chased after him. He was about twenty yards from the end of the barracks when Don, Mickey and Guy who had been watching from the corner of the building, jumped out in front of John. John didn't hesitate as he made a sharp left turn and began running for the door to the barracks at the back end of the gap between them. He was almost on top of Lucas before he saw him. He spun to turn and run the other way when Lucas tackled him. He tried to get up but Luke held him down and punched him a couple of times in the arm and shoulder. T.J. and Robby grabbed his arms and Bobby and Guy grabbed his legs. It only took a moment before he quit struggling as the boys pinned him down. Lucas sat on top of him with his knees on John's biceps.

"So, you punk, how do you like it now?" Luke taunted. "You're not so tough without your brother and Terry with you, are you?"

"Get off of me!" John shouted. "You're gonna be in so much trouble if you hurt me. My dad will make sure your dads all get DRs."

The boys all laughed at him. It was the usual threat from John. His dad was an officer and was very protective of his two sons. Major Dolan had intervened in the past when one of his boys got into a hassle with someone. The gang wasn't too worried about it. There were too many of them and they would all deny any involvement.

"Whatcha gonna do, John, cry?" Guy asked. "Let's see John cry!"

"Go ahead, Luke, smack him!" Bobby yelled, as the other boys all chirped in with similar taunts.

Then Lucas was hit by an overwhelming feeling as he sat on top of John Dolan. The "let's see John cry" struck a nerve in Lucas. This was what his dad did to him. He hated it and now he was here doing it to another person. He knew it wasn't right but he couldn't just let him go after orchestrating the whole affair. As he looked into John's face, he knew he couldn't just beat him up. As the boys continued their encouragement for Luke to punch him, an idea popped into Luke's head.

"I ain't gonna hit him anymore," Lucas said to the disappointment of the other boys. "Let's de-pants him instead." This brought a cheer from the group. They all started chanting, "De-pants, de-pants, de-pants …"

Lucas undid John's belt as he struggled to get loose, protesting the humiliation that was about to be unleashed on him. He had tears in his eyes but was trying desperately not to cry as Jason took off his shoes and Bobby and Guy yanked down his pants. Jason threw the shoes out into the field as Lucas got up. Lucas grabbed John's pants and ran to the tall tree near the corner of the barracks. It took him three throws before he finally got them to stick in the upper branches of the tree. T.J. and Robby let go of John. As he stood up in his underwear the boys all started to head back to the housing area laughing. John stood below the tree looking up at his pants, trying to figure out how he was going to get them down.

"Tell your brother, he's next," Lucas said matter-of-factly. The group all took off and headed back to the playground to hang out.

"I'm glad you didn't beat him up," T.J. said to Lucas as they walked side-by-side back to the playground. "He and his brother are both assholes but I think de-pantsing him was a better way to get back at him. He's never gonna get those pants down in his underwear. He's gonna have to walk home and put on another pair to climb the tree."

"I'm glad, too," Lucas replied. He really liked T.J. His entire family was nice, but T.J. just seemed so even-tempered and level headed for his age. Lucas had been hanging out more and more with him and Joey North in the evenings in front of their stairwell. He always seemed to say things that would make Lucas think about what he did and the consequences of his actions. He didn't have anyone else besides Coach Tyler giving him that kind of feedback.

As it turned out, they never did get back at Jeff Dolan. It was fun for a while as Jeff would do everything he could to avoid Lucas and the rests of the Cricks. When Andy Kirkland gave him a hard time about being afraid of some 6th graders, he pointed out to Andy they were almost 7th graders and besides, they were a tough bunch and he wasn't about to fight them all. Eventually, the boys all got back to more important things in their lives, like playing baseball and hiking off post.

Chapter XV

Spring Had Arrived

The end of March Benny's family moved back to the States. Lucas was getting used to his friends leaving. Pat Simmons, Jimmy Parker and Bonnie Lee had all left for the States. Except for the time that Ricky Mason left, Lucas just took it in stride. It was just part of Army life. He wasn't as close with Pat or Jimmy and as much as he had wanted to be, never was close to Bonnie. It was tough on his brother Ike, though, when the Simmons left. Ike was more upset than when Billy Washington left because Kyle Simmons was Ike's best friend.

"It's not fair," Ike whined to his older brother.

"Sorry, Ike," Lucas responded. Then he repeated something Coach Tyler had told him when he got cut from the baseball All-Star team because he was too young. "Life's not fair, Ike, it's just life. Things and people come and go. You just go on."

Ike looked down at the floor. Joey had been sitting on the top bunk bed, not uttering a word. He only nodded his head. Luke looked up at him. *How does he take it when his friends go?* He realized he had never paid attention to Joey when his friends had left. He hadn't noticed any reaction out of him. *I never thought to take the time to ask him.* Nothing kept Joey down, so if he was upset it didn't linger. Still, Lucas vowed he would be a better big brother. In the future he would just ask Joey how he was feeling.

Luke put his arm around Ike, and said, "They'll be other friends and who knows, you may see Kyle again someday."

"Yeah, maybe … but no one could be as good a friend as Kyle was."

The three boys all sat in silence for a while, immersed in their own thoughts. It was just the way life was for army brats. A few weeks later, Bobby and Todd's father got transferred.

It was now April and the Boy Scout Troop was making their plans for their June campout. They met in the day care center, in one of the wings of the hospital. There were two big rooms.

One was full of mini chairs and different little play areas. The other had a few desks, some tables and files. On this night, the Scouts were gathered in the first room while Captain Harley, *Sergeant* Tyler, who had just gotten a promotion, Spec 4 Cooke and *Private First Class Tate,* who also had been promoted since the hike to the castle, were in the adjoining room, leaning over a table. The Scouts were told to "hang loose" while the Scout Masters put the finishing touches on the plan for the set-up at the picnic grounds.

To the boys, "hang loose" meant "horse around" which they did with great enthusiasm. They wrestled each other, played paper, rock, scissors and other games that involved punching or hitting each other. On several occasions, one of the GIs would poke his head through the doorway between the rooms and tell the boys to keep it down. They would all stop what they were doing for exactly the time that the GI was in the doorway, but as soon as he popped back into the other room, the rowdiness would continue.

Earl Clayton and Terry Smith were punching each other in the arm, playing a game called "Inch Punch" in which you couldn't get farther away than an inch with your fist. You then would hit the person in the arm as hard as you could from that distance. The problem that inevitably occurred was one of the participants would draw their fist back farther than the inch and punch his opponent. Lucas had been watching Earl and Terry, who were best of friends, play this game. As it began to escalate, Earl punched Terry pretty hard and being the big guy that he was, almost knocked Terry over. Now it was Terry's turn.

Lucas decided that Earl had cheated and Terry should have an equalizer. He snuck behind Earl and got down on all fours. Terry picked up on it right away and as Earl was bracing himself for a retaliatory punch, Terry shoved him backwards, flipping him over Lucas and crashing into a couple of the mini-chairs that were off to the side. Everyone laughed. When Earl got up he had a big grin on his face and he pointed to Lucas.

"You'll pay for that one, Luke," he said.

True to his word, a few minutes later Earl saw Lucas bending over to pick up a box of crayons that had fallen off one of the shelves, and as he did, Earl picked up a min-chair and hit Luke across his back, knocking him to the floor. Lucas immediately jumped up and started after Earl, who dropped the chair and took off for the other room. Lucas was steaming. This was a bit more than just a "get even" from Earl. The chair may have been small but it hurt when slammed against Luke's back. As Luke started through the doorway between the two rooms he could see Earl standing next to Captain Harley, sticking his tongue out at Lucas and grinning. Lucas pulled back from the doorway.

Knowing that Earl would come out eventually, Lucas stood by the doorway with a mini-chair lifted over his head just waiting for Earl to peek in. Lucas was sure he would before he came back in. For a moment all the boys stopped what they were doing which almost panicked Lucas. Earl would know something was up. Terry picked up on it right away and began waving his arms to the rest of the Scouts in a circular motion to have them continue to make noise and be rowdy. The problem was they did but this time they overcompensated for the silence and began a flurry of noise.

With Lucas standing next to the doorway, chair in the air, primed for Earl's head to pop through to look for him before coming in the room, all the other boys continued making a commotion while keeping an eye on Luke and the doorway. Things took an unexpected turn. The head that popped through the doorway to see what was going on wasn't Earl's. It was Captain Harley's. Lucas realized this as he began the downward movement of the chair but could not stop it before it crashed upon the Captain's head, sending him sprawling out across the floor. Everything stopped as the whole troop looked on, mouths agape, at their troop leader face down on the floor.

Sgt. Tyler and Specialist Cooke saw the whole incident from the other room and came running over to Captain Harley. He was conscious, but dazed as they sat him up. Coach Tyler turned to Lucas, still standing there, in shock, with the chair in his hands. "Luke, you better go home."

"Is he … is he okay?" Lucas sputtered. "I'm so sorry. I didn't mean to hit …"

"Luke," Tyler continued as he took the chair out of Lucas' clenched hands, "just go home. He's going to be okay but you need to go while we sort this out, okay?"

"Okay," Lucas said softly. Then he turned, and after looking around the room at all of the now silent boys, headed for the door.

"Jason!" Cooke yelled. Then more softly, "Go with him. Make sure he's okay."

Jason nodded and took off after Lucas, reaching him just outside the day care center. Jason could see Lucas had tears in his eyes and didn't say anything as he walked down the hall of the hospital alongside his friend. Lucas was the first to speak.

"I'm dead, Jason … DEAD!" he said as they walked out of the door of the building and started up the road towards the housing area. "When my dad finds out he is going to kill me. I really didn't mean to hit Captain Harley."

"I know you didn't mean to, Luke," Jason said, trying to comfort his friend. "Maybe we could all say it just fell on him?"

"JUST FELL ON HIM?" Lucas shouted as he stopped and turned to look at his friend who turned back with his hands raised questionably by his side and his eyes wide open. They both broke out in hysterical laugher, then, wiping the tears from his eyes, "Oh yeah, a damn chair just mysteriously fell out of the sky, through the ceiling and hit Captain Harley squarely on the head."

"Sorry," Jason replied as they both continued to chuckle about it, "it was all I could come up with."

"Let's go to the playground," Lucas said as they continued to walk home. "I don't want to show up at home early or my mom will know something is up. I need some time to think about it."

"When do you think they'll tell your parents?" questioned Jason.

"Hell, I don't know!" exclaimed Lucas as they neared the playground. "I hope they don't call my dad at work. He really will be pissed if they do. He got mad when the school called him to pick me up that time I got the flu. I can just imagine how he's gonna be when he gets called for this."

The boys sat on the sand box when they reached the playground, staying in the most dimly lit portion of the area. The streetlights from the cul-de-sacs on both sides gave some light to the playground but not too much. If his parents should happen to look out the window or go out on their balcony, they wouldn't be able to tell who it was in the playground. They had been sitting for a few minutes before Lucas noticed Jason shaking. Turning to face him, Lucas asked, "Jason, are you okay?"

Jason spun around and burst out laughing so hard he sprayed Lucas with spit.

"What the hell?" exclaimed Lucas, wiping the spray off of his face.

"I'm so sorry Luke," Jason sputtered. "I just starting picturing Captain Harley sprawled out on the floor in there and you standing … ha, haaa, haaa … over … haa … over him with the cha … cha … chair in your hands."

Jason couldn't say any another word as he continued to laugh uncontrollably. Lucas couldn't help himself and he, too, began to laugh just as hard. They both laughed so hard they had tears in their eyes. They could have gone on like that for a long time but they turned suddenly as they heard someone coming up behind them. They pulled themselves together quickly and stood to face the three shadows coming their way.

"We thought we might find you here," Guy's voice rang out. "They sent us home early while they all discussed your future, Luke."

"Shit, Luke!" exclaimed Mickey. "You whacked a fuckin' Captain!"

"Laid him out on the floor seeing stars," added Terry Smith, the third shadow of the group.

Jason cracked up again. He started that hysterical laughter that was so infectious it soon had all the boys caught up in it. Guy pretended to hit Mickey over the head with an imaginary chair and Mickey spun around a few time, fell into the sand box and flopped around like a fish out of water. The boys continued on like this for a good ten minutes before Lucas, holding his side from laughing so much, pleaded with his friends to "Stop … please stop! Enough!"

When they finally settled down, Terry looked at his watch. "Well, I better be gettin' home. I'm supposed to come home directly after Scouts. Don't want my old man pissed at me."

They all nodded in agreement and after a few words of encouragement to Lucas, headed home. When Lucas got home his parents were sitting at the table going over some papers and barely acknowledged his presence. Ike was working on his homework at the other end of the table and Joey was in the bedroom looking through his baseball cards. Lucas thought of this as a blessing. He didn't know how he would answer any question they might have regarding the Boy Scouts. He plopped on his bed and picked up a comic book but his mind wasn't really on it. When it was bedtime, Luke lay awake for a couple of hours after the lights were out. *What's gonna happen when Dad finds out? Will he be 'Ivan the terrible' like when I lose a fight or will he be like he was when I flipped Susan the bird? I mean, it was an officer I hit. Maybe the old man'll give me a fuckin' medal.* He finally drifted off to sleep.

The next day, Lucas got caught up in his school day and except for a little teasing on the bus to school, nothing was said about the incident the night before. Lucas knew it was spreading through school like wildfire, but no one said a word to Lucas about it.

"I think they're afraid of you, Luke," Jason told him as they were heading for the bus back to Münchweiler. "I mean, a lot of kids are afraid of you anyhow because of the fights you get into but now they think your just fuckin' crazy! I mean, who would hit a Captain over the head with a chair unless he was crazy?"

"I'm trying not to think about it, Jason," Lucas responded. "I could hardly look at Katie Harley today. I hope her father isn't hurting too bad."

"Some of the rumors going around say that you warned him not to mess with you or you'd hurt him," Jason told his friend.

"That's just plain stupid." Lucas replied. "Who would believe that kind of bull?"

"Kids that weren't even there are telling it like they saw it," continued Jason.

The two boys climbed the stairs of their bus and moved to the back, Jason slid next to the window and Lucas sat by the isle. To their surprise, Katie Harley sat in the seat across the aisle from Luke. Lucas turned to her and meekly said, "I'm sorry about your dad, Katie. I hope he is doing okay today."

Smiling, she replied, "Don't worry about it, Lucas. Daddy is fine. He does have a big lump on the back of his head, but he said he is fit for work and was on his way to the hospital as I headed to the bus this morning." After a short pause, she continued. "He knows you didn't mean to hit him and that you guys were horsing around. He actually likes you and he doesn't know yet what to do, I mean, your father being like he is and everything. He doesn't want you to get beat up by your dad but he feels he has to do something. He is supposed to meet with the other Scout Masters tonight to decide. I just wanted to tell you I know all the stories going around and I know better. Also, to let you know neither my dad or I are mad at you."

Lucas was dumbfounded. It wasn't something he had expected from Katie. He had known her as long as just about any other kid there. Captain Harley had extended his time there so he could continue to provide "the best dentistry" possible for the GIs there. Turning to Katie he smiled, "Thanks Katie, I really do appreciate you tellin' me that."

"You're welcome, Luke." Then with a broad grin coming over her face she added, "But I don't think you should have any fillings done any time soon."

Jason burst out laughing and Katie and Luke joined in. The rest of the kids on the bus just looked on curiously. Seeing Katie Harley sitting next to Lucas was a rare enough sight. Now, knowing what had transpired the night before, to see her laughing it up with Luke left them all wondering.

The next day, school was pretty normal. Except for Miss Larkin pulling him aside just as recess was beginning to ask him if everything was okay.

"Lucas," she started, "I just want to make sure you're okay. With all of this talk going around ... I know you are a decent boy that sometimes gets into trouble, but I cannot imagine you being as bad as everyone is making you out to be over this incident with Captain Harley. What really happened?"

After assuring Miss Larkin that he was fine, he proceeded to tell her what really had taken place. He did tell her that he didn't know what kind of punishment he would get from his dad when his dad found out but told her not to worry about it. He would be able to handle it. Then he went and joined his friends for recess.

When Lucas got home after school, he finished his homework and went out to play. As he left his stairwell he saw PFC Tate walking down the sidewalk towards him. Albert waved as he saw Luke spot him. Lucas turned and started walking down the sidewalk to meet him.

"Hi, Al! What's up?" Lucas asked as the two met.

"Hey, Luke," PFC Tate answered.

"What are you doing here?" queried Lucas.

"I was chosen to take care of a task no one wanted to do," Al said after taking a deep breath. "Is there any place you want to go so we can talk?"

Lucas, now a little apprehensive, said, "Sure, we can go over to the playground and sit on the concrete wall around the sand box."

The two of them walked over to the playground and sat down. "The Scout Masters met last night to decide what to do about the mishap that took place the other night."

"Mishap!" Lucas exclaimed. "Mishap! Shit, Al, I hit Captain Harley over the head with a fuckin' chair! That's a little more than a *mishap!*"

PFC Tate smiled and nodded, "No, you're right, Lucas. This was more on the line of a fucking disaster. Anyway, call it what you want, the verdict of the Kangaroo Court was that you are to be suspended from the Boy Scouts for six months. You won't be able to join the Troop for their annual campout and I'm supposed to tell your parents."

Lucas just hung his head. He knew they would tell his parents but he really hadn't expected to be suspended. In fact, he had never thought about any possible consequences from the Scouts. He was only focused on the punishment he would get from his dad.

They sat in silence for a few moments. Then Lucas looked at Al and said, "Well, my dad ain't home now but my mom is. Guess you better do your job, now."

PFC Tate did not relish this job. In fact, he hated it and knew that he was picked because he was the lowest ranking soldier on the Scout staff. He wasn't surprised when they told him he would have to be the one to carry the bad news to Lucas' parents. All during their meeting, the statement "I just would hate to be the one that has to tell Sgt. Baryshivka" kept popping up. He told Luke he had a feeling the job would fall on him, especially since he had just informed them that he was being transferred to a Company in Ulm, West Germany and would be leaving in a week.

"Luke, I've been thinking about this a lot. First, I want to let you know I am being transferred to Ulm," Al stated. "I've heard enough stories about your dad not to want to tell him about this. So this is what I'm gonna do. I'm going to tell them I told your mother and if she tells your dad, well, that would be up to her."

"She'll tell him," Lucas replied.

"No … I don't think you get what I mean. I am going to tell Captain Harley and the rest that I *told* your mother. I didn't say I really would *tell* her."

"What?" Lucas asked, baffled.

After a deep sigh, Al continued. "Look, Luke, if they want to court marshal me for lying to them, then, hell … they can, but I am not going to be responsible in any way for you getting the shit kicked out of you by your father. None of these guys ever talks to your parents except maybe briefly at one of your Little League games. I just ask that you keep this between us 'til I am outta here next week. Can you do that?"

Lucas was just getting a grasp on what Al was actually telling him. As it sunk in he looked PFC Tate in the eyes and said, "I don't want you to get in any trouble because of me."

"It's okay, Luke," Al replied. "I'm not worried about it as long as you can keep it a secret for just one week. Then, to hell with them! If they really want your dad to know, they can damn well tell him themselves instead of making me do their dirty work."

Lucas could tell Al was upset. He hardly ever heard him cuss and he was spewing cuss words now. "I promise you, Albert Tate, I won't say a word to anyone until you are gone. Even then, well … I'll have to tell Jason and the rest of the Cricks, but I sure won't let it get back to the Troop."

"That's good, Luke. I will let Captain Harley know I told you and your mom. Remember, you're suspended so you can't be comin' to the meetings." Then Albert extended his hand to Lucas. "I've enjoyed knowing you, Lucas Baryshivka. I hope things work out for you. This is goodbye, too."

They shook hands and PFC Tate turned and headed back towards the barracks. Lucas knew he would never see him again. He watched Al walk back the way he had come. *Is it bravery or cowardice that made him decide not to tell Mom and Dad?* Then a warm realization fell over him. It was compassion that made him stick his neck out for Lucas. *I hope I meet more Albert Tates in my life.*

Now Lucas faced another dilemma. He knew if he told his mother she would have to tell his dad. As he walked back towards his stairwell entrance, Joey North and TJ Carson came out carrying their ball gloves, a bat and baseball.

Joey greeted him. "Hey, Luke! We're going to get a game of 500 going. Get your glove."

"What? Oh yeah, sure, I'll run up and get it," Lucas answered.

T. J. looked at Lucas, then tilting his head he asked, "Something wrong, Luke? You look a bit frazzled."

TJ always seemed to be able to read Lucas. Lucas wasn't sure how he looked but he was in deep thought about his problem. He let out a big sigh and then told his two friends about his situation.

"That's not good, Luke," TJ stated. "Whatcha gonna do?"

"Not sure, yet," Luke responded, drooping his shoulders, as the weight of the problem seemed to fall on him like a ton of bricks.

After a few moments of silence, Joey spoke up. "If I were you, I wouldn't tell your parents. Your old man will knock the crap outta ya."

"What can I do?" Lucas asked.

Again there were a few moments of silence and again it was Joey who broke it. "Hey, when all you goof balls are off doin' your Scout thing, TJ and I just hang out down at the Teen Club or we catch a movie or sometimes we just hang out at the playground. Why don't you just hang out with us and go home the same time you would if you were at your Scout meeting. No one would have to know. Anyone else seeing you would just think you quit Scouts."

"I'm not so sure that's such a good idea," TJ said. "If you get caught, you're really gonna get beat."

Before Lucas could respond, Joey piped in, "That's if he gets caught and, hell, if he's going to get the crap beat out of him anyway, how can it be any worse?"

That hit a cord in Lucas. "You know, TJ, Joey's right. At least I can put it off until I do get caught. In fact … I think that's a damn good idea."

TJ just shook his head and grinned at Lucas. "Well, it's your ass. If you want to chance it, I'll hang with you."

"Me, too," exclaimed Joey. "Now go get your glove."

That's how they left it as Lucas ran upstairs to get his glove. ᵗʰree of them went out into the field and started playing

500. It wasn't long before they were joined by most of the rest of the gang as well as a lot of younger kids. When they finished up, Lucas got with his buddies and told them of his plan, or rather Joey's plan, that he was going to follow.

It was Earl Clayton that posed the big question. "How are you going to pull it off? I mean, someone is going to let it slip that you aren't in the Scouts anymore."

"Well, technically, I still am in the Scouts, just suspended," answered Lucas. "Look, our parents don't know a quarter of the shit we do, why would this be any different? As long as everyone that knows about it keeps their mouths shut, it could work."

"Hell, why not?" Guy added. "If my old man whopped me like Ivan the Terrible whops Luke, I'd be doin' the same thing."

It was settled. Every Boy Scout meeting night from the following week until Lucas left Münchweiler, he left his house and headed towards the hospital with Guy and Jason, leaving them at the entrance and meeting up with TJ and Joey. Sometimes they would catch a movie that ended about the same time as the Scout meeting. The boys seldom paid to see the movie. The Sergeant who ran the movie theater would allow the boys to go in free after the doors were closed and the Newsreels started. He allowed them to stand at the back of the theater. At some point about half an hour into the movie, he would let them find seats and watch the rest of the movie. Other times they would go to the Teen Club but as Lucas found out, this was more risky. Once, his sister Sue had come to the Club when they were there. Luckily for Lucas, he was in the bathroom when she came in and Joey ran in to let him know. TJ distracted Sue as Lucas and Joey slipped out the front door.

Most of the time the three of them just wandered around the post talking baseball. This lasted until Lucas moved back to the States. His parents never found out.

It was May now. The weather was getting nicer and the boys spent more time playing baseball and hiking off fort. School was a little boring for Lucas since he had learned a lot of the classwork the year before; and he wasn't hanging out with Molly Durbin anymore. That had lost its appeal for both of them.

It wasn't like they formally split up. They just both started seeing less and less of each other. Molly started hanging out with one of her brother's friends who lived in Pirmasens and Lucas was happy to hang with his buddies. He did miss smooching with Molly, but they hadn't had that many opportunities to be alone so it wasn't like they'd kissed a lot. Besides, Lucas, Jason, and Mickey had played Spin-the-Bottle a few times with Don Davis's older sister Sally; her best friend, Maggie Penn; and Joey North's older sister, Shelia. The three boys thought it was pretty cool that the older girls wanted to play it with them instead of the boys their age.

"Look at the dorks our age," Maggie told Lucas once when he asked. "They're either ugly or they're not very nice guys. You guys are all cute and you act older than your age. Besides, you are a lot more fun to hang out with than they are."

It was true that when the girls saw the boys at the Teen Club they had a lot of fun. The younger boys made them laugh a lot. It was after one of those Saturday afternoons at the Teen Club that Sally and Maggie invited the boys up to the Davis' apartment to play Spin-the-Bottle. It became a Saturday afternoon regular event through the month of May, until school got out.

As much fun as it was for the boys, once summer started they were more excited about their hiking trips off Post. It was warm and the trek to Three Lakes was always a blast. They often walked in the creek that led up to the lakes and swam in the lakes if it was warm enough. School was out and they had been to at least one of the lakes every day. On the second week of June, five of the boys left for the lakes. Jason, Mickey, Guy, and Roby Smith joined Lucas on the hike. The first part of the trail paralleled the train tracks. Very seldom did they see a train on this track so they often walked on the track, especially if the trail was muddy. It had rained the day before so the boys were walking on the tracks. As they approached the train tunnel and were about to leave the tracks for the trail, Lucas stopped. Looking at the steep trail that went up the hillside that the tunnel went through, Lucas could see water still trickling down the middle of the trail. It looked slippery. Then he turned and looked into the tunnel. He couldn't quite see the end of the tunnel because it had a slight bend to it. They had ventured a short distance into the tunnel in the past, but just far enough to see the light at the other side, then, they turned and came back out.

"Hey guys!" Lucas shouted as his companions started to leave the tracks and head for the trail. "Let's take a short cut!" Pointing towards the tunnel, Lucas continued, "We talked about what a short cut this would be if we went through the tunnel. We'd save going up and down the hills and some time."

"What if a train comes?" Guy questioned.

"What are the chances of that?" asked Jason. "In all the times we've hiked along here we've only seen a train go through a couple of times and that was on a Saturday."

"I'm up for it," Robby stated.

"Me, too," Mickey added. "We'd feel the train coming long before it'd get to us and I don't think it's that far to the other side."

The time the boys had gone into the tunnel they had tried to guess how far it was to the light they could see at the other end. It didn't seem like it was that far, and they had often talked about going through but never got up the courage to do so.

Lucas stooped down and put his hand on the tracks. They had done this on the spur that went into the fort once when Lucas and Jason were with Bobby and Todd. It was Todd that told them they would be able to feel the vibration long before the train came. They had gone to the tracks to put pennies on them. They knew the train was coming in that day by all the activity at the loading docks. Lucas remembered how it felt as the train approached. What he wasn't thinking about at this time was that the train going to the hospital was slowing down as it approached the station. The slowdown didn't occur until it was through the tunnel and switched to the spur for the fort. Any other train coming through the tunnel now would be at full speed.

Guy, not wanting to be the only one that seemed hesitant to go through, shouted, "LETS GO FOR IT!"

Guy's yell was so loud, the boys jumped, then broke out in laughter. "Okay, let's go," Lucas said.

They all headed into the tunnel side-by-side. The going was slow at first, until their eyes adjusted to the darkness. It wasn't totally dark inside, but close. Once they adjusted to the lighting they were able to pick up speed but still had to move cautiously. As they looked around they could see that the tunnel was not shaped quite like the entrances, which were pretty vertical along the sides. Throughout most of the way the tunnel tapered down from the ceiling to the sides. They were unable to see very far either way in the darkness but could make out areas of the rock walls that had large chunks of rock that protruded into the tunnel. This was also evident along the tapered ceiling. As they passed through the bend they could see the entrance on the other side.

"Wow, it looks a long ways off," commented Robby.

The going was a little slower as it was more difficult seeing their way with the light in front of them instead of behind them as it had been until they hit the bend. They stumbled a few time on the railroad ties and gravel that covered the area between and next to the track. They were no longer all side-by-side. Lucas and Guy were in front with Jason and Mickey behind them and Robby in between them but back a few feet. All of them were anxious to get through the tunnel. Even though the entrance at the other end was growing larger as they cautiously walked along, it was taking them longer than they had anticipated. There wasn't much conversation except for a few "Hey watch it!" from Jason or Mickey as Robby stumbled into the back of them trying to speed it up some.

They were just starting to relax as the tunnel exit was growing in front of the when all of a sudden Luke stopped.

"What is it, Luke?" Guy asked as Jason, Mickey and Robby bumped into them, with Lucas' sudden stop.

"Do you feel that?" Lucas asked, stooping down to touch the rail.

"Cut it out you dick." Jason chided Lucas. "You're not pullin' one on me."

"No, no, Jason! I'm serious. Feel the track!" Lucas stated in a panicked voice.

All the boys bent down to feel the track. They all felt what Lucas did, a small vibration that was growing stronger as they were feeling for it.

"Oh shit!" Guy uttered.

"How far away do you think it is, Luke?" questioned Robby.

"I have no idea," answered Lucas. "But we better pick up our pace and get the hell outta here fast."

He didn't have to say it twice although they were still limited on how fast they could go by the darkness and the difficult footing. They could feel the vibration getting stronger as the hurried towards the end of the tunnel. The boys' hearts were pounding. Just as the lighting began to get better as they got nearer the tunnel's end, the tracks almost shook beneath them and suddenly they could see the train racing towards the tunnel entrance.

"GET TO THE SIDE OF THE TUNNEL! COVER YOUR MOUTH!" Lucas yelled at his companions. He didn't have to say it twice as they all jumped off of the tracks and stumbled towards the side, ducking their heads as they rushed towards the side. Lucas had remembered the smoke that came in the train when he opened the window on his first train ride in Germany. At the same time as they raced to the side of the tunnel … the train reached the tunnel. The roar was deafening, but just before he could hear nothing else, Luke thought he heard Mickey cry out. Then there was nothing to do but cover his face with his tee shirt and close his eyes. The ground shook like they were in an earthquake as they were engulfed in smoke for what seemed to be an eternity.

The train passed in what was probably less than a minute. It took a few moments longer for any of the boys to open their eyes. The tunnel was still full of smoke but was clearing fairly quickly as a breeze followed the train through to the other side. Luke could hear his friends coughing and feel them waving their arms trying to clear away the smoke. Then he could hear Mickey moan.

"Mickey!" Lucas called. "Are you okay?" Then, squinting, "Where are you?"

Lucas could see the figures of the other three boys but not Mickey. The others began looking around in a panic for their friend.

"I'm here," Mickey answered as he began climbing out of a hole the size of a grave, but only about three feet deep. The other boys, after their vision became clearer with the dissipation of the smoke, rushed over to help Mickey climb out of the hole. He was holding his arm across his body.

"Are you hurt?" Jason asked him.

"My arm hurts like hell." Mickey answered. "Let's get the hell out of here."

"He's right, we need to keep going," Lucas said as they moved back to the tracks. By now, the smoke had almost totally cleared. They could still feel the vibration of the train that had just passed. With Robby and Guy on each side of Mickey they helped him along the tracks to the tunnel's end.

"Damn!" exclaimed Jason. "We were so close! Another couple of minutes and we would have been out before the train came."

As they exited the tunnel the boys looked at each other, wide eyed. "We look like Eddie Cantor!" exclaimed Robby. They were all totally covered with soot and with their eyes as wide open as they were, Robby was right. They all did look like Eddie Cantor, the Vaudeville singer.

"Let's get away from the tracks," Luke told his friends. "Can you climb the hill to the trail, Mickey?"

"Yeah, my legs are okay. It is my arm that hurts like hell. It might be broken."

After they scrambled up the hillside to reach the trail, they all sat down. Jason looked at Mickey's arm. With his father being a doctor, he did have more knowledge than any of the rest of them as to what kind of injury Mickey had sustained. Jason held Mickey's wrist and turned his arm back and forth. It hurt him some but did seem like he had pretty good movement.

"We should head back to the post," Guy stated.

"We can't go back lookin' like this." Mickey said.

"He's right," agreed Lucas. "We have to clean up. Let's head to the little lake. Are you good enough to make it there, Mickey?"

"Yeah, the arm is killin' me, but if I go home lookin' like this, my mom is gonna kill me. This is a new shirt."

"I don't think his arm is broken," Jason added.

"Okay, let's go," Lucas said as he led the way along the trail as it sliced along the hillside. The trail soon dipped through a draw and turned to the south as the tracks continued to the east. As they entered a heavily wooded hollow, they could hear the waterfall. The waterfall wasn't a straight drop but was made up of multiple small drop offs with the water cascading down the hillside from one little pool to another until it reached the hollow. It was one of Lucas' favorite places and always seemed to bring him a sense of calm. It was so lush along the stream at this time of year. During the winter there were often icicles along side of the stream and hanging on the rocks that lined the falls as it dropped down the slope. The trail now paralleled the stream as both continued to drop in elevation. It wasn't long before they reached the first lake. This was one of the gang's favorite hangouts. The pond was surrounded by trees and thick vegetation with a small two-track dirt road coming down the hillside from the west, opposite of where the trail was. This was the road the German forestry workers used to stock the pond. One of the times the boys had hiked to Three Lakes they had come across the workers just after they had released fish into the stream from the pond through a gate next to the overflow structure to the pond. One of the workers spoke English and explained to the boys what they were doing and how the fish that were released into the stream eventually stocked the two lakes downstream, just as Todd had told them on their first hike.

The boys moved over to the open area at the end of the road. It got the most sunlight and although it was a warm day, the difference in the temperature between the sun and shade felt like at least ten degrees. As the other boys stopped, Lucas continued along the narrow path that ran at the edge of the pond until he reached the upper end where the stream entered the pond. Kneeling next to the stream he took off his shirt and stuck it in the stream, rubbing it together in his hands in an attempt to get the soot out. Following his lead, the others did the same. After they had washed their shirts and hung them in the trees they emptied their pants pockets and did the same with their pants. There was very little conversation as they all were recounting their ordeal in their heads.

Finally, breaking the silence, Mickey whined, "Crap, my shirt isn't black anymore, it's grey. So are my pants!"

Looking at the clothes hanging on various tree limbs, Lucas spoke. "I don't think we'll be able to get them any cleaner with just water." They all were grey looking.

"To bad you dicks wore light colored clothes!" Robby yelled at his companions just before turning and jumping into the pond in his underwear. Robby had a dark blue tee shirt and jeans on. They had a grey tint to them but didn't look nearly as bad as the other boys' lighter colored clothes.

"That looks like the best idea yet!" Guy shouted as he jumped into the pond, joining Robby. Soon all the boys were swimming. One by one, they exited the pond and sat in the sun to dry off. Lucas hadn't said much. He was feeling a little guilty since it had been his idea to take the tunnel short cut.

"Are you okay, Luke?" Jason asked.

"Yeah, just thinkin," Lucas replied.

"Oh, shit!" Guy said with a mock startled look. "Lucas is thinking! Isn't that what got us in this sucky situation in the first place. The Idea Man … the great planner … the …"

"Shut the fuck up, Guy!" Mickey shouted at him, cutting him off in mid sentence. He could tell Lucas was feeling bad and that if Guy kept it up he would only piss Luke off. Then the two would get in a fight. It seemed like it didn't take much to get a fight going between Lucas and Guy. They fought each other more than any of the others fought anyone, period. The outcome was always the same, with Luke coming out on top. "Luke will end up kickin' your ass and I don't want to have to listen to you cry all the way home."

Guy did stop. Turning to look right at Lucas he said, "Hey, sorry Luke. I was just kidding. But look at us! We're all sittin' around shiverin' in our underwear, waitin' for our clothes to dry. This wasn't what I thought our day would be like."

"Hey, look at it this way," Jason said, "we could all be just hanging out at the Teen Club or playing 500 but instead, Luke led us on another great adventure."

At that, Lucas let out a chuckle. *Yeah, a great adventure that may have left Mickey with a broken arm and all of us probably getting in trouble when we got home with grey clothes.* The other boys all lightened up and began chatting about the tunnel. They shared how they were feeling with train bearing down on them in the dark and how they could barely breathe for a few minutes while they were engulfed in smoke.

"It doesn't look like we will make it to the big lake today," Lucas said matter-of-factly. "It's going to take at least another half hour or hour for our clothes to dry. We won't have time to get there and get back to the post by five o'clock."

"That's fine with me," Robby said as he fell back to the ground from his sitting position. "I could stay here all day."

He was right. As the sun moved overhead, the lighting kept

changing how their little piece of paradise looked. It was so beautiful; the reflection of the trees on the pond; the sound of the waterfall tumbling down the hillside, the leaves rustling with the light breeze. As it turned out, it was more like an hour and a half before their clothes were dry enough to put on. When they finally dressed, all but Robby shook their heads as they looked at each other in their grey outfits. Robby's clothes didn't look much different. As Mickey finished lacing his sneakers, he looked up to see the rest of the boys already starting for the trail.

Turning to Mickey, Lucas asked, "You ready, Mickey?"

"Yeah, let's go home."

Off they went. No short cut back though, as they stayed on the trail as it went up and down two steep hills leading them back to the post. As they neared the very southeast corner of the post, Jason stopped. "Whatta we gonna tell our parents about how our clothes got like this ... and where we've been?"

In unison, the other boys all shouted, "THE SAND PITS!"

It was the place they always told them they were at when they left the fort. It was at the southeast corner of the post and they often did play there. If they were in the pit, which was a material pit that the Army used whenever they needed dirt for some project on the post, they couldn't really be seen very easily and they usually did come home from it pretty dirty.

"So, I think we should go through the hole in the fence instead of the back gate," Jason continued. "At least if we walk through the sand pits on our way home we won't be lying to our parents."

"Good, idea, Jason," Mickey said.

The boys turned and walked along the outside of the fence until they reached the hole in the fence that was next to the pit. They scurried through the hole and marched through the middle of the sand pit past the old abandon cars and continued to the road. Instead of going past the barracks and through the hospital, the shortest route, they followed the road all the way around the complex, past the train depot, and up to the housing area. They had their story down on how they got soaked at the low spot in the sand pits and then got dirty playing Army. All of the boys received a scolding but none of them got into any serious trouble. Mickey had a nasty bruise on his arm but didn't break it. He was lucky.

Lucas was exhausted as he climbed into bed that night. *Whew! Dodged another bullet.* Then he drifted off to sleep.

Chapter XVI

Last Summer in Germany

June had finally arrived. The last day of school was great for Lucas and his classmates. They were now going to be in junior high school when school started again. It was hard for Miss Larkin to keep the class in any sort of order. School was only a half-day and they really didn't do any work. She went to Lucas and asked his help in keeping the class from getting too unruly. He was happy to help and quickly went to the front of the class and began banging a dictionary on Miss Larkin's desk.

"EVERYONE QUIET! LISTEN UP!" Lucas shouted. The class immediately became silent, much to both Lucas and Miss Larkin's surprise. Even Luke didn't expect such a quick response. Then he continued, "Miss Larkin has made me *GENERAL* of the Safety Patrol of this class for the last hour. (Luke looked over at Miss Larkin. Her eyes were opened wide, but she said nothing.) It is my duty to make sure we do not get our favorite teacher in trouble on the last day by being too rowdy. So I am going to have to smack anyone who gets outta line."

At that Miss Larkin jumped up, "Lucas! I did't ..."

"Just kidding!" Lucas said with a big wide grin. "Miss Larkin would like us all to have fun on our last day, but without as much noise as we've been makin'. Any objections?"

"Yeah, I have one." It was Katie Harley who spoke up to everyone's surprise. "There is no way you can be a General, Lucas. I mean ... you're like a criminal. You can't have your record and be a General."

The whole class broke out in laughter. Katie didn't say much all year and now she was giving Lucas crap. In the middle of the laughter, Lucas ran up to Katie and as she started to cower from his onslaught, he gave her a big hug and a kiss on the forehead. The class erupted in screams and laughter as Lucas, again had to quiet them down. The last hour was a wonderful experience for them all as they recalled funny incidents that had happened to them during the year. They even teased Miss Larkin about Mr. Knoll.

The whole school was abuzz as the final bell rang. It was time to catch the bus. Most of the class had said their good-byes to Miss Larkin during the final minutes of class. Lucas smiled as he and Mickey walked up to her to say their final good-bye. To Luke's shock, Miss Larkin gave him a big hug and a kiss on the cheek. He turned beet red as the remaining students "oohed and aahed" at the exchange.

"Lucas, thank you for being you. I have enjoyed teaching you these last two years and I will truly miss you," she said as she fought back tears. "I wish you the best."

It took Lucas a moment to find his voice as he, too, had to fight back his emotion. She had been such a great teacher and he knew he had learned so much because of how she taught. She had put up with his antics for two years and always supported him.

"You're the best, Miss Larkin," He finally got out. "I am the one that's so lucky. I had you and Mr. Knoll for the last three years. I hope everything works out with the two of you. "

Then realizing he had been holding her hand, he slowly let it go, giving her a little squeeze as he did. He smiled and headed toward the door. Just outside of the door he ran into Mr. Knoll. They said their good-bye quickly as Mickey was urging Lucas to get going. They didn't want to miss the bus. School was out!

Summer meant baseball, hiking and a lot more adventures ahead for all of the kids. In the third week of June, the Cub Scouts were having their campout. The Cub Scouts had grown and changed since Lucas last was with them. They were much better organized and had GIs helping them just as the Boy Scouts did. When Lucas was in the Cub Scouts they didn't go on a campout. Now that Ike was in it, there were about fifteen Scouts and they did a lot more activities then the original Scouts had. On this day, Friday, the Cub Scouts all took off for the off-post camping site. Sgt. Tyler was with them, as was his friend Spec. 5 Conner. They were helping the Cub Scouts, too, at least with their campout. They were going to a nice spot that had a spring and small pond next to an open meadow where they would be pitching their tents. Lucas was hanging out with TJ, Joey and Mickey as the troop marched out of the back gate following the same trail that took them to Three Lakes. There was a turn-off onto a trail that headed east just past the southeast corner of the post. The trail went for about half a mile before getting to the spring. This spring actually was one of a few springs that fed the stream that led to Three Lakes.

Lucas and the other boys decided to follow the Scouts, trying not to be detected. It was just a little game to occupy their time. They lagged several hundred feet behind, almost being spotted several times as they got too close to the younger, slower kids. As the troop reached their destination and began setting up camp, TJ tossed a pine cone at Ike, hitting him in the back. Ike quickly turned and looked around but didn't see anyone. The four of them were hiding behind a huge boulder surrounded by shrubs. Lucas, Joey and Mickey joined in, tossing an occasional pine cone at the Cub Scouts when no one was looking. After all of the tents were up, and the Scouts gathered around the middle of the campsite where the Scout Masters had set up the fire pit for that evening, Ike and the rest of the Cub Scouts were blaming each other for tossing the cones. A couple of the boys got into a little scuffle so Sgt. Tyler took control.

"All right, Scouts! Knock it off!" he shouted at them. Then in a milder tone, "We are going to eat lunch then go on a short hike. There is a neat little lake that this stream drops into where the Germans stock the nearby lakes and stream with fish. That is where we will hike to today."

Lucas and Mickey just looked at each other and smiled, recalling their last trip to that particular lake. They huddled together silently and watched as the boys ate their lunch. The pond had a small green meadow next to it where the tents were set up. There was a stand of reeds where the small stream left the pond on its bubbling journey to the first of the Three Lakes. The small stream was filled with stones that made it much more turbulent that the stream that left the weir at the first lake. The trees around the pond and meadow were pines with very few leafy trees, unlike the lake below.

Sgt. Tyler and another GI, PFC Bill Quincy, who was new to the 225th, set up the latrine. It was a good distance from the camp, with one roll of toilet paper that they sat next to it, leaving the remaining rolls with other supplies next to the pond. Most of the rest of the supplies were stowed in one of the tents that the Scout Masters used at the opposite end of the campsite from the pond. Quincy was left to guard the camp as the Cub Scout Troop set off on their hike. As soon as the group left, Quincy pulled a folding cot out of one of the tents and set it up in front of the tent. He then proceeded to lie on the cot so that he had a good view of the campsite.

"Should we follow the Scouts?" Lucas whispered to the other three boys.

"I don't feel like it," Joey answered. "Let's see if we can mess with their campsite."

"Yeah," Mickey chimed in. "Maybe we can pull all of the stakes."

"I bet if we give that guy, Quincy, a few minutes, he'll fall asleep," added TJ.

"Okay," Lucas said. "We better be quiet for a few minutes, then." The other three boys nodded in agreement. They all peeked out from behind their hiding spots to start to formulate a plan to sneak into the camp. If they didn't make any noise it would be fairly easy. Although PVC Quincy had a good view of the center of the camp and the trail coming in and leaving the camp, it would be easy to use the tents as a screen when they made their move. They decided that Joey and Mickey would go along the tents closest to the pond while TJ and Lucas would take the tents lined up on the other side. There were six tents not counting the two for the GIs. The plan was to pull up the tent stakes holding the ropes that held the tent poles at each end of the tent but not let the tent collapse. They would use rocks to hold the rope lightly so that the slightest bump of the tent would cause it to fall.

It didn't take very long. The boys had to fight back laughter as Quincy began snoring very loudly. They could see him with his head tilted back and his mouth wide open. Stealthily as they could, the four youths got up from their hiding spot and, splitting up, went to their assigned tents. It was easy. There was a slight breeze that whispered through the trees, blowing from the GIs' tents towards the pond, which helped keep any sound they were making from reaching the sleeping Quincy's ears. On the first tent it took TJ and Lucas a few moments to get the right sized rock. They needed one that would hold the tent rope lightly, but not too lightly or it would collapse before the troop got back. Although the breeze helped them with not waking Quincy up, it did make it a bit more difficult keeping the tents from falling prematurely. In less than ten minutes, TJ and Lucas were heading back to their hiding spot.

"I guess we beat them," TJ said to Lucas as they arrived at their spot. Then looking across the pond TJ could see Joey and Mickey working their way back by going past the supplies by the pond.

Lucas' eyes followed the two as Joey stopped at the supplies. Mickey continued to sneak back to their hideout. Luke looked at TJ. "What the hell is he doing?"

"I'm not sure … oh shit!" TJ whispered as he watched Joey set the box of toilet paper in the pond. Just then Mickey arrived, breathing deeply.

"Hey, I had nothing to do with that," He said as he pointed to Joey. "When he told me he was gonna do that I told him I didn't think it was a good idea."

Joey came plowing back to the hiding spot with enough noise to stir Quincy. He lifted his head and looked around before he lay back down on the cot. It looked like he would go back to napping. Meanwhile, Joey was smiling broadly as he joined his companions.

"What the hell did you do that for?" TJ angrily asked Joey.

"What do you mean? We wanted to mess with 'em. What better way than for 'em to run out of TP while in the middle of the woods," Joey answered with a hurt look as he caught the glare of both TJ and Lucas.

"Shit, Joey," Lucas said trying to control his irritation. "It's one thing to make their tents collapse but it's another to destroy property. Now, they're gonna try to find out who did it, and I can't afford to get into more trouble with Coach Tyler."

"Luke's right, Joey," TJ said a bit more calmly. He could see Joey was getting upset. He thought he was adding to the fun and didn't think that it was such a big deal. "We're gonna have to take off instead of hanging around to see the tents fall. I don't wanna be around when they find the TP in the pond."

Mickey and Lucas nodded in agreement as Joey looked at

them in astonishment. "Really! We're not gonna wait?"

"You can if you want, but I can't be around Sgt. Tyler when he finds out. He's gonna think it's me anyhow. Whenever some prank happens, who does he think of first? Just like with the traps at the fence and even if it isn't me, I'm the first one he thinks of when somebody else pulls one," Lucas told Joey.

After a moment of silence, Joey looked at the other boys and said, "I'm sorry guys. It seemed like a good idea when I thought of it."

"Don't worry about it, Joey," TJ said. Then all of the boys held still as they heard Quincy get out of the cot and moan as he stretched. They had been talking in their normal tones, forgetting about the sleeping GI. Now they all got very quiet as TJ continued. "Let's get going."

The four boys, keeping low to the ground, snuck back around the far end of the pond and caught the trail about a hundred feet from the campsite. They began walking back towards the post in silence until they were a good quarter mile away. Just the walk helped to lighten their mood.

"Hey, Joey!" Mickey shouted at him as they met the dirt roadway and were able to walk side-by-side. "We can enjoy it when we hear about it. I'm sure Ike will tell us all about it when he gets home."

"Yeah, guess you're right," Joey said as his spirits picked back up. The other boys weren't really angry with him. It wasn't like any one of them hadn't pulled a bonehead stunt before. "Anyone up for 500 when we get back?"

That's what they did when they got back. They had sworn an oath not to tell anyone that they were the ones who mossed up the campground. That did take some of the fun out of it, but when the Cub Scouts got back the next day, the four conspirators were eagerly waiting at the bottom of the apartment stairwell for Ike to return.

"Here he comes!" Lucas said as he saw Ike with his small backpack walking up the sidewalk towards them. "Hey, Ike!"

"Hey, Luke," Ike replied. "What are you guys doin'?"

"Just hanging out," Luke answered as Jason came walking up from the direction of the playground. "Did you have fun on the campout?"

Ike looked at the boys suspiciously. "Yeah, except for a couple little problems. Where were you yesterday, Luke?"

"We were all here playing ball. Played 500 most of the day," he replied. "Why?"

"Someone set our tents up to fall when we got back from our hike. Coach Tyler said he bet it was you, Luke, probably with Jason, Mickey and Guy."

"Luke and Mickey were with Joey and me all day yesterday," TJ inserted into the conversation.

"Well, you better let them know. They were all mad at me for a while cause you're my brother, but they were madder with that new GI, Quincy. He was supposed to guard the camp while we were on our hike and that's when it happened. He told Coach he fell asleep and didn't see anyone. He thought it had to be some of us that pulled it off 'cause there was no way he wouldn't have heard something. Whoever did it threw the extra rolls of toilet paper in the pond. Coach made Quincy hike back to the barracks and get a couple more rolls. He was pissed."

The boys were trying to suppress their laughter. Jason didn't know what exactly was going on but he had picked up on the fact that the other four boys did. He sat quietly, waiting until Ike left before asking any questions.

TJ asked Ike, "Who was pissed, Tyler or Quincy?"

"Well, both," Ike answered. "I think Coach was pissed at Quincy for letting this happen on his watch. He really lectured him behind their tent about how if it was wartime, and if that were how he handled guard duty, they would be all dead. He was trying to do it so we wouldn't hear, but the wind was blowing our way and we could hear everything he said to him. Then he sent him to get the toilet paper."

"I'm sorry, Ike," Lucas said to his brother. "I hope it didn't ruin your campout."

"Naw, we had lots of fun and it was pretty funny when the tents started falling when we got in 'em to rest after the hike. The Scout Masters didn't get mad about it until they saw the toilet paper in the pond. Quincy tried to say that the wind must have blown the box in but no one was buyin' that."

Mickey and TJ glanced at Joey. He mouthed 'sorry' to them, which was also caught by Jason. Jason couldn't wait for Ike to leave.

"Well, I'm glad you had fun, Ike," Lucas said to his brother as Ike brushed by them and headed up the stairwell.

As soon as they heard the door to the apartment close, Jason asked, "Okay, you guys did it, didn't you? You didn't start playing ball until after lunch and I couldn't find you all morning."

Lucas glanced at his other three partners in crime and said, "We can tell Jason. He's kept a lot of my secrets over the years." Everyone nodded their approval and Lucas proceeded to tell Jason what had happened. Surprisingly, Jason thought the toilet paper in the pond was hysterical which made Joey feel a little better. After having been admonished by the other three boys, he felt a little vindication. At least it wasn't just him that thought it was a funny thing to do.

The incident turned out to be one of those mysteries that was never solved, at least by anyone one out of the circle of five. The other surprise was Coach Tyler never brought it up at baseball practice on the following Monday. In fact, he never brought it up at all. After the first week of hearing the story being retold by Ike a few times, the whole incident faded into the past.

★ ★ ★

The 1962 baseball season was starting out great for the Münchweiler Pirates. Lucas was the Pirate's number one pitcher and when he wasn't pitching he was playing the outfield, mostly right field. A new boy, Lenny Turner, had moved to the fort and was a very good shortstop. When Coach Tyler told Lucas, he thought Luke would be upset. After all, he had made the All Stars at that position and the coach thought Luke was of the mindset that he had to play shortstop to make the All Star team again. Lucas actually had learned to like playing the outfield more. He had taken away a couple of opposition home runs in both the games he didn't pitch during the month of June and really liked catching fly balls much better than fielding grounders. The transition to the outfield was easy for him and Luke thought with his improvement as a pitcher, he had a better chance to make the All Stars as a pitcher and outfielder, than as a shortstop. He was 4-0 in the month of June and was set to pitch the big game on the 4th of July.

The Little League game was the first game of the eventful day, starting at 11 o'clock. Then the usual rivalry between the 225th and the 15th would start at 1:00 p.m. The 225th had dominated in recent years, but this year they were without their biggest star and the Pirates' second coach, Specialist Cooke, had received his transfer orders in May. Spec. 4 Quincy had replaced him as Coach Tyler's assistant coach. Lucas had to control himself several times when he wanted to joke to Quincy about "sleeping" on the job but knew he couldn't give away the secret of the Cub Scout outing.

When the game started, the bleachers were already packed. Their home games were well attended but Lucas had never seen a crowd like this before. His heart was racing when he took the mound to a roaring ovation. He was a little too pumped and proceeded to walk the first batter. Coach Tyler made an early trip to the mound.

"Lucas," he said as he put his hand on Luke's shoulder, "you have to take deep breaths and settle down. Right now your adrenalin is pumping way too much."

"Okay Coach," Lucas replied and proceeded to take a deep breath as Tyler walked back to the dugout. Luke then struck out the next two batters and got the third to ground out to Guy at third base. It was smooth sailing from there. The game went quickly. The Giants managed only three singles against Lucas and the Pirates won, 7-0. Lucas picked up his fifth win and the Pirates moved into first place in their division. All seemed great as Lucas walked off the field after shaking hands with the Giants. Then he saw his dad approaching his mother in front of the stands. Whenever Ivan did watch Lucas play he usually tried to hide from sight. Something was going on. After the guys were all given an after-game popsicle and soda, Lucas and Joey Baryshivka, who was the team's batboy, started heading towards their parents when Ike came running up to them.

"DAD GOT HIS ORDERS! WE'RE GOING TO THE STATES!" Ike shouted at the top of his lungs.

Lucas came to a dead stop. He felt a grip in the pit of his stomach. Coach Tyler and many of his teammates heard Ike, too. Lucas looked stunned. He always knew this would happen someday but he never could bring himself to accept it. He loved living in Germany and the thought of leaving this place was something he would not allow himself to even think about. As he stood there looking at his parents some thirty feet in front of him, he found he couldn't speak or move. He just stared, his mind racing, as he felt the big hand of Gus Tyler on his shoulder.

"It'll be okay, Luke," he said softly. "You'll go back to the States and make some All Star team there. Baseball is the same no matter where you play it. You'll make new friends, too. Think about how many of your buddies have left since you've been here. Life goes on. You'll have a lot of new adventures and friends wherever you go."

Ivan turned and left. Tears started streaming down Luke's face. He had no words, just sadness. Maria came rushing to her son's side and with Gus backing away slightly, gave Lucas a big hug, holding him tightly. The rest of the team surrounded them. Each patted Luke on the back as he and his mother walked slowly away. Lucas still had not said a word and he started to take deep breaths to control his sobbing.

"Mom, I don't want to go back to the States," he finally squeaked out.

"I know, Luke," Maria replied. "We always knew we would have to be going back someday. I guess I should have warned you boys that it was coming soon. Your dad has been here four years. We should have left last year but he extended his tour by a year so I could be around my relatives for a little longer. I don't know if I will ever see them again."

Lucas knew he should be feeling bad for his mother, too, but he was too self-absorbed in his own sadness to have any empathy for his mother. Ike and Joey seemed pretty excited about the move but both tempered their excitement as they looked at Lucas. For Ike, his closest friends had already moved, so he was just following suit. In his mind it made sense and he didn't have the same attachment to Münchweiler that Luke did.

"Listen, Lucas," his mother said, "why don't you hang out with your friends here for awhile before coming home. I am going to head home now to start my list of things we have to do to get ready. Your dad is waiting for me but I want you to stay and have some fun, if you can. There are a lot of activities going on and the big game between the 15th Evac and the 225th is coming up. You have to support Coach Tyler the way he does you.

"Okay," Lucas meekly replied. "I don't really feel like staying, but he has been really good to me. I think I'd feel worse if I didn't stay for his game. I'll be home after the game, Mom."

Maria gave her son a kiss on the cheek and another quick hug before heading toward the parking lot. Lucas took a deep breath and turned around to head towards the stands. He almost jumped when he turned. Standing there in silence were most of the team. They all looked sad. Luke knew it was for him and it brought a smile to his face. *What great friends I have!*

"Well, hell," he said as a little sob took his breath away for a second, "we can't stand around moping all day. Let's get ready for Coach's game!"

All the boys started yelling and shouting as they swung around and headed to the first base side of the stands that were located behind the backstop. The team filled in about four rows as the other spectators moved to make room for the group. Lucas sat directly in front of TJ with Jason and Mickey on each side. TJ patted Luke on the back.

"Things will work out, Luke," he said.

TJ was only a year older than Lucas but he seemed much older and wiser. He had been like an older brother since he had moved in downstairs. He always had a good word to say about any situation, no matter how bad it seemed at the time. The funny thing was most of the time he was right. Things did always seem to work out. Maybe not quite the way Lucas had hoped for, but they did work out okay.

Lucas tried to focus on the field as the starting lineups were introduced. His contorted face seemed to show he had to fight hard to keep his thoughts from going to his looming departure. He fought back a swell of emotion as he looked at the two friends on his sides and the one at his back. *Nobody ... nobody has better friends.* It was going to be painful leaving them. Jason looked at Lucas' faraway look. Tears began to fill Jason's eyes, too. Then both boys were jolted back into the moment by a crack of the bat. The 225th's leadoff batter had just drilled a double. For now, his wandering mind was put to rest as he focused on the game.

Chapter XVII

Return to the States

The next two weeks were pretty much a blur for Lucas. He got to play in one more Little League game. He went 4 for 4 including a home run and while playing right field he made a game-saving, diving catch to end the game. It was one of the best games he had ever played. Most of his time, though, wasn't spent playing ball, but was spent helping to pack their belongings. It was Lucas' job to help his brothers pack their toys so that they fit in the boxes that Ivan gave them.

"If it doesn't fit in these boxes, I'm throwing it out," Ivan declared.

Lucas had a great ability for making things fit together. He had helped his friends pack their daypacks when they did a Boy Scout hike or just in organizing things when he and his brothers cleaned up their room. He was getting everything in the boxes with room to spare. When his father came in to check on the boys, Lucas could see him look around the room and then at the boxes. Lucas caught him smiling. Lucas knew he was pleased with what he saw. Luke always felt he got this ability from his father. He had spent enough days with his dad working at the Property Disposal yard to watch him directing the German civilians and the GIs that worked for him in placing the items coming in. When officers and NCOs came in, Luke heard many of them praise his dad for how orderly the yard was.

As Lucas finished putting the last of the toys into the final box, Joey jumped on his back yelling, "Wahoo, Luke! You got everything in!" Ike joined his younger brother and the two wrestled their older brother to the floor. Lucas let them have the upper hand until the door popped open suddenly, their father standing in it looking at his three sons. The horseplay came to a halt.

"Good job boys," Ivan stated. "Wash up and come out for lunch." He then turned, leaving the door open, and headed back to the front of the apartment. The boys dashed for the bathroom, quickly washing their hands before joining their parents. This was to be their last lunch in this home. The last of the dishes would be packed up after their final dinner later that night. Ivan, Karla and Susan were going to pick up food at the NCO Club and bring it home. They were leaving so early in the morning they wouldn't have time for breakfast until they were on the train.

Lunch went quickly. The boys listened intently as Ivan explained to their mother how they would proceed in the morning. Ivan had been driving a jeep the last couple of weeks. Their station wagon, a Dodge Rambler, had been shipped out a couple of weeks earlier. Ivan was going to take the jeep back that afternoon and return with a ride from a soldier in his company. A taxi would take them to the train station in Pirmasens.

"How are we all going to fit in one taxi?" Maria asked.

"Same way we did comin' here," was Ivan's blunt reply. "We'll sit up front with the cabbie and Karla, Susan, Lucas and Ike can squeeze in the back seat with Joey on Karla's lap."

"But the boys are bigger and it was crowded then," Maria stated.

"This taxi is bigger. It ain't that long of a trip. We'll just have to make the best of it. Now quit worryin' about it," Ivan said with some finality.

After lunch the three brothers went outside and headed towards the playground. It seemed like all of their friends were there. Lucas couldn't remember anyone else getting this kind of send-off but then, he didn't know anyone else besides Jason, that had been stationed there as long as they had been. As he looked around at the shouting kids he did not see who had been there before him.

"Anyone up for 500?" Guy asked.

"Gloves are packed," answered Lucas. "Besides, I just want to hang out and talk to you guys."

"And we all know Luke gets what he wants," retorted Guy.

"I think that maybe some of us will miss you less than others, Luke," TJ said giving a menacing look at Guy.

"It's okay, TJ," Lucas joked, "I'm kinda tired of beatin' Guy up. I don't think I'll miss him too much either."

Guy just grinned at Lucas as the other boys laughed. They did have a bit of a rocky relationship ever since Guy's arrival at the post. It was no secret, but in spite of the friction between the two, they had still managed to make it tolerable. Guy was involved in most of what the Cricks did and had even talked about continuing the "gang" after Luke left. Jason had whispered to Lucas after Guy had made the statement, "It ain't gonna happen. Nobody likes Guy that much to follow his lead. Besides, he never has the kinda good ideas you always come up with ... you know, as far as things for us to do."

Mickey, overhearing Jason then began with "Remember the time ..." This led to storytelling that lasted until dinnertime. Lucas and his brothers headed home when they saw their father and sisters return from the NCO Club with dinner.

"See you all later!" Lucas shouted at his friends as he left. The plan was to go back to the playground after dinner. It would be the last time he would get a chance to see his friends. His family was leaving at 5:00 in the morning, so his final good-byes would need to happen that night.

There wasn't much conversation going on at the dinner table that night ... the family listened to Ivan layout the plans for the next few days.

"We take the taxi to Pirmasens and then the train to Frankfurt. We board the plane around 7 o'clock. The plane will fly to Edinburgh, Scotland. I think we have an hour and a half layover there before we fly to Gander, Newfoundland to refuel and then on to Fort Dix in Jersey. We should be there early mornin'. You'll all stay at Fort Dix overnight while I go to New York to pick up the car. I'll be picking you up from Dix around 9 o'clock. You better have had your breakfast by then, 'cause I ain't waitin'. It is about a five-hour drive to my sister's house. Any questions?"

Lucas was sure that they all had some questions, but by now they all had learned not to ask until the time was right. His father always thought he made things clear enough there shouldn't be any questions. The boys had taken a few smacks to the back of the head as their father drove home the point many times over the last several years. By now they knew to wait and ask their mother later. Sometimes Susan would ask just to aggravate her father, but this evening she wanted things to go smoothly. She had her plans to say her good-byes to her friends, too. As soon as dinner was over, with no dishes to do that night, they all excused themselves from the table and asked to go out.

"Keep an eye on your brothers, Lucas," Maria instructed her eldest son.

"Will do," Lucas replied as he and his two younger brothers headed for the door.

Lucas would always remember his last night there. It was one of the most fun times he had all summer. When Ike, Joey and Lucas got to the playground only a handful of kids were there. Jason and Mickey were two of them. They just sat and reminisced. They talked about the shortcut through the tunnel; digging up the German helmets and the partnership with Hans; pulling the tent stakes on the Boy Scout campout; and Lucas getting kicked out of the Boy Scouts and the fact that his parents still didn't know.

"Oh crap, Mickey!" Jason exclaimed. "You just jinxed him. Now IVAN THE TERRIBLE will beat the livin' crap out of him."

"Hey, quiet, Jason!" Lucas said as he looked around him to see if his brothers were close. "I don't want Ike and Joey to hear you or my old man *will* find out."

"Sorry," Jason said softly and then he started laughing hysterically, causing the other two boys to burst out, too. "You hit the fuckin' Scout Master over the head with a chair!" His laughter was just too contagious. Ike and Joey were hanging out with their friends at the swings. They all came running over to find out what was so funny. The three boys tried to stop laughing enough to explain, and then realizing it was Ike and Joey that came over made them laugh even harder. These were the two Lucas had to keep the secret from! How could they explain their laughter to them?

It took several minutes before they finally regained control of their laughter and a lot more kids had drifted into the sandbox. There were other stories that came up as new people joined the group. This went on for several minutes when Guy jumped up and said, "Hey, look at how many kids are here. We could have a great game of Hide and Seek!"

It seemed like everyone agreed with Guy on this one. Kids were already getting up to their feet and heading to the light post by the edge of the playground. Lucas, smiling, caught Guy's eye and nodded to him. Guy broke out into a big grin and nodded back. It looked like the Cricks had a new leader from this night on. In spite of Jason's comments, Guy was a leader. Maybe not as well liked as Lucas had been, but he was a take-charge person and others would follow him.

The neighborhood was full of sounds of the kids playing Hide and Seek for about an hour and a half. It was 8 o'clock and many of the younger kids had to head home, but Joey was able to stay later since he was with Lucas. The three brothers all had to go home by 9 o'clock. Usually, Lucas could stay out until ten on a summer night, but they had to get up early and it was going to be a long journey.

As the crowd thinned out, Lucas found himself with his two good friends. Guy had to leave to take his youngest brother home and whenever that happened his parents would tell him it was too late to go back out. Most of the other kids that remained were playing on the swings or slide. Mickey, Jason, Ike, Joey and Lucas were all that were left in the sandbox. They told a few good stories about school and teased Lucas about his crush on Miss Larkin, no matter how vehemently he denied it. When the time neared nine o'clock, Lucas got up. The rest soon joined him.

"Thank you guys for being such great friends," Lucas said as he faced his two pals. "We've had a bunch of good guys go through here with us. Maybe someday we'll see each other again."

"You bet!" Mickey responded.

"Got that right!" was Jason's response as he pushed away Lucas' outstretched hand reaching to shake Jason's and instead, wrapping his arms around Lucas and giving him a big hug. When Jason released him, Mickey spun Luke to the right and gave him one, too.

"See you, guys!" Lucas said as he turned to his brothers, "Come on, guys, time to get home for one last night."

The three brothers went home to the apartment that had been their home for almost four years. Lucas was over his crying. He had gotten that out of his system the first day he found out they were going back to the States. He had been trying to get a little information about Fort Riley from people, but none of his friends had ever been there or knew anyone who had. That made the coming change even more of an adventure. That was how Lucas was looking at things now.

There's nothin' I can do that would keep me in Münchweiler, might as well find out what the new place is like.

The morning was cool for the end of July. It made the morning drive to Pirmasens less of a pain than Lucas had anticipated. As cramped as the cab was with all of them in it, the mood would have been much worse had it been hot and muggy, too. As he looked out the window he fought back the sadness. *I've had great friends and so many fun times with them. Will my life ever be as much fun again?* The train ride to Frankfurt went quickly for Lucas. His eyes closed when leaving Pirmasens and he fell into a sound sleep.

When they arrived at the train station in Frankfurt, a van was there to take them to the nearby Air Force base. The van drove them onto the tarmac where they unloaded from the van and found themselves standing with the rest of the passengers made up of military personnel and their dependents.

"Oh my God!" Karla exclaimed as she looked at the airplane they were about to board. "I am not getting on that thing!"

"Quiet, Karla!" Ivan said rather loudly as they all looked at the antique looking airplane in front of them. There were other grumblings from some of the other passengers as they began to examine the Flying Tigers Airlines four-propeller passenger plane while lining up to board it.

"I mean it, Dad! I am not going on that plane. It doesn't look like it can get off the ground, let alone fly across the Atlantic!" the almost twenty year old Karla exclaimed in a loud enough voice that most of the loading passengers could hear. "She's got that right." another voice from the crowd added as Ivan began pushing Karla forward to close the gap in the boarding line.

"I'm sure the Army wouldn't be sending us on it if it wasn't fit to fly," Ivan stated with a not so confident voice as a couple of the other NCOs in line looked at Ivan and raised their eyebrows. Lucas was taking it all in. He caught the little glances some of the soldiers were making to each other and was getting the feeling this plane wasn't as safe as Ivan was trying to get them all to believe. Karla, reluctantly, proceeded to move forward and board the plane. Their father directed them to their seats with the boys sitting in a row over the wing, Lucas by the window, Joey in the middle and Ike by the aisle. Their parents sat in the row in front of the boys with an empty seat between them. Susan and Karla were in the row across the aisle with a teenage girl who was sitting in the window seat. It took perhaps half an hour for everyone to get situated as the crew started up the engines. This was Lucas' first airplane flight and he had no idea if this was normal or not. Karla had flown before and he could tell by her face that this wasn't like any flights she had taken before. The sound from the four large propellers was deafening. Moments later, after the airline stewardesses went over the flight safety instructions, the plane was taxiing down the runway. Lucas and his brothers were excited.

As the plane lifted off, Lucas was focused looking out the window at the ground below. As the plane banked to the right his two younger brothers were stretching their necks to look out the window. Lucas had promised them they could switch seats at some point so they could all see, but within minutes after liftoff they were in a cloud cover and the glimpse they got at takeoff was the only one they would have until they started their descent into Scotland. This made the flight rather boring for the boys. They occupied themselves by reading the comic books they brought with them. With the drone of the plane, coupled with its vibration, Lucas drifted off to sleep.

Lucas slept the entire flight to Scotland and only awoke when Ike shook him, speaking directly into his ear. "We're landing!"

The clouds were still thick and there wasn't much of a view until the plane was only a few hundred feet off the ground. The surrounding landscape was green and lush. The landing was smooth and as the plane rolled to a stop, the pilot announced there would be an hour and a half layover. The passengers could depart but had to remain in the gate area of the terminal. They would be boarding again in one hour.

"You boys stick with me," Ivan ordered as they all got up to leave the plane. The brothers were able to wander around the gate area, always within view of their father. They tried to see as much of the surrounding countryside as possible but their view was limited. Their best view came as they were boarding again. The clouds had lifted and there were a few spots of blue in the sky. From the top of the stairs, Lucas could see the surrounding hills. They were beautiful. They looked a little like the hills surrounding Münchweiler, but were a different shade of green. The trees were leafy and he didn't see any pine trees. Luke stopped at the top of the stairs to look around but quickly entered the plane when he heard his father shout out his name. Although he was holding up the other passengers from boarding and knew his father wouldn't be happy, he took the moment anyway. It was another of those calculated risks that this time had no dire consequences. When he got back to his seat, Ivan didn't even give him a look.

Off again. They would be crossing the Atlantic Ocean. This was the longest leg of the trip. The next stop was Nova Scotia and not Newfoundland. Lucas thought it best not to point out that his dad had been wrong when he told them the plan for the flight. When the plane was about an hour from Nova Scotia it began encountering some turbulence. The pilot had warned everyone to keep their seatbelts on tight. It was going to get rough.

The plane began to bounce around dramatically. There was no going to the bathroom at this point. Lucas began to feel sick. He never did well with rides that tossed and turned, and now he was on the worst ride of his life. The passing minutes seemed like an eternity to him. He looked at his watch. *Fifteen more minutes and we'll be on the ground.* He was fighting the urge to throw up, but soon it was an urge he could no longer suppress. Reaching for the vomit bag, he barely had time to get it to his mouth when he began to throw up. He was very loud as he "tossed his cookies" which started a chain reaction throughout the plane. The last ten minutes were some of the worst of his young life.

Ike threw up, Karla threw up and Joey would have but just as he reached for the vomit bag, Ivan turned to his youngest son and shouted, "JOEY, DON'T YOU DARE THROW UP!" Joey put the bag down and never did toss. Lucas looked at his younger brother. *Unbelievable!*

As the plane began its landing approach, it encountered heavy rain once it dropped below the cloud level. By this time, there was nothing left in Lucas' stomach to get rid of. He was feeling lightheaded but managed to look out the window. The visibility was terrible through the hard rain, and as the plane touched down, the water from the landing gear hitting the runway splashed against the windows as hard as the rain falling from the sky. Lucas glanced around the plane, peeking over the back of his seat. He could see a lot of fear in the other passengers' faces as the plane skidded a little sideways. It appeared that it was going to go off the runway but finally came to a stop just a few feet from the end of it. After a brief pause, it turned and taxied to the terminal.

This was supposed to be a brief refueling stop with all of the passengers staying on board. It did not happen that way. The peak of this storm was still over the airport and wasn't supposed to lighten up for another hour. Because of the odor from all of the sick passengers and the mess caused by some not quite getting to their vomit bags on time, the passengers disembarked while the ground crew came in and cleaned up the plane.

Lucas felt better once they were off the plane. His father never said a word. He just glared at his oldest son. He overheard his mother telling him, "It's not Luke's fault he got sick. I got sick, too!"

"Yeah, but Jesus, he was so damn loud he started everyone throwin' up!"

"Well, he's always been very vocal when he throws up," Maria said with a little smile. It lightened Ivan's mood a bit and his scowl turned into a grin.

"I remember the first time I heard the boy in the middle of the night when he got that flu in Zweibrüken. Scared the shit outta me," Ivan said.

It was still raining as they boarded the plane again, but this time less hard. Lucas took a deep breath once he was aboard. *Ahh ... not bad.* The crew had done a great job getting the plane ready for the last leg of the journey. There wasn't even a whiff of the smell that permeated the air when they got off. The flight to Fort Dix was a little bumpy but nothing like the approach to Nova Scotia. When the plane landed there was a light rain there, too. The Baryshivka family took a bus from the airport to a building that was the Army's equivalent to a hotel. Ivan got them all checked in then took off to pick up their car in New York. By the time he returned, the rest of the family had already retired for the night.

The following morning they woke up to sunny skies. Ivan began hustling them along. He was impatient to get going to Uniontown where they were going to stay for a few weeks with his sister, Sharon. It had been almost four years since they had seen Aunt Sharon and Uncle Peter and their cousins. The family climbed into their Dodge Rambler station wagon and off they went on their five-hour drive to Uniontown.

Lucas had enjoyed his three weeks in Uniontown, getting reacquainted with his aunts, uncles, and cousins. He had forgotten how much fun it was to play wiffle ball with his cousins. *I was so much younger then.* They never played it in Germany, only baseball.

Lucas woke from his sleep in the back of the car. They were approaching Fort Riley as the sun was rising. It was 8 o'clock in the morning when Ivan pulled into the parking lot of the Headquarters of the 1st Infantry Division, his new company. "You can get out and stretch but stay close," Ivan said as he headed to the doorway of the Big Red One, the nickname for his new unit. Ivan had to check in and find out where he and his family would be quartered. The boys got out of the car to a warm sunny morning on this last week of August. The surrounding landscape was green and a lot hillier than Lucas was expecting based on all of the photos he had seen of Kansas. In spite of having been cooped up in the car for a little more than sixteen hours, Lucas didn't feel much like moving around.

It was half an hour before Ivan came back out with a handful of papers and a map of the Fort. "We're going to be staying at the temporary housing at Whitside. They're old barracks turned into apartments. There's limited housing on North Fort." Everyone piled back into the car for the short drive to Whitside. As they drove east on Huebner Road, Ivan pointed out to them the original Territorial Capital building on their right.

"LOOK!" shouted Joey. "There's buffalo in the corral."

"I SEE THEM, TOO!" Ike yelled as Lucas tried to look over his brothers' heads to see if he, too, could see them. He caught a quick glimpse of them before a tree blocked his view. "Can we go back and see them, Dad?"

"Later, Ike. We need to get settled into our new home first. I'll take you boys over after the furniture gets delivered."

"Neato!" Joey replied.

Ivan made a left just after the Capital. It looked like rows of old barracks and Lucas half expected to see GIs running around instead of a bunch of kids. As the Rambler closed in on Building D, Lucas caught a glimpse of two boys running towards them from behind one of the other buildings. By the time the Baryshivkas got out of the car, the two boys Lucas had seen came flying around the building.

Just as Lucas heard, "Hey Luke!" he recognized the boys. It was Robby and Terry Smith. "What the hell are you guys doin' here?" he asked, utterly amazed.

"Watch your language, Lucas," his mother warned.

"Sorry, mom." Then turning back to face his two friends, "What are you guys doin' here and how did you get here before us?"

Robby said, "I can't answer how we got here first but the day you guys left my dad got orders for Fort Riley, too. We left Münchweiler two weeks later. I thought I'd see you when we got here but nobody here knew about you."

"They do now," Terry added. "Where have you guys been?"

"Oh, we stayed with our cousins in Pennsylvania for a few weeks before we came. Guess my dad had some leave time."

"Okay, now that makes sense," said Robby. "We came straight here and have been here a week. Got to know most of the kids our age in Whitside."

Turning to Terry, Lucas said, "Whatcha mean when you said 'they do now' about kids knowin' 'bout me?"

"Aw, Robby's been telling them what a bad ass you were and if they messed with us they were going to have to deal with you."

"WHAT? OH SHIT!" and then catching himself as he glanced to see where his mother was, he said much softer, "Shit, Robby, if I have to get into more fights because of you I'm gonna kick your ass."

Terry said, "I don't think so Luke. You know how Robby can spin a story. You wouldn't believe all the guys he told 'em you beat up. I think most of 'em are scared of you, just hearing 'bout it. Then there's this one kid from Pirmasens, he said he didn't know you but backed up all of the tales Robby told them. He knew a kid that knew some of the guys you had fights with and your reputation just ballooned."

"Hey, Luke!" Ivan shouted out the doorway of the apartment. "Get your punk buddies to help you and your brother bring in the luggage."

"Yes, sir!"

The boys began unloading the luggage and moving it inside. Lucas wasn't at all impressed with his first look of the apartment. He glanced around. *What a dump!* There were dead cockroaches everywhere and the walls were a dingy white. He could hear his dad telling his mother and sisters that it was only temporary until better housing opened up. He told them not to worry about the cockroaches. The apartment was just fumigated so there shouldn't be any more. The ones lying around the apartment, dead, were the biggest Lucas had ever seen. *Our old apartment in Münchweiler was The Ritz compared to this place.*

Robby and Terry were giving Lucas the low-down on the kids in the neighborhood, Junction City Junior High School that they would be attending, the closeness of the Kansas River, the buffalo at the Territorial Capital, and anything else they could think of telling him that they had learned in the week they had been there.

By the time they got everything inside it was 9:30 a.m. "Dad, can I go check things out with Robby and Terry? I'll take Ike and Joey!"

"Yeah, get outta here. Don't lose your brothers. And, be back at noon!"

"Yes sir!" Luke shouted to his dad as all the boys turned and headed west towards the hospital with Robby leading the way.

Robby led them past the hospital to a park that had a locomotive engine with a coal car attached. As they neared the engine, the two youngest Baryshivka brothers took off in a dead run and immediately began climbing up the stairs of the engine.

"Hey you little twerps," Lucas yelled, "be careful! If you get hurt I'll kill you!

"If we get hurt," Joey yelled back as he entered the engine compartment, "Dad will kill *you!*"

Lucas said as he grinned at his two companions, "The little smart ass."

They grinned back. "Just like his older brother," Robby said.

After playing around the train for an hour, the boys started to head back by a different route. They went north of the hospital along the base of the hillside that ran parallel to the highway with Whitside and all of the other buildings and facilities located in the flatter area between the hill and highway. North of Whitside and the hospital there was a higher plateau-like area. The drop off to the lower elevation where Whitside was located was a couple hundred feet with most of the hill being fairly steep. From there it continued to drop off slowly until it met the river on the south side of the highway. As the boys discovered later, the slopes along the hill that were not covered by trees made great sledding areas when it snowed. From the upper elevation there were several little canyons that started on top and quickly dropped to little low areas or streams as they went south towards the river. Where the cliffs were fairly sheer, there wasn't much large vegetation along the sides of the canyons, but at the top and bottom and in the little drainages that emptied into the canyons, the woods were thick, filled with elm, ash, mulberry and oak trees.

The five boys walked along the base of the hill with Robby leading. About a quarter mile from the hospital there was a dirt road that cut up the side of the hill. Following Robby's lead, the boys began to climb the hill via the road. When they reached the top, the road turned to the northeast and the trees disappeared, exposing a huge field covered with waist high grass. The bottom portion of the grass was green, but the top two-thirds was a dull gold color. On the far end of the field were more woods.

Lucas stopped. *This is what I thought Kansas would look like!* Turning to the other boys Lucas said, "We better stop here for now. I don't want to be late for lunch or the old man won't be happy."

"There is supposed to be a neat canyon across that field," Terry said. "The guy that lives in the unit next to ours says it is full of fossils."

"Fossils?" Joey asked. "Come on Luke, let's go check it out."

"Not today, Joey. Lunchtime's comin' up. Maybe tomorrow we

can get an early start and go." Turning to Robby and Terry, Lucas asked, "You guys busy tomorrow?"

"Oh wait," Robby answered, "let me check my social calendar, you dork!"

"We've been waiting for a week for you to show up so we can go exploring Luke," Terry added. "We'll come by in the morning."

The boys all headed home for lunch. The van with their furniture was being unloaded when the boys got there. There wasn't much for them to do until the movers got everything in place. They were done by 1 o'clock and true to his word, Ivan took the boys to the Territorial Capital. They got to touch the two American Bison that were in the pen next to the building. The boys were fascinated by all the history that the museum had on display. They spent a good two hours there before returning home where they spent the rest of their day unpacking.

The next morning the three brothers had barely finished their breakfast when Robby and Terry showed up at their door.

"You guys ready?" Terry asked as Luke answered the door.

"Come on in. We'll be ready in a couple of minutes."

The three boys quickly got their teeth brushed and were ready to go.

"Bye, Mom!" Lucas yelled as they headed out the door.

"Watch over your brothers, Luke!"

Soon the boys were climbing the dirt road behind the hospital to the top of the hill. It was a cool morning with a slight breeze. The leaves were starting to change and the breeze brought down some of the early fall leaves. As the boys reached the top of the hill, a red-tail hawk swooped over them, releasing a shrill cry as it banked hard to its left and disappeared over the hill.

"Neato!" Joey said as the other boys just nodded in silence.

"Which way do we go from here?" Ike asked.

"I don't know," answered Robby. "We only heard about the canyon. We've never been there."

Lucas looked across the field at the tree line on the other side. He turned to the guys and said, "Let's just head for those trees. It's hard to tell, but it looks like it drops off there. We can tell when we get there." Lucas took off towards the tree line across the field with the rest of the boys following. The grasses were higher than Lucas' waist and it was up to Joey's shoulders so they hiked in a straight line with the bigger boys beating down the grasses as they went, making it a little easier on Ike and Joey. When they reached the other side, they could see that the terrain indeed dropped off. They came to the top of the tree-packed gully that dropped down to the canyon below although until they actually started following the gully, they didn't know they were entering the canyon. Once they reached the bottom of the canyon, they came across a small stream and began to follow it upstream. As they advanced farther up the canyon, the walls became steeper with the trees now being either on the top of the canyon or scattered along the walls of the canyon in whatever flat spot they could take root on. The trees had thinned in the bottom of the canyon. As they reached a rocky outcropping in the middle of the canyon, Ike yelled. "Fossils! Look you guys, fossils!"

As the other boys quickly scooted to where Ike was, they began to look around. They could see lots of fossils in the rocks around them. They looked like snails and shells, some like insects. The boys felt like they hit a gold mine.

They gathered what they could, although most were in the bedrock itself and they didn't have any tools to be able to retrieve them. They did manage to pick up some in smaller rocks and loaded their pockets with their find. The time passed quickly. Looking down at his watch, Lucas said, "Oh shit! We need to start heading home for lunch. I can't believe how much time has gone by."

After a bit of complaining, they all picked up the last of what they could carry and began to follow Lucas out. When they reached the side canyon they had entered by, Lucas saw the broken branch he left on the side of the big oak tree in the middle of the canyon to mark the spot where they entered the canyon. Some of the things he had learned in Boy Scouts did pay off. It would have been difficult for them to find the gully where they came in without the marker he had left, since there were several that entered the canyon. It wasn't long before they were crossing the field again. When they got close to home, Joey bolted ahead to show off his fossils to his mother.

Over the next several weeks Lucas and his brothers were busy adjusting to their new home and schools. Lucas wanted to try out for the football team but his father nixed that idea when he learned he would have to chauffeur him home from practice every day and take him to the games. In spite of his disappointment, Lucas didn't dwell on it long because there were so many new places to see and explore. The boys often were joined by another boy that lived in Whitside, Howard Kaufman. Howard was a year older than Lucas and there was something about Howard that Lucas didn't totally trust. He reminded him a little of Guy Henderson in Münchweiler. Nevertheless, he became part of Lucas' new unofficial club and hiked with them every weekend. They took hikes across the highway to the river and discovered a small pond between the highway and the river. They saw beavers downing trees in the area between the pond and the river. The trees were different nearer the river. There were a lot of cottonwoods, poplars, and willows. They saw deer numerous times and often saw coyotes when they were in the canyon.

During their outings, they explored more of the canyon and expanded their knowledge of it and the surrounding area. On the first Saturday of October, Lucas was making the hike to the canyon with his brothers and Robby and Howard. In spite of finding friends their own age, Ike and Joey loved to explore with their older brother. They were both eager to go and as Lucas filled his canteen, they followed his lead and filled theirs.

"Where we goin' today, Luke?" Joey asked.

"I thought we would go to the beginning of the canyon this time. We always go down the canyon from that first spot we found with all of the fossils. We'll go up it this time. I don't think it is very far to where it starts."

"Cool!" Joey said, using his latest 'new' word that he was now using instead of 'neato' all the time.

"See you later, Mom," Lucas said as he and his brothers started out of their home and before Maria could answer or acknowledge, Lucas he added, "I know, 'watch out for my brothers.' Don't worry, Mom, I always do."

As the three boys headed towards the Smith's home, Robby, Terry and Howard were heading in their direction. They stopped and waited.

"I see you brought your dorky little brothers," Howard said.

"Yeah, and they aren't always dorky."

"Oh well, I guess they ain't so bad."

"They been hiking a lotta miles with us," Robby added.

Ike turned to Joey and whispered, "Look who's calling who a dork."

The boys took their usual route up the road behind the hospital and across the wide field to the gully that led to the bottom of the canyon. It had rained earlier in the week and the small stream in the canyon was running more than they had seen during their past hikes. They played around in the stream as they made their way up the canyon. Not far up the canyon from their original "fossil spot" the stream shrunk and then disappeared completely. Lucas could see a cluster of trees near where the walls of the canyon started.

"I think we're almost at the head of the canyon," Lucas said as he paused to look ahead, placing his hand across his forehead to shade his eyes. "Yeah, I think once we're past those trees it looks like another big field, but I can't really see past the trees."

The boys continued the few hundred feet to the first of the large oak trees. As Lucas passed the tree he could not believe what was now before his eyes as the canyon opened up to a huge field. "OH MY GOD!" he cried, "BUFFALO!!!!!"

The other boys didn't need Luke to tell them there was a herd of buffalo in front of them. There were at least a hundred of them covering the field with the closest not more than a couple hundred feet from them. The boys were dumbfounded as they gazed upon the sight of the herd of American Bison stretched out in front of them.

"Wow, this is like something you'd see in a movie!" Robby exclaimed as all of the boys cautiously moved towards the herd. They were scattered all over the field with most of them lying down, maybe a third of them standing.

"Wow!" Robby kept repeating over and over again.

"Too bad we don't have a camera," Howard said.

"You know, I heard the guy at the museum tell some people that the two buffalo in the pen were part of a herd that was kept on the Fort, but I never thought it was anything this size," Lucas said.

"I wonder how close we can get?" Ike asked as he inched closer to the herd.

"Be careful, Ike," Lucas warned his brother. "We don't know what they'll do."

"Oh, come on, Luke," Howard said as he puffed his chest out and started to boldly walk towards the three closest to the boys, just below the last tree at the top of the canyon. "Are you really such a big chicken shit you're afraid of a few buffalo? I'll bet they're just like cattle. They ain't gonna bother us." Then Howard began picking up stones and tossing them towards the bison.

"What the hell are you doin'?" Luke asked.

"What's it look like I'm doin'? I'm tossing rocks at the big guy there, trying to see if he'll move."

"Well, stop it butthole." Luke told him.

"I'm with Luke on this, Howard. You oughta stop before you piss him off," Robby added.

"What a couple of pussies you two are," Howard said as he hurled one last rock. It landed about ten feet from the big bull closest to them. All of a sudden the buffalo stood straight up and when he did all of the other bison got up at the same time creating a huge 'whoosh' sound that echoed in the mouth of the canyon. Then they all started coming towards the boys. At least it looked like all of them from Lucas' view. They started walking but that turned into a slight trot.

"COME ON! FOLLOW ME!" Lucas shouted at his brothers. Joey and Ike took off after Luke with Howard, Terry and Robby right behind them. The bison were gaining on them as Lucas reached the side of the canyon where the cliffs started. He checked to make sure his brothers were right behind him before starting to climb up the side of the canyon, coming to rest on a large ledge that was about twenty feet above the bottom of the canyon. The ledge was large enough to hold all six boys.

When he finally got situated on the ledge and made sure his brothers were safe, he turned to Howard and said, "You dick! What the hell did you think would happen? Fuck … look at us now! Stuck up here!"

Howard didn't say anything to Luke. He turned beet red and looked like he wanted to come at Lucas, but after sending Luke a nasty look, he turned and looked at the more than a dozen bison milling around below them. Once the boys got up the side of the canyon, the bison all stopped where they were, for the most part, and began grazing. Many of them returned to lying down. After several minutes of silence, Howard turned to Lucas, his face no longer red and seeming more relaxed.

"Sorry, guys. I don't know what I thought they'd do, but I never thought the big fuckers would come chargin' at us."

Lucas, too, had settled down now that they were all out of danger. He had been looking around and assessing their situation. There was only one way for them to get back off the cliff and that was the way they had come up.

Lucas began to laugh as he responded to Howard. "I never thought they'd come at us, either, Howard. Now we gotta get them to leave or we're gonna be here a long time. The way we came up is our only way down."

The other boys began to look over their surroundings and Robby and Howard nodded in agreement. They were going to have to wait for the bison to move.

Howard started, "We can always throw more …"

"NO!" came a shout from all the other boys.

"We ain't throwin' any more damn rocks at the beasts!" Lucas shouted.

Howard just broke out into a grin. "Okay, bad idea."

The boys had to wait almost an hour before they got their chance to get down. It was quite warm as the morning sun came over the trees on top of the canyon and shined on the ledge they were on. The bison slowly drifted to the north, away from the canyon. The last two were no more than 100 feet from the base of the cliff when Lucas' looked at his watch.

"We need to try to get outa here. We'll be cutting it close for lunch."

"You're worried about lunch?" Howard asked.

"Naw, he's worried about gettin' his ass kicked if he's late," Robby said.

"Doesn't matter," Lucas said. "There are only two buffalo close now and they could wander back this way so we need to get down now."

The words were no sooner out of his mouth when Lucas began his descent and motioned to his brothers to follow. Joey moved so quickly he was almost on top of his older brother before they were halfway down. Getting down was easy and quick but it was also noisy. As Lucas jumped the last five feet, landing with a thud, the two huge bison, which were both facing away from the boys, turned and looked back at the commotion being made behind them. The boys wasted no time retreating down the canyon once they reached the bottom of the cliff and headed for home.

As Luke and his brothers neared their home, Joey turned to Luke and asked, "Can we tell mom we saw the buffalo?"

Lucas thought about it for a moment. He knew it was going to get out somehow. This was too big a deal to think that the word wouldn't get out and back to his parents.

"Yeah, Joey, we can tell mom, but don't tell her we got suck on the cliff. You can tell her we saw the herd while we were exploring the canyon but no more. I mean you can tell her how big the herd was and how they all got up at once, but don't tell her it was because that dork, Howard, threw rocks at them, okay?"

"Gotcha, Luke!"

"Good! You got it, too, Ike?"

"Yeah, I understand. Don't tell her nothin' that can get us into trouble with the old man."

Lucas nodded to Ike as they entered their front door. Joey couldn't wait to tell their mother who was amazed to hear their story. She helped them retell it that evening at the dinner table. Ivan seemed pre-occupied and just listened. Later, Lucas found out what was consuming his father's thoughts as he overheard his parents talking. Ivan wasn't happy with his new assignment and to make matters worse, he had just found out that in February his company would be getting a new company commander and that commander was the same Major (now a Colonel) that Ivan had had problems with in Germany. Ivan hated him.

"My re-enlistment is coming up in the middle of January," Lucas heard him tell Maria. "Maybe its time to get out. Twenty-two years is enough."

The two continued to talk. Lucas headed back to his bedroom so they wouldn't think he was eavesdropping on them. He didn't say anything to his brothers as he wondered what changes would occur if his dad did decide to retire from the Army. *Wonder if we'll move back to Pennsylvania? Would we stay in Kansas?* It gave Lucas a lot to think about.

Time moved on and Lucas did not think too much about the future. Instead, he, his brothers and the Smith brothers, continued to explore their surroundings as the weather turned colder and the leaves changed colors. Lucas loved going through the woods at this time. He thought it was awesome to have all of the multi-colored leaves on the ground. The kids made several more trips to the canyon, discovering an Army obstacle course at the southern end. They had a blast going through the course. The most fun was crossing the stream using the thick cables hanging across it. At this point in the canyon, the stream had widened considerably from the little rill it was higher up. There were two cables, one above the other, that were too far apart for Joey or Ike to reach but Lucas and the Smith brothers could grab the top cable and place their feet on the bottom cable, using the two to cross the creek.

These outings to the course were usually uneventful but lots of fun. Only once did they have a problem. It was early November and there had just been a snowstorm that blew through, leaving almost a half a foot of snow on the ground. A little snow never deterred the boys from a good hike and this storm didn't either, at least not Lucas and the Smith boys. That Saturday morning, Ike and Joey decided to go to a movie with some of their friends instead of playing in the cold snow. Robby, Terry, and Lucas were headed straight east to intercept the stream and the obstacle course. As they passed Howard's apartment he popped his head out of the front door.

"Hey, where you guys going?"

"The obstacle course," answered Terry.

"Can I come?"

Terry glanced at Lucas and after seeing his approving nod said, "Yeah, but you better hurry. We ain't waitin' around in this cold for you to get ready."

"I'll catch up," Howard said as he darted back into his house to get his gear on. It didn't take him long to catch up to the rest of the guys. He had run most of the way and when he reached the boys, steam was coming off of his head and his breath created such a fog it looked like a fire was burning in is stomach.

"Where the fuck is your ski cap?" Robby asked him.

"Oh, I got it. It's in this inside pocket. I couldn't get the zipper to the pocket undone."

"Well, you better figure it out," Lucas said. "You be freezing your butt off if you don't get that hat on."

They all stopped while Terry helped Howard get the zipper to his inside pocket open. It took a few minutes and by the time they got it and Howard got his coat closed, he was shivering almost uncontrollably.

"Come on, let's get moving so Howie here can warm up," Lucas said. He knew Howard was cold and focused on it since he didn't react at all to Lucas calling him Howie. He hated being called Howie. "DOUBLE TIME!"

The boys all knew what that meant and began jogging towards the course. By the time they got there, Howard was quite warm. All of the boys were panting and Robby had to open his coat up for a few moments to cool down. After a brief rest they decided to attack the course and since it was covered with snow they had to brush off most of the obstacles before they got on them. When they came to the creek it was a daunting situation. The cables had a lot of ice on them and the creek was flowing strongly, weaving around the snow-covered boulders that dotted the stream. The sun was starting to break through the clouds and the sunlight sparkled off of the snow and stream with rays shining through the woods in their immediate area.

"Luke, you go first," Robby said even though he really didn't have to. Lucas almost always went first if there was danger involved.

Lucas stepped onto the lower cable and reached up and grabbed the upper cable. He was wearing standard military gloves. They were black leather with cloth liners. Even though they were made for just this kind of weather, Lucas could feel the cold metal through the gloves as he began to slide along the cables towards the middle of the creek. They all had done the cables enough times to know only one could cross at a time without causing them to bounce, making it impossible for two to be on them at once. For the other boys the good thing of having Lucas going first was he knocked all of the snow off of the lines as he slid his feet and hands across them. The cables had become icier with each passing boy and they were quite slippery by the time Terry crossed last. Luke, Howard and Robby all crossed without incident, although Robby almost fell while joking around and bouncing on the cable. Lucas looked at him and smiled. *You dumb shit. See how you feel if you fall in that icy stream.*

As Terry reached the other side and started to climb off onto the small wooden platform at the end of the crossing, he couldn't let go of the upper cable.

"Shit! My gloves are frozen together," Terry said as he struggled to free his hands.

"Quit dickin' around, Terry." his brother said.

"I'm not. I'm fuckin' stuck."

Howard was the tallest and closest to Terry so he got up on the platform to try to help him. As they struggled to pull apart the gloves, Lucas and Robby moved below them for a better look. This put them right on the edge of the creek amongst a lot of icy, slippery boulders. Terry managed to get his hand out of one of the gloves, which relieved some of his discomfort of being stretched between the two cables. Just as Howard swung his leg around Terry to get a better grasp of the glove, Terry's feet slipped forward off of cable. He came out of his gloves, butt landing on the bottom line, knocking Howard off behind him into Luke and Robby, with all three tumbling into the stream and Terry bouncing off of the cable backwards on top of them.

"Damn!"

"Shit … shit … shit!" Howard sputtered.

All the boys were on their asses in the creek with Terry half sitting on his brother, that is until Robby shoved him off, sending him into the creek shoulder first. By the time they all got up and out of the water, they were thoroughly soaked. It didn't take long for them to start feeling the bitter cold.

Stating the obvious, Lucas turned to his companions, "We better get the hell home before we freeze."

Looking up at his gloves still frozen to the upper cable, Terry asked, "What about my gloves?"

"I guess you gotta come back when it warms up or you can stay and try to get them now. That, you'll be doin' alone," said Lucas.

"You got that right," added Robby.

That was the last view of his gloves Terry ever had. The boys practically ran all the way home to keep from freezing. A few days later when Terry went to look for his gloves they were nowhere to be found. They had probably dropped into the stream when they thawed and floated all the way to the river, never to be seen again.

Time flew for Lucas over the next few months. Being in junior high school was an adjustment, but one he enjoyed. He loved moving from class to class and … the cute girls. Lucas spent most of his spare time at school flirting with girls he had gotten to know in a couple of his classes, but he didn't get much of a chance to see them outside of school. All of the girls he liked lived on the North Fort and it was a bit too far to walk there from Whitside; besides, once the weekend came, Lucas couldn't get enough hiking and exploring done in the limited time he had. *Can't wait 'til summer vacation.* He and his friends and brothers took many hikes to the river. They also spent some time playing on the now frozen pond that sat in between the highway and the river. It was a beautiful landscape, with the trees felled by the beavers scattered around the pond, often covered by icicles and patches of snow.

Finally, Christmas vacation was upon them. A few days into the vacation, Luke, Ike, Joey, Robby and Terry decided to hike to Fossil Canyon, their unofficial name for the canyon, via their usual route across the field to the arroyo that led to the bottom of the canyon. It was a Wednesday. All their previous outings to the Canyon had been on weekends. This was the first time they had gone in the middle of the week. It didn't occur to any of the boys how significant a difference that was. They reached the top of the hill and began to cross the field. Lucas noticed that at the top of the hill, on the far northwest end of it, there were soldiers assembled there. *Are those cannons?* He didn't think too much of it. Growing up in the Army, it was a sight he had seen plenty of times in the past, just never while hiking to the canyon. They were just about to the middle of the field when the heard the booming of howitzers coming from the GIs on the hill. There were four rounds fired within seconds of each other. The boys stopped. Almost immediately, they could hear the rounds going over their heads, landing to the southeast, exploding around huge targets that were located no more than a few hundred yards on the opposite side from them.

"What the fuck?" Robby blurted.

Then Lucas looked back at the soldiers at the top of the hill. *What the hell just happened?* The boys could hear whistles and horns blaring from the soldiers' position. As Lucas looked at them he could see red and white-checkered flags waving back and forth and all kind of commotion. Men had jumped into several jeeps and were heading towards the boys.

"RUN!" Lucas shouted as he bolted for the tree line and arroyo. He didn't need to say it twice. All the boys took off after him. Glancing over his shoulder, Luke could see the jeeps rapidly closing in on them. When they reached the arroyo they began sliding on the fallen leaves that thickly covered the ground. As they began dropping down into the woods, Lucas realized they weren't going to be able to outrun them. With the leafless trees, the top of the drainage they were in was visible on three sides.

"Quick, cover yourselves with leaves!" Lucas ordered. They had done this many times in Germany when they were playing War at the bunker. Hiding under leaves, then popping up and ambushing the "enemy." The boys quickly went to work covering themselves with leaves. Lucas helped Joey before getting himself covered. Using a branch, he could lift the leaves just enough to be able to see an area at the top of the drainage and the edge of the tree line. A jeep popped right into his line of sight. He could see four GIs get out. He could hear many others as they yelled for the boys to come out. One of the soldiers was shouting orders to the others to fan out and head down the arroyo.

"Find those fucking Army Brats!"

Lucas couldn't see his companions but knew they wouldn't panic and run. *As long as they don't get stepped on, they'll be okay. The soldiers will think we're still runnin'.* He could see a couple that had come down from the jeep on the ridge. They looked behind a couple of boulders as they passed, but continued to move fairly quickly downward. Then he could hear the rustling of the leaves as someone was walking towards him. His heart began to race. He held his breath. It was all he could do not to panic and run as he saw the army boot land less than a yard away. He could hear the soldier's heavy breathing, almost feeling it on his face. The boot blocked out his entire view of anything else for a brief moment. Fortunately for Lucas, the GI in those boots continued to move down the arroyo towards the canyon bottom. Lucas let out his breath. Now he again could see the jeep on the ridge. It was backing up and Lucas could tell it was driving away. He had to pee. No … he had to pee bad! He listened intently, hearing the voices of the GIs getting farther away when he couldn't take it any more and slowly lifted his head for a better look. He could see the slight mound in the leaves where he had covered his brother. He wasn't able to tell where the others were. Scanning his surroundings and seeing no one, he jumped up from the leaves and began peeing next to the closest tree, looking in every direction to see if any of the soldiers were still around.

"Hey, Luke," came a muffled voice from the bump in the leaves. "can we get up?"

"Yeah, Joey, you can get up but keep quiet," Lucas said in a low voice.

The others heard and all began to shake off the leaves and stand. Robby looked at Luke taking a piss and had to hold back a laugh. "I gotta go, too."

When Lucas and Robby finished, the boys gathered around a large boulder. "What're we gonna do, Luke?" Ike asked.

"Wait here. I'm goin' to the top of the ridge and see if I can see them." Lucas climbed up the slope, slipping at times in the leaves. The boys watched as he crawled the last twenty feet or so to the top. He was only there a few moments before turning on his butt and sliding down the first forty feet of the slope, then stood and walked to his companions. "I can see a bunch of jeeps and people up to the right. I think they are following the canyon but I've never seen that side of the canyon from there so I'm not sure. It looks like a couple of GIs are on a platform up by the guns with binoculars. We're not going to be able to go back the same way."

"No shit, Sherlock," Robby said. "Like I'm gonna go through

the middle of a god damn firing range again?"

They all started to laugh. "I think you should, Robby, but wait until you hear the first howitzer go off," his brother said. Then turning to face Lucas, "Well, Luke, you're the trail boss, how the hell are we gonna get outa here?"

"I think we only have one choice. We gotta follow this down to the bottom of the canyon and then follow the canyon down to the obstacle course."

"What if they're still down there?" Ike asked.

"I don't think they will be, but if we see any of them we're just gonna have to hide. There's a lot of boulders at the bottom we could hide behind," Lucas answered. "Come on. Let's get goin."

The boys quickly scrambled down the arroyo to where it met the canyon. From there they cautiously began moving down the canyon, keeping to the west side. It didn't take them long to reach the end of the canyon as it began to widen out at the obstacle course.

"Stop!" Lucas said, as he held his hand out behind his back. The boys stopped. There was a group of GIs on the course. Again, as with the firing range, the boys had never been to the course during the middle of the week.

Robby slid past Ike and huddled up next to Lucas. "What'd ya think we should do, Luke?"

"Shit, Robby, I don't know." It was a very uncharacteristic statement from Lucas. He was tired and worried that somehow the soldiers at the firing range would be able to track them down and his father, just three weeks from getting discharged from the Army, was going to go out with a Delinquent Report because of his sons. *We're all gonna get it … but I'm the oldest … I'll get it worst.* The boys all sat in silence for several minutes. Finally, Lucas just started shaking his head back and forth; he looked each of his companions in the eyes, one by one; then he stood.

"Let's get the fuck outta here," he said. "We can swing behind those trees along the side of the canyon where it rolls into the hill. Just stay behind the trees until we get out of view of the course. It's real brushy over there so we should be hidden until we're right above the dirt road that runs along the base of the hill."

Lucas took off along the side of the hill, hiding behind the trees as he went. He never looked back to see if his brothers or the Smith brothers were following. He kept going until he was on the road. Once the boys reached the dirt road, Lucas relaxed.

"Whew, that was a close call today," he said as he waited for the rest of the boys to catch their breaths. They had been moving at a very quick pace.

"Man, oh man, that was scarier than the time with the buffalo," Robby said.

"No shit, numbskull," Terry said as he turned to face his brother. "Those were fuckin' live rounds that went over our head."

They started walking … at a much slower pace. "I think it was cool," Joey said. "I can't wait to tell my friends at school."

"No … no, no, no Joey, you can't tell anyone about this. It can't get back to dad or we'll all get our butts kicked," Lucas said. "This is another one of those secrets we gotta keep to ourselves."

"It was pretty cool, though, wasn't it?"

"Yeah, Joey, it was," Lucas said, laughing. *Lucky we aren't fuckin' dead.*

The boys reached the Baryshivka residence first, and as the three brother headed towards the door, Robby, smiling, yelled at them, "Hey you fuckin' Army Brats, lets see what trouble we can get into tomorrow!"

Lucas just waved. Little did he know at the time, but this would be their last adventure as Army Brats. A snow storm hit the following day and the boys spent the rest of their vacation time sledding on the hills behind Whitside. Lucas wasn't chancing another encounter with the Army. Ivan retired three weeks later. The Baryshivkas were going back to Pennsylvania …, civilians

The Baryshivka family headed back to Pennsylvania in the middle of January. The girls and Maria were going back by train while the boys were going with their father by car. Earlier in the day, Ivan had taken Maria, Karla, and Susan to the train station in Junction City. Lucas was finishing his last day at his Junction City Junior High School. As he looked out the window of the school bus taking him home for the last time, he passed his Dad's company headquarters. When he had gotten on the bus, he watched a GI kiss his son, tell him he loved him, and he would see him when he got back from Viet Nam. *I don't remember Dad ever telling me or Ike or Joey he loved us.*

As the bus came to Lucas' stop, he climbed out onto the snow-covered ground. He started to turn around and felt snow going down his back.

"Shiiiiitttt!" Luke yelled.

"There you go you dork!" Robby Smith said as he ran back a few steps. "That's what you get for leavin' us!"

"Yeah!" his brother Terry added.

Then both brothers came up to Lucas and hugged him.

"Man, who are we gonna get in trouble with when you're gone?" Robby asked.

"Shit, man, you guys can get in enough trouble without me," Luke answered.

"But it won't be as fun," Terry said.

It was time to go. Lucas knew his father was waiting for him to come home. They were going to spend the night in a hotel that night and drive back to Pennsylvania the next morning. Lucas smiled at his two friends as he backed away and started heading home.

"Thanks for being my buddies all these years, guys!" he shouted as he turned for home.

"YOU TOO, LUKE!" they both shouted in unison.

When Lucas reached the apartment, Ivan had just picked up two suitcases. "Hold the door, Luke." Then sliding by Luke, he headed for the car. "Grab that last one."

Lucas picked up the last suitcase and followed his dad out. Ike and Joey were already in the car. They looked excited and cold. With the temperature as low as it was the car heater had not been running long enough to warm it up inside yet.

"I'm gonna lock up, Lucas. Hop in with your brothers."

It only took a few minutes to get to the hotel in the town of Manhattan, east of the fort. They had two connecting rooms, each with two double beds. Ike and Joey were in one, with Lucas sharing the other with his father. They dropped off the suitcases and went out to get some burgers and fries for dinner.

They watched some TV when they got back, then the two younger brothers went to bed. It didn't take them long to drift off to sleep. Lucas was still wide awake as he sat on top of his bed. He reflected back to the scene of the soldier saying goodbye to his son. It was still bothering him that his dad had never told him he loved him. He wanted to say something. *Wonder if it'll piss him off if I just ask him why he's never told us he loved us. I don't think he would smack me for askin'. Now that I think about it, the old man hasn't hit me in quite awhile. I'm gonna ask!*

"What the hell are you thinkin' about, Luke?" Ivan asked. Then grinning, "Your face is going through all kinds of contortions."

"Dad, can I ask you something?"

"Sure, you can."

"I've heard my friends dads tell them they loved them, but you never have told me or Ike or Joey. Why?" Lucas asked in a shaky voice.

At first a scowl came over Ivan's face as he looked at his son. Lucas' heart raced. Then the man's face softened. He took a big sigh before answering. "I put a roof over your head, food on the table, clothes on your back … you should know I love you and your brothers."

"How are we supposed to know if you never tell us? We're not grown-ups. We can't just figure it out ourselves."

There was another long pause as Ivan looked at Lucas for what seemed to be an eternity to the boy. Then he got up and sat on Lucas' bed. Lucas wasn't sure what to expect. Then his father put his arm around his son's shoulders. "Lucas Baryshivka … I love you."

Lucas was fighting back tears as he hugged his dad. He held the embrace for a few moments.

"Okay, Luke. Time for bed. We have a long drive ahead of us tomorrow."

"Goodnight, Dad. I love you, too."

"Goodnight, Son."

Ivan turned off the light and went into the bathroom as Lucas rolled to his side. He could feel the tear roll down his cheek, across the smile on his face.

A whole new chapter in his life was about to begin.

About the Author

Michael G. Cerepanya was born in western Pennsylvania. He spent most of his early childhood as a military dependent, living on various U.S. Army bases in Germany and the United States. After his father retired from the Army, the family moved back to Pennsylvania for a short period before relocating in Tucson, Arizona.

A desert rat from the first time he stepped foot in Arizona, Michael has had a passion for hiking and climbing the mountains of Arizona, as well as a passion for almost all outdoor sports. After serving two years in the U.S. Army from 1969 to 1971 he spent time traveling around the country, both hitchhiking and traveling in various vehicles from a VW Bus to a pickup truck. During these travels he landed on and fell in love with Cape Cod, Massachusetts, where he lived for a year and a half. His wife Cheryl is from there, and although his main residence is still in Southern Arizona, they maintain a second home on the Cape and spend as much time as possible there.

Michael always had a passion for telling a good story and writing. His hope is that his first book, *Army Brats* (and future books) will be as fun for the reader as it was for him to write.

Connect with Michael G. Cerepanya

I really appreciate you reading my book! Please visit my website at army-brats.com.

59003032R00179